A LONELY AND CURIOUS COUNTRY

TALES FROM THE LANDS OF LOVECRAFT

EDITED BY MATTHEW CARPENTER

ULTHAR
PRESS

Published by Ulthar Press
700 Metacom Avenue, Warren, RI 02885
http://www.ultharpress.com/

First Edition

Cover design by Steven Prizeman
Ulthar Press logo by Mike Corley
ISBN: 978-0692501962

CONTENTS

INTRODUCTION

Matthew Carpenter

"When a traveller in north central Massachusetts takes the wrong fork at the junction of Aylesbury pike just beyond Dean's Corners he comes upon a lonely and curious country.

"The ground gets higher, and the brier-bordered stone walls press closer and closer against the ruts of the dusty, curving road. The trees of the frequent forest belts seem too large, and the wild weeds, brambles and grasses attain a luxuriance not often found in settled regions. At the same time the planted fields appear singularly few and barren; while the sparsely scattered houses wear a surprisingly uniform aspect of age, squalor, and dilapidation." – H. P. Lovecraft, "The Dunwich Horror"

If he expected his work to be remembered at all, perhaps the best H. P. Lovecraft might have hoped for was to be recalled as an author by a few fans of pulp publications. World domination would have astonished him. But, more than 75 years after his death, that is what we see. His influence is inescapable in science fiction and horror literature, his creation Cthulhu is iconic and even fans who never read the old gent's stories themselves are familiar with the basics of Lovecraftian horror. Others have speculated on the whys and wherefores about this explosion of interest in all things Lovecraft, be it the fulfillment of the early promise of the Internet in terms of connecting groups of fans, the rise of materialism in popular thought or the influence of artists who have been influenced themselves by Lovecraft such as Guillermo Del Toro and Stephen King. I first read Lovecraft in the early 1970s in the old Lancer paperbacks, and I have followed this avalanche of Cthulhu Mythos fiction with emotions running from bemusement to disbelief. Ever since I was in eighth grade I have voraciously consumed Lovecraftian fiction. Even as recently as 2010 I could with some certainty say that I had read almost every single Lovecraftian novel, single author collection or anthology available. Very little escaped me. Now, however the task is hopeless. The pace of publication has exceeded anyone's ability to read all of it. Over the last five years more than 50 Cthulhu Mythos story anthologies have been published; this does not include such genres as comic books, novels or children's books. Even more remarkable is the change in character and quality in what we read today. In the 1970s most of what was written was derivative pastiche. The prototypical Lovecraftian story had a new tome added to the Eldritch Library, a listing of the entire pantheon of mythos entities and a reiteration of a well-worn plot. Today authors are not content to echo Lovecraft; they use his themes and monsters as a springboard into new horizons. Cosmicism, as popularized by Lovecraft, reflects the uneasy and insignificant place of humanity in a vast indifferent universe, and is used to create horrors that perturb even modern readers inured to daily reminders of the fragility of existence in the daily news. Even if familiar entities or locations are used, today's writers do not feel bound by the structures created by Lovecraft and perhaps made rigid by Derleth. What else is striking is that the quality of writing has now become astonishingly good. Previously anyone could include a few whippoorwills, a chanted "iä iä" or two, mention the Necronomicon, and hope to see print. Now in almost every venue where Lovecraft is spoken the prose glitters like jewels. Before it was almost unthinkable that Elizabeth Bear could win the Hugo Award for "Shoggoths in Bloom." Now no one blinks an eye when Charlie Stross wins the same award for his novella "Equoid," that details a plausible explanation for Shub Niggurath. When Sam Gafford of Ulthar Press approached me with the idea of editing another Cthulhu Mythos anthology I hesitated for a moment. All of my publications have been in medical journals. And then I thought here was a chance to discover something new and wonderful, and share it with fans like me who can't get enough mythos fiction. Why not take advantage of a burgeoning popularity of Lovecraft and the remarkable improvement in the quality of writers to explore some new byways? We placed few restrictions on submissions for the book you are now reading. We wanted to hear from new writers, established writers, anybody interested in the Cthulhu Mythos. All we asked was they not deliver us a pastiche. We wanted our authors to take that wrong fork just past Dean's Corners, sending us to some new location in Lovecraft country. All I had hoped for was a few worthy new additions to the ever expanding Lovecraft circle. I was flabbergasted by the excellence of the stories we received. We agonized over which ones to include but I think you will be very happy with the results. Here are 17 never before published tales of horror and madness. Some are set in the familiar environs of Innsmouth or Miskatonic University. Some take us to places we've never been. All are new, and none is like any of the others. Get ready to be surprised and disturbed. Turn the lights in the house down, nestle into your favorite reading chair with a cup of hot tea by your side. You may find adding a wee nip of medicinal brandy will help. As the shadows press in and silence descends, allow yourself to be transported into that lonely and curious country we love so well. Apart from having a few chills and the seeds for future nightmares, you will return from this book just fine…probably.

The Dreamer of Nothingness

Steven Prizeman

Paris. May, 1968

Yves leaned back, tilting the café chair onto its rear legs, and exhaled a haze of smoke. He watched the gray dissipate slowly, revealing the clear, blue sky, dazzling in the afternoon sun. With his left hand he revolved the last of the pastis in his glass. Beside him, in his ears, yet again, were Anne-Marie and Eduard.

"I said: *'Are you coming to the demonstration tomorrow?'*"

It was Anne-Marie. Yves plucked an answer from the air.

"What is the point of another demonstration until the objectives have been defined? *A demonstration without objectives is merely a crowd.*"

"A crowd…" Eduard's lager-and-Gauloises breath was offensively close. "…is the spearhead of the proletariat. A crowd will tell you *its* objectives. Crowds don't need to be led; *crowds lead.* Crowds don't need manifestoes; the will of the crowd *is* the people's manifesto."

"Spoken like a true anarcho-syndicalist!" Yves said it with a smile, but he thought: *'Christ! This again!'*

Anne-Marie raked her fingers through her long, russet hair.

"Actually, the committee is meeting this evening to set out its demands. *Do come!* We need you, Yves. How can we build student-worker solidarity if even the students aren't solid? Everyone else in Political Science is going." She leaned close and whispered in his ear. "Claude's anarchist friends have heard a rumor the riot police are going to try and reoccupy the Sorbonne. They're stockpiling cobblestones and Molotovs. We can make love on my balcony while they fight below."

"Perhaps. If the workers and students need me." Yves had been to Anne-Marie's apartment before – the balcony wasn't high enough to be out of the tear gas. He didn't fancy that, any more than having his skull cracked by the batons of those fascists in the CRS. Anne-Marie was quite suggestible, so he could probably get her to do the bourgeois thing: go indoors, close the windows, snuggle up. He drained his glass. Surely, this ought to feel more pressing? Was he actually feeling anything at all? Only in a very muffled way.

"You with us? *Hello?*" Eduard snapped his fingers in Yves' face. "We're talking about bringing down De Gaulle and his cronies and there you sit, puffing your Gitanes like you didn't have a care in the world! What's wrong with you today?"

"Nothing's wrong. Not really. I was just..." Yves waved his cigarette vaguely toward the cloud it had created. "I was just watching how the smoke looks so dense for a moment – you can hardly see through it – then all at once it thins out and disappears, as if it had never been. And it suddenly struck me how much that's like... life."

"Life?" Eduard was too surprised to inject the word with his usual venom. Just for a moment. "*Life!* Stone me!" He drained his vodka chaser and slammed the glass on the iron table. "You need to sort yourself out, mate! I thought you existentialists were meant to be engaged, not bourgeoisly indifferent. *'Life! Ooh! It's all floating away!'* Stone me! You sure it's just tobacco in that cigarette? You smell of hash, come to think of it."

"I thought it was poetic." Anne-Marie murmured the reassurance softly, before adding: "You do smell of pot, Yves. This really isn't the time for it."

Eduard's mockery switched to English as his fingers flicked two V-shaped peace signs: "*'Hey, man! Far out! Drop out, man! Is cool!'* I keep telling you, Yves: dropping out is the antithesis of engagement. The Man is perfectly happy for you to sit on your arse and smoke dope. Just so long as you let him run things his way."

"It isn't pot," Yves protested. "It's my new apartment." The smoke that came out this time was more ragged. "I'm stuck on the sixth floor, right at the top of the building, and there are some Arabs on the floors below – Algerians, I think." He saw Anne-Marie and Eduard open their mouths and moved quickly to head them off. "*Arabs are fine; Algerians are fine* – but some of them must be smoking a hell of a lot of dope. There's always this weird odor in the room. It seems to filter up through the floor and rise up the side of the building, too, because it wafts in through the window – especially at night. It gives me strange dreams; I haven't been sleeping properly." He took a drag, anxious now, earnest. "What's galling is that I've only got the one window and it's nailed shut. The shutter outside is closed, too. I don't get any light or any air. It might as well be bricked up."

"I would have thought that'd be right up your street," Eduard snorted. "Struggling philosopher-writer in his lonely garret. *The new Camus!* Why did you have to move there, anyway? You've made things very difficult for Claude and me. If we don't get a new lodger by the end of the month your share of the rent will fall on us." And then he was straight into his defender-of-the-downtrodden persona. "One window that

8

doesn't open? Bad air? No light? Your landlord's a capitalist all right! Want me to have a word?"

"No, no!" Yves made placatory gestures. "I don't want any trouble – the whole reason I went there was I needed some peace." Eduard and Claude argued every night and each had his own clique of friends who came round to join in. And all the students in the adjacent rooms, and floors, and down the street, and across it, acted likewise. The new apartment was cheaper, too. Much, much, cheaper. "Just let me handle it. Once I've fixed the window, I'm sure it'll be fine."

"Where did you say it was?" Anne-Marie lit another cigarette and picked a loose strand of tobacco from her lips. "Are you going to invite us round?"

"Rue d'Auseil. You're welcome whenever you like, of course."

"Rue d'Auseil?" Anne-Marie's brow creased. "Where's that?"

"It's about a twenty-five minute walk from here; a couple more from the university. It's in that odd little district – I don't know what it's called. You know that dirty river – it must be a tributary of the Seine – dark and scummy-looking? It's lined with a lot of rundown warehouses that don't look like they've been used since the war, and some factories that still do something or other."

"I know!" Eduard wagged a finger. "That whole area's a health hazard. Stinks! I pity the exploited who have to work in those factories – must ruin their health. That's why you need workers' control of production, otherwise…"

"Anyway…" Yves pressed on. "…there's an old stone bridge across the river, and it leads to a lot of narrow, cobbled streets – they're quite confusing, if you don't know the area." *'And to me,'* he thought. *'And I've been there almost two weeks!'* "They go uphill. It really gets quite steep – flights of steps and everything – and the Rue d'Auseil is the highest and steepest of all. It's closed to traffic, of course – and it's a dead end. Just stops at a high brick wall covered in ivy. Anyway, my apartment is in the third house from the top – but it's much taller than any of the other houses, so it's the highest point in the area. Sometimes it feels like the highest point in the city – Eiffel Tower included."

"There must be a magnificent view," said Anne-Marie.

"Yes," laughed Eduard. *"If he ever gets the window open.* Seriously: have a word with the landlord."

"I don't want to give him a hard time." Yves shrugged. "He's old and has health problems. He's pretty much paralyzed. I think he must have been gassed in the war – the first one."

"*You'll* have health problems!" Eduard stubbed out his Gauloises as if it were a kulak. "Going up and down that hill every day."

"I don't know." Anne-Marie squeezed Yves' thigh. "Perhaps it'll make him strong, all that exercise."

"Strong enough for a demo?" Eduard stood, his chair grating across the cobbles behind him.

"Maybe." Yves shrugged again. "If I get a decent night's sleep."

"Good man! *Solidarity!*" Eduard raised a clenched fist and strode away, keen to see how his friends' black flags and brickbats were coming along.

***

Two Pernods, six Gitanes, and a stroll along the Left Bank later, Anne-Marie and Yves parted with a kiss. It was now a firm date: demonstration tomorrow morning, lunch and miscellaneous agitation in the afternoon, indoor lovemaking in the evening, with or without a riot. Yves paused for a moment to watch the early evening sun reflecting on the Seine. He didn't need to check his watch to realize that if he didn't turn his steps toward home – if you could call it home – it would be dark before he'd negotiated the circuitous cobbled alleys leading to the Rue d'Auseil. He wasn't in a mood to deal with them in the dark. The second night after he'd moved in, he'd gone out for a stroll – late – looking for a bar. Didn't find one. He ended up wandering for what felt like hours, although his watch told him it was less than one. He must have been going in circles, but there was little enough that he recognized. There were few streetlights, and those there were shed only a sickly nicotine-yellow glow. Little pools of gloom in which, sometimes, small knots of shadowy men congregated, muttering and smoking. Arabs, he believed. And, though he thought badly of himself for doing so, he would invariably turn around or cross the street.

Today, even before he reached the bridge over the muddy river, its surface flecked with panchromatic slime, the feeling of uneasiness returned. It climbed, as Yves climbed, the roads and alleys and steps beyond, rising, rising, rising to the Rue d'Auseil. He felt the hill beneath him, the hard mass of it pressing up through his calves and knees as he pushed himself toward the gray-blue twilight. *'This is no good,'* he thought. *'This? Every day? I'll have to start looking for somewhere else as soon as I've scraped some money together. I can't go back to Eduard and Claude: I'll look a fool and I'll never hear the end of it.'* He pressed on.

This evening – and evening was well advanced by the time he got there – Yves found the Rue d'Auseil at the first attempt, catching himself as he almost passed the turning. The road, as usual, was dark and quiet. His house, unusually, exhibited noise and light. Raised voices. Someone was haranguing Monsieur Blandot – the half-crippled landlord – in broken French.

"Where is he? Eh? *Where?*" Three young Arab men stood in the doorway of Blandot's shabby office, set back a few meters from the foot of the stairs. Yves felt obliged to put his head round the door.

"Everything all right?" Although Yves nodded briefly at the Arabs, the question was directed exclusively to Monsieur Blandot, who sat, milky-eyed and unshaven, at his desk. *'God knows what he does about that hill,'* he thought.

"Ah, Monsieur Leulliette!" Blandot caught at Yves verbally the way a beggar clutches at a man's lapels. "Monsieur: *have you seen Youcef?* His friends here have not seen him for days. They are worried."

"Youcef?" The name meant nothing to Yves.

"The young man in the room below yours. On the fifth floor. The Algerian gentleman. These are his friends."

The three Arabs nodded at Yves and – surly, suspicious – muttered their names: Hakim, Moussa, Ahmed.

Yves smiled at each in turn.

"I'm sorry, I don't know him. I haven't seen him." He might have, for all he knew: on the stairs, checking the ever-empty pigeonholes downstairs for mail, lounging on a street corner. How would he know? They didn't all look alike, of course not, he'd never say that. But he didn't *know* any of them, and there were quite a few. The one who had identified himself as Hakim faced Yves and made staccato points with a jabbing cigarette:

"Youcef say man upstairs smoke hashish all time! Smell make him sick! Sleep bad! *Sick!* Not answer door yesterday! Not answer today! Borrow key – room empty! Stink of hashish – ash all over floor! No Youcef!"

"Hashish? I've noticed that, too. I thought it was coming up from below."

Blandot nerved himself: "I do not want anyone smoking hashish in my house, thank you very much, gentlemen. There are plenty of tenants who will not give me such trouble. Should I call the police?"

A sudden flurry from all in the doorway indicated that, no, they would prefer it if Monsieur Blandot did not call the police. Hashish was merely something of which they had heard tell. An idea struck Yves.

"The police. Could your friend have crossed the bridge and gone into the center of town? There are so many cops around these days, what with... everything. And, with him being Algerian... Well, you know how the police feel about you. Have you checked the hospitals?"

"Not yet." Hakim's eyes fell and he muttered despondently to his companions, resigned to finding his friend, if at all, in a hospital bed, cell or morgue.

"You can use the pay phone in the hall," said the landlord. "Had that installed in '53 – knew it would come in handy."

The Algerians flowed past Yves toward the dusty telephone, hanging neglected on the wall.

"It's not unusual for people to leave unexpectedly," whispered Blandot. "It happens! Especially with..." He nodded in the direction the Arabs had taken. "But this one was paid up to the end of the month, and I have his deposit, too (which is forfeit), so that *is* a little curious." Blandot shrugged. "That's life! He seemed all right, for one of..." He nodded toward the Arabs again.

As Yves turned to go, he paused on the threshold as a thought struck him.

"I don't suppose, Monsieur Blandot, that he could be in the other room on my floor?"

"No, no." Blandot spoke urgently and paled beneath his stubble. "That room is unoccupied."

Hakim stamped back along the hallway: "What room? I thought *he* had only room on top floor." His cigarette indicated Yves.

"No," said Yves. "My room is on the *west* of the sixth floor, but there is a door opposite, on the *east* side. Could your friend have gone in there?"

"No," asserted Blandot, rising in his seat insofar as he could. "There *is* a little room, as you say. But it is unoccupied. No one has been in there for years."

"Oh, that can't be right, Monsieur Blandot." Yves shook his head. "No, I've often heard someone moving about on my floor at night. I assumed that room was in use."

"You must be mistaken. The door is kept locked."

Hakim stubbed out his cigarette on the doorframe: "We go look."

***

With the keys relinquished reluctantly by Blandot, Yves and Hakim ascended the chimney-like staircase, every step a creak. Another one of the Algerians followed close behind. Moussa, was it? Or Ahmed? The third remained downstairs, persisting with expensive, erratic and fruitless phone calls. At each landing, Yves glanced at the doors of what must have been the Algerians' rooms, and those of the other, more furtive tenants whom – he presumed – had already been quizzed. On the fifth floor, Hakim walked to Youcef's room and pushed open the door.

"See! All his thing here." Hakim raised his head and flared his nostrils. "Smell hashish, yes? *Hash?*"

Yves stepped forward and found his nose and lungs filling with an intoxicating aroma that made him, for a moment, light-headed. It was without doubt the smell he had noticed in his own room, but fresher, stronger.

"Yes." He nodded. "Hash." And yet, even as he said it, Yves was thinking: *'No, that's not hash. At least not any kind I've ever smelt.'* Blinking hard into the gloom, he saw that the window opposite stood wide open, the strong breeze blowing through it carrying the odor his way. The sharply defined square of the window, high above the city, revealed a patch of blue sky, still illumined by the long-set sun. Then he heard a click as Hakim flicked on the room's one weak light bulb, hanging unshaded from a cord in the center of the ceiling.

"See! There is clothe! There is shoe! Why go, no clothe, no shoe? See! Is ash on floor! Ash on table. Ash on chair. Ash on bed."

"Yes." Yves nodded. "Ash."

It was very fine, very pale, very light, blowing against them, carried by the breeze. Yves and Hakim and Moussa (or Ahmed) slapped their legs to brush it from their trousers.

"Did you open the window?" asked Yves.

"No." Hakim shook his head. "Was like."

"You don't think he could have jumped, do you? Or fallen?"

The missing Youcef had obviously taken something – the smell alone proved that. Could there have been some LSD involved? Made him think he could fly? Yves had heard of such things. He made so bold as to tiptoe across the room, planting his feet in ashy prints he presumed to have been made earlier by the searching Algerians. He was halfway to the window when Hakim said, wearily: "I already look."

Although Yves did not doubt the Arab's ability to look out of a window, the opening – and the lingering image of the deep blue horizon – drew him on. Two weeks he had lived upstairs without a window to look through. This could only be, what? Three meters below his? He wanted to see the view. He rested his hands on the sill but immediately drew them back as he felt the grit: they were covered in ash. It was odd to find it here too, given the breeze. Yves put his hands back on the windowsill and leaned out. Below him, vertiginously and infinitely far, was the murky neighborhood of the Rue d'Auseil, speckled with scabs of light enough to pick out its hovels and alleyways, its steps and weed-broken pavements, the smoky factories beyond and the warehouses beyond them. The bridge and the sewer-like river were, thankfully, shielded from view. Yves pulled up his gaze and cleansed his palette: Paris dazzled brilliantly all around, dressed for a spring night, beautiful as ever. His immediate vicinity was the only morbid lesion on her face.

Yves breathed in the evening air, cool, refreshing. He twisted now and looked up to confirm his orientation was correct. It was: above him, below the steeply angled eaves, barnacled to the side of the house, was the black mass of his dormant window, encased behind inert shutters. *'I must look through that window,'* he thought. *'I will look through it. Tonight.'*

"Hey, come on, yes? What you do?" Hakim was getting impatient. Although the Algerian had wrested control of the keys as soon as Blandot handed them over, Yves now realized that he was essential to the proposed search. He was to be Hakim's witness to whatever would be found in the room facing his, and to testify that the Arabs removed nothing. He stepped back briskly, nose wrinkling at the dust he kicked up, and pulled the door shut behind him. Then he led the Arabs to the sixth floor.

"That's my room." Yves pointed across the cramped, top-floor landing. Hakim threw a brief, suspicious look his way. "He's not in there!" Yves added, before sighing in resignation. "All right! Let's be thorough." He unlocked his own door and pushed it hard, generating an air current strong enough to circle the room and come back out before he had even switched on the light. The air smelt much the same as the room below. *"See!"* Yves said this boldly, though embarrassed by the dishevelment of his room: the piles of clothes (some washed, some not); the posters that did not fully conceal the stains on the walls (Godard's *Breathless* sharing honors with screen-printed agitprop by Anne-Marie's arty friends); the stacks of Camus and Sartre beside a cramped writing desk; the small typewriter and disarrayed papers (neglected, half-finished essays), weighted down by an overburdened ashtray; the waste basket choked with paper.

Yves was a little offended that the Algerians did indeed step into his room to see, opening his wardrobe and peering under the bed.

"OK," said Hakim. "Is good." With three quick strides, he crossed the landing and pushed the key into the lock of the eastern door. He groaned with the strain as he forced the key in a slow, grating circle. Still the door did not open, until he put his shoulder to it. It revealed only darkness. Hakim reached in and Yves heard his hand sweeping up and down the wall in search of a light switch, but not finding one. The Arab muttered something over his shoulder to Moussa and the two pulled out cigarette lighters and sparked them into life. Yves drew his own. Led at arm's length by the three flames, they moved inside.

Vague shapes came into view and faded away again as the area of light expanded and contracted amorphously as the three men moved their arms independently, before realizing that they needed to huddle and concentrate the illumination.

"Youcef!" Hakim called the name as if shouting into a cavern – which the room might have been, for all they could see of it. "Hallo! Youcef! Anyone here, please? Hallo?" The words fell dead and echoless from his lips, bringing no response. In the silence that followed, they heard the breeze brushing the tiles and rafters just inches above their heads, the floorboards creaking beneath their feet. Nothing else.

"What is?" Hakim headed in one direction and the others followed. Their pooled light revealed a chair piled high with papers. Nearby, a music stand with a cello propped against it, together with its bow. All were covered with what they thought, for a moment, was more of the ash, before realizing that, no, it was dust. Just dust.

"Same as the chair in my room," said Yves, unsure if that meant anything. He picked up the topmost sheet of paper and shook the dust from it. It was music; something with a German title. The sheet below: also music. Yves could not read music and put it back. The men moved slowly around the small room, defining the edges. There were some boxes and an old, old suitcase, packed with clothes, a Homburg hat beside it. Yves picked it up and peered inside in search of a label. 'E. Zann' was inked in a shaky hand on a grimy white patch. He set it down on the case. Moussa said something sharp; Hakim nodded.

"*Junk!* He says is junk."

"Yes." Yves nodded. "Looks that way."

"But you say you hear someone. You sure."

"I was. I could have sworn. Obviously, I was mistaken. Sorry." Hakim said something guttural to Moussa, tilting his head to indicate Yves as he did so. There were a couple more harsh words and a gesture – none of which Yves understood – as the Algerians ushered him out of the room, dragged the door shut and wrestled the lock back into place. "Sorry!" he said again to their backs, as they stamped downstairs to return the keys to Blandot and continue their search elsewhere. Yves still had his lighter in his hand. He lit another Gitanes, returned to his room and sprawled across the bed.

Youcef. Had he ever seen him? He hadn't known any of the Arabs' names before tonight, or which one lived in which room. Now that he knew Youcef was the occupant of the room below his, he was able to conjure a face: about twenty, tightly curled hair, hollow cheeks, pale (for an Algerian), and, quite distinctly now – a frightened expression. Terrified. When had he seen him? When had he ever seen anyone that scared? If it wasn't for the sickly-sweet fug of the room, maybe he would recall. Yves watched the smoke from his cigarette move horizontally, carried by the breeze that blew again – or, rather, blew still, unceasingly – through the split and moldering frame surrounding his otherwise sealed window.

'I'm opening that!' He stared at the dusty pane, reflective in the pallid bulb-light because of the black shutters immediately beyond. *'I'll find a hammer, pliers –something – take those nails out and force the lock. I'll smash it, if I have to. Eduard's right: I need air. And I want to see! As soon as I've finished this. Five minutes.'* But the Gitanes smoldered down to his lips, before being stubbed reflexively on the floorboards, as Yves drifted into a half-sleep. A half-sleep studded by dreams and memories, and memories of dreams, and dreams of memories. Of a wind and a sound and a scent that carried meaning and a spirit and a whisper. Of eyes staring, staring, staring into an abyss and eyes – or what served as eyes – staring back. Of an outsider that sought admittance. Of fugitive footsteps in a nighted building, descending and ascending like a Minotaur in a vertical labyrinth. Of stealthy searching and stolen keys and unlocked doors. Of a sleeper waking in terror, hands about his throat, choking, unable to move, choking, choking. Of windows flung open and a howling cosmic Sirocco that scours bodies to powder with the breath of aeons.

***

Eduard was annoyed that Yves did not, after all, join the demonstration the next day; Anne-Marie chagrined that he did not show up for their date. It was only some days later that they noticed he had stopped attending all meetings, happenings and – once they resumed – lectures. Having no proper contact details for Yves, the best Eduard could do was wander the endless cobbled alleyways beyond an unhealthy river, one hot June afternoon. But he gave up at last, unable to find the Rue d'Auseil. He, and all Yves' friends, concluded that he must, after all, have dropped out. It happened.

In the third house from the top of the Rue d'Auseil, it took very nearly as long for Monsieur Blandot or any of his tenants to realize that the sole occupant of the sixth floor did not, in fact, appear to be in occupation. When a search was made, all that was found was the typical untidy array of a student's room, dusted with a thin layer of aromatic ash (or something very like ash) and a shattered windowpane. The prevailing wind must have been blowing against the unlatched shutters, and blowing hard, for Hakim (Blandot's favored agent that day), was unable to push them open. He did not try for long, and, to placate the crippled landlord, dragged the missing student's possessions into the room across the landing, as requested. With both rooms secured, he returned the keys. Blandot, for reasons he did not discuss, decided that he would not, in future, permit any further tenants on the sixth floor.

Paudie O'Brien and the Bogman

Seán Farrell

Paudie walked carefully, his slow steps lit by the moon. Right foot, then left, no hurry. Had to be careful. He'd left his home an hour ago and still had many miles to travel. But he knew exactly where he was going. This gave him great comfort.

He'd walked this path many times in his life before, from a babe to a boy, and though each time was different, he had a good feeling now. He had a great gift with him, and this coupled with his knowing where he was going, so to speak, left him beaming; his dirty brown teeth gleaming dully in the moonlight. He was dressed in the clothes he'd woke in - tanned boots and trousers, and a worn paintstained shirt. The night was quiet and vast. There was no one around for miles.

The path Paudie walked wasn't well known anymore. It whispered across fields and streams, up and down damp hills, traces here and there. Sometimes it changed, one night as straight as the beam of light that peeked through his keyhole each morning, the next, as curved as the swirling black pool in the river that ran from behind his home.

He used to try and plot his progress in the stars when he was younger. But he'd been led astray so many times, that he'd learnt it was best to just take your time, and follow the route that seemed right.

Paudie'd learnt about the path from his mother. On the night he was born, through wind and rain that had clattered off her back like sheets of leathered straps, she brought him out here herself, the birthmark on his face a thumbprint from that night. He used to say to her that he remembered it. Black and moist, and stinking, its inkline grooves filling slowly with the blood of his newborn body, before finally taken away, leaving a permanent mark below his right eye. He'd dream of that night again and again.

Although his mother disagreed, as he grew up, Paudie became well known as a fool. So stupid was he, that he could have been the king of the fools if there was such a thing.

Paudie O'Brien was simple they said. Touched in the head. His skull filled with water and a brain like a sod of turf. 45 and barely able to boil an egg. He'd be seen at the back of mass on a Sunday, and heard, talking endlessly about whatever seemed to come into his head.

"There's Tierney now, he has the pigs up at the farm. Awful smelly those pigs are. Awful smell of shite off them."

18

Or you'd see him walk out of Kelleher's grocery, bread and bacon peering out the top of a brown bag, and a couple of bottles of porter to wash them down with.

"Ah hello Mrs. Murphy, how are you keeping I'm good myself now but I've an awful pain in my leg, I can barely walk on it without being reminded of it. And how is the baby doing is he healthy? Ah good, good and how are you yourself, I heard that Mr. Murphy has fucked off has he? Ah that's terrible terrible but Mrs. Murphy didn't my father do the same and didn't I turn out OK in the end, and even after Mammy dying when I was just 17 and barely able to fend for myself, and sure it's all in God's plan that's what the priest says, and what's the use in worrying."

People tolerated Paudie, said hello when they passed him, and blessed themselves when he was gone. But they didn't laugh or joke. Or shake his hand. Or compliment him the way you'd normally congratulate a simpleton for managing to get up in the morning and put on his clothes and brush his teeth without causing himself serious injury. There were rumours, whispers really, about him. Nothing that even amounted to anything as substantial as a story. But they treated Paudie differently, gave him a wide berth. Because for all of Paudie's dimness there was one thing you couldn't call him, and that was harmless.

***

"Hello my dear"

"Hello to you too Tom Breathnach"

He had a smile on his lips. He looked rocken. Elemental. The smooth face of seacarved stone - flushed cheeks and wet black hair filled with movement.

"How was it?"

"Glorious. I'd say one of the best days the sea has ever seen."

He put Lucy down in her mother's arms, and wiped his head with a tea towel.

"How are you feeling? Better?"

"Much better. Needed the nap. But the headache's gone, as well as the stomach pains. Feeling much better really. And how was Lucy?"

"Ah great. Her little blue eyes were stuck on the water."

Putting a cigarette to his lips he sparked the flames of the cooker briefly, and bent down to light the tip. Puffing out, he looked calmed, settled.

Nora put Lucy's hands around her thumb.

Tom leaned on the cooker and spoke again:

"Imagine seeing the sea as a baby. Seeing it for the first time. What would you think?"

He exhaled, and the smoke curled into the air like icy lines on a frostdewed window.

"It always makes me wonder actually, when you're down there, down past Joe's road, and up past the old lighthouse. You know, down where the sea's made the stone so tangled, like knotted hair. When you're there, and it's just you and Lucy and the lapping of the waves, and the whole world behind you. What must it have been like? Way back when. To have been the first person to go out and see it. To see the sun break through the clouds, over the water. And not a candle or stitch of cloth to your name."

"I know what you mean", Nora said. "Is it any wonder we have old stories of giants and witches, and God and the saints?"

Lucy gurgled in Nora's arms, hands twitching with new control.

"I went down to the cove as well, gave Lucy a bit of sand to run through her fingers. Get a bit of texture into her paws."

Nora could feel the tiny grains between her skin and Lucy's, held in perpetuity. Spots of rockglue joining their hands together.

***

Black flies filled the chipped brown mug. Flecks of light flicked off their twitching wings, like sun through sandglass. A dark hand appeared, shuddering. Haired nails at the end. It grabbed milk from a bowl, running through its fingers and filled the mug. Now brought to dark lips drinking deep.

Nora heard the crunch and saw wings, jutting out between curved fishhook teeth, like a pike's jaw almost. Looking closer, and the wings changed, to fingernails, eyelashes, toes, ears. An eye. She put her hands among the teeth, opened the slack soggy jaw further and further, until like tar it fell away in her hands. She dug deeper.

To her right and left, black crows crawled beneath dark soil, beaks filled with muck and worms, drowning in the sullen earth. It was getting warmer and warmer the deeper she went, and soon she felt a beating pulse. A dull thud in the dirt, like a hammer from miles and miles above. Smashing the surface - beating through eternity.

Jesus the heat was almost unbearable now. But she had to dig deeper. Clawing through, tombed in a dirty sodden womb she had to break through until finally. Air. A gleam of light reflecting from a small corrugated shed. A black scorched symbol on the door. Two vertical lines crossed by a horizontal. As straight and perfect as if God himself had written it.

She opened the door and saw she was at the edge of a bog. Paudie O'Brien was curled up in the distance, on his haunches at the bog's edge. Naked, he looked at her, a black spiraled mark beneath his eye, almost glowing in the depth of its darkness. His hands were in the bog, up to his wrist, and he was pushing something down, down beneath the surface.

But her eye was drawn to the figure behind Paudie, standing quietly. Tall, at least 15 feet, lumpy and misshappen, but always changing, slightly. Black as dirt from head to toe, clumps falling off his body. Moving slowly, suddenly. Imperceptible almost. As if through time not space - existing here in one second, there the next.

An inward nose, no eyes, but shadows that dwelled in sunken holes. His black mouth was open and quiet.

In his right hand he held a sceptre made of ash. It was adorned at the top by a rough wooden circle. Looking closer, Nora saw it was a withered brown eye, fenced by a widening gyre. It grew larger and larger, turned and creaked. She closed her eyes, as tightly as she could.

***

They beat the shit out of Paudie when they brought him in.
"But what'd I do?"
Bang. Wallop. Another clobber to the jaw.
"Cut it out now Paudie. What the fuck have you done with her."
The blood drooled out of his mouth, bubbles of saliva down the middle.
"Ah but sir. I've done nothing."
"Paudie."
"Fuck youse lot", and he spat at Inspector Moran. A red gob landed on his cheek, beside a sweat-dropped moustache.

It was another five minutes of mauling Paudie got before they began to talk again.

"Paudie, you'll hang for this if you don't talk. And that's before we mention what'll happen after. You're going straight to Hell Paudie, you're not going to get anywhere even near St. Peter if you don't put that poor woman out of her misery."

"Ah sir, I've me own life to be worrying about. Sure wasn't it only last week that cunt Maureen left her dog do his business in me front garden - why aren't you after her? It's a hard life sir, keeping things going when you've no-one to care for you."

Moran gave him a final punch, breaking Paudie's nose. Paudie looked at him as if he'd finally woken up.

"You were seen walking down Joe's road the night that Lucy Breathnach went missing. We have multiple witnesses who will testify against you. You're done for Paudie. Repent. Let us help you, if not to save your life, then surely your soul."

It was hard to explain, but Paudie seemed to grow bigger

"Ye fucking cunts going on about ye're souls. What use have I for a soul."

If Paudie'd thought he'd got a beating before then, he was dead wrong. An hour later, Inspector Moran brought Paudie to his cell, dribbling out the side of his mouth, spitting curse words through swollen bloody lips.

***

The day that it happened, Nora knew, as soon as she woke, that Lucy was gone. She didn't know how, but she knew. Later she thought that maybe she was so used to the house, right down to the settling dust atop each surface, that a balance had been upset. Fragments of the air left to settle that should have been met with quiet small breaths.

Panic didn't overcome her until she looked over the ridge of the cot, and saw its empty carriage. Blankets folded, undisturbed. As cold as the dirt in the ground outside the window. She didn't wake up Tom.

She looked around the cot. Footprints, dirt, mud, anything. Nothing.

She looked at the window for scratches cuts, fingerprints hair. But is was bare, clear, reflecting her pale face back at her.

When she woke Tom, they would search for weeks, starved of sleep and food and rest. But they both knew that morning, grief gestating in their breasts, that she was gone.

Nora would think back over that morning endlessly. This morning was no different. She was sat in their bed, after everything, this whole sorry mess had settled down, and the world began to turn at its usual rotation.

"I feel as though a razor has come across my eye and removed a milky film."

Tom lay awake, his eyes staring at the cracked ceiling.

"Tom, I'm glad. I'm glad she's gone. What is all this really? All this meaningless conversation, a constant waiting, and for what?"

"Nora," Tom started, but she cut him off.

"When I was younger, I thought, and with you and her, that there was something, some spark, some meaning to all this. But I see now there's nothing. We may as well be cattle, bags of meat on two legs, just breathing. That's all. And, Christ, I'm just glad. Wherever she is. Because it doesn't matter - any of this."

"You can't keep talking like this, Nora." They were both exhausted.

"No. This means nothing. I don't even feel for her. I see you, and I just don't know Tom - just how far we all are. We're all just waiting, waiting for it all to pass, and just counting down the grains and the tears until they're gone. Until there's nothing left, and your lungs are so sore with the sadness you're inhaling, and trying to get out. That you just stop. See all this waste for what it really is."

Tom said nothing.

"At least her life mattered", Nora said, whispering with fury. "He wanted her, and now she's gone beyond us all. There's nothing more to say."

There wasn't and they both stared, starved with gaunt emotion.

***

An eye, plucked from a baby's head, stuck through by a rusty nail. The nail, peeking out through the splinters of a barbed wooden post. The post, stood still, atop a lonely green hill, looking over a sloping stonesided valley. First, no one noticed it. Then a fly, passing through, landed on its tiny black centre. Only a small fly, he took a while to cover the little orb. He felt the ridges of small frostened veins, and looked into the blue ethereal triangles of a still developing iris. He saw the tortions of an optic nerve torn in two, squeezed from its socket and split by brown steel.

He then flew off, to land on cowshit, and trees and other things.

A day later, a lonely sheep in a neighbouring field came to the top of the hill, to see if the grass was any better. She noticed the tiny eyeball, came close, and investigated with a long wet tongue. She thought of eating the little eye, of feeling the soft crunching between its grasshardened teeth. But she thought better of it. Better to stick to things that were green.

It wasn't until much later, days later, when Murphy, the farmer who owned the field, came across it. By this time it was already withered and dry, hardening away without the cover of a lid. It looked like a little grey snail. But he called the guards, and said that it looked like part of the baby Breathnach had been found.

***

Tom lay with his head on Nora's chest, listening to the slow small breaths of Lucy, four feet away. His hair was still wet from the trip to the cove with Lucy, but Nora could begin to see the shine of silver and golden sand on his crown.

"Actually", Tom said, "I forgot to tell you, something really odd happened on the way home. When I was leaving up from the sea, back up the trail to the road home, I got this terrible sense that someone was looking at me. A really strong sense."

Tom felt Nora's heartbeat softly quicken.

"And Lucy was still awake at the time, and you could tell that she got it too, she went really quiet and alert, and sort of buried her head into my chest. It had gotten very quiet as well, but I looked around to where I thought whoever it was was, out to one of the fields just West of the cove that's jutting way out into the ocean, and makes the bay."

Nora nodded, her heartbeat was fast enough now, and she didn't know why.

"And I swear, for about a split second, just in the corner of my eye, right before I was able to look properly, I swear I saw this tall, really tall actually, big black figure, right in the middle of the field, just standing there."

Nora didn't say anything.

"Like right in the middle of the field. And the oddest thing nearly, was that the sense I got, or whatever it was, it was just so uneasy, because, whoever it was, was just so tall. Not just tall though, or fat or skinny either. Just misshapen, almost as if, and I know this sounds mad, but as if their body was always moving, like changing shape nearly, or losing bits and gaining bits. But black, and dirty, almost, from head to toe."

Lucy had fallen asleep, her breaths became deeper, each small lung filled slowly.

"But, you know, maybe it was just my mind playing tricks on me, or the sun for a second casting a shadow on the big ash tree in that field. But I got such a sense of uneasiness for that split second. Anyway, it had left me by the time I'd got back to the road, and Lucy had gone to sleep by that stage too, but it was very strange I have to say. Sorry, it just came into my mind there looking at the shadow of the lilies in the window."

Nora didn't say anything, and they soon both fell asleep until well after the sun had set, lying on the leathered couch in the corner of the kitchen. Lifting their sore bodies, they brought Lucy to her cot, and each other to their bed, before all three drifted off to quiet, undisturbed sleep.

***

Inspector Moran woke, as he usually did, with the stretch of the dull blade of sun as it crossed across his face. Rising slowly, he lathered some soap in a bowl of hot water, and shave with a blue safety razor, clipping the dull grey hair that blinked from beneath the folds of his chin. Once complete, he washed his face, before getting dressed, and driving down to the station. He opened the door, said hello to the sergeant at the desk, before asking how Paudie had behaved throughout the night.

"You'd have got more trouble from a suckling lamb", Sergeant Murphy replied. "Not a peep out of him."

"Sure we'll go down and see how he's getting on will we?"

Paudie was in 7B, a cell away at the back of the station, far away from the other prisoners. As they turned the corner, Moran stopped.

"7B, Murphy, are you sure?"

"Yes sir", Murphy shouted from down the hall, "sure didn't you put him there yourself last night?"

He was right, Moran had dragged Paudie down the hall to the cell, and even turned off the light before leaving. But that still didn't change the fact that the cell was empty.

And just like that, Paudie O'Brien was gone, never to be seen again.

***

Years after Paudie had disappeared, Nora had a dream. At this stage she was nearly an old woman, and the events that defined her life seemed a distant memory. People rarely mentioned what had happened to her, but even when they did, they never went into the particulars.

She was sat on her bed, back around the time Lucy had gone. The bed was empty, and Lucy's cot was in the distance. Paudie was sat in a chair beside it.

Nora went to reach her hand out, but it was stuck, and slow, moving as if through glue.

Paudie raised his finger to his lips slowly, and told her to shush. He reached to the ground, and with rotting charcoal drew a symbol on the ground. Two lines crossed by another. They both watched silently as the black fragments floated up into the afternoon light in the room.

"Who are you to grieve?" Paudie said softly.

"Why should you care what happened? It doesn't work in straight lines. It's different to how you think."

Nora understood.

"Your life, anyone's life - you've only a lend of it. You've no purchase on it. So why would you care what I did."

As he spoke, Nora noticed his eyes were all black, and that he didn't blink. He remained calm, and Nora, in dreaming felt as though he spoke truth to her. She accepted, and was happy for it.

"If I plucked your babies eye and fastened her mouth shut with the bone I threw out for the dog. Or if I brought her to the Bogman. That's not his name, but the name I have for him."

Paudie became noticeably more hushed now as he spoke.

"If he wanted her, who was I to say no? I'm merely acting on his behalf. He's been here much longer than you or me, and he knows far more than we do about the real way of things. Your baby will live on Nora. I put her there meself, with him looking over my shoulder. I pushed her down. Deep into the ageless black. And she didn't scream, didn't wail, didn't cry, didn't say one word. She knew that was the way it was, and she let go of my thumb as left our time to enter a new."

Nora began to cry, joy breaking her heart.

"Be proud. As much as you can be. She was a fine baby."

Nora was.

***

The morning sun tracks time, thought Tom. Scorches the ground softly. How many suns have touched me? Bathed in golden light. How many moons for that matter, have I seen in the sky? Or slept under.

He sat at the edge of the cove, his feet in cold water. Lucy was in his arms.

***

In the deep dark of a country night a black cow slept in a field. Curled up on spindly legs, warm piles of flesh in the middle. Slow puffs of air curled from her wet nostrils, with hot hairy wafts of steam rising up from her meatpacked body. Rising and falling, she slept peacefully.

It's hard being a cow. You spend all day working for the farmer, chewing the cud, getting fat, keeping the grass down, from sunrise to sunset. And when you're not working, you're being milked, pulled by cold hands that are never gentle with delicate udders. Then you're packed off to eat more, and get fatter and fatter and work and work. Until you drop dead from tiredness, or are sent to the butcher to be put out of your misery and fed to hungry children. To be born a cow in rural Ireland - what rotten luck when you think of how they're treated in other countries. If I were a cow, I'd be as bad tempered as the rest of them. But then again, there's not much difference between us and the cows.

I don't know if all cows think like this, but I do know that this particular cow had other things on her mind when she was woken by the crack of a kick right in her belly. She felt the wind knocked from her, and trying to breathe, nearly fainted with the pain of splintering ribs that had burst her lungs. She looked around, panicked, and dazed, before feeling the pressure of hands at her bosom. With soft tension four long nipples were torn from her body.

Bellowing, she fell, and ran blind from pain, over fences and into darkness, before she stopped at the edge of a bog. Unsure of where to turn, she studied the quiet black pool, mad with panic. But then another kick pushed her in.

The sting of black peat and mud, of tarry ancient soil, mingled with the tear in her breast, entering her lungs through ribcracked protrusions in her side. She breathed in, blood and peat, the milk of a mother swirling in the soil. A black fleshy creature, buried in the earth, the pale light of the moon and the soft buzzing of a kitchen bulb (turned on in a nearby farmhouse with the commotion), the only witnesses.

Standing at the window, trying to gaze through the darkness, Murphy, the farmer, could see nothing. But the faint sense that the world still turns, and things still live in the dark of the night couldn't leave him, even as he pulled the silverballed cord, and quenched the filament flame in his kitchen. He turned on his linoleum floor, and went upstairs to his bed to lie awake, knowing that once his gaze was gone, the night would return to its usual order.

And sure enough, heavy feet tramped back across the field, away from the dead cow in the bog, and on with their journey, their only company the heavy silence of darkness.

Turn on, Tune in, Infiltrate, Disrupt

K. H. Vaughn

Terry stared at the lamp. Globules of viscous blue oozed upward in a column within the milky white fluid, broke apart, and drifted languidly to the base again. The room was brick with a worn couch and a mattress resting on old shipping pallets. The ceiling was high, and pipes ran across the walls, asbestos wrapping coming apart in chunks. He picked up a piece of the insulation, and it crumbled between his fingers like a dried white honeycomb. The stuff was everywhere. Out on the main floor of the Mill, he could hear a smoky mélange of laughter and political debate over the sound of Iron Butterfly. Students and drop-outs, mostly. Pretending to be beats, hippies, and revolutionaries. A few gurus selling Aquarian voodoo. He hated these people, or most of them at least. A handful were dangerous, but most of them were simply fakes.

"You o.k.?" Connie said from the doorway. "You're missing the party." He'd met her on campus protesting the ROTC recruiters. Pretty, blonde, smart. She was leading a crowd screaming "One, two, three, four! We don't want your fucking war!" when the cops started firing teargas. The riot didn't last long, but they broke the windows in the student union, flipped over a tow truck and set it on fire. Afterwards some of them said it was a symbol of protest. Terry didn't follow the semiotics, but later that night Connie smelled of burnt tires and the apple-blossom scent of phenacyl chloride.

"Just trying to get my head together," he said. "That dope is pretty strong."

"Sure, baby. Dwight said it came from Hawaii. Or California. Good shit, man."

"Yeah, good shit," he said, and rubbed his eyes. "I don't know, Connie. I'm tired of listening to coffee-house revolutionaries. That asshole Lonnie thinks growing a beard and wearing a beret is gonna change the world."

"Lonnie thinks it's gonna get him laid."

"Then I guess he's not that dumb. Chicks seem to dig it."

"Not all of them," she said. The lamp continued its languid dance of merger and separation in a slow-motion boil.

"You ever seen one of these things come uncorked?" he said. "Unbelievable. It explodes everywhere. Glass in the ceiling. Wax all over the place. Fucking mess."

"Come on, let's get out of here," she said, pulling him from the couch. They maneuvered through the open floor of the Mill, clusters of people drinking beer, smoking. Dean Martin pretended to stagger drunkenly on a silent television off to the side. He caught a glimpse of Professor Baloq, wild-eyed, lecturing to a small assembly.

The air on the loading dock was cooler, helped to clear his head. Beer bottles stacked along the ledge. A skinny hippy with wilted flowers braided around his neck picked at a guitar. He was too stoned to notice one of the strings had snapped.

"Hey look," Connie said. "'Guy with a guitar' is playing."

"Damn, I love that band."

They laughed. The Cuyahoga River drifted past sluggishly below, slick greasy surface reflecting industrial lights. Upstream, the stacks of the steel mill fumed.

"Some of them just want to get fuck around and get stoned, but we're gonna stop the war and we're gonna win on civil rights," she said. "If you pay attention, there are people who know what they're talking about."

"I'm not sure it really matters whether they do or not," he said.

###

Another night at home. His mother and sister. A conversation about the Pill that he was not supposed to hear, and that ended with his mother crying quietly. He snuck upstairs and took the phone from the stand in the hall into the bathroom.

They made him memorize the number. Warned him not to write it down anywhere. Clicking noises on the line. Tapped? Tapped by whom? His FBI handler came on. Asked him a list of perfunctory questions before getting to the point.

"What's your progress with Dr. Baloq's group?"

"I've been able to get in with students in his set. He's at the Mill most nights. What should I be looking for? Is he a Red? An Anarchist?"

"It may go beyond anything that simple. Assume nothing. Except that he may be dangerous."

"Yes, sir."

"There is another Bureau asset assigned to his case. Do not attempt to make contact. Do not identify yourself as part of this operation. Do not intervene. As a Confidential Agent, you do not possess the training or authority."

"I have to report a violation. I smoked part of a marijuana cigarette. I didn't think there was any other way to keep my cover. It's a test. If you don't join in, you can't get close. They dose each other to prove no one is a cop."

"Hold on." Dead silence on the line. Five minutes. Below, he heard the door slam and his sister's car start.

"Are you experiencing any psychiatric symptoms? Psychosis? Paranoia? Suicidal ideation?"

"No, sir."

"Hold on." More silence, punctuated with clicking noises. Ten minutes. A brief, muffled argument between his mother and father downstairs.

"We've encountered this before. Marijuana is authorized if necessary to maintain your cover, but minimize use. Make excuses, fake inhaling. Whatever you have to do. Under no circumstances are you to take heroin or cocaine. Be aware that they may lace a reefer cigarette with other substances."

"Yes, sir."

"Don't trust anyone. Report back in one week. Sooner, if you have actionable intelligence."

***

When he went back downstairs, his sister was gone and his mother was pretending nothing had happened. His father was watching the Indians game on the big color console. Terry flopped on the couch. The Indians were at Country Stadium, and the old man sure hated the White Sox.

"Oh, you should shave and get a haircut," his mother said. "Robert, can't you make him shave those awful sideburns?"

"If he wants to wear his sideburns like Chester Arthur, I can think of no finer tribute to our twenty-first President. Say, honey, would you grab me a beer from the fridge? One for Terry too."

His mother left a pair of Strohs and retreated to the kitchen. Dad in the recliner, Terry on the sofa.

"It's fine for college, sport, but you'll need to do something about that when you start interviewing for jobs. Nobody with a beard ever amounted to anything."

"I missed the news earlier," Terry said. "Anything happening?"

"Same as every day. Demonstrations. Riots. The whole country is losing its mind."

"People have a lot to be angry about. No one wants to be in Nam. The cops are beating people."

"What are the cops supposed to do? All those blocks on Hough and in Glenville burned in riots. National Guard called in twice. Snipers killing cops in the streets. It's the communists starting it all. I didn't fight the Chinese in Korea so commies could start riots in my own back yard."

Sweat beaded on Terry's beer bottle. Hopkins took Tiant deep to tie the game. His dad sighed, looked around for Terry's mother then went to the fridge for another beer.

"Your mom was pregnant when I got activated and sent to Korea," he said as he walked back to his lounger. "I thought I was done after we beat the Japs. Came home, got a job, married your mother, but I stayed in the reserves for the money. A lot of us did. Nobody thought anyone would be stupid enough to start another war, so when Kim Il-sung and Stalin invaded South Korean we got caught with our pants down. So they called up the reservists and threw us in there until they could get their shit together. Sorry about the language. I guess you're old enough to hear it. Anyhow, I made it home for your second birthday in one piece. More or less. Anyway, what I'm saying is no one wants to be there, but the damned hippies aren't going to solve the problem and most people understand we have to be there whether we like it or not. We didn't start this thing, but the Army's getting it under control now. They've got the A Shau Valley cleaned out and they whipped the NVA at Binh Ba. Nixon says they'll pull 25,000 more troops by the end of summer. We'll have it sewn up before too long. This time we're doing it right."

***

Lonnie was reading the new *Playboy* in the back of the van as they drove down toward the Mill. "Hugh Hefner is a great man," he said. "Opening minds, throwing off the Patriarchy. He's liberating our sisters."

"He's sure liberating their tits," Maliq said. "I don't see how that helps the cause. That's not treating our Sisters with respect." Maliq had moved from Hartford a few weeks before, just in time for final exams and an attempt to hold a sit-in at the Courthouse to protest the death sentence for an activist who had led a running gun battle against the cops in Glenville last summer. He'd moved quickly into the Mill crowd.

"You got it all wrong, man. In twenty years, everyone will be fucking everyone whenever they feel like it. There won't be any judgment. No more rape. Men and women will be free and equal."

Connie drove while Terry fiddled with the eight-track.

"Hey, Maliq," Terry called back over his shoulder. "I heard you got roughed up by the pigs last week. What'd you do?"

"Got born Black in America, man."

"Right on."

***

It was dusk when they reached the Mill, abandoned by a bankrupted company and taken over by the people. Lonnie, Connie, Maliq, and Terry piled out of the van, made their way across the weedy, trash-strewn lot. Inside they found beer and dope, and mingled on the main floor. Tie-dye and denim. Military jackets and Cuban sunglasses. The air was thick and humid and it felt close despite the wide open space and high ceilings. They separated, drifted from cluster to cluster. Some talking music, others politics. Terry was finishing his fourth beer when Connie pulled him from a small group where a kid with a PLA hat with a red star was explaining that Mao, Castro, and Che were champions of the struggle.

"People all over the world are throwing off the oppressor and the imperialists. The capitalists and the racist slave-owners. There will be peace, man. By the year 2000 we'll look back at how much better the world was because of heroes like them."

"Hey Terry, the Professor wants to see you," Connie said, looping her arm inside his.

***

Baloq had set up in what had been some sort of supervisor's office off the floor. More couches and an oriental rug on the concrete floor. He had a pair of battered oversized leather chairs framing a small table. Books and papers littered an army surplus desk. He smiled when Terry appeared at the door and gestured to a seat. He wore jeans, sandals, and a mustard turtleneck shirt.

"I don't remember you from any of my classes, Terry. But I hear good things about you."

"Thank you, sir."

"No need for that. We're all equals here. Call me Peter."

"Right on."

"I was wondering what you want with the Mill. Why are you here?"

"I'm not really sure. I just feel like that scene in *The Graduate*, you know? Hoffman's at his graduation party and all these old guys are giving him bad advice and laying all these expectations on him about what he's supposed to be. I just want to hide at the bottom of the pool. I want something authentic, and it isn't there."

"I understand you attended the police academy. Why did you drop out?" "I guess I was trying to please my old man when I joined up, you know? He was in the army, real patriot. I always trusted the government. I heard people talk, but I couldn't believe our own government killed King or the Kennedys. Then I saw the cops beating people outside the convention in Chicago last year. They put tear gas and dogs on a bunch of kids just trying to stop the war. I felt like I was on the wrong side."

"Your eyes are partway open, at least. There's a process of consciousness-raising to disrupt the narrative of history and patterns of thought you have been force-fed your entire life. But there is more. We can open your eyes further. You can attain the spiritual awakening that the Age of Aquarius promises."

Baloq removed a book from desk, an old leather-bound volume, and took a sheet of paper from within. It looked like a sheet of stamps, with yellow squiggles on a brown background. No, not squiggles, more like a spiral. It was hard to say.

"Take this. Place it on your tongue."

"Naw, I think I'm good. I'm already pretty high. I've heard that stuff isn't good for you."

"Alcohol isn't good for you. It dulls the senses and atrophies the brain. You know, one of the most difficult challenges we face is reprogramming our mind from the lies that we have been told by the system. Those in power, or who believe that they have power, lie to you. They depend on your willingness to believe their lies. We depend on your willingness to see the truth. To slip the bonds of ignorance and illusion. This is your first time, so it is a minimal dose. You'll see. Do you trust me?"

Terry hesitated. Another test. If he didn't comply, he'd never get close to Baloq's plans. He placed the piece of blotter paper on his tongue. For a moment, Baloq's eyes expanded so that cold blackness filled both orbs, and stars glittered within like ice crystals.

***

The lights sparkled and rainbow trails followed his hands as he waved them before his face. He giggled. Connie was saying something he could not follow.

"They will say 'does not drown but decays. Does not drown but decays,'" she said, but then she walked further away through the smoke and he lost track of her. The room was febrile. People moved at strange angles as he tried to make his way through the crowd. They were hazy, strange.

But the lights were beautiful.

He stood and stared as a lamp suspended on a long thin wire like a globe or pure fire, or a star in the heavens. Moths fluttered around it and he heard the television announcer say that Yastrzemski had hit a ball off Ellings deep into right field at Cleveland Stadium. But it was too dark out now for them to be playing. He turned and there was a guy he hadn't seen before in a worn Army uniform standing in the doorway. His beard was thick and ratty.

"Were you in the war?" Terry asked. He wasn't sure he was saying the words out loud, but the soldier nodded at him.

"What's the worst thing you saw over there?"

"I killed a baby."

"By accident? Shooting at some Viet Cong and the kid got in the way, right?   "No, man," he said. "It wasn't like that at all."

And he walked away, leaving Terry on the loading dock alone.

He looked out across the oozing river, at the lights of Cleveland across the way. Hazy smoke from joints, incense, and cigarettes blended from the smoke from the factories and mills along the river. A train crossed the railroad bridge just downstream, giving off a long mournful whistle for the impending death of the American heartland. The blue lights of a police car flashed in the distance.

"Fucking pigs," he said. He laughed. He tried to repeat it but he was laughing so hard that he could do no more than squeal incoherently. There was a message spray-painted on the wall that he could not make out, but that seemed incredibly significant to him, and overhead, the stars whirled and twisted madly.

***

"What is your report?" It sounded like his handler had him on a speakerphone.

"I'm getting closer to Balog. He talked with me privately for a little while. Everything he says is the same consciousness-raising mumbo-jumbo. He offered me something - LSD I think. I didn't take it. Said I was already too high."   "Describe it."   "Blotter paper. Brown with a yellow design on it. A spiral. Or maybe a question mark. It was hard to-"

"Hold on." Dead static on the line again. "We need you to obtain a sample. Do not take the substance. We will leave a package for you at the dead drop. Use it to establish that you are 'hip' or make a trade, but don't use it."

"What is it?"

"Pure LSD-25. You can say you got it from a pharmacy student you know. Her information will be included. Burn it afterwards. If they contact her, she'll vouch for you."

"Look, I feel like I'm getting in a little over my head with this. I don't think there's anything going on at the Mill except people talking and getting high."

"You know that the Black Panthers tortured and killed a man in Connecticut last month because they thought he was an informant."

"Was he?"

The line went silent again. In the morning, he found an envelope filled with sheets of flower power designs in the university library stacks, hidden in an issue of *Terrae Incognitae*.

***

"Man, they rioted in Ann Arbor last night," Connie said. "Fifteen cops taken to the hospital." They were laying on the green near the library. Clouds scudded overhead. Terry was supposed to be in a 9:30 English lecture; he didn't know about the others.

"Right on," Lonnie said. "How many student?"

"Seven."

"Two to one? Shit, if that was news from Vietnam, they'd call it a victory," Maliq said.

"You got any more of that acid, Terry?" Lonnie asked.

"Yeah."

"Where'd you get that from?" Connie asked. "I never figured you for a chemist or a dealer."

"Pharmacy student I know. I can hook you up. Not as good as the professor's stash though."

"You tried that?" Maliq asked. Could he be the other FBI asset? He was from Hartford. He came right around the time the Panthers killed that guy, too. Shit, if he was an informant, it would get back to them that he had lied. He'd have to tell his handler. No. He could say he was just showing off to impress the Mill crowd.

"Yeah, just the one time," he said. "I'd like to get some more though."

"I bet that can be arranged," Lonnie said.

"I wish we could get more going on campus," Connie said. "All the action is in the streets around here. My dad's in Berkeley. They're on the front line out there. Fucking Cleveland, man."

"Your old man's protesting?" Maliq said. "That's cool. Mine's too worried about keeping his job. Says I should just keep my head down and make sure I don't get kicked out of school and lose my draft exemption."

"Yeah, my pop's pretty square too," Terry said. "He doesn't do anything but watch ball games and photography."

"Photography?" Lonnie said. His eyes narrowed. "He let you touch his cameras and shit?"

"No. He says there's chemicals. Plus the equipment is expensive."

"Dig it. All these old guys, locked down so tight? Photography clubs? They're taking pictures of naked ladies. All those old guys, pretending to be so upstanding. Bunch of old panty sniffers, man. Every last one of them."

"Hey, you better watch what you're saying about my dad," Terry said, anger surging suddenly in his chest.

"I'm just saying, they're all pervs like everybody else."

"Maybe like you Lonnie," Connie said. She touched Terry's arm, just a pat. Just enough to keep him from getting up and saying the next thing that would lead to a fight.

***

"Pop, you home?" Terry called. "Mom?" The house was empty and still, except the curtains blowing slightly and the sound of the television on in the living room. Almost two o'clock. His dad must have run out to the store before the game. He'd have to be quick.

His dad had built a small darkroom in the back of the garage. There was a latch on the inside of the door to keep people from walking in when he was developing film, but that was all. He relied on his authority in the home to keep people out of his private domain otherwise. Terry closed the door behind him and pulled the chain for the work light. The space was cramped, and smelled of cigarettes and Aqua Velva, with an underlying funk of vinegar and spoiled eggs. Pictures from last Christmas hung on lines over the wooden work bench. Terry, his mother and sister. The white aluminum tree with red balls and garland. "It'll last forever," his dad pleaded when his mom saw it for the first time. She had been so embarrassed by it when her friends and family came to visit.

He searched efficiently, moved through the boxes and cans of materials. Envelopes of negatives, and files of developed pictures. Family events and holidays. His uncle with his new Cadillac from a few years ago. Some experiments with nature shots: birds at the feeder and sunlight shining through icicles. A file of correspondence sent to photography magazine contests, consisting almost entirely of submission forms and rejection letters. There was no hint of Lonnie's accusation. The closest thing was a few pictures of his mother in a modest one-piece from their trip to Hawaii when he was little.

He closed the darkroom up quietly and returned to the house, through the kitchen and into the living room. His dad was in his lounger with the game on.

"Hey, sport. Didn't hear you come in."

"No, I was in the garage."

"Did you--ah, dammit, he sure got all of that one."

Terry looked up to see Yastrzemski trotting around second while Ellings looked on. His stomach churned and the hair on his head bristled. His dad shook his head.

"Two-nothing to start the game. Well, we were third in the whole League last year. They'll right the ship. With the new divisions they got, it'll be even easier to make the playoffs. Hey, you alright? You look a little sick."

"Yeah, Pop." He said. "I'm o.k. Everything's fine."

***

"Some girl Connie called," his sister yelled from the doorway as he ran out to Lonnie and Maliq in Lonnie's pickup.

"If she calls again, tell her I'll call her back."

"Ain't you going to mass with me an' mom?"

He gave her a disgusted look and got in to laughter and the Rolling Stones.

He'd never seen the Mill in daylight. Trash and weeds choked the parking lot and riverbank. Rainbow slicks sparkled between shoals of clotted sludge in the river beyond. There were a lot of cars. Not as many as on a weekend night, but there were a lot of people inside. Their feet crunched on broken glass as they walked across the broken asphalt toward the dim space within.

The sun filtered through the skylights and high windows well above the floor. Dust motes whorled in hazy columns that played upon the uneven concrete. It looked as though most of the trash from the night before had been swept out the back, or at least to the corners where oil-stained machinery mounts still protruded from the floor.

"There any beer?" he asked. Lonnie shook his head.

The Mill crowd shifted about on the floor, groups forming and dispersing, talking angrily about the war and the government. "The problem is escalation, man," Maliq said. "Nixon's gonna nuke Hanoi, and then the Russians will retaliate. If we don't take steps to control and prevent the propagation of this shit, there will be more and more violence. We've got to take control from the warmongers and capitalists. By any means necessary, man." It seemed to Terry that only the more intense personalities had come, and the room was agitated by the time Professor Baloq appeared.

His voice was a quiet murmuration at first, but it slowly picked up in volume an intensity as he preached against Nixon and the war, against the bankers and factory owners. Terry had heard it all before. Rage and fear and demands for change that led only to snipers and bombings and riots. They were going to burn the country to the ground. He'd heard more than enough when Baloq shifted into a rant about expanded consciousness and ancient wisdom, spewing an inchoate mix of Eastern mysticism, astrology, and other mythologies that Terry had never heard of.

"But the words themselves are empty, my friends," Baloq shouted. "It is only in the lived communal consciousness of experience with the alien Other that we realize our place within the cosmos. And that time, my friends, is now." He held a sheaf of brown blotter paper aloft. "You have all had a taste. Today, we throw the gates of perception open."

Terry began to back away, but Lonnie and Maliq pressed him from the sides.

"You need this, brother," Maliq said.

"We're gonna be shipping this all over, man," Lonnie said. "Gonna force everybody's eyes wide open."

"You guys go ahead. This is too intense for me."

"Bullshit," Lonnie said. "Unless you're still with the pigs, man. There's always that option, isn't there, Terry?"

"What? Fuck you, man."

But they had his arms tightly and there were too many others around him to fight. Dozens of them glaring at him now. They'd beat him, maybe try and force him to confess. Or worse.

"Everyone calm down," Baloq said, coming toward them. Terry could see the yellow symbols on the blotter squirming. "Terry is one of us. Remember that it is an essential truth of all revolutions that most people must be dragged kicking and screaming into the fight. Try not to think about it, son. If you do, if you resist, you'll drown. If you don't, you won't."

"Always whining about wanting to get to what's true," Lonnie said. "You want to know the real world? Trip to this." Lonnie held his mouth open painfully. He tried to turn his face away, but Baloq forced squares of brown blotter inside. It took seconds for the ceiling to open up and the void to enter his head again.

All around him, the Mill crowd were changing. Some stood like wax statues, their bodies twisted in strange poses, black tears oozing from their eyes. Others staggered or rolled on the floor. A man in a tuxedo with slick black hair produced bouquets and snakes of rainbow scarves on a stage while a woman in a dress stood beside him and looked on at the growing mounds of silk at his feet. He saw Connie reaching for him before she was shoved away and then he was running naked down the road from the village, screaming, his back burning while a photographer snapped photos.

His thoughts became less clear after that, disrupted by strange intrusions and synesthesias, while the stars churned in his mind. Later, or maybe earlier, he saw students standing slack-jawed and comatose, black tears running down their faces in torrents to pool upon the floor, soaking through their sneakers, running over the tops inside. Maliq was lying on his side, moaning. Gut and chest wriggling, squirming. Something trying to get out. Bloody froth bubbled from his mouth. Strange tubular creatures with fan-like wings moved across snow-blown basalt as Terry watched a golf ball fly away from him, far across the lunar landscape and into oblivion.

Then Connie was there again, helping him to his feet, and his FBI handler appeared in the middle of the Mill floor, chanting something that made him nauseated and afraid. Agent Fallon made a strange gesture with his hand and Baloq's arm shriveled, curled, and blackened. Two balls of fire fell from the starry rift in the ceiling and flew around the room at the Agent's direction. The fireballs scattered the crew across the floor of the Mill, and one picked up Lonnie and carried him high in the air while he shrieked and burned. His legs kicked as he turned to ash and the charred stumps clad in western boots and smoking denim cuffs fell to the floor. Terry tried to scream, but he could only choke out words in languages he did not know while urine ran down his legs.

In the lot outside the Mill, cars pulled away spraying rocks and ground glass. The fiery motes screamed from the building, passing over the river before returning to the sky again. Within moments, the oozing river was on fire, pungent black smoke roiling from the sickly orange flames. Connie was yelling at him but he could not hear her.
###

He woke up in the hospital. Connie - he never found out her real name - had called the Bureau when she realized he was in trouble. Their handler informed him by telephone that the Cuyahoga had been ignited by sparks from a passing train and that the Mill investigation was closed. Baloq had been taken to Lima State Hospital for the Criminally Insane.

"Sir, I saw you-"

"Son, you were under the influence of an unusually powerful psychedelic. You don't know what you saw or didn't see. You'll be monitored for residual symptoms, including so-called 'flashbacks,' but our experts tell me that you should not experience any permanent effects. I can tell you that, thanks in no small part to your efforts, we have neutralized a significant threat to our national security."

***

His mother came by that evening, fussed at the nurses and frowned at his hair. She sat in the chair by his bed in silence for a long time.

"I'm leaving your father," she said, when she finally spoke.

"I didn't know you two were having problems," he said.

"Then you haven't been paying very much attention," she said.

She left a short time later. He lay in the bed, staring at the ceiling, listening to the evening sounds on the ward. Outside his room, a small television set sat in the hallway. Ed Sullivan introduced Fantasio, who began his scarf routine. He couldn't see the set, but he knew what color the scarves were. Tears formed in the corners of his eyes and he sobbed silently while the audience applauded.

***

A week later he was home. His mother and sister were at his aunt's house in Evanston. He sat on the floor in the upstairs hallway and listened to his handler on the phone. Connie had been reassigned. They wouldn't tell him where.

"You've received the package."

"Tickets to 'An Aquarian Exposition' in August," Terry said. "Wallkill, New York."

"It's been moved to Bethel. Zoning issues. The organizers are planning for 600 toilets for 50,000 people and they'll have twice that many. Fucking hippies will be rolling in their own filth. We'll wire you cash. You received the other materials necessary for this operation?"

Terry looked at the sheets of blotter paper clipped neatly to the poster and tickets.

"The brown acid," he said.

"Not on the phone, son. You know better than that."

"Yes, sir."

He hung up the phone, hid the envelope in his dresser, and walked downstairs. His dad was in the living room watching the ball game. Terry grabbed a pair of beers from the fridge and joined him.

"Good timing, sport," his dad said, setting down his empty bottle. It tipped and rolled with a clatter against another.

"Who's winning?"

"Tribe's up on the Senators, seven - two. Tiant's pitching a gem. Hey, you want to go see the Independence Day fireworks up on the lake tomorrow night? Gonna be a nice show."

"Sure."

Terry fiddled with his beer, tried to keep his hands from shaking.

"Say, Pop? Can I ask you something?"

"Sure."

Williams was sending Shellenbeck out to face the Indians in the bottom of the 8th. Droplets shook from the bottle to spot the floor. He tried to clear his throat.

"Well, what's the matter?"

"What's the worst thing you saw over there? In Korea, I mean."

His dad shifted in his chair, stared at the television.

"I killed a baby."

"By accident? Shooting at some Viet- I mean, North Koreans and the kid got in the way. Right?" His voice shook, and he could barely get the words out. "No," he said quietly, and paused to take a sip from his beer. "It wasn't like that at all."

Down through Black Abysses

Pete Rawlik

". . . to Cyclopean and many-columned Y'ha-nthlei, and in that lair of the Deep Ones we shall dwell amidst wonder and glory forever."

Are those the words my cousin wrote? Was he that naïve? Was I? It all seems so long ago, but in truth it has been only days, weeks at the most. They said I was a lunatic, all those years ago, and my father and grandfather shut me up in that Canton madhouse. But Uncle Douglas and Grandmother knew the truth and it cost both of them their lives. Only my cousin Robert was strong enough to discover the facts and embrace them. He engineered my escape and planned for both of us to go east to Innsmouth and then into the sea where our great-great grandmother Pth'thya-l'yi was waiting, calling us to the sub-aqueous metropolis of Y'ha-nthlei, calling us home.

We were fools.

I haven't much time to write this. I can hear them outside. I've taken refuge on the second floor of an abandoned warehouse that overlooks the Innsmouth waterfront. I write these words on pages I found in a long forgotten desk. When I am done, I shall secure them into an abandoned mason jar and throw it into the harbor. It is perhaps the only way to tell my story and assure that it reaches the outside world. The world must know the truth, my cousin Robert must be stopped, before he too reaches Innsmouth and undertakes the journey to Y'ha-nthlei.

Robert had a plan, but I, who had been locked away for years, could no longer wait. The voice of my ancestor was so loud, so insistent, so demanding. I stole his car, his money, his supplies and I made my way to Innsmouth without him. I could have gone anywhere really. I could have slipped into Lake Erie or the Ohio River, or any of a dozen waterways and then made my way to the Atlantic. Yet somehow all these options seemed wrong. I was drawn by something to the Manuxet. Some ancestral memory or impulse made it impossible to go anywhere else but the headwater of that dark river. Like some strange salmon I had no choice but to follow the path that my breeding had laid out for me, no matter how maddening, dangerous or ridiculous it seemed. I stopped only for fuel, rolling down the window only enough to slip the attendant the required payment, I collected no change. Never did I let my crude disguise of a hat and muffler slip. I relieved myself in the woods along deserted and desolate back roads, always with the motor running. I subsisted on the rations of dried foodstuffs and bottled drink that my dear cousin had assembled for the two of us. I followed the course Robert had laid out for us, passing through Erie and then wilds of western New York, before coming into Massachusetts and crossing the Round Mountains to pick up the Aylesbury Pike toward Arkham. I was careful to turn east and skirt Bolton before finally stopping the car at the headwaters of the Manuxet which steals water from the Miskatonic through a vast marshy land.

It was there, at the end of the land leg of my journey and the beginning of the waterborne that I let my guard down and was suddenly endangered. As I stood there in the stream, in a godforsaken marsh, in the morning hours, a man suddenly appeared in my field of vision. His uniform identified him as a soldier; one I supposed of those that Robert had told me had been deployed to occupy Innsmouth. He was alone, with a gun slung over his shoulder. That he surprised me goes without saying, but I think it was he who was the most startled, for he seemed surprised simply by my presence. I was naked, half submersed in the cold spring water of the creek, my gills flexing in the cold air, a strange crested fin running down my back. Without a word he raised his rifle and took aim, I panicked and leapt through the air more out of reflex than conscious thought. In an instant I was on him, his throat was slit, and the claws of my right hand were warm with blood and gore. I left him there on the road to die; his hand clutching his throat his eyes wide in fear of the knowledge that he was close to dead, his mouth gasping for air and instead gurgling bubbles of blood.

Spurred on by the horror which I had inflicted on another man I slipped into the icy black waters and let them carry me downstream, toward the Manuxet, toward the harbor and the reef beyond, and deep beneath those fathomless waters lay my goal of Y'ha-nthlei! The stream twisted and turned, grew deep and then shallow. In places I could swim freely, my huge, unblinking eyes able to see even in the black-stained waters. Elsewhere I had to crawl across muddy shoals and rocky deposits. Each time I rose above the water I knew I put myself at risk and my actions during these exposures were swift and direct. Finally I emerged from the stinking fen and the small stream consolidated with others which ran faster and deeper as a large creek. A little further downstream and the creek joined with others and the channel deepened to become the Manuxet River. So deep and dark were the waters that surrounded me that I no longer feared being observed. I relaxed and let the current carry me.

I rounded a bend and then suddenly there was a curious taste, metallic and electric at the same time, and my skin began to itch. I passed by a cavernous industrial pipe and could somehow sense the lingering accumulation of lye and other chemical wastes that still leached into the waters. Irritated I kicked my thick legs and sped away from the area as fast as I could. Another bend in the river and suddenly my speed was increasing without any effort on my part. There was an odd sound in the water like a thousand tiny drums being beaten. It took me a moment but only that to realize I was approaching the falls, the three-tiered water fall that was the heart of Innsmouth. Slowing my movement I caught sight of a bridge pillar and latched on to it. Instinctively I had no fear of going over the falls, my body was resilient enough to resist the pressure of the deepest of seas, but consciously I was still just a man, one who needed to prepare himself for what was to come next.

I don't know what possessed me to rise to the surface and observe my surroundings, but I did, and I immediately regretted it. There were soldiers on the bridge above me, and the one further down the river, and along the roads that ran on both sides. In the bright morning sun, the shadows of the bridges were all in the wrong places and offered no protection. They saw me just after I broke the surface. Guns went from shoulders to hands and took a bead on my position. There was a rifle crack, and then another. Something whizzed past my head and smashed into the stones beside me exploding fragments into the river around me. One grazed my shoulder, cutting deep and sending a wave of burning pain through my arm. I didn't scream but instead reflexively sought the refuge of the deep water. They were yelling as I dove back under, and more rounds sped through the water around me.

I was immediately caught up in the current and whisked downstream. I hit a rock, and then something that wasn't a rock, but rather a mesh of rope. There was a net across the river and I was suddenly caught in it, but not yet tangled. More gunfire. Even through the water I could hear the rifles cracking. I suppose they were shooting at the bulge I made in the net. I crawled my way across the webbing, searching for a way through. Suddenly the lines tensed and the net was being reeled in, with me in it. I was like a fish in a seine, but unlike a fish I knew how to escape from this trap, and had the strength and tools to do so. I slashed at the ropes and felt them cut beneath my claws. I slashed again, and again, desperate to escape the closing trap. Then with another cut the ropes broke and I tumbled out of the enclosure. As I fell into the water, bullets whizzing past me, I hit a submerged rock worn smooth from ages of rushing water and sand, but my wounded arm throbbed from the impact. I rolled over the edge and down the falls. The pool below caught me and swirled my wounded body around before shooting me out and down over a second plunge. I barely had time to recover before I was caught in the speeding waters and shot down the river over a third drop. This time I was able to avoid any rocks and regain my bearings. I pushed off the hard bottom of the pool and sped down river.

In the lower part of the river I could taste the freshwater of the Manuxet mixing with the brine of the harbor. I swam forward and with each stroke I could sense more of the open sea and less of the river. I cleared the river mouth and moved quickly through the harbor. The small bay tasted of diesel and rotted wood and dead fish and something else, something chemical that reminded me of gunpowder and dynamite. It only took a few strokes to propel myself across the harbor and out of the inlet. In the open ocean all the smells and tastes of the Manuxet faded, and soon all I was left with was the feeling of the sea as it passed through my gills, and the voice in my head calling me, urging me forward, louder than ever.

I swam east towards the rocks that marked Devil Reef. The sun was bright and flooded the surface layers of the sea with light. Around me small fish, cod and blues, swam gracefully in the clear green waters. A bull shark, presumably drawn by my blood, stalked me from a distance, circling, looking for a weakness it could exploit. When it finally decided to move off and leave me alone I felt a wave of relief pass through me. Not that I couldn't have taken the animal, he was no match for me, but I had no desire for a confrontation. I had had enough of conflict, of doctors, of nurses, of soldiers, and of boats that suddenly were coming for me. I could hear their engines and the men screaming orders. Soldiers were searching the waters for me. I slipped under the surface and dove deep, leaving the sunlit world of soldiers behind.

The water was thick with oxygen and my gills felt rich as it ran past them. I sped down with powerful kicks and not a backward glance. I had thought that the descent from the surface to Y'ha-nthlei would be a phantasmagorical transition from one world to another, but the only thing that happened as I fell into the deeper ocean was that the sun slowly died and the darkness grew. I went deep, deep beneath the surface, down past where the fish danced in the last dim light from above. Beyond that there were still fish, but they were no longer joyous creatures of the shining sea, but rather dark brooding things with huge mouths that lumbered through the thick dark waters and menaced each other with long predatory investigations. As I fell, there began a kind of precipitation, not unlike snow in appearance, but entirely unlike it in composition. This strange pale fall was neither rain nor snow, but the accumulated particles from the upper levels which, for one reason or another, had lost their buoyancy and were now slowly falling through the abyss. It was a detrital rain, composed of plankton, algae, plants and even the carcasses and bones of fish. We all fell together, and I hoped that I was more than just another piece of decayed refuse raining down in the dark.

The great flat expanse of the ocean floor, covered with rock and silt was a desolate place, filled with batrachian beasts that could barely be called fish. Huge black shapes that were little more than mouths with fins hunted chimerical horrors that lay on the floor sifting nourishment from the rain of decay. Horned and hungry crabs picked through the carcass of an ancient whale, while great gelatinous worms bored through the bones with grinding teeth. I dared not pause but instead followed that siren call in my head and angled myself to fall below the surface and into the secret trench in the sea floor that seemed to crack the very world itself. I cut through the waters like I belonged there, like I had been made to dwell and sail in the dark and empty depths of the sea.

I was there, floating in an ocean that was both abyssal and subterranean, when I first caught site of the lights of the sub-aquaeous metropolis of Y'ha-nthlei. My cousin described it as many-columned, but more appropriately it would be said to be many-arched, for great sets of arcs rose up from the center line and the outer edges bearing great tattered sails that billowed in the current. Terraced palaces covered in barnacles, corals, and twisting fronds of things that were only semi-vegetative surrounded the central row of arches and flapping tissues. Outside, beyond the fringes of the city, giant shadows moved about, ancient things, that I knew to be kin, descendants of our ancestors Father Dagon and Mother Hydra. These things were old even when my great-great-grandmother Pth'thya-l'yi was young, and I knew she had been born nearly three hundred millennia ago, and had dwelt here in Y'ha-nthlei for the last eighty-thousand years. They were to be feared, these things of age, and avoided, for they were terrible and capricious.

A score of shadows rose up out of the city to greet me, and as they did the voice in my head, that whispering siren call that had haunted me for so many years finally ceased. Instead my mind was filled with information, I was being spoken to, informed, and educated. These were the Daughters of Y'ha-dra, spawned by Pth'thya-l'yi through parthenogenesis. They were sisters, but more than that because they were genetically identical, not only to one another but to their parent as well, one of the primordial Deep Ones Y'ha. It was from her title "dra" meaning "virgin" that men had come to know her as Hydra. Only her daughters perpetuated that name, mostly amongst men, such as those in Innsmouth, they had cultivated as worshippers. Here in her city of Y'ha-nthlei she was known only as Y'ha, and I quickly learned that nthlei was the word for those bound to her service. I found this sudden influx of knowledge invigorating, and was reminded of Greek place names which often were bound to a particular deity, such as Athens and Hermopolis.

Pth'thya-l'yi was amongst the Daughters, and she came to me and took me by the hand and led me down into Y'ha-nthlei. We floated down to a great open space at one end of the city. Around us, many other Deep Ones had gathered, all were female, though how I knew this I can't explain, but I knew it to be true. There in the floor of the city, located in the center of a slow descending grade, was a great reflecting pool, yards and yards apart, I thought it was glass, but as I stared at the glossy darkness I could see liquid running across its surface. It was strange to see one fluid of a different color and density entrapped in that great circular pool while all about me the waters of the ocean itself flowed.

The Daughters, my ancestor included, intoned some ancient choral, and soon were joined in by those masses that lurked about the edges. It was a queer thrumming noise, generated from within the bodies of my companions, and filled the space around me with a fantastic, electric vibration. I realized immediately that I was participating in an initiation rite, one that had likely played out repeatedly over the vast epochs the city had existed. Thrilled that I was so quickly accepted, I allowed my limbs to be gripped by the Daughters and paraded above the black semi-translucent pool such that all gathered could see me. Any sense of modesty or shame had been lost, for there was no such concept amongst these things. The fear and humility involved with one's own body was discarded, left behind on the surface as the human construct and taboo that it was.

At some signal that I did not note, my retinue moved away from the pool, and I, not knowing what else to do, followed. We proceeded down the length of the city moving past the great arches wrapped in billowing material and down along a ridge where similar arches had either been destroyed or never completed. Beyond these, the structure of the city grew thin, though in the distance I could see another set of furled arches, which seemed even larger. I thought perhaps these massive spires were our destination, but instead we floated off to one side and skimming over the surface of the great barnacled city we ducked beneath a huge tubular outcropping that seemed to connect two different lobes of the metropolis.

There in the shadow of this weird bridge I was ushered into a kind of cave or tunnel, which seemed not only artificial, for it was symmetrical, but also natural for the walls seemed to be composed of imperfect layers and veins. The chamber inside was vast and throbbed with a strange rhythmic vibration, the water was strangely warm and carried with it a peculiar scent that reminded me of blood and other bodily fluids. Across the floor a trail of globular cysts lay imbedded in semitransparent, gelatinous ooze that trailed off to the walls of the cavern which were lined with row upon row of telamons, sculpted male figures that functioned as columnar supports.

If only that had been true.

Pth'thya-l'yi pointed at the carvings and I heard the word nthlei. I saw that there was a vacancy amongst those grim statues of amphibious men, and toward it I was ushered. As we drew closer I saw the details on those strange carvings. I saw the fine scales, the muscular arms, the veins that ran beneath, the blood that coursed there. I also saw the queer tendrils that seemed to hold them in place against the wall, the same tendrils that slowly unfurled from the wall and reached out from the vacancy and groped in my direction. In my mind I suddenly understood the true meaning of the word nthlei.

As that terrible realization suddenly dawned on me and I recognized where I was and why. I recognized the horrific position I had been led to and was expected to voluntarily submit. I broke free from the gentle grip of my escort and fled toward the strange cleft that we had passed through. My captors seemed startled and I somehow knew that in the eons that this ceremony had been carried out, that no one had ever rejected the honor. The Daughters of Y'ha-dra had been entombing their male brethren in this place for more than a hundred thousand years, and none had ever rebelled.

Until now. Until me.

They didn't know what to do. My reaction was unprecedented and so I was allowed to escape. Through the fathoms I sped, desperate to reach the surface and escape the fate I seemed destined to. I looked back only once, and that was enough to drive me to move faster, for what I saw, what I finally comprehended, what I finally understood about Y'ha-nthlei was enough to drive me over the edge. If I wasn't mad before, surely this revelation was enough to accomplish the task and set me firmly into the mantle of lunacy.

I broke the surface and discovered that the sun had set and the moon now reigned in the sky. That dim light glistened off of the surface and illuminated the rocks of the Devil Reef. In the distance the village of Innsmouth glowed weakly, barely breaking the darkness that marked where the night was eclipsed by the land itself. Hours earlier I had had but one desire, to leave the world of the surface behind, now it beckoned to me and seemed my only salvation. With every effort I struggled against tide and time to lessen the distance between myself and that decayed refuge. I feared that in an instant the sisters would overtake me and drag me back down into the darkness, down through those black abysses.

That was hours ago. It had taken them time, but once the Daughters had recovered from their shock they had no choice but to pursue me. Their voices called to me in my head, searching, pleading, and even commanding me to return. With each passing moment those voices are growing stronger, which I can only assume means that they are getting closer. My time is short. The trail I left from the harbor cannot have gone unnoticed. Either the soldiers or my ancestors will have found it by now. My discovery is inevitable.

The clues were there all the time in our dreams, and in the history of Innsmouth itself. How did I and my cousin not see the truth? For eighty-thousand years that which had been our great-great-grandmother had dwelled within Y'ha-nthlei. Were we to believe that for all that time that hidden metropolis had lain off the coast of Innsmouth and never before interacted with her neighbor? Why was it that only the men of Innsmouth were forced to take veiled brides? Why weren't the women forced into unholy matrimony with new and terrifying husbands?

I know why now. I know the secret of cyclopean and many arched Y'ha-nthlei. I know what lascivious purpose those rare, fertile male members of the Deep Ones and their hybrids are enslaved to. Stupendous and unheard of splendors indeed! We shall dwell amidst wonder and glory forever, that was the promise. Yet that wonder is the thing called Y'ha-nthlei, an ancient and titanic thing, so huge that monstrous barnacles and corals and her own children have colonized her flesh, dwelling like parasites; like remoras and hagfish, like leeches on their own birth mother. And the glory for her rare sons is to be entombed in her own flesh, chained inside her birth canal to fertilize her eggs as they move through that terrible channel. My destiny is to live forever as a slave to the inhuman needs of an ancient and terrible goddess as she gives birth to thousand upon thousand perhaps millions of hideous spawn. This is the honor, the wonder, the glory promised me by Pth''thya-l'yi and her sisters. It is the promise made by Y'ha herself, who was once Y'ha-dra, but is now Y'ha-nthlei, the city-goddess Y'ha and her betrothed the nthlei, insignificant things that do not even warrant names. As I made that casual and cursed glance back toward her and saw from above that great black pool and realized that as I gazed into it, that huge single eye of cyclopean Y'ha-nthlei, so too did it gaze into me. I heard her speak as I she watched me leave, heard her terrible and monstrous words as she called me, her own rebellious child, back to where she said I belonged. I heard her, and her very voice bellowing in my head drove me mad.

They are in the streets. Are those the furtive, cautious steps of men in boots, or Deep Ones with claws? Are those the sounds of guns on shoulders, or scales rubbing against themselves in the cold night Innsmouth air? Does it matter?

In my head they call to me, and tell me of their plans. Innsmouth is finished; it is too dangerous to stay. Y'ha-nthlei must move, she and those who are bound to her in unspeakable betrothal, and all of her children must migrate to deeper waters, where men with bombs cannot find them; a place where they can once more lie and feed and breed in peace. They want me; they need me to come with them. She needs me. There is a place prepared, and it is a sin to leave it unoccupied.

They're at the door below, smashing through.

I have only moments before I am captured. Whether I have been caught by the Daughters of Y'ha-dra or the soldiers that occupy Innsmouth, I cannot yet tell.

I hope it is the soldiers; they at least might kill me.

Project Handbasket

Rebecca J. Allred

02/28/2017
Name: George W. Denton
Gender: Male
DOB: 12/10/75
Admitted from outside facility, Lincoln County State Prison
Chief Complaint: Danger to self and others

    History of Present Illness: Mr. Denton is a former family medicine physician with no known personal or family history of mental illness. According to the patient's daughter, Mr. Denton went on a six month humanitarian mission to South America last year. When he returned, Mr. Denton—a lifelong atheist—began regularly attending church services. When questioned about his sudden change of faith, Mr. Denton was said to reply only that he was "preparing." Approximately six months ago, there was an acute change in Mr. Denton's personality. He became paranoid and spoke obsessively about "The Eleventh Plague." Despite concerns of both family and colleagues, Mr. Denton continued to see patients in his clinic. Indeed, it is noted that in the final weeks leading up to his arrest, the former Dr. Denton was seeing upwards of fifty patients per day, often remaining in the office after hours and holding appointments on weekends. It wasn't until later that it was discovered the doctor had been soliciting patients to bring themselves and their children in to the office for "urgent treatment."

    Using the panic surrounding the current Simian Flu epidemic to his advantage, the former Dr. Denton administered injections—which he described to patients as a new, more effective vaccine—to nearly two thousand individuals, including hundreds of children. It is still unknown precisely what Mr. Denton injected into his victims, only that after several weeks, a subset of his patients became acutely ill and died.

    Among the victims were Mr. Denton's wife, Cecilia; their son, Nicholas; and his granddaughter, Lily.

    Deemed unfit to stand trial by the courts, he was remanded to our care.

Objective: Patient is a Caucasian male in no acute distress.

    Physical Exam: Heart, lung, abdomen, and neuro exams all within normal limits

    Labs: CBC, BMP, Urine - within normal limits

Tox Screen - Negative
Medications: None
Family History: Noncontributory
Assessment: Patient is a 42-year-old male admitted for homicidal tendencies and delusions.
Plan: Enroll in Project Handbasket.

***

Informed Consent form for Subject #314-69-4245
Part I: Information Sheet
INTRODUCTION: My name is Dr. Harper, and I work for Shady Acres Neuropsychiatric Institute. I am doing research on the effects of life after death on the behavior of subsequently revived individuals and its application as a rehabilitation tool. I am going to give you information regarding Project Handbasket as you are now a participant in this research. There may be some words you do not understand. Please feel free to ask questions as we proceed through the information, and I will answer your questions on a need-to-know basis.

PURPOSE OF RESEARCH: Violent crime has been a problem for as long as man has roamed the earth. Various modes of punishment and rehabilitation have been implemented over the centuries; however, few—if any—have resulted in long-term behavioral changes, and recidivism rates remain high. The purpose of this research is to determine if short-term exposure to the afterlife is superior to traditional sentencing penalties in achieving and maintaining reformation in serial offenders.

TYPE OF INTERVENTION: This research will involve a series of sessions during which a single infusion of potassium chloride will be administered intravenously (IV) into your arm, followed by a period of brief observation, resuscitation, and appropriate clinical follow up.

PARTICIPANT SELECTION: All patients remanded to the Shady Acres Neuropsychiatric Institute by the courts are eligible to participate.

VOLUNTARY PARTICIPATION: Your participation in this research is mandatory. You have no choice regarding the duration of enrollment in this study and may not withdraw at any time.

DESCRIPTION OF PROCESS: During the study you will make between one and seven[1] visits to the research theatre.

---

[1] The maximum allowed therapeutic interventions has been reduced from ten (10) to seven (7), secondary to an interim analysis of the data. See updated risks and side effects for further information.

On the first visit, baseline data will be obtained during a one-hour, pre-treatment interview and administration of psychometric testing. The interview will include questions regarding religious beliefs, past criminal offenses, the presence or absence of remorse, and intent to reoffend.

Following the interview, you will be secured to an operating table, and a single infusion of potassium chloride will be administered to you intravenously, resulting in arrhythmia and subsequent cardiac arrest. You will remain clinically dead for a period of no less than ninety seconds.

During this time, your soul will exit your body and you will experience an eternity of suffering, torment, and despair at the hands of Hell's minions[2]. Unfortunately we cannot accurately predict the nature of your particular encounter with the afterlife; however, participants from pilot studies have reported the following:

- A limitless void, "red as death and cold as sin"
- Repeated consumption by a yellow, eyeless serpent
- Drowning in a vat of liquid fire
- Pursuit by "The Devourer in the Mist"

After the ninety-second interval has elapsed, resuscitation techniques will be employed, including but not limited to: manual chest compressions, defibrillation, and the administration of pharmacologic agents, e.g. epinephrine, calcium, insulin, diuretics, and antiarrhythmics. These agents, when used in combination, will counter the effects of the potassium chloride, allowing for reversal of the death state and the subsequent return of your soul to the confines of its earthly body.

Post-therapeutic evaluation will include a complete medical examination, three (3) one-on-one follow up visits with a study psychiatrist to record your experiences and assess your mental status, and administration of follow up psychometric testing.

SIDE EFFECTS: Potential side effects include: sleep disturbances, insomnia, persistent nightmares, hallucinations (both auditory and visual), seizures, and short-term memory loss[3].

RISKS: As with any therapy, there are risks to undergoing treatment. Known risks associated with the above-described intervention include:

· Infection at the IV site

---

[2] In the unlikely event your near death experience is one of peace, love and/or joy, you will be immediately excluded from the study and returned to police custody for reevaluation and processing.

[3] Incidence is proportional to number of treatments received. Most side effects are mild and resolve within 12 months of the last treatment.

· Broken ribs
· Irreversible psychosis[4]
· Increased incidence of developing suicidal tendencies
· Coma
· Permanent death and disability
·

BENEFITS & REIMBURSEMENT: While you may experience no direct benefits, others will benefit from your participation, in that a successful trial will decrease the recidivism rate of violent offenders, making society safer for everyone in the long term. All medical and living expenses incurred during the interventional and subsequent observational periods will be provided at no cost.

CONFIDENTIALITY: By participating in this research, you are undergoing an intervention unfamiliar and unavailable to other patients within the Shady Acres facility. While many patients are aware that experimental therapies are under investigation, we do not share the identity of any participants with other patients. However, due to the nature of your crimes, law enforcement officials, judges, lawyers, and victims or their surviving families may be made aware of your participation status as one of the conditions of your release.

RIGHT TO REFUSE OR WITHDRAW: As stated above, participation in Project Handbasket is mandatory. At no point will you be permitted to withdraw from the study.

PART II: Certificate of Consent

~~I have read the above information. I have had the opportunity to ask questions about it and all questions I have asked have been answered to my satisfaction. I consent voluntarily to participate in this research.~~

Print Name of Participant   N/A
Signature of Participant   N/A

I have witnessed the accurate reading of the above information to the participant, and the participant has had the opportunity to ask questions. ~~I confirm that the participant has given consent.~~

---

[4] While psychosis and suicide has been documented in participants following a single treatment, these effects are significantly more common in participants receiving greater than seven (7) treatments.

Print name of witness   *Jacqueline Harper, MD*
Signature of witness   *Jacqueline Harper, MD*
Date   *March 4, 2017*

***

03/05/2017

S: Patient reports he did not sleep last night. Refused meals both last night and this morning. No other overnight events.

O: Mental Status Exam: Patient is alert and oriented.
Affect: flat.
Mood: "defeated."
Thought Process/Content: Linear without evidence of delusions, hallucinations, suicidal or homicidal ideation.
Vital signs within normal limits.
No acute distress.

A/P: Patient is a 42-year-old male with a non-specified psychotic disorder on experimental protocol. Proceed with experimental treatment 1/7 scheduled for this afternoon.

***

03/05/2017   Subject #314-69-4245   Pre-treatment Interview - Transcript

JH: This is Dr. Harper. Today is March 5, 2017. The time is 08:35. This is Mr. Denton's pretreatment interview. How are you feeling this morning, Mr. Denton?

GD: (inaudible)

JH: Do you know why you are here?

GD: I failed.

JH: That's an interesting perspective. Can you describe your failure?

GD: You understand, don't you? We're both doctors. It's our job to prevent illness and death.

JH: Yes, but Mr. Denton, you didn't prevent illness and death. You inflicted them.

GD: If you could save a million people by killing a thousand, would you do it?

JH: Mr. Denton, this isn't a sophomore ethics class.

GD: How about a billion? How about the entire world?

JH: Mr. Denton—

GD: I'll change the context. Triage. Right? In an emergency you save the ones you can, sacrificing some so that others can live. You understand that, right? Of course you do. He knew I understood it, too. I think that's why he chose me.

JH: Who chose you? For what?

GD: What? Nothing. It doesn't matter. You wouldn't believe me anyway. I'm crazy, right? That's why I'm here.

JH: You're here, Mr. Denton, because you have been deemed mentally ill and unfit to stand trial for your crimes.

GD: Was Copernicus crazy? Or Pasteur? Or Mendel? They knew things no other man knew. The Bible says, "You will know the truth, and the truth will set you free." I know the truth, and now I'm a prisoner to it.

JH: Can you tell me about this truth? Or about the one who chose you and for what purpose?

GD: I could, but it would only lead to more death.

JH: Is that a threat, Mr. Denton?

GD: No. I'm sorry.

JH: Very well, we'll leave this discussion for another time. As we discussed yesterday, you will be receiving an experimental therapy to treat your illness. Later today you will undergo the first of seven treatments, but before that can happen, I need to ask you a few questions so that we might better understand your response to the treatment. First question: On a scale of 1-10, one being not at all and ten being definitely, if you were to be released today, how likely would you be to resume killing?

GD: Ten.

JH: I see. Question two: On a scale of 1-10, one being none and ten being extreme, how much remorse do you feel regarding your crimes?

GD: Ten. I didn't want to hurt anybody. One. I did what I had to do. Ten. It wasn't enough.

JH: So, ten?

GD: (inaudible)

JH: Very well. Last question: In your own words, how would you describe your religious beliefs?

GD: There is no God.

JH: Really? It's my understanding that over the past year you spent a significant amount of time in church, and not five minutes ago, you were quoting Bible verses.

GD: There is no God.

JH: Very well. What about a higher power other than God. Do you believe in that?

GD: (inaudible)

JH: Mr. Denton, are you all right? You look pale. Would you like a glass of water?

GD: (inaudible)

JH: Are you sure?

GD: (inaudible)

JH: Very well. Let me know if you change your mind. I'm sorry? Would you please repeat yourself?

GD: Belief is irrelevant.

JH: It's relevant to the data analysis. The presence or absence of religious beliefs is a standard question we ask all study participants.

GD: I'm not talking about your study.

JH: What then?

GD: You'll see.

***

Treatment Note: Subject #314-69-4245 Session 1/7
Date: 03/05/17
Procedure start time: 13:07:00
Procedure end time: 13:14:37
Total time elapsed: 00:07:37
Total dead time: 00:02:27
Complications: None
Subject comments: "The angles are wrong."

***

03/07/2017	Subject #314-69-4245 Post-treatment Interview #1 - Transcript
JH:	This is Dr. Harper. Today is March 7, 2017. The time is 16:07, and this is the first of three post-treatment interviews with Mr. Denton. He has completed one of seven treatments. How are you feeling today, Mr. Denton?
GD:	I'm tired.
JH:	You didn't sleep last night.
GD:	I did not.
JH:	Would you like me to prescribe something to help you sleep?
GD:	I would not.
JH:	Very well, but insomnia is a common side effect of the therapy, and I'd be happy to prescribe something if you change your mind. Now. Can you tell me about your experience on Sunday?
GD:	I was murdered.
JH:	How did it feel?

GD: It didn't feel like anything.

JH: What did you experience following the injection?

GD: (inaudible)

JH: No sight or sounds? No conscious thought?

GD: Not conscious. Dreaming thoughts. Dead and dreaming.

JH: You thought you were dreaming?

GD: Not I.

JH: What then do you mean by "dreaming thoughts?"

GD: He showed me.

JH: Who showed you? What did you see?

GD: The Eleventh Plague.

JH: Can you describe it?

GD: Undying death returns in the absence of sacrifice.

JH: What kind of sacrifice?

GD: The kind that comes before eleven.

***

Treatment Note: Subject #314-69-4245 Session 2/7
Date: 03/12/17
Procedure start time: 15:00:00

Procedure end time: 15:24:44
Total time elapsed: 00:24:44
Total dead time: 00:06:51
Complications: Sedative required following resuscitation.
Subject comments: Uncontrolled laughter for 15 minutes prior to sedation.

***

03/13/17

S: Patient reports poor sleep and nightmares. Decreased appetite. No overnight events.

O: Mental Status Exam: Patient is alert, but only oriented to self. He is unable to correctly identify the date and when asked where he is, the patient is overcome by seemingly uncontrolled bouts of laughter.
Affect: irritable.
Mood: inconsistent.
Thought Process/Content: Tangential with delusions and obsessive discussion of a coming plague.
Vital signs are within normal limits.
Other than bouts of inappropriate laughter, the patient appears to be in no acute distress.

A/P: 42-year-old male with an unspecified psychotic disorder on experimental protocol.
1. Begin risperidone for psychotic symptoms
2. Begin zolpidem for sleep
3. Continue experimental protocol as scheduled.

***

03/14/2017 Subject #314-69-4245 Post-treatment Interview #1 - Transcript

JH: This is Dr. Harper. Today is March 14, 2017. The time is 11:15, and this is the first of three post-treatment interviews with Mr. Denton. He has completed two of seven treatments. How are you feeling today, Mr. Denton?

GD: [laughter]

JH: I understand you've been having nightmares. Would you like to discuss the content of your dreams?

GD: My dreams are not my own.

JH: Whose dreams are they?

GD: [laughter]

JH: Mr. Denton, please sit down.

GD: [laughter]

JH: Sit down, or I'll be forced to—

GD: [laughter]

JH: Security!

GD: [laughter]

***

03/16/2017 Subject #314-69-4245 Post-treatment Interview #2 - Transcript

JH: This is Dr. Harper. Today is March 16, 2017. The time is 12:55, and this is the second of three post-treatment interviews with Mr. Denton. He has completed two of seven treatments. How are you feeling today, Mr. Denton?

GD: I'd like to go home now.

JH: I'm afraid it will be several months before the decision of whether or not you are well enough to return home can be made. I'd like to talk about your last treatment. There were some unexpected side effects, though I'm pleased to see they seem to have resolved. Tell me about Sunday's session.

GD: I don't want to go back. I want to go home.

JH: Satisfactory progress must be illustrated prior to patient release. You know this. Mr. Denton, you must go back if you're ever to go home.

GD: If I don't go home...

JH: Where do you go during your treatments, Mr. Denton?

GD: It's here. I can see it.

JH: What do you see?

GD: A city. Deep. Forgotten. Filled with towers. No! Mausoleums. Built from...not stone. The angles are wrong. They scrape the sky and cry out to dead stars the color of migraines, begging them to live again.

JH: Mr. Denton, are you all right?

GD: (inaudible)

JH: Mr. Denton?

GD: What day is it?

JH: What day do you think it is?

GD: Easter?

JH: It's March 16th. Easter isn't for another month.

GD: Then there's still time.

JH: Time for what?

GD: I'd like to go home now.

***

Treatment Note: Subject #314-69-4245 Session 3/7
Date: 03/19/17
Procedure start time: 09:00:00
Procedure end time: 09:19:19
Total time elapsed: 00:19:19
Total dead time: 00:08:01
Complications: None
Subject comments: "The day of resurrection approaches."

***

03/21/2017 Subject #314-69-4245 Post-treatment Interview #1 - Transcript

JH: This is Dr. Harper. Today is March 21, 2017. The time is 12:41, and this is the first of three post-treatment interviews with Mr. Denton. He has completed three of seven treatments. How are you feeling today, Mr. Denton?

GD: Like death warmed over.

JH: Is that supposed to be a joke?

GD: Everything is a joke. You. Me. That tape recorder.

JH: How so?

GD: The problem is that not all jokes are funny. Sometimes the punchline is just mean.

JH: Tell me more.

GD: (inaudible)

JH: No? Very well. Let's talk about something else. I'd like to discuss something you said during your last treatment.

GD: Sure. Okay.

JH: You said, "The day of resurrection approaches." What do you think you meant by that?

GD: I think my brain was deprived of oxygen from being killed and brought back to life for the sixth time.

JH: Third time, Mr. Denton. And I disagree. Last week you thought it was Easter, and this morning, one of the nurses brought me this. She found it under your bed. Would you care to read it?

GD: "He is not here; he is risen, just as he said."

JH: Anything else?

GD: It just says the same thing over and over again. "He is risen."

JH: Do you recognize that phrase?

GD: Yes. It's from the New Testament.

JH: How about the handwriting?

GD: It's mine.

JH: For a man who doesn't believe in God, you seem awfully preoccupied with the resurrection. Can you explain to me why that is?

GD: Can you explain to me why Easter falls on different dates from year to year?

JH: I fail to see the relevance of that question.

GD: Then you fail to understand the basis of my obsession. The truth that threatens my sanity.

JH: Enlighten me.

GD: Enlighten yourself.

JH: You sound upset, Mr. Denton.

GD: Your goddamn right, I'm upset! I shouldn't even be here! I don't deserve to be here! And I wouldn't be here if it weren't for our incompetent guide leading us into that forsaken village! I wouldn't know any of this! My wife. My son. My granddaughter. [crying]

JH: Tell me about the village.

GD: Ravaged. Ravaged by plague. I wanted to help. We had supplies. But it was a trap. I never wanted this! You think you're the first one to show me what it's like in Hell? [crying] You have to stop, Doctor.

JH: Stop what?

GD: They know about you.

JH: Who knows about me?

GD: They've seen me come and go. They know you can make them live again.

JH: Who? What are you talking about?

GD: Hell's dreamers.

***

03/23/2017 Subject #314-69-4245 Post-treatment Interview #2 - Transcript

JH: This is Dr. Harper. Today is March 23, 2017. The time is 09:05, and this is the second of three post-treatment interviews with Mr. Denton. He has completed three of seven treatments. How are you feeling today, Mr. Denton?

GD: Go to Hell.

JH: No need to be hostile. Maybe this will put you in a better mood. I took your advice and did a bit of self-enlightenment last night. To answer your question from our previous session, Easter is celebrated on a different day every year because it is based on the lunar calendar, falling on the first Sunday following the paschal full moon.

GD: That's the long answer.

JH: What's the short answer?

GD: The stars have to be right.

***

Treatment Note: Subject #314-69-4245 Session 4/7
Date: 03/26/17
Procedure start time: 17:00:00

Procedure end time: 17:35:06
Total time elapsed: 00:35:06
Total dead time: 00:12:11
Complications: Patient revived after four minutes, but decompensated and required a second round of resuscitation.
Subject comments: Unintelligible. Phonetically interpreted as: "R'lyeh," "Tharanaak," and "Gotha hai uln."

***

03/27/17
S: Patient reports persistent sleep disturbances despite pharmacologic intervention. Appetite better today. No overnight events.
O: Mental Status Exam: Alert. Oriented to self. When asked to write a sentence, the patient produced the following:
"Ph'nglui mglw'nafh Cthulhu R'lyeh wgah'nagl fhtagn."
Affect: anxious.
Mood: anxious.
Thought process/content: evasive, delusions ("Eleventh Plague"), auditory hallucinations ("whispers from the abyss").
Vital signs within normal limits.
A/P: 42-year-old male with non-specified psychotic disorder on experimental protocol.
           1.   Increase risperidone for psychotic symptoms
           2.   Increase zolpidem for sleep
           3.   Begin clonazepam for anxiety
           4.   Continue experimental protocol as scheduled.

***

03/28/2017 Subject #314-69-4245   Post-treatment Interview #1 – Transcript
JH: This is Dr. Harper. Today is March 28, 2017. The time is 14:45, and this is the first of three post-treatment interviews with Mr. Denton. He has completed four of seven treatments. How are you feeling today, Mr. Denton?

GD: Fine.

JH: You seem less anxious than yesterday. It seems the medications are working.

GD: Maybe I wouldn't need medicine if you'd stop killing me. Or stop bringing me back.

JH: Yes, well, that's one consideration. And perhaps once your treatments are over, the need for medication will subside. In the meantime, I need your help with something. Can you read this for me?

GD: What is it?

JH: Read it, please.

GD: I can't... I don't... [sighs] "Ph'nglui mglw'nafh Cthulhu R'lyeh wgah'nagl fhtagn?" Is that right?

JH: Your guess is as good as mine. Does it mean anything to you?

GD: No. No, of course not. Why are you showing me this? Is this part of the therapy?

JH: You don't recognize it?

GD: Should I?

JH: You wrote it.

GD: (inaudible)

JH: Yesterday. After breakfast. And you spoke similar—I'm not sure I'd call them phrases, gibberish might be a better description—after your treatment last Sunday.

GD: I'm sorry. I don't know what it means.

JH: Are you sure?

GD: I said I don't know!

JH: Okay. Calm down. Let's try a different one. I copied this from a page in your therapy journal.

GD: I thought that journal was private.

JH: You thought wrong. Read the paper, please.

GD: It says, "Nyarlathotep."

JH: What is Nyarlathotep?

GD: Not what. Who.

JH: Very well. Who is Nyarlathotep?

GD: He was once a great house. A bringer of plagues.

JH: I don't know what that means. You're going to have to be more specific.

GD: In the time of Moses, Nyarlathotep was a Pharaoh.

JH: Back to the Bible?

GD: Not everything in the Bible is bullshit.

JH: That's an interesting assertion. I'd like to discuss that further in the future, but for now, I'd like to know more about Nyarlathotep and how you came to believe you met a Pharaoh from ancient

Egypt in the jungles of modern-day South America.

GD: You read my journal. You already know what happened.

JH: Still, I'd like to hear you say it. Sometimes when we hear our thoughts out loud, we recognize something obvious that is otherwise obscured when those thoughts are kept inside our head.

GD: [sighs] We were on a humanitarian mission in South America. Our guide got lost and we wound up in a village that had been all but destroyed by a series of seemingly natural disasters. One after another—nine in as many years. We had supplies and medicine, so I sought the tribe's leader to ask permission to distribute them to survivors.

JH: Did you find him?

GD: You know I did.

JH: And?

GD: And it was Nyarlathotep.

JH: Did you know then that he was an Egyptian Pharaoh?

GD: Of course not.

JH: What did he say?

GD: He said I could administer any aid I saw fit, but that it would do no good.

JH: Why not?

GD: Can a bandaid effectively treat a traumatic amputation?

JH: So, he thought they were beyond help?

GD: He didn't think it. He knew it. And it wasn't just them. It's all of us.

JH: Why?

GD: [sighs] Because. He's only one plague away from bringing about the end of days.

JH: Ah. There it is. Did you hear it, Mr. Denton? The contradiction?

GD: What contradiction?

JH: As someone who doesn't believe God, how do you reconcile the idea that the antichrist is alive and well in South America, quietly plotting the end of the world?

GD: Because Nyarlathotep is not the antichrist. He's not even a man.

JH: What is he then?

GD: You wouldn't believe me even if I told you.

JH: You said yourself that belief is irrelevant.

GD: [laughter] So I did. Fine. He's an immortal prophet of the Old Gods. The ones that ruled the Earth in a time before man, and although they fell from power before the first four-legged creature crawled out of the primordial ooze and onto dry land, they still exist. Beneath the oceans. In the furthest reaches of space.

JH: You're right. I don't believe you. And what's more, I don't believe that you believe it, either.

GD: It doesn't matter what either of us believes. The truth remains.

JH: I think that's enough for today, Mr. Denton.

GD: Just one more thing.

JH: What's that?

GD: If you think the second coming refers to the return of Jesus Christ, you're in for a nasty surprise.

***

Treatment Note: Subject #314-69-4245 Session 5/7
Date: 04/02/17
Procedure start time: 11:45:00
Procedure end time: 12:27:13
Total time elapsed: 00:42:13
Total dead time: 00:22:10
Complications: Patient experienced significant blood loss from epistaxis secondary to hypertensive crisis.
Subject comments: "He's coming."

***

04/07/17
From: chris.w.meyer@lincolncountylaw.gov
To: jaqharper@sani.org
RE: George Denton and the Eleventh Plague
Dear Dr. Harper:

Thank you for your message regarding Mr. Denton's case. Pardon my delay in response, but your request required more time than I originally anticipated. Upon further investigation, your suspicions have been confirmed—each of Mr. Denton's deceased victims was, in fact, either an only child or the eldest of their siblings. I'm not certain how this detail managed to escape attention during the initial investigation, but if your assessment is correct, I believe this is further evidence supporting the court's decision that Mr. Denton be remanded to your institution for intensive psychiatric care.

Please don't hesitate to contact me if I can be of further service.

Sincerely,

Christopher W. Meyer

***

04/08/2017 Subject #314-69-4245   Post-treatment Interview #3 - Transcript

JH:	This is Dr. Harper. Today is April 8, 2017. The time is 13:35, and this is the third of three post-treatment interviews with Mr. Denton. He has completed five of seven treatments. How are you feeling today, Mr. Denton?
GD:	Do you have children?
JH:	Excuse me?
GD:	Children. Do you have them?
JH:	I do not.
GD:	Siblings?
JH:	No.
GD:	Me either. Not anymore. Never had siblings, my older brother died before I was born. And my kids? I sacrificed my son, and now my daughter won't speak to me. She doesn't understand.

74

JH: This isn't the first time you've used the word "sacrifice" in reference to your crimes. I'd like to explore that a bit if you don't mind.

GD: (inaudible)

JH: It's come to my attention that all of your victims, the ones who died, they were only children or the eldest of their siblings.

GD: (inaudible)

JH: You were recreating the Tenth Plague of Egypt.

GD: Yes.

JH: Why?

GD: Have you ever wondered why Passover and Easter are so close together?

JH: I guess I never considered it.

GD: Think about it.

JH: I'm sorry. I'm not seeing a connection.

GD: Okay, let me ask you another question. What is the purpose of blood sacrifice?

JH: I don't—

GD: Appeasement!

JH: Who were you trying to appease?

GD: You haven't been paying attention.

JH: Nyarlathotep?

GD: [laughter] Blood! Death! Resurrection!

JH: Mr. Denton, I'm going to have to ask you to lower your voice.

GD: [laughter] He failed once before! Ten became eleven, suppressed by the blood of the innocent! Eleven! Eleven! Eleven! Only ten can unmake eleven!

JH: Security!

***

Treatment Note: Subject #314-69-4245 Session 6/7
Date: 04/09/17
Procedure start time: 13:30:00
Procedure end time: 14:57:03
Total time elapsed: 01:27:03
Total dead time: 00:33:11
Complications: Subject revived, briefly coherent, then slipped into a catatonic state.
Subject comments: "One more."

***

04/12/17
S: Patient remains catatonic.
O: Patient has not slept in four nights. Hydration provided by IV. BP: 155/95, Vital signs otherwise within normal limits. No acute distress.
A/P: 42-year-old male with non-specified psychotic disorder and new onset hypertension on experimental protocol.
      1. Discontinue oral risperidone
      2. Begin risperidone injection IM for psychotic symptoms
      3. Hold zolpidem
      4. Hold clonazepam
      5. Start atenolol IV for hypertension
      6. Continue experimental protocol as scheduled.

***

04/15/2017 Subject #314-69-4245   Post-treatment Interview #1 - Transcript

JH: This is Dr. Harper. Today is April 15, 2017. The time is 11:00, and this is the first and last of originally three post-treatment interviews with Mr. Denton. The previously scheduled interviews were cancelled due to Mr. Denton's recent catatonic state. He has completed six of seven treatments. How are you feeling today, Mr. Denton?

GD: One more.

JH: One more what?

GD: One more.

JH: Treatment? Yes, you have just one more treatment. Do you feel they have helped? That you're unlikely to commit murder if released back into society?

GD: One more will complete the ritual.

JH: It's a clinical trial, not a ritual.

GD: Ph'nglui mglw'nafh Cthulhu R'lyeh wgah'nagl fhtagn.

JH: Mr. Denton?

GD: Ph'nglui mglw'nafh Cthulhu R'lyeh wgah'nagl fhtagn.

JH: Mr. Denton? Your nose is bleeding.

GD: Ph'nglui   mglw'nafh   Cthulhu   R'lyeh
            wgah'nagl   fhtagn.   Ph'nglui   mglw'nafh
            Cthulhu R'lyeh wgah'nagl fhtagn. Ph'nglui
            mglw'nafh   Cthulhu   R'lyeh   wgah'nagl
            fhtagn.   Ph'nglui   mglw'nafh   Cthulhu
            R'lyeh   wgah'nagl   fhtagn!   Ph'nglui
            mglw'nafh   Cthulhu   R'lyeh   wgah'nagl
            fhtagn!   Ph'nglui   mglw'nafh   Cthulhu
            R'lyeh   wgah'nagl   fhtagn!   Ph'nglui
            mglw'nafh   Cthulhu   R'lyeh   wgah'nagl
            fhtagn!

JH: Mr. Den— Security! [screams]

                            ***

Treatment Note: Subject #314-69-4245 Session 7/7
Date: 04/16/17
Procedure start time: 99:99:99
Procedure end time: 99:99:99
Total time elapsed: 99:99:99
Complications: I killed Dr. Harper. The ritual is complete, but I was
misled. Instead of closing the door, I opened it.
Subject comments: He is risen.

INCENSE AND INSENSIBILITY

Christine Morgan

Mrs. Aylesbury, being a widow with two daughters, had fallen rather into dire straits since the death of her husband. When, therefore, a cottage at Star-Winds became available by the graces of a distant cousin, she was gladly obliged to accept.

That cousin, although born John Yaddith, had taken to going by the name of Brother Zoar. A large man, caftaned and sandaled, possessed of a leonine white mane, he welcomed them with immense affection.

The cottage proved both humble and cozy, smallish but adequate to the needs of the Aylesbury ladies. They found the environs most agreeable, set as it was in a cool, pearly-dawned coastal forest of fog-drenched ferns and redwoods.

Within a matter of days, they felt very much at home. During the daylight hours, they busied themselves with the activities of the community. They helped in the garden and kitchen, learned to macrame, wrote poetry, practiced the arts of tie-dye and beading.

Evenings, when they gathered cozily together, they would touch flame to some scent of incense or other – sandalwood, cinnamon, strawberry, less identifiable fragrances. These fragrant concoctions, along with blends of tea, potpourri, natural remedies, soaps and candles, were made and sold to augment the community's modest income. Some had an invigorating effect that went well with card games or chatter; others, more calming, lent themselves to the enjoyment of quieter pursuits.

The elder of the sisters, Eleanor, had a particular interest in the botanical and found herself fascinated by the various processes. She struck up particular friendships with a girl called Hesperia and a striking youth known as Chaos. They, for their part, were more than glad to show her around and instruct her.

Dried and ground substances – tree bark, seeds, leaves, fruit rinds, flower petals, moss – all went into the making. Men and women perched upon stools, working the mixtures together with soft resins, gum arabics and pine saps. The resulting material, they formed into cones or pellets, or molded around thin sticks, or packaged into small round tins for use in incense-burners.

Eleanor noted the predominance of patchouli, lemongrass, sandalwood, cloves, charcoal and essential oils. Each breath brought minglings of aroma: floral and spice, sweet and bitter, fragrant and pungent.

Some, she almost knew but could not name. They danced enticingly, evocatively, at the very edges of her memory. Others, she did not know at all, and the merest whiff of them stirred a strange and vague expectancy of something almost akin to dread or revulsion so deep it was almost subconscious.

"I don't recognize the …" she said, faltering. "I can't quite identify …"

Chaos's dark eyes glinted. "We know all the places where the most rare and secret things grow."

"Rare and secret?" Eleanor echoed. She took up a pinch of the gritty, sticky stuff and rolled it between her fingertips and thumb. It felt like grainy clay, like wet salt dough, like wads of damp cornmeal. She sniffed it and sensed again that strange, vague expectancy … that something-akin-to-dread … and wasn't sure if she wanted to recoil, or inhale more of its weird perfume.

"Like, so rare and secret, you won't find them anyplace else," Hesperia said.

"This blend," said Chaos, savoring it, "is among the rarest of them all."

Again, Eleanor sniffed at the incense, crushing it against the pad of her thumb to release more of its aroma.

Its predominance was a strong, damp earthiness … not quite like mildew, nor mold, but similar. Loam? Peat? The moss that grew thick and furry in crevices of redwood bark? Yet … fleshy, somehow … slightly sour, even acrid … or was it?

And there was some undercurrent of … spice … carnation? Marigold? Anise? Was that a hint of anise she detected? Or possibly fennel; it lacked the sweetness particular to licorice root …

"When it burns," said Chaos, leaning close, so close that his cheek almost brushed against hers as he spoke, and his breath tickled warm and soft in her ear, "when it burns, you'll see the colors in its smolder, glowing spires like faint suns in skies of flame, and red-gold thrones where gods no longer sit."

She trembled, though with what precise emotions, she couldn't quite define. His words seemed both profound and utterly without meaning, imbued with passion and promise. She felt poised at a threshold to some greater knowledge, some epiphany. A step further, and she might find her way to the enlightenment that would open new worlds of understanding.

Hesperia leaned in just as close on Eleanor's other side, long hair falling in a shimmering drape. She held out a cupped hand, in the palm of which were strewn several loose petals.

Eleanor caught her breath at the sight of them. They were unlike anything she'd ever seen before. The nearest resemblance she could think of was less botanical than entomological, putting her in mind of the veined, glassy-clear wings of dragonflies.

The fragrance wafting up from them was that of fading, unearthly, dying starlight.

The very thought struck her as strangely poetic to have come from her own usually more prosaic consciousness.

Fading, unearthly, dying starlight?

The petals showed only a slight wilting that suggested they'd been recently plucked from the bloom … petal by petal, in the loves-me/loves-me-not manner with which a romantic might pluck the petals of a daisy.

When she picked one up, she found it – though delicate-seeming – strong and supple, somehow silken to the touch, yet also oddly … membranous. She held it beneath her nose and inhaled deeply of that strangely poetic fragrance.

Yes … fading, dying, unearthly starlight.

Images that were not images, but more akin to half-remembered visions from someone else's dream, drifted through her inner darkness.

"What is that?" she asked.

"We call it *nithon*," Chaos said.

"We'll need to gather more soon; this is the last handful left." Hesperia dropped the petals into a mortar and took up a pestle to begin grinding them into a thick, clearish jelly.

"Gather it where?"

"Oh, past the sphinxes," said Chaos, in a casual, off-hand manner.

"Past the garden gate," Hesperia added.

"What garden gate?" Eleanor asked, the words sounding faint and far even to her own ears.

"The sphinx-guarded one," Chaos replied. "The labyrinth of wonder."

This made no sense to her, yet she found herself nodding as if in comprehension of some deep and abiding truth.

"Can you imagine," murmured Hesperia, "what else might grow there?"

"Yes …" she sighed.

They smiled the way indulgent adults might smile at some whimsy from a child.

"Oh, but you can't," Chaos told her. "You can't imagine. No one can."

"Then show me. I want to see."

"When you're ready," he said.

She wanted to protest that she was ready there and then, but something in the glinting darkness of his eyes convinced her she would do better not to push yet for more answers.

Instead, she settled onto a vacant stool. The men and women at the table were glad enough to make room for her as they demonstrated their techniques. Soon, Eleanor had the knack of it. Her palms and fingers became discolored, stained from the damp, granular residue.

Had she thought the mixture smelled vaguely unpleasant before? Mildewy and sour? It still did, a bit, but … she did not mind it so much now. Perhaps it was an acquired taste, improving with familiarity and exposure? Or had the thick, clearish jelly of the *nithon*-petals tempered its scent?

Her nose tingled. She thought of what Chaos had said, the colors in its smolder when it burned, and wondered anew what he had meant.

But when she looked up from her work to ask him, she saw that while she'd been occupied, he and Hesperia had drifted away. Resolving to seek them out later, she remained making incense the rest of the afternoon.

It rained that night, a heavy, steady rain, a grey and sodden dreariness that hung a dense pall over everything. A shifting in the weather carried murky tidal smells inland from the sea. The eaves did not so much drip as flow with miniature rivulets. Mud and puddles replaced the paths.

A general irritation built despite the cottage's coziness. Before long, the Aylesbury sisters had taken to bickering over phantom trifles. They found even their dear mother's attempts at kindly cheer to be grating, while she began to find them irksome in a way she never had before. Opening the shutters to let in the air let in only wet chill and brine. They lit candles and incense in hopes of chasing out the lingering disagreeable atmosphere … both figurative and literal, as it were.

Eleanor watched the granular cone smolder in a ceramic dish. Threads of fragrant smoke curled up from the deep red fire-ruby of the ember. It issued forth the very scent she remembered from earlier.

"Where did that come from?" she asked.

"Your friend Hesperia brought it by," her mother said said. "She told me we should try it tonight, that it's more potent when it rains. Something about how the moisture intensifies the scent. I saw her taking some to everyone."

"I don't much care for it," said her sister. "It smells of gone-off mushroom soup."

They sat quietly for a few moments, watching the smoke spiral up, spreading and drifting, diffusing, effusing. Eleanor found her gaze drawn to the ember, to the deep red ruby ring smoldering into grey ash.

What had Chaos said? *"... glowing spires like faint suns in skies of flame, and red-gold thrones where gods no longer sit."*

And the strange perfume of it ... loam and spice, a fleshy acrid sourness ... that hint of something not-quite-anise ... but tempered by the scent of fading, unearthly, dying starlight.

They conversed in desultory fashion for a while, then fell silent again, each lost in her own thoughts.

Eleanor's dwelt upon the glassy and somehow membranous petals Hesperia had shown her. *Nithon*, but who had ever heard of such a thing? She wished she'd had a better chance to examine them. Or, better yet, see the blossoming plant itself –

"... past the garden gate," Hesperia had said, and asked her if she could imagine what else might grow there.

After a while, the younger Miss Aylesbury opened up her page-worn notebook and began to write, the scratching of pen on paper an oddly eerie counterpoint to the drumming of the rain. After a while longer, hardly seeming aware of it, she began murmuring as she wrote, her words gradually becoming audible.

"From Leng comes Death to strip us of Life's mask ... silken folds of skin torn free to bone and entropy beneath --"

"Goodness," Mrs. Aylesbury said, rousing as if from a torpor. "How morbid."

"I'll read another instead." She turned a page. "Old when Babylon was new, sleeping beneath its mound, vast pavements and foundation-walls, stone steps leading down, to eternal night's black haven where the primal secrets frown --"

"That's still rather grim, dear, don't you think?"

"We found the lamp, the brazen bowl." Her eyes gleamed strangely in the reflected candle flames. "The oil, how it blazed! In its mad flash, the shapes we saw, vast shapes! The maze-wall, and the gate sphinx-guarded!"

"I think," said Eleanor diplomatically, herself feeling rather as if she'd emerged from some half-dream, "that we've had enough poetry for now, don't you?"

One by one they sank again into their private musings. They lit another cone of the same incense when the first was spent. The irritations and annoyances with each other did seem far and silly. It was better to sit here. So peaceful, so relaxing. Watching the fire-ruby ember shift and change as it burned its slow way down, releasing the musty, mossy, mildewy scent.

***

The younger Miss Aylesbury swayed in her seat. "Through what sphinx-paths winding in the night, pointed to by far blue rays! Where vine-choked gates of graven dolomite open to the stone-lanterned maze!"

"What was that, dear?" queried their mother, again like one stirring from a doze.

"It is the hour … the hour when the moonstruck … moonstruck …" Then she settled her cheek onto her notebook, yawned once, and fell asleep.

Mrs. Aylesbury blinked drowsily. "Oh, how odd. She must be very … very …" Her head lolled onto her shoulder and she exhaled a slow, sighing breath as she, too, succumbed.

Eleanor stirred herself from her chair, and from her own attendant lethargy, with considerable effort. The uppermost third of the incense cone had become an ashen mound, the widening ring of the ember a strange twist of gold. As she reached for the dish, her hand struck it, knocking it askew. For an instant she suffered an image of scattering sparks on the braided-rag rug, igniting myriad hungry tongues of fire. But the incense merely wobbled, shedding flecks of ash, and did not spill.

She picked it up and carried it outside, holding her breath as she did so. Raindrops splashed on ceramic, hissing when they met the smoldering cone, forming a sooty puddle around it.

Soon, neither smoke nor steam arose from the sodden lump. Eleanor decided this was still an insufficient measure, and tipped the dish entire into a ditch of muddy water, where it sank with a gurgle.

As it vanished into the murk, she let herself breathe again. The distant low-tide miasma of the sea crept into her nose and throat and lungs. Her mind, however, felt more clear.

Had the incense been … drugged?

She almost could not believe it. Did not want to believe it, that much was certain. True, certain illicit substances were far from unknown at Star-Winds, but those who partook did so of their own knowing, willing accord.

Didn't they?

Or did they?

The incense ... the tea ... the potpourri and soaps and candles ... all the things they made ... and sold ... local farmer's markets, street fairs ... mail order ... herbal remedies and traditional medicines ...

The rain fell. Her wet hair hung limp along her cheeks, her wet clothes clung to her skin. Water trickled down her neck and back.

It seemed so quiet. She heard no voices, no laughter, no crying babies or barking dogs. Not even any music. No one else was out and about. Everything looked bedraggled, shabby and run-down, dispirited in the sodden, dreary weather. But for a few lights flickering through curtains and shutters, the neighboring cabins might have been deserted.

She went to the largest, a redwood lodge that served as home to Brother Zoar and his innermost circle. When her knocks brought no reply, she peered through a window. Sheets and swags decorated the walls and hung from the rafters, giving the effect of the interior of a nomadic tent. Bean-bags and oversized cushions heaped the floor, serving as beds for partially-clad people. Amid a clutter of water-pipes and wine jugs was a large incense-holder in the shape of a beaming, chubby Buddha. Several spent cones made gritty mounds of ashes in the burning-dish.

Her taps at the windowpane, then more knocking and calling, elicited no response. They merely slept on. If not for the steady rising and falling of their chests, she might have presumed the worst.

Hesperia had given it to everyone; did she know of its potent effects? Was this result her deliberate intention? If so, then *why*? And if not ... if not, then ...

It occurred to her that Hesperia was not among those slumbering figures. Neither were Chaos, nor Brother Zoar himself.

Despite the openness of the community, she nonetheless felt a qualm of manners as she let herself into the lodge. None of the three were to be found within. She passed through and came to the back deck, pausing briefly to glance out at its rain-sluiced redwood planks. A gleam out in the forest beyond, some shining amber beacon, caught and held her eye.

Why anyone would be in the woods at night, in this miserable weather ...

"We know all the places where the most rare and secret things grow," Chaos had said.

And Hesperia ... *"We'll need to gather more soon; this is the last handful left."*

How they had whispered, soft, conspiratorial.

"Past the sphinxes."

"Past the garden gate."

"The labyrinth of wonder."

How they had leaned so close and intimate, breath tickling silkily in her ears ... the tantalizing allure of the *nithon* petals, like nothing she'd ever seen ...

As she stepped closer to the sliding doors, her hip bumped the edge of a table. Something heavy and rounded wobbled atop it. Eleanor caught the item before it fell, and gasped at how warm it was to the touch.

It was made of bronze, and she initially took it for some sort of lidless little teapot – short and stout, as the rhyme went; there was its handle and there was its spout – but it held no liquid, no dregs of leaves. She thought next that it might be an incense-burner and cautiously sniffed at it, anticipating that same dank, mossy, fleshy scent.

What she smelled instead made her think of hot oil left too long on the stove, not quite to smoking but very nearly to the point of bursting into flame.

Fine lettering embossed the object's curving metal side. She ran a fingertip along it as she puzzled out the archaic-looking script.

The Nameless One For Whom We Raise A Thousand Smokes.

The voice that recurred to Eleanor then was that of her own sister. *"We found the lamp, the brazen bowl,"* and something about a mad flash, great shapes, gates and mazes.

The residue coating the inside of the brass –

"... lamp, the brazen bowl ..."

-- container looked greasy, like streaks of paraffin or petroleum jelly.

Acting on an impulse – even a compulsion – she could neither understand nor resist, Eleanor found and lit a match. The matchhead flared, then guttered in the breeze. Before it could blow out, she dropped it through the lidless opening.

With a flash – *"a mad flash!"* – the oily substance ignited. It burned glassy-clear flames etched and shot with lightning-blue. Thin beams sprang from the lamp's spout, a dancing, dazzling intricacy of –

"... far blue rays ..."

They pointed in the direction of the light, the amber beacon. There, the rays touched upon and illuminated –

"... great shapes ... the gate, sphinx-guarded ... gates of graven dolomite ... the stone-lanterned maze ..."

She set a hand to her head, which seemed filled with voices, all speaking at once.

"... the hour when the moonstruck poets know ..."

The rays *did* touch upon and illuminate shapes she swore had not been there before. Statues, two hulking granite statues, of winged lionesses with the heads and breasts of women. Sphinxes. They stood moss-encrusted and climbing with ivy, flanking a gateway topped with a carved arch of some pale-hued, crystalline-glittering mineral.

Through the archway was a narrow path, a high-walled maze, marked by lampposts also made from granite and set with golden lozenges of glass. She caught a glimpse of someone just turning a corner – fleeting though it was, she was sure she recognized the long white hair of Brother Zoar.

Without pause for concern or consideration, Eleanor slid open the doors and stepped outside. Heedless of the rain, she dashed across the deck and down the steps toward the forest.

The far blue rays and amber beacons vanished as she left the brazen bowl behind, but she did not need their guidance. Within moments, slipping on wet grass, she reached the place where she had seen the sphinxes.

They were not there.

She blinked and wiped raindrops from her face.

They *were* there.

Looming above her, stern-visaged, terrible and strange, the sphinxes *were* there. And between them, the gate with its carved arch … but the gate held only nothingness.

Not blackness, not blankness, not emptiness.

Nothingness.

Eleanor hesitated, then stepped through.

The rain stopped as decisively as if she'd gone indoors, but no ceiling stretched above her. The maze's high, vine-choked walls were open to the sky. Open to the pink sky, a sky not rose-pink with dawn or blushed with sunset's fires but pink nonetheless, a pink sky where the stark outlines of birds like herons flew.

She stood, dripping, on a path of dry bricks, porous-seeming as if cut from thirsty pumice. The air felt balmy. It smelled not of cold fog and wet brine but of a more stinging alkaline; she thought of salt-flats and deserts.

When she looked back the way she'd come, she saw the silent sphinxes continuing to loom there. She saw the backside of the arched gateway, and the nothingness it held.

Spindly insects buzzed faintly as they ticked and batted against the lozenge-shaped panes set into the stone lampposts. She recognized them no more than she recognized the vines that grew up the high walls, or the kinds of trees whose boughs interlaced above the decorative stonework at their tops.

This was not the world as she had always known it. This was someplace else altogether. Someplace strange, unreal and unfamiliar.

To call out, to raise her voice, seemed a terrible transgression. Eleanor hastened on instead. The path was indeed a maze, bending and switching, splitting off in every direction, filled with hidden alcoves, intersections and dead-ends.

"The labyrinth of wonder," Chaos had said.

And, indeed, so it was. Within moments, she'd all but forgotten in her fascination her true purpose for coming here.

Or *was* this her true purpose in coming here?

Were they not, perhaps, one and the same?

Each pace she took brought new angles of view. Apertures in the walls, slanting from width to narrowness like castle windows, offered peeks at tantalizing features – terraced gardens, crumbling slabs and statues, puzzling shrubs laden with shiny clusters of fruit, low bridges spanning pools where what resembled monstrous lily-pads and lotus-blossoms floated against the reflected pink-hued sky.

These always seemed but a turn or two ahead, yet when she reached where they should have been, she found only more of the winding maze itself. She saw broken towers, decaying spires twisting upward to weathered white turrets, and a gaping hole where stairs descended into a blackness darker than eternal night –

Or had that been something her sister said, reciting from her poems?

"... stone steps leading down, to eternal night's black haven where the primal secrets frown ..."

The vines rustled against the walls. A bird cried somewhere on high, its screech that of a madman. Thin, brittle leaves whirled around Eleanor in a frenetic blowing dance. The insects buzzed and ticked against the amber glass of the stone lampposts.

Somewhere, it seemed, a cracked flute played, the music splintered and atonal, the sort of music to which lunatic throngs might caper.

Another turn in the maze brought her to a gate, this one not flanked by sphinxes or topped with an arch but a simple gate of corroded metal bars. It hung askew on a hinge, wedged partway open and weedily entangled as if it had not moved in centuries. The pumice-brick path she walked on continued a ways past this gate, but more and more weeds straggled through cracks, and it was swiftly overgrown and lost.

The scene beyond it was one of fetid greens and greys. Mossy hills humped up from marshy moors. Ground-mist seeped in steamy vapors.

Ancient stumps and fallen logs lay half-buried by layers of mold. Pallid, fleshy growths of fungus sprouted from their decomposing crevices … not mushrooms in any sense that Eleanor could comprehend, but horrid rugose stalks topped by caps somehow both bulbous and pendulous … and the ground-mist, she realized, was not *ground*-mist at all but issuing from the sporulating folds and gills forming the undersides of those caps.

The prevailing odor was both mildewy and acrid, slightly sour, with the barest hint of something almost spicy, something not-quite-anise. She felt again that sense of expectancy and dread, vague but overwhelming.

"We knew you'd come," Chaos said from behind her.

Eleanor spun to see him emerging from an alcove concealed in the stonework of the maze walls. He smiled, his dark eyes glinting. Behind him, Hesperia and Brother Zoar also appeared.

"We knew you couldn't resist," Hesperia added. "Now you can help us gather what we need."

"You … you make incense from … *these*?" She shuddered as she indicated the clumps of sighing fungal growths.

"Not only those." Chaos held up a jagged, spiky stem tipped with a single glassy-clear flower. The petals – veined and membranous like dragonfly wings – blossomed out in a radiating spiral from its vile heart.

She caught its scent of fading, dying, unearthly starlight. This time, it repelled her and she drew back.

"Child." Brother Zoar raised empty, upturned palms. "My dear Eleanor, you do not understand. Our search for enlightenment is the Nameless One's poison dream. It lures us into the idiot vortices, and loses us amid the cosmic spheres."

"Looking for awareness," Hesperia said, "looking to expand the consciousness and open the inner eye."

"They don't know," Chaos continued. "They're making themselves more vulnerable."

"Vulnerable to what?" cried Eleanor.

"The madness of the Outer Gods," said Brother Zoar. "The streams of Time, the voids of Space."

She gazed at him in incomprehension.

"There is no harmony," Chaos said. "There is no purpose, only visions in the muttering dark. We are nothing."

Hesperia nodded. "We have seen into the gulfs, and retained our minds. We've seen ourselves upon the altar. We've stood alone before eternity, and nothing since has looked the same."

"Think of it as an inoculation," Brother Zoar said. "To save us from ourselves."

They showed it to her then, the truth beyond the truth. They showed her where unknowable things flopped and fluttered – formless things, shapeless, perhaps once human but no more – to the shrill piping of insane flutes.

She beheld with her own living eyes the dead eyes of blind Azathoth, and ceased to hope ... because she understood.

Salt Water Bodies

Susan Hicks Wong

We cruised through the warm moist night air with our favorite band blasting out the open windows; two eighteen-year-old beach town rats dressed to look twenty-one. Our band was in town tonight. The most amazing, incredible band you could imagine. We two freckled, salt-mouthed mermaids talked about them all the time.

Tube tops pulled down, acid-washed jeans with the knees and bottoms strategically torn, black velvet mascara and glitter eye shadow, hair flamboyantly roostered, lip gloss as slippery as a porpoise's backside. My cousin Mar-Lyna and I had planned this night for months and *nothing* was going to go wrong. As we barreled past the AME Zion church a wrinkled old lady shot us the wary eyeball from under her big flowered hat as she snatched the cross at her neck and kissed it.

We was bad news.

Traffic slowed to a molasses pour of rocking vans, pick-up trucks and rusty band-stickered imports full of kids as we neared the auditorium. Our old Falcon throbbed as we waited to turn into the parking area. A smoke-filled van next to us honked wildly and some guy inside waggled his tongue at us. "Moon him," Mar-Lyna commanded and I waited until the cars ahead of us cleared, yanked down my pants and aimed my backside out the window. She stomped the accelerator with a screech and I fell back into my seat, slithering into my pants as the air behind us filled with male hoots and raucous laughter.

Mar-Lyna cackled and waved her middle finger out the window as she cut off another car and slid into a parking space. A spotty-faced parking attendant shone his flashlight at us and shook his head no with a frown. She blew him a kiss and jumped out, grabbing my arm. "Come on, girl. We don't have all night."

We strutted down the dusty parking lot aisles and into the heaving crowd of hormone-stoked teenagers. Her hand clamped my elbow as we were sucked into the vortex of the auditorium entrance. A guard motioned me and I opened my bag for her to inspect it with what I hoped was a look of peach-fuzz innocence. The ticket was taken from me and someone stamped my hand. It said UNDER 21 in smeary red script. I looked around for Mar-Lyna on the other side of the turnstile and for a moment lost her in the sea of denim.

"Bet you thought you got rid of me." Juicy bubblegum popped next to my ear. "Let's hit the Ladies' Room, if you know what I mean." She elbowed me hard in the ribs. I hooked two fingers through the back collar of her fake snakeskin jacket and she pulled me through the crush at the door of the Ladies' like a water skier behind a motorboat. Someone cried out in protest, no fair jumping in line! Mar-Lyna pushed a pasty brunette out of the way, yanking me into the stall as she slammed the door in the girl's face.

"Here, hold my bag while I pee and then you can go." She smirked as she slid something out of her boot. "Mama's got treats." She waggled some pink and white pills in a baggie and a small leather flask. "Was my dad's. He don't need it no more." She gestured at the flask. "Drink up," she commanded, unscrewing it with a sharp smell of whiskey.

I wobbled a bit as we found our way to our assigned seats. The arena was already filled with a furtive haze of acrid smoke. "Nosebleed section," Mar-Lyna sneered. "Follow me." We talked loudly as we scooted down the stairs, swinging our hips. Nearer to the stage, a group of teenage boys gave us appreciative looks.

"Need some company?" she slithered in next to the cute one with long hair. Bitch. She always got the best-looking ones. She pushed her lips in a cherry-red pout as I scrambled into a hastily vacated seat on the other side of her. "Ya'll party?" Mar-Lyna inquired.

The opening band was some indie outfit I'd never heard of but Mar-Lyna and the guys nodded their heads along as the musicians squealed through their set. One of the boys at the end of the group went wooooooo and stood with his hand raised in a devil's sign. I think his name was David or something. Jerking her head in his direction, Mar-Lyna rolled her eyes at me and mouthed, *Loser.*

The opening act finally finished and she snuggled in closer to Alex, the guy she'd sat beside and batted her eyes. She was casting her spell, throwing her sparkly little net over him and he was mesmerized, hanging on her every word.

"Mar-Lyna!" I elbowed her and she brushed me off. "You're not supposed to *do* that anymore. Remember what happened last time?" She ignored me even more elaborately than usual but I could see the rapt expression on Alex's face.

It wasn't her fault exactly, the things Mar-Lyna did. Nobody was around much to tell either of us what to do.

Our mothers were half-sisters from the same mother, the two youngest of a vast and complicated family with a tendency towards inbreeding. I had a wrinkled snapshot of the two of them up to their waists in the waves and laughing showing their teeth but they had very little to do with one another these days. My mama had found a spiritually higher path, playing organ for prayer meeting at the Holiness Church. Mar-Lyna's mama was out greeting sailors at the base and spreading hospitality. Or at least that's what she called it. Since her last boyfriend ran off and she lost her job at the Undercurrent she's been doing that a lot. She just shrugs, grabs her little pocketbook on her way out the door and says, Hon, a girl's gotta get by.

I sighed and settled into my seat. Laser lights swooped through the crowd and as each section was highlighted cheers erupted and bodies moved in waves. When the lasers swept over us I felt a gurgle in my stomach. After the Southern Comfort and pills I felt a little woozy. I stood up trying to catch Mar-Lyna's attention but she had her back to me, her gaze on Mr. Excellent Hair. "S'cuse me," I mumbled as I brushed past them. "I'll be right back."

As I climbed the stairs to the exit there was a rush of excitement at some movement onstage and I struggled against the tide of people running back to their seats. Someone sloshed a beer on me. Guitars growled behind me and the crowd roared approval. Ladies and Gentleman, the Demons of Darkness, the Gods of Noise, the Beast With Five Heads! My heart sank as the opening chords cranked up. It was all so awesome. And I was stumbling toward the empty Ladies' Room gagging with my hands over my mouth. I made it just in time too. Everything came up: liquor, funny pills, plus some other stuff. Brrrrrr. I looked sickly green around the gills when I finally emerged from the stall. I arranged my hair, studying the effect with narrowed eyes and rinsed my mouth at the sink and put on some more lip-gloss. My mascara had run so I dabbed at it with a tissue.

I wondered if they missed me. A sob of self-pity bubbled up out of me. Mar-Lyna *always* got the cute guys. Her mama said that she was coming into her womanly powers. Me, I was still an ugly dork, always conscious of trying to fit in. When, if ever, would *I* come into my womanly powers? With a huge wet, shuddering sigh I emerged from the restroom and ran full force into someone's large hard arm.

"OW. What the fuck? What're you doing here?" My nose throbbed. Was it spurting blood? "Look what you did!"

It was David, the Loser Guy from the edge of the group. "I followed you to make sure you were alright. Are you . . . ?"

"Of course I'm okay. What do you mean, you followed me?" I aimed an offended flick of my bony leather-jacketed shoulder in his direction. "Weirdo. Do I look like I need help?"

He shrugged, hunching over me slightly because he was so tall. Muffled music boomed from inside. "Come on, you're missing all the good stuff. My friend won backstage passes for after the concert. We might be able to get you girls in."

Not a jock, not the cool dude Mar-Lyna was plastered onto, but one of loser David's friends.

We made our way back. My least favorite song, *Backside of the Planet* was playing so maybe I hadn't missed that much. Halfway to our seats David placed his hand at my back as if to guide me. I bounced the two-fingered party sign at Mar-Lyna and she shot me a crabby look as David and I slid past the jocks, her and Mr. Hair. He introduced me to his pals by name, which surprised me because I didn't think he knew it. His friends nodded and smiled at me and offered me a surreptitious toke. I sighed, slid down into my seat and turned my attention to the spectacle onstage.

***

There *he* was out front and center, tight black leather pants accentuating his manhood. Dirty blonde hair streamed behind as he pranced across the stage; smoke and flames billowing around him. He was holding the huge microphone so close to his lips that he threatened to swallow it. By this point in the concert his eyeliner had just begun to run and the effect was one of a highly assertive and debauched barbarian.

I shivered and crossed my legs tightly and imagined him and me in our castle lying on a bearskin sipping cognac. We would own white Lipizzaner stallions and mastiff dogs that ran after us when we went for our long rides on the rocky beach. No, scratch that, no beach. A meadow, an alpine meadow with edelweiss and blue larkspurs and . . . what was the name of that tree? An aspen that's what it was. There'd be lots of those. The band launched into a thunderous version of *Open Wide* and, as I galloped through my daydream, he slid to his knees at the edge of the stage and looked down, down, down to . . . me. He looked tenderly into my eyes as he sang to me, and me only. Open wide, my little flower. Give to me all your power. Yeah, ROCK ME! Rock, rock, rock me, bay-buh!

The moment ended with a jolt. The lights broke away from him to illuminate the guitarist, who ripped into a long screeching solo with lots of masturbatory riffs and dramatic flailing.

I leaned over and whispered across to Mar-Lyna, "I think this guy David's friend can get us backstage." She made her eyes big. I could tell she liked the idea but was probably not happy with the fact that I might make it happen. I stuck my tongue out at her. The rest of the show was a blur of light and thudding sound. I hoped *he* would look at me again and he didn't. But he would be backstage after the show. Backstage? I felt a little dig of nerves that threatened to escalate to terror. What, exactly did you do, *backstage*?

Mar-Lyna would know what to do.

I was on my feet along with hundreds of other chanting fans, holding a lighter over my head, swaying back and forth. There was stomping and the floor beneath our feet shook with the strength of our devotion. The band rushed back onto the stage to a pounding roar of applause. They played two more songs. More applause, this time a little quieter, more satiated and the band left the stage like gods off to Valhalla.

Darkness. Then the blinding house lights came up. Low-lying tendrils of dry ice smoke hung over the bottom of the arena. Everything sounded muffled and my ears rang with unpleasant pressure. "What?" I asked as David mumbled something into my ear and Mar-Lyna reached over and grabbed my arm hard at the same time. "We follow these guys and go back this way," I whispered to her. She hissed something to Hair Guy. He looked at David who shrugged and said, "I guess Alex can come too."

The auditorium was emptying out. We stumbled, following David through a barely visible door at the bottom of a ramp. Dim red light on the other side showed block walls and a concrete floor. A janitor's mop bucket blocked the hall. A very large shaved-bald man with gold earrings and a black As The World Burns Tour t-shirt grunted as David's friend presented his pass. "Pass says four. I'm only supposed to let FOUR in."

Mar-Lyna shouldered past me and planted herself in front of the guard with a perky grin, "But I'm small. I won't take up much room."

"Yeah, I just bet you won't. How old are you anyways? Gotta be twenty-one to go backstage."

"Even for a kiss?" she laid that adorable pout on him, "a nice one?" He hesitated for just a split second. I don't know if he was considering her offer or about to throw us all out on our behinds. The walkie-talkie in his back pocket let out a blast of static and he held up one finger halting us as he half turned away to answer it.

"Come on." Mar-Lyna gave me a yank. "Let's GO!"

I scampered after her. David, Alex and the other guy gaped at us. I looked back, "What are you waiting for?" There was a dissenting murmur from behind but everyone pounded up the metal staircase, following Mar-Lyna and me. Below us the bald man spluttered into the walkie-talkie. We darted through a heavy metal door that clanged shut after us.

Blocking our way stood a girl with a skimpy bandanna top and a battered leather cowboy hat, holding a clipboard. "Rafe knows he's not supposed to send you up those stairs." She made a little snort, and said something under her breath. She had a tattoo of a scaly clawed something running up her collarbone and I tried to see what it was without actually staring at it. "Let me see your pass." She narrowed her eyes at the clipboard and frowned, "Won passes, huh? You're just real VIPs. I guess I can let you go through." She looked us girls up and down. "Y'all ready for the inner sanctum?" she snickered in a not entirely pleasant way. When I looked back at her she was still staring at us and thumping her boot toe against the bottom of the wall.

***

The Inner Sanctum. Mar-Lyna's fingernails bit into my arm as we entered the room. It was small, cramped and full of sweaty people, all talking at once. A crowded table held bottles of Jack Daniels, mixers, ice and snacks. Somehow I had pictured something a little grander, maybe with tinkling chandeliers or crushed velvet pillows and mirrors. Mar-Lyna was cruising for the liquor table when I saw him. Him. My internal organs turned to water and jumped up through the top of my skull in a warm roar.

He was sitting in the middle of the room slightly off to himself though I could see there was a watchful swirl of young women around him. He looked like a lonely Viking king with a long black leather coat draped around his shoulders like a cape. He must have caught me staring because he raised a bottle of beer in my direction and my remaining insides contracted. He beckoned me with one finger. Me? I looked around to see if he was motioning some other girl and tapped my chest questioningly. He smiled and pulled out another beer from a big cooler and opened it with a crack and held it out to me.

"So, how'd you like the show, kiddo?"

Somehow my throat had locked up and nothing came out but a scraping noise. I grabbed the beer and took a fast swig. The bottle was so cold that white vapor came out of the opening.

"My close friends call me Killer." He winked and the whole room telescoped down to just us two. "You know, as in Ladykiller. Have a seat." His eyes were very blue. Like those mountain larkspurs.

My knees gave way and I plumped down onto a case of beer at his feet. One of the swarm of young women separated and hovered over at his side, buzzing something into his ear. "It's okay, Honey," he said to her, "she's not bothering me." He stretched back in his chair and turned his intense blue gaze full on her and ran one finger down her bare golden arm. "So pretty. You are just so beautiful. Hey, you know what would be really good right now? One of those White Russians you make. Awwwww, c'mon you make 'em the best. Purty please." He dragged his voice, trying to sound sultry and southern. Honey gave me a dirty look and pulled herself away, half-turning for a few steps until she finally gave up and went over to the bar table where Mar-Lyna had found a bottle of tequila and was setting up shots for the guys.

He fixed those blue eyes on me again and I scooted just a bit closer. "So, tell me all about yourself. What's your favorite album?" he said.

I cleared my throat, "All of them . . . maybe not the second album as much, it's kinda slow."

"Ah, yes the acoustic folk one. That wasn't really my idea. I'm more of a plugged-in artist, myself. I have to really feel the music in my body, know what I mean?" He tapped my knee and looked at me as if we had a special understanding.

I nodded. How many times had I listened to them turned up full blast, the music rocking my bed until my mother hit the ceiling with a broomstick to make me turn it down. Yeah, I felt their music in my body.

He leaned his face in nearer to mine. "I'm really looking to go someplace darker with my work. More real." Up close the eyeliner had seeped into a fine network of lines around his eyes and he smelled of beer, leather and man sweat.

"I know what you mean." My voice shook a little. "I'm all *about* darkness."

There was a blast of cheers and wolf whistles from the bar table and he broke eye contact. As I looked up, Mar-Lyna had just slammed down a shot. She licked a lime wedge with a tiny baby pink tongue, tossed her rippling hair back and strode over with her hand stuck out in front of her.

"Well, what have we here? A queen. Is this your friend?" he asked without looking back at me. Mar-Lyna stood in front of him as if she expected him to kiss her hand. He took it, in his two hands and laughed as he brought it to his lips. She gave him an abrupt little slap on the cheek and his eyes widened in surprise.

"You fresh thing, I was only going to shake your hand," she said. Her face glowed and her heavily lashed eyes sparkled against the blue eye shadow. Behind her at the bar Alex the Longhaired looked up in her direction like a wary deer at a watering hole that has just heard a wolf in the surrounding woods.

"Why don't you have one of your handmaidens make me a drink. Margarita. Rocks. Extra salt on the rim." It wasn't a question. She was being awfully bold, even by Mar-Lyna standards. He was a rock star, for god's sake. He stared at her for a moment and then burst out laughing and gestured at poor Honey, who had just walked up, White Russian in hand. "Honey, darlin' see if you can make Miss—"

"Name's Mar-Lyna."

"—Make Miss Lili Marlena here a proper margarita with ice and extra salt and what-all. And, Honey . . . "

Honey sniffed and threw the White Russian on him and stalked off. Cream ran down his draped coat and bare chest.

He shrugged and shook off the ice. "So hard to get good help these days." Sighing, "Well, I guess I'm just going to have to make you a drink myself, Miss Lili. A Killer Special. And your little friend, what does she want?" He barely nodded in my direction. "I really should be making you both Shirley Temples, right? But life is short in the fast lane as they say. Y'all little ol' southern belles invented the fast lane, didn't you?"

Mar-Lyna glanced in my direction and hesitated one fraction of a moment and commanded, "Make that two margaritas then." He heaved to his feet to go make the drinks, leaving the black coat in a leather puddle on the floor. Mar-Lyna eyed the coat and I knew what she was thinking.

"Don't you dare. That's his coat."

"Me-yow! Relax, don't be such a B. He don't care about it." She looked at me with pretend-innocent eyes, "Besides, I got bigger fish to fry, girlie."

"I was talking to him," I sulked.

"What? You *was* talking to him. What is he, your boyfriend now? All's fair in love and war, babes, you know that. RIGHT?"

I muttered something.

"What did you say?"

Feeling crazy brave like going over the top of the first big hill of the roller coaster down at the Pavilion, holding your hands up over your head and screaming, I said, "Don't you dare do what I think you're going to do. You . . . we're not old enough."

She pushed her face up into mine and bared her sharp little teeth. Her eyes were very black, the pupils dilated. "I'll DO whatever I WANT. Besides, it's time. I'm tired of waiting. He's the One—I'm sure this time."

"That's what you said about those others."

The ugly animal look on her face was wiped over by a huge smile as he walked up with the drinks. "There you are," she cooed. "Did you make your Killer Special for me?" Her eyes slid to someone behind me, "Oh wait, my little friend has to go home. It's past her bedtime."

I turned around. It was David, flushed and gawky. There were pink blotches on his cheeks and beads of sweat on his forehead. His black hair stuck up in all directions. "That guy Rafe caught me. Thought I was never going to get in here." Faintly accusing, "You girls ran off and left me." He looked down at me, "Everybody in here looks . . . *older*."

"I think she's had too much to drink," Mar-Lyna said to David as if I wasn't there. "Why don't you take her home now."

"Fuck you," I said.

"Definitely too much to drink. Go on, get her out of here."

"Girls, temper, temper," the Killer interjected. He looked lost somewhere between concerned and enormously pleased. He held a drink out to Mar-Lyna. "I think you'll like this one. I put something special in it." He took a slug from the other glass. "Yeah, that's more like it." His blue eyes were fixed on her as she sucked liquid through the red straw.

"Let's get out of here," David said, leaning down to me. "Mar-Lyna, you should come too, if you want. I think my guy is ready to go. Alex went off somewhere with that Honey chick."

She licked the straw, "Go on home, pussies. I'll be okay." Grandly, "Re-e-e-ally, I'll manage somehow." Looking straight at me for the last time, "See ya later, Alligator." It was a litany of our girlhood and it demanded a response.

I leaned over, whispered in her ear *after a while, Crocodile* and my voice broke hoarsely. Then I turned around and walked out with David and onto the dry land of the rest of my life.

***

"Are you sure you feel comfortable taking care of her by yourself?" I asked.

Our baby girl, swaddled in crocheted pink, gurgled in her carrier on the motel bed. I stood in the bathroom door wrapped in a towel with a toothbrush stuck in my mouth, watching her father as he played with her. The television was on for background noise, some fishing show, but he wasn't really watching it. As usual, the baby was our center of attention. "You know you two can come with me, if you want."

He shook his head yes for the baby girl, hard no for coming with me.

"I haven't seen any of the family in years. Now with Mama gone, I'm . . . curious about them. You understand, don't you?" I dressed and carefully applied makeup: a little pale foundation, a soft peach shade of lipstick. I blotted my lips on a tissue. There, I was ready. I turned sideways to the mirror, eyeing myself critically, a habit I'd had since girlhood.

"You look nice," he said. "Don't worry."

I kissed him and our precious daughter and went out and started the rental car and pulled out onto the highway. The flat coastal landscape, littered with brand new retirement villas, fancy beach cottages and strip malls gave way to raggedy old shotgun shacks and trailers that hadn't changed much since I'd left. I turned down what felt like an endless sandy dirt road, hoping my rental wasn't going to bottom out. I passed a windswept farmhouse that looked deserted, wondered what had become of the family who lived there but kept going through a grove of skimpy pine trees and out to the marsh. The tide was starting to come back in and it smelled like rotting fish.

There it was. I got out and slammed the car door shut. The eerie peep of tiny frogs stopped and started up again. I felt a moment of shock. The house they used to live in was gone, torn down. In its place stood a huge raw-looking brick monstrosity that loomed on the small hill over the incoming water. There were no vehicles outside but windowpanes reflected blankly from a multi-car garage behind the house and there was a neglected algae-clotted swimming pool.

I guess that's what they did with his money.

I rang the doorbell. It boomed deep fathoms within the silent house. I leaned, with my ear against the door, not breathing, listening for the inhabitants in its depths. I rapped the cavorting dolphin-shaped doorknocker. Nothing.

I was fighting the nervous stomach-tingle urge to flee when I heard something faint but getting closer from inside. A scuffling noise and the door flew open. It was Mar-Lyna's mother holding a dirty little white dog. "Say hi to Tiny," she said, jiggling the animal in my face.

The dog let out a ripping growl and snapped in my direction. "Do you recognize me?" I asked.

"Of course. You're still one of us." She looked much as I remembered her, slender with wavy jet-black hair that flowed over her shoulders. "Missed you. Sorry couldn't none of us make it to your mama's funeral." She turned and gestured for me to follow her into the darkened house. "We sent flowers."

She waved a hand back in my direction, "Mar-Lyna'll be happy to see you. Of course there'll be the baby. There's a fresh one for you to look at." She muttered, as if to herself, "The other ones got so *big*."

She led me to a dark-paneled den at the back of the house, crammed full of enormous furniture. Velvet curtains covered the windows so that no sunlight entered. Mar-Lyna's mother flopped down on an overstuffed sofa, of which there were several. She stared at the blue underwater flicker of a large television with the sound on low. Tiny nursed a basketful of squirming white puppies.

Mar-Lyna was curled up in a huge round chair carved in the shape of a shell. "Aw, come here and give me a hug. I'd get up but I'm just tuckered." She wheezed and said in a hoarse voice, "The baby, you know. Just wears me out." She appeared bloated and her features were rubbery. Her skin felt clammy. Surely she couldn't be pregnant again. Hadn't one just been born?

"I know about that. I have a baby too. She's six months old now, a handful." I thought of our little pink bit wriggling on the hotel bed with David and wished I were there with them.

"Well where's she at, hon? Should have brought her."

"Her father is taking care of her back at the hotel. She was feeling a little . . . under the weather."

"David?" she sneered. "Well, I guess he's okay. Y'all married now?"

It was then I realized we were not alone in the room.

"I can't get him to do nothing." She glared at a corner. "Worthless."

"Well, hello," I said. "How have you been?" and immediately regretted it when I saw his face.

He crouched like a toad next to the cold empty fireplace. His once-fine physique had melted into a pale ruin and the long blond hair was gray and stringy, pink patches of scalp showed through. In the dimness I thought I saw a flicker of recognition in the thickened blank of his face. He looked at me with the beseeching expression of a dog about to be kicked for piddling on the rug.

His cracked white lips struggled to form a word.

"Hey, I know what," Mar-Lyna said, "Bet you want to see the new baby. She's big now. I mean huge. Probably way bigger than your kid." Her eyes were very bright. "Mumma, go get us girls something fun to drink."

I felt faint. The air was too stuffy in here.

"Kil-*ler*! He trembled at the sound of her voice. "Go down to the water and get the baby. Time to feed her."

"That's okay," I was backing away now. "I really need to be getting back. My daughter's not feeling well . . . "

"Oh yeah, I reckon you better check on your little girlie. Make sure she's all right. Be certain nothing's wrong with her." She stood up with effort and patted her enormous belly with satisfaction. Something moved under her stretched t-shirt. Not moved exactly. *Roiled.* "I got another li'l bun in the oven, in case you were wondering." Her head swiveled around toward him, "Killer, don't make me ask you again."

I muttered something about my husband needing me and stumbled for the hallway. The dog, Tiny yelped behind me. I bumped into massive furniture in the darkness and bruised my shins against a low-lying something before I twisted the front door handle and stumbled down the cracked concrete steps to the walkway.

"That's right, you better run away," Mar-Lyna's voice rose at me like a wave, crashing at my back. "That's all you was ever good for anyway."

I dropped the key trying to open the car door. My legs shook as I crouched down in the sand, fumbling under the car for them. I groped, tearing my hands on weeds until I finally caught the glint of the key ring, grabbed it and stood up so relieved I thought I had wet myself.

He was standing on the other side of the car.

"OH. Oh god. Look, I have to go now. Expected back . . . " I yanked the door open and had slid in, locked the doors, and put the key in the ignition when he tapped on the passenger window. Shaking, I waited a moment and pushed the button to roll the window down a crack. He bent down until his face was level with the opening. His eyes were no longer blue. He was holding one of Tiny's white puppies under his arm.

Help me.

Please.

Did I only imagine he said this? There was a high tinkling sound like broken glass from the house and he looked back toward it for the space of a pounding heartbeat, stood up, turned and staggered away from the car and across the yard and into the marshes. I thought the dark figure with a white patch under its arm hesitated and turned back toward me again but it was hard to tell. Thank God I couldn't see his face anymore when he disappeared into the dilapidated shack near the water.

I put the car firmly into reverse and backed hard out of the drive until I reached the deserted farmhouse and turned around and headed to the hotel. Fly home to the fields of Kansas, far from all salt-water bodies. Home with the man who adored me and our precious little one. My wiggly pink girl. My perfect little fishie.

As I drove I rubbed the slit opening in the side of my neck and my finger caught on one of the tiny barbs. I yanked my hand away. There was a smear of blood on my fingertip where I'd hooked it.

I'd always worked so hard to cover that opening with makeup, scarves, hairstyles. It was barely noticeable.

Please God let her turn out just like her father.

Please.

Interrogation

Damir Salkovic

The corridor was cold and dark and stank of fear. Dull electric light bathed the iron galleries and rows of grim doors, threw long shadows up the stark white walls. The silence was absolute, funereal. Solovkin watched his feet move across the concrete floor of the passage without making a sound. His mind reeled: it was a mistake, had to be. They would realize it any moment now. Beneath his confusion he could taste fear, bright and hard and metallic, cutting through the daze like a knife.

The guard in front opened a heavy steel door. Beyond it lay a wide, windowless chamber, its walls and floors covered in stained gray tile. A long wooden table stood halfway across the room, and behind it sat two uniformed men. Before the table was an empty chair. Further back was small desk with a secretary hunched over a typewriter, a metal cart covered by a dirty sheet. Dim, terrible realization dawned on Solovkin, something his bowels understood before his brain did. He felt his legs give way. The guards half-led, half-dragged him across the threshold, dumped him into the chair without ceremony. Behind him the door slammed shut.

Harsh white light streamed from a naked bulb, blinding him. The faces of the two men were shadows in the painful glare. Solovkin recognized one of them, a tall, slender officer of the People's Commissariat for Internal Affairs who'd been present at his arrest. The other one was stocky and brutish, with coarse dark hair and a cruel set to his mouth. His huge, scarred fists lay knotted on the table like mallets. His eyes, flat and black and lifeless, stared at Solovkin like the eyes of a shark.

They had come for him in the dead of night, hammering on the door of his apartment, the ill-lit landing echoing with their shouts. It was an old trick, one Solovkin himself had used with no small success: catch a man off guard, half-asleep and dazed, his mental and physical defenses lowered. He was given ten minutes to dress and pack his belongings. An arrest warrant had been thrust into his face. Before he knew what was happening, he was in the back of a huge black car, roaring through the sleeping Moscow streets. Then the prison, a vast, sprawling nightmare of brick and concrete, bristling with searchlights and machine gun towers. That had been days or months ago: time slowed to a trickle in the mute, shapeless darkness of the cell. No one had spoken to him until the two guards came and ordered him to get up and follow. He hadn't dared ask where they were taking him, afraid of the cell door closing again, of the thick, viscous silence that descended like a shroud, shutting out the world.

"Smoke, Comrade?" The tall interrogator pushed a crumpled pack across the table. Solovkin thanked him and reached for it with a trembling hand. The wood of the chair dug into his back. He lit a cigarette with the proffered lighter, feeling the eyes of the men on him. "My name is Malenkov and this is Commissar Kazakov. We have been commissioned to question you about the events leading to your arrest." The pack vanished into an inner coat pocket. Malenkov leaned back in his seat. "Do you know why you're here?"

"There has been a mistake, Comrades." It took Solovkin tremendous effort to keep his voice steady. His gaze betrayed him, crept to the covered metal cart. Terror rose in him like an icy tide: he knew what lay beneath the stained sheet, had used it himself more times than he cared to remember. "I assure you I had nothing to do with the matter. I'm the deputy head of the Special Tasks Section, not a-"

"Surely you don't think we don't know who you are, Vitaly Dmitrovich." Malenkov chuckled, a low, unpleasant sound. He rummaged through the thick folder before him. "A decorated veteran of the Great War and a stalwart of the Revolution. Before joining the Special Tasks Section, you served as acting chief of the Seventh Directorate. Your exploits in the fight against the enemies of the people, at home and abroad, are legendary. You're something of a hero in the Commissariat. One of the Old Guard." He put the folder down and steepled his hands under his chin. "This makes your betrayal all the more baffling."

Solovkin fumbled for words, but found none. Malenkov's eyes bored into his, glinting with cold amusement. "You claim your arrest is a mistake. Very well. It might be so. Think carefully before you answer. Where were you in October last year?"

A knot of hope and anticipation tightened in Solovkin's chest; his mind grasped at it like a drowning man at a straw. "I was in Paris, on assignment. I stayed at-"

"-the Hotel Quai Voltaire." Malenkov was skimming over a tightly typed page. The expression on his face was suddenly stern; Solovkin felt the glimmer of hope die out. "Attending a trade exposition. Your cover was that of a publishing house representative. What was the nature of this assignment?"

"It's in my report." The light hurt Solovkin's eyes. From somewhere behind the table came the distant clatter of a typewriter. "We – the Section – received orders to find and eliminate Konrad Odinets, a former White officer and reactionary ringleader. I went to Paris to gather intelligence and coordinate the operation."

"How did that go?"

"It was a failure," Solovkin said. "An agent was assigned to visit the target in his quarters and kill him with a cyanide bullet. Somehow Odinets must have gotten wind of it. He fled the city, took the overnight train to Marseilles. I dispatched two men to find him there, but they were unsuccessful."

"I see." Malenkov pretended to study the file again. "According to this report, on the third day of the exposition you met with a Finn by the name of Vartiainen. An antiquarian from Helsinki."

"As you said. It's all in the report. I met with him to preserve my cover"

"He gave you a package. What was in it?"

"Yes." Solovkin could hear the tremor in his voice. The other Commissar's silence was beginning to unnerve him. "A rare copy of Philidor's *Analysis of the Game of Chess*, published in Paris fifty years ago."

"Come now." The thin man gave him a reproachful look. He reached under the table and brought out an old, leather-bound volume, the covers lettered in gold. "We found the book while searching your apartment. It is of no interest to us. We want you to tell us what you did with the letters."

"Letters?" The walls seemed to close in on Solovkin. "I don't know anything about any letters."

"This Vartiainen," Malenkov said, as if the prisoner hadn't spoken, "is an enemy agent, in league with reactionary immigrant groups. He used you to transport ciphered messages to subversives and criminal elements within our borders. We want to know the names of his contacts here, in Moscow."

"There were no letters," Solovkin said blankly. The words sounded like they came from the mouth of a stranger. A horrible uncertainty seized him for a moment. What if Malenkov was right? Nonsense, utter nonsense: he knew how the game was played. This was what they were taught to do – instill confusion, try to get the suspect to contradict himself, to question his own sanity. How many times had he sat on the other side of the table, smoking cigarette after cigarette, staring at the condemned with cold, calculating eyes? "There are no contacts."

"He's lying," said the thick-shouldered Kazanov. His voice was very even, void of accent or inflection. He leaned back in his seat and laced his massive hands across his stomach. "The bastard is sitting in front of us, lying to our faces."

Malenkov shot an annoyed look at his comrade, turned back to Solovkin. "Do you know a man named Bogatsky? Mikhail Bogatsky?"

"He was second-in-command of the foreign intelligence branch."

"Was?"

"He was arrested and executed for treasonable conspiracy."

"Indeed." Malenkov nodded and shuffled papers. "In his confession, the accused Bogatsky stated that he maintained contact with counter-revolutionary terror groups in Berlin, Warsaw and Helsinki. That he used his influence and position to betray state secrets to foreign powers through a network of dissidents and exiles. That he assisted them in planning assassinations. Are you aware of this?"

"I am aware." Solovkin rubbed his temple. His mouth was suddenly very dry. A sinking realization settled into the pit of his stomach with frigid certainty: he would never leave the prison alive. He was the one who had dictated the confession to Bogatsky. He recalled how the old man's hands shook while signing the statement, the desperate terror in those watery blue eyes. Another one of the Old Guard. It had taken Solovkin less than a week to break the former Directorate chief; he wondered how long he would last.

"   Two reactionaries arrested last week named Vartiainen as Bogatsky's man in Helsinki." The Commissar crossed his arms over his narrow chest. "According to them, you acted as the courier, delivered correspondence from abroad to the leader of a secret counter-revolutionary cell in this city. Who is this man?"

"This is absurd," Solovkin said, knowing all was lost. The trap had been laid with great skill. If he tried to confute Bogatsky's confession, they would accuse him of putting an innocent man to death to cover his tracks. If he didn't, he would be admitting his guilt.

"There's no use denying it."

"There is no man." He stared at the drab floor tiles. A dark, rusty stain had seeped into the grout, into the tiny cracks. "I'm telling you, I never-"

The blow caught him unawares, knocking him off the chair. For a man of his bulk, Kazanov moved like a panther. Shadows gathered in the corners of Solovkin's consciousness. Malenkov's voice reached him from a vast distance: ... restraint... handled delicately... well-known figure. A great hand picked him up, deposited him back into his seat with a boneless thump. The pain came in a dull bolt, almost an afterthought. He was vaguely aware of the cut above his eye, the warm stickiness crawling down the side of his head.

"We'll have none of that," he heard Malenkov say. A noncommittal grunt came in response. The blur before Solovkin shifted, resolved into the faces of his interrogators. "Why do you so stubbornly maintain your innocence? We know you're not a subversive at heart. It is the belief of the Commissariat that you have been manipulated by the criminal reactionary movement. You can be reformed."

Solovkin shook his throbbing head. To his right, the troll-like form of the hulking Kazanov hovered on the fringe of his vision. Malenkov sighed and rubbed his eyes.

"Is it ready?"

Behind the interrogators, a metal chair scraped across the floor. Footsteps approached and receded. Solovkin kept his stare riveted to the scratched surface of the table. It was an awful dream; any moment he would wake up, away from the interrogation room, from the hideous silence of the prison.

A typewritten page was thrust in front of him. He tried to read it, but his mind refused to make sense of the words. References to clandestine meetings, unfamiliar places, names he didn't recognize. A drop of blood fell from his cheek to the paper, a red circle spreading across the whiteness.

"Sign the statement," Malenkov said, pushing a pen across the table. The tall man's countenance was weary and sallow; dark shadows ringed his eyes. "It's an admission of guilt, concocted to minimize your culpability in the affair. Ten years at most, but you can get amnesty in one or two." The Commissar's tone was businesslike. He rapped his fingers on the tabletop. Solovkin sat with the pen poised over the page for what seemed like an eternity. Finally he looked up and placed the pen to the side.

"As you wish." Malenkov shrugged his shoulders. Kazanov took a menacing step forward, but his companion waved him away. A bell rang in the depths of the endless corridor beyond the door, and within minutes two prison guards appeared in the room. Solovkin was escorted down the dark passageway, through the great circular galleries, back to his cell. Thoughts roiled in his head, each one more dismal than the next. He didn't think he'd be able to fall asleep, but exhaustion overcame him as soon as he settled on the hard, uncomfortable cot, and his sleep was full of nightmares.

***

In his dream he sat behind a chessboard in a vast, shadowy hall, its walls melding with the darkness. Across the board sat a tall figure, pale-skinned and gaunt and swathed in black robes. Its long, bony fingers flickered over the black and white squares with uncanny speed. Solovkin couldn't make out his opponent's face amid the shifting shadows; its contours seemed to meld and change with each shift of the flickering light. The only thing that didn't change was its grin, huge and frightful: a hungry grin, looming in the darkness like the crescent of a diseased moon. The teeth in the grin were like a shark's, folding back from the gums in double rows, too many to count. Bone-deep cold sank into Solovkin's flesh; he was thankful for the shadows that hid the rest of that hideous face. Dream or no dream, he suspected the sight might drive him mad.

Frozen as his mind was with fear, his fingers danced across the chessboard with unusual confidence and cunning, seemingly playing the game on their own. The dark man played with blacks, cackling and tittering after every move, regardless of the outcome. At times his actions appeared erratic and haphazard; yet no matter how well Solovkin plotted his tactics and developed his position, his opponent remained a step or two ahead of him, weaving a tangle of moves and countermoves, the mad, glassy smile never wavering. Slowly the realization that he was going to lose dawned on Solovkin with chilling certainty. His second thought, groundless but persistent, was that there was more to the game than met the eye, that he was playing for the highest stakes imaginable.

A black knight blundered into the right file, leaving the middle exposed. Solovkin saw through the gambit and riposted deftly. The cackling ceased; Solovkin thought he could see the dark man's eyes now, dull red embers glowing in the shadowed face. The robed figure leaned forward, grin twisted into a grimace, skeletal fingers grasping the sides of the chessboard. Sick, baking heat came off it in waves. Silence held for a moment; then the creature threw its head back and hooted with laughter.

"Excellent." The dark man's voice was the whistle of wind across a corpse-strewn battlefield. He shook and clapped his hands with mirth. A black piece slid across the board without making contact with the pale, thin fingers. "You're a crafty player, Vitaly Dmitrovich. But how many moves do you have left?"

Solovkin stared at the board, a furrow of concentration etched between his brows. He launched a counteroffensive, but his opponent evaded, ever a maddening step or two out of reach.

"The game draws to a close," the dark man said, shaking his head. For a moment the room took on the shape of Solovkin's cell, wavered, dissolved once more into dimensionless shadow. "A pity. All for a handful of letters."

"I already told you," said Solovkin through clenched teeth. "There were no letters."

"That's of no importance." It was Malenkov's voice issuing from the man's black lips. The tiny figures on the chessboard came alive, writhing in mute agony. "Your guilt has already been decided. By refusing to sign your confession, you're preventing justice from taking its course. You're a bourgeois parasite, a scab and a traitor to the Motherland."

"Who are you?" The notion that the dark man might be the devil crossed Solovkin's mind, but deep down he knew that the truth was far more complex than that. His eyes had adapted; he could now see into the crawling darkness, where blind, ravenous shapes lurked. The thin veneer of reality had cracked and he looked upon the truth beneath it, chaos and madness spinning in the absolute nothingness beyond the rim of the universe. "What do you want from me?"

"I dwell in the cracks, in the small, hidden spaces," came the cryptic answer. "I need to do nothing but watch and wait. Speaking of which, I fear our time together has come to an end."

Solovkin glanced down and his heart sank: the white king was checkmated. Bit by bit, the robed figure faded into the blur until all that was left was the voracious grin, triangular, razor-sharp teeth gleaming in the darkness.

"Wait," Solovkin said. The darkness grew thicker; something moved inside it, vast and unformed and older than time. "What do you want from me? What do they want?"

"You are being forgetful, Comrade." The face of the First Secretary stared out of the dark man's cowl, the broad, stern peasant features stamped with malignant glee. Solovkin screamed and sprang backward, the chair beneath him tumbling to the floor. The robed figure shrieked in awful hilarity. "Some doors close, others open. You shouldn't have taken what wasn't yours."

An image came to Solovkin: the inside of a filthy peasant hut, a symbol drawn across the rotting floorboards, a crude many-pointed star. Black candles burning at the intersections of the lines. Crude wooden shelves along the far wall, lined with musty, yellowing manuscripts. In the corner, something small and bloody, wrapped in a tattered potato sack. He had seen the hut before – but where?

"The faithful are eaten first," the mouth said. There was torment in its voice, a crooning hunger that the mocking tone couldn't quite conceal. "Open the doorway, Vitaly Dmitrovich. You don't want to be left behind by the Rapture."

The slavering shapes circled closer. Solovkin raised his arms to ward them off, flailed wildly. He blinked at the darkness surrounding him: the cell was empty and he lay on the cold concrete floor, a dull pain in his elbow and side. A gruff, disembodied voice from the other side of the door shouted at him to be silent. He climbed back under the thin blanket and tried to fall asleep, but the white, featureless face floated behind his closed eyelids, the pestilent grin like a raw, suppurating wound.

***

The prisoners shuffled round the courtyard in a rough circle, their footsteps the only sound breaking the silence. Solovkin kept his head down and stared at the tips of his scuffed shoes. If he didn't let his eyes stray far, he could pretend he was strolling down the city's main promenade, far from the immense stone walls and iron-grated windows, from the scowling, uniformed guards at the center of the yard. He forced himself not to look at the other men; he was afraid he would recognize someone he knew among the blank, hollow faces. The Old Guard devoured by the monstrosity of their own creation.

A shadow fell across the flagstones. Solovkin lifted his gaze. A man was standing in the shadow of a doorway, dressed in a long robe, like a priest's. Long, greasy dark hair framed his bony face, eyes like hot coals in the darkness. He nodded at Solovkin and his lips parted in a leer. His teeth were black, rotten stumps.

Solovkin glanced toward the guards. Communication was forbidden, as was stepping out of line. Yet neither of them seemed to have noticed the man in the doorway. The stranger raised his hands and beckoned to Solovkin. His palms were red with blood. The burning eyes seemed to pull Solovkin toward the shadows. He lost his step, stumbled, nearly fell. The guards laughed and cursed at him. The prisoner next to Solovkin shot him a wary look, but kept his silence.

The whistle sounded, signaling the end of the exercise hour. Solovkin stood in line, waiting to be conducted back into the building. He didn't have to look over his shoulder to know that the doorway was empty, that the robed man was no longer there. He remembered the pale, ascetic face, the burning eyes. He remembered the village, the smell in the peasant hut: dirt and dried blood, and tallow from the dripping candles. The chatter of the guns, the smoke and ashes rising from the conflagration. Almost twenty years had elapsed, but the priest had not changed, had never grown old.

Heavy concrete doors scraped open. Solovkin stepped inside, the dark, vaulted corridors closing around him like a fist.

***

111

At some point he'd fallen asleep, because when he opened his eyes the cell swam in pale light and a guard was shaking him awake.

He was taken back to the interrogation room and seated in front of the two sullen, unshaven Commissars. The covered metal cart had been wheeled closer. Laid out neatly on the table were the typed confession, a cigarette, a match and a pen. Solovkin pushed the paper away. Malenkov gave him a look of weary hatred, but Kazanov seemed almost cheerful, his dark, beady eyes shiny and malicious.

They made him stand in a corner of the room and kept him awake with a continuous stream of questions. Hours went by; at some point the two interrogators were replaced by others, and those by others again, shouting at him, waving the fabricated confession. Solovkin suffered in silence, his legs and back riven with cramps, the world around him a blur of angry faces and loud, echoing voices. Memory came to him in disparate fragments. In his delirium he saw a crack in the wall grow into a wide fissure, the pale sickle of the dark man's grin rise up from its depths.

What is the name of your contact?

Where did you meet?

What did you carry from Helsinki?

The questions ran together, numbing his sleep-deprived mind. The answers had already been entered into the statement Solovkin refused to sign. The name of the men he was expected to denounce were vaguely familiar, but he couldn't put a face to them. From what Solovkin could gather, he was being accused of plotting to assassinate the First Secretary and a number of Party officials. Two men arrested as participants in this alleged conspiracy had already denounced him as a collaborator. All the Commissariat needed now was a confession from the disgraced official to close the circle.

Several times he nearly broke down with exhaustion, but fear and desperation gave him strength. He knew that a signed deposition would spell certain death. A bullet to the back of the head, or, worse yet, whatever lay covered on the metal cart. He knew he was only delaying the inevitable, but for the moment that didn't matter.

Hallucinations set in. There was a hole in the center of the concrete floor, a black pit that dilated like a great sightless eye. The room was collapsing into it: he could feel the irresistible pull, see the objects around him stretch and distort. The hole blotted out everything; an abyss opened under his feet and he was falling, into the bottomless, viscid dark, into the maw of the thing that slithered below.

An eternity passed. Rough hands lifted him to his feet, shook him awake. Kazanov's heavy, expressionless face hovered over him. Malenkov stood in the background, smoking a cigarette and leafing through his file, flicking ash carelessly across the pages. Behind the table sat the priest from the dead village, grinning at the two Commissars who appeared to be oblivious to his presence.

"I trust you've come to your senses," said Malenkov. He closed the file with a snap and sat down in the chair. Solovkin blinked once, twice. His eyes had played a trick on him: there was no robed, leering figure behind the table, only a shadow. "The sooner you sign, the sooner you'll be released."

"I can't confess to a crime I haven't committed," Solovkin said. Fragments of half-formed memory leapt to the front of his mind. The beaten, bloodied priest dragged out of the darkness of the hut, babbling about unseen spheres and hidden realms, about forces beyond human comprehension. The sparks dancing in his dead eyes, fading into the darkness. Solovkin in his olive-green Commissar's uniform, feeding crumbling old pages into the fire, watching them blacken and curl. The symbol on the hut floor falling away, opening on swirling galaxies. A vast cosmic cloud dimming the cold radiance of the stars.

"Don't be a fool." Malenkov's face twisted in a sneer of disgust. "Whom are you trying to protect? We've arrested many of your accomplices, and it's simply a matter of time before we find the rest. There is nowhere for them to hide. You can still save yourself."

Solovkin was silent. He was staring at a crack in the wall, from which a cancerous blackness seemed to emanate. "Too late for that," he finally said.

***

They had rounded up the peasants in the center of the village and executed them one by one, even the children. The last light of day faded and died, the evening air filling with the crack of rifle-fire. The priest knelt and watched the killings, his visage blank and impassive. Only when the hut with the altar was set ablaze and thick black smoke began to curl up from under the wooden roof did his expression change. Solovkin peered down at him. The man was smiling. His face, lit red by the spreading flames, shone in the gloaming.

A soldier appeared at Solovkin's side, a bundle of yellow manuscript pages in his arms. "What should we do with these, Comrade Commissar?"

The paper was ancient, covered in strange symbols. Solovkin's skin crawled at the sight. "Enemy dispatches, in some sort of code." He

113

dismissed the soldier with an impatient gesture. The priest was looking up at him and grinning.

"Who are you?" The question slipped from Solovkin's mouth before he could stop himself. "What's happening here?"

"He wants to meet you." The priest's dark eyes found Solovkin's and held them. "The Dark One who dwells in the forest. He sees something in you. Something more than just dead meat waiting to be devoured. They are old, these woods, and the Dark One is older still."

"I don't believe in the Devil." Solovkin followed the kneeling man's gaze past the killing ground, past the burning huts. A tall, thin figure stood at the edge of the thick forest, slipping in and out of shadow before the eye could fix upon it.

"He believes in you," said the priest and laughed. The dirt beneath his knees slowly turned to red mud. "Besides, you got it all wrong -- God and Devil, good and evil. The truth lies well beyond such tired scriptural platitudes."

"What is He, then?"

"What you see around yourself is not a place, not a location." The priest closed his eyes. A look of ecstasy crossed his thin face. "It is a process. Think of Him as a bridge, as the instrument by which Creation perfects itself. Oh, He'll show you wondrous sights, and whisper forbidden knowledge in your ear. You will pass through the terminus and be changed. Reshaped in His image. Living the life everlasting."

Solovkin pressed the muzzle of his gun to the priest's temple and pulled the trigger. The body slumped into the mud, the dark eyes never leaving Solovkin's. He found his reflection in them, saw it melt and become something else, turned away.

The soldiers worked quickly, without hesitation; there was no need for orders. Later they would convince themselves the village had been razed by the enemy, and the Army Command would not question their account. By the end of the war, Solovkin had almost managed to forget all about it. He had shot a religious agitator, burned a bundle of reactionary pamphlets. He'd done far worse things in the years that followed; regret was not something Solovkin entertained often.

But the priest had not forgotten, and neither had the black man of the woods. They could afford to wait; time ceased to matter in the living, pulsing dark.

Solovkin grunted and came to. He was on the floor of a prison cell, the stub of a pencil in his right hand. For a moment he didn't know where he was, his heart beating a frantic tattoo in his chest. Then it came back to him: the arrest, the interrogation, the cruel faces of the men of the Commissariat. Sooner or later they would come back for him.

He stared at the broken pencil as if expecting it to move on its own. A recollection lit up the recesses of his mind, bringing a smile to his lips. He had committed the priest's manuscript to the flames, but not before reading it, the peculiar symbols burning themselves into his mind. Twenty years had passed, but he would remember.

The lead heart of the pencil traced a line across the concrete floor, haltingly at first, then bolder. The secret sign, hidden in the tangle of lines and curves, burned in his mind's eye. Solovkin hummed as the image took shape, lost to the world around him. When the pencil was used up he tore his skin open and dipped the shards in the dark ink welling from beneath.

***

The guards were caught unprepared.

Several times they had escorted the quiet elderly prisoner from cell 336 to the interrogation room, and he'd never tried to resist in any way. When they came for him that morning, he seemed even more subdued and distracted than usual. He shuffled along between them, his eyes glassy and unfocused, until they reached the staircase that connected the iron galleries. Then he spun round and shoved the guard behind him with all his strength.

The unexpected attack nearly sent the guard over the railing; he flailed his arms as he fell back, clutching at the metal bars. The man in front was too slow. By the time he turned, the prisoner was already halfway up to the upper gallery, bounding up the steps with desperate speed.

Shouts exploded in the staircase, footsteps thundering from below, the noise immense in the dead silence of the prison. Other guards joined the pursuit, but the fleeing man evaded them with ease. Yet there was nowhere to run: he was almost at the top of the staircase, two guards waiting for him on the uppermost gallery, truncheons at the ready. The prisoner scrambled over the railing and perched above the drop for a moment, arms thrown out like a grotesque bird of prey. Before the nearest of the guards could reach him, he stepped off into the emptiness.

They found him in a pool of blood at the bottom of the stairs, crumpled and twisted like a broken doll. He drew in a ragged breath, then another. His finger smeared a dark scarlet curve on the concrete, the start of a drawing or a strange symbol. His dying eyes gazed around the circle of faces; blood bubbled on his lips as if he were trying to speak. By the time the doctor arrived, the prisoner was long gone.

***

"Are you all right, comrade?"

"Yes," Malenkov said through clenched teeth. "Leave me now. I have to go through the prisoner's personal effects."

The guard moved away, his steps noiseless on the carpeting of the corridor. Malenkov waited until the man was out of sight, exhaled a whistle of breath. The interior of the cell spun round him, mad designs and patterns inscribed into the floor and walls robbing him of all sense of dimension. He stepped in and closed the door behind him. The cell had to be cleaned up by someone reliable, someone who'd keep his mouth shut. There would be enough unpleasant questions to answer: not only had he failed to secure a confession, but the prisoner was dead. In the paranoid atmosphere of the Commissariat, even the smallest mistake could easily place one on the wrong side of the interrogator's table. No one could know about this.

He crossed the room and peered at a shape that resembled an eight-armed star, surrounded by small, twisting symbols. Devil-worship of some sort, occultism. There had been nothing in the old man's file to suggest anything of the sort. It only went to show no one could be trusted. He made a mental note to find out who had compiled Solovkin's surveillance file and punish them for the oversight.

In the meantime, he had this mess to contend with.

Drawings covered every centimeter of the bare walls and floor like a hideous, tightly woven tapestry. Some had been drawn in pencil, others in the prisoner's own blood, the strokes crude but precise, measured. A central piece above the cot featured a tall, slender form emerging from a crack in the wall: a huge, predatory grin cleft the face in two. In spite of himself, Malenkov shuddered. Something about this gruesome icon made his skin crawl, turned his mind to deep, sunless places in which screams could echo forever without being heard.

The silence was oppressive, the roar of blood in his ears deafening. Suddenly he no longer wanted to know what had happened, only to be as far from the call as possible; some long-dormant fragment of his consciousness screamed in alarm. The walls faltered, lost solidity. He turned round. The door had disappeared under the obscene scrawl. He clawed at the stone until his fingertips split and bled, distantly aware of the animal whimper coming from his throat. From behind him came a crumbling noise, the crevice in the wall widening, something pushing through. Fetid air rushed at him, the sickly sweetness of corruption. An irresistible force grasped his head, turned it against the resistance of his neck muscles and vertebrae. Malenkov heard the crack, saw the grinning maw yawn open, a razor-lined tunnel glowing with infernal light.

Radical Division

Jonathan Titchenal

In my dreams, a bell tolls.

***

Boone sets down the papers and fixes me with his good eye. "In your own words," he says. "Explain to me what happened."

"Pennington's report should-"

"I've read Pennington's report. I'm asking you."

He's fixed me a gin and tonic. I sip it. It tastes like rubbing alcohol in my mouth. I set it aside. "Blakely was first through the door," I say. "Then Harkaway, Robertson, me, and Pennington. We came in with weapons drawn, but they caught Blakely with a scatter gun all the same. They were expecting trouble."

"They usually are, now." Boone takes a sip of his own drink, sits back in his chair. "How many?"

"Four, maybe five Batrachians, including the priest. Eight or ten people who looked more or less normal, best as I could tell. It was smoky. They doused the candles as they ran."

"And this nonsense in Pennington's report, about some kind of giant or something..."

"A statue," I say. "A giant fish statue, in the back of the temple."

"Pennington claims it was moving."

"It was very smoky. We were all of us nerved up." I shrug. I keep my eyes on Boone. "The air was full of smoke. All those people were howling and dancing. I wouldn't be surprised if there was more than incense in the air."

Boone nods, as if he's thought of that already. He takes a cigarette from the pack at his elbow, lights it, breathes out smoke. It hangs in the stifling air. Behind him, two windows look out on Kingsport from their third-floor vantage point. From here, all I can see is a forest of buildings, but I know that somewhere beyond them lies the harbour. I can feel it.

"Well," Boone says. "You've come through for us again, Guilford. Any of those creatures get a good look at you?"

"No, sir. We came in masked."

"Good man. Shame we didn't bring one back. Bastards get more slippery all the time." He barks a laugh, startled by his own play on words. "What we need us is a proper witness."

"What about the man we brought back? The wounded one?"

"Ah. Yes. Your man." Boone tamps ash into a cut-glass dish. The light from above highlights every crease of his jowls. He looks up, one eye staring through milky film into the middle distance. The other eye is fixed on me. "Your man," he says. "Broke a chair leg into a stake, put it to his eye, and fell down on top of it." Boone's bad eye seems to water, as if in sympathy. "Old Dave Gilman's in there right now, cleaning up the mess."

***

I am very young. There is little in my head but sky and water. I sit on a rotten stump of dock that juts out from below the overhanging eaves of an abandoned building. My legs dangle over the edge, into the salty swill. My sister cuts the webbing between each of my toes with a pair of medical shears. It hurts. My blood dyes the water red. She packs gauze into the wounds, then swathes each foot in a dirty, oversized sock. She stands hip-deep in the water, her tools on the dock beside me. The tide washes in and out, in and out, around her. The sun comes out like a pale eye from behind a filmy scrim of cloud, and she turns her unblinking gaze up to it, eyes full of wet, pearlescent colors.

***

Royal Pennington stares into a mug of beer, his face set and hard, as if expecting something unpleasant to emerge from the foam. The bar is empty on this dreary afternoon, and the air hangs still and stale, sour with the ghosts of spilled pints.

"Christ," Pennington says. "This whole county's wrong. You know that?"

Jim Robertson, half obscured by the smoke of his own cigar, cocks an eyebrow but says nothing.

"I mean it," Pennington says. "It's like being dosed with something. I can't hardly stand it. He turns on his barstool to face me. "You were born here?"

"In Kingsport, yes."

"Well I'm from Boston, and I'm telling you this whole goddamn part of the world ought to just sink into the mud. Christ." He grimaces. "We should have had back-up. Where was the goddamn back-up?"

119

"We ain't all that important," Robertson says. "Rad Div has got teams all around here, up in Arkham, down in Vermont. If you're saying we're understaffed-"

"I am."

"I agree with you. What do you want to do about it?"

"I'm like to quit and go drive a bus, at this rate."

The door opens and Robert Harkaway steps inside, doffing his hat and shaking the rain from his coat. He joins us at the bar, but does not sit. His height, and the light in the room, combine to make him loom. "I've just come from Boone's office," he says. "Eamon Blakely is dead."

Nobody says anything.

Harkaway orders whiskey. He holds it up to the light, as if examining it. "You gents think maybe Washington hasn't got our backs anymore?"

Pennington turns to him. "What're you saying?"

Harkaway's eyes flick from his glass to Pennington. "What do you think I'm saying?"

"Hoover's as concerned about the froggies as anyone."

"You spoke to him, did you?"

"There are *monsters* walking around in our world- in our country- preying on our citizens. Our wives and children."

"There are monsters in Russia who want to turn all of us, our wives and children included, into slaves. Monsters with tanks and bombs, monsters with airplanes." Harkaway downs his whiskey in one go. "You think our government cares about a pack of inbred freaks up in the asshole of New England- no offense, Guilford."

I wave the comment away.

"I won't hear this kind of talk," Pennington says. "Not from you, not from anybody." He moves as if to stand up from his barstool.

"Look," Harkaway says. "I apologize. I'm angry and I'm shooting my mouth off. I lost a friend today. We all did. Listen, have a beer on me."

Pennington, not looking at him. "Already got a beer."

"Have another one. Christ knows we'll need it." Harkaway slides onto a stool and motions for the bartender. "We've a funeral to attend tomorrow."

We live in the empty shell of an old hotel. When nor'easters blow in hard along the water, the sea will come into our home, emptying into the basement, bringing strange wriggling things in from the depths. On those storm-tossed moonless nights, I sometimes wake to hear cries, or sounds like cries, echoing over the harbour, as if something is calling to the deep water, or from it. Deep calls to deep, in the lonely hours of the night.

I swim with my sister. We swim as far north as ancient Kingsport, following the deep water currents. We swim about the harbour, out to the tall stone where the white gulls tarry. One night, we swim up to the rocky headlands that form the bowl of the harbour, and into the caves at the water's edge. My sister takes me to the chamber where the great statue of the Father stands, surrounded by candles that never go out. My grandmother is there, and her grandmother, and hers. I am given a new name, which I may not utter, and rites are performed in the glittering waters of low tide.

When I awake the next morning, I see the world with new eyes.

* * *

The day is overcast, chilly even at noon. Gray clouds race across the sky, framed by trees whose skeletal arms are already visible behind their dwindling leaves. The funeral is a field of coats, hats held onto heads to keep the biting wind from snatching them. I stand off as far away as I can decently manage, listening to the birds call to one another. Apart from the gathering, and the rusty cries, ancient Kingsport is silent.

Boone arrives late, parks his car at the cemetery gates, and approaches. His toadlike bulk, swaddled in a massive tan trenchcoat, plows through the windy air like a ship. He approaches me, the plumes from his cigar trailing behind him.

"McGovern and the Arkham team telephoned me," he says. "They want you to come and take a look at something."

I nod. "All right."

"Something that might help us deal with the fr- the batrachians."

"I'll go tonight."

"Guilford."

I turn to look at him.

"He was very evasive," Boone says. "Wouldn't tell me anything on the phone."

"Never know who might be tapping the lines," I say.

"Is all of this..." Boone holds up his hands, as if groping for words. "On the up-and-up? I'm supposed to be in command here, but no one will tell me anything."

"I'll drive down to Arkham and see. Lot of clever boys at Miskatonic."

"I know," Boone says. "That's what I'm afraid of." He pauses. "Are you prepared to start again in Innsmouth?"

"My cover is intact, if that's what you mean."

"You're certain no one suspects you?"

"I'm a shirt-tail relative of the Waites. Grandmother's side. They're used to seeing me about."

"Mm." Boone watches the funeral service for a long moment. "You suspect anything, anything feels off, you get out of there. I can't afford to lose anyone else."

"I know."

"And while you're down in Arkham, see if you can get us any back-up. I don't want anyone going back in there without proper support. Christ." He looks up at the sky, as if reading the scudding clouds. "Monsters. What we do to make this country safe, eh Guilford?"

"This is a legend-haunted part of the world, Mr. Boone. It's old, and it's full of superstitions. But by light, and rationality, and science, we'll drive them all out."

"I hope so, boy. I surely do."

***

The nameless old man leads me up the steps to the ruined courtyard. The sky overhead is an endless, blameless blue. The gray stone, speckled with gull shit, looks white in the glare of the noonday sun.

"The world is so very, very old," the man says. "It was old when Mother Hydra and Father Dagon first came from Outside. It was old before time began to mark the passage of year. When the ape-men first learned to crack skulls with the thigh bone of the antelope, it was already so old. It had seen countless civilizations come and go."

A wind blows out of the hills to the west, stirring the leaves on the trees. Beneath my feet, the vegetation is already reclaiming the courtyard, pushing up through stone with slow, patient feelers.

"When the ape-men are gone, there will be others," the old man says. "Come from Outside, or brought up from the bosom of this Earth. Perhaps the Old Ones will reclaim the world, and drag it back through gateways of forgetting to the black abyss. Perhaps others will come from the starry oceans, swimming through the void to find us. An abyss of height and an abyss of depth. Do you ever think, child, that when you gaze at the night sky, you look not up, but *out*?"

He traces a strange sign on the air before me, and my head begins to swim.

-there is-

A gap. A void.

I wake, shivering, on the bare stone. I stretch my cramped limbs and stand. Night has come. The courtyard is empty. Up above me, cold stars look down on the citadels of Man. I look up. I look out.
An abyss of height, and an abyss of depth.
Something passes overhead, obscuring the stars. Something with great, silent wings.

***

I drive to Arkham in the afternoon, and park on the university campus. McGovern and his men are using an empty fraternity house as their base of operations, making regular forays to and from the science wing at all hours. The beer-stained boards of their ramshackle house still resonate with the unsettled, frenetic energy that comes from a concentration of young men. McGovern's team seems to be putting out plenty of their own, on top of it.
Neiman McGovern is deep in conversation with a local priest when I arrive.
McGovern: And this church- you know where to find it?
Priest: No.
McGovern: Do you know anyone who could find it?
Priest: No.
McGovern: If the boy could find it, there must be others. Wasn't there a crowd gathered around, when-
Priest: I don't know.
McGovern: Father Paulson...
Priest: It is not a good place. You would not wish to go there.
McGovern (standing): Piece of luck, since no one will tell me how to get there. You're dismissed. Keep in touch. We may have more questions for you."
The priest leaves without comment. McGovern does not see his backward look, but I do.
"Guilford!" he says, and crosses the room to shake my hand. He has to weave his way around heavy tables scattered with papers and artifacts to get to me. Beside me, close enough for me to grab it and brain McGovern with it if I had a mind, stands the carven black statue that

123

McGovern's people took from the witch-cult in southern Maine. The University had requested that it be deposited into the Armitage archives for study. McGovern, it appeared, had ignored them.

I shake his hand. "Looks like you aren't making many friends in town."

"Fucking locals." His pugdog face twists itself up. "Won't say a word because their daddies told them not to. Because it's 'evil'. Because there are some things Washington wasn't meant to know. Shitbags." He is leaning on the table, pushing around papers without realizing it, putting creases in old manuscripts. Near his left hand sits an open copy of Geoffrey's *People of the Monolith*, notes scribbled in the margins in fountain pen. Next to that is a book I don't immediately recognize until I crane my head around to read the text. It's a page-for-page copy of the Wormius *Necronomicon*. Apparently there are still some things the university can't be bullied into parting with.

"Guilford. Up here." McGovern snaps his fingers under my nose. "I want your full attention on this. Washington needs you, boy."

I stare at him.

"Rad Div can't spare the men for a raid on Innsmouth."

"No kidding."

"Washington is a busy place, Guilford. They have bigger fish to fry-" He pauses to laugh at his own joke. "Hem. Bigger fish to fry than a town full of inbred freaks." He leans toward me and lowers his voice. "Our boys are out there, right now, making America safe. There are Communists and Fascists and fucking bomb-throwing anarchists just waiting in the wings to come and take down what we've built up. To wreck this great country of ours. Think about it." He straightens. "Anyway. That's where you come in."

"How so?"

McGovern gives me what he probably thinks is a hard, appraising look. Then: "Are you familiar with the concept of psychological operations?"

"No, sir."

"Come with me. I want to show you something."

He leads me through the tangled mess of tables into a back room that might once have been a sitting room or library. The shelves have been cleared off and piled willy-nilly with artifacts, boxes, crates, and loose papers. McGovern goes over to a sturdy lockbox, fishes in his pockets for a set of keys, and selects one. He fits it to the lock, opens the box, and takes out a pint-size lab-glass bottle full of liquid. The liquid appears clear to me at first, but when McGovern holds it up to the light, it flouresces briefly with the kinds of colors I see when I rub my eyes too hard. "Any guesses what this is?" McGovern says.

I shake my head.

"About twenty years ago, there was a meterorite fell to earth not far from here. It evaporated, but before it did, the bright boys here at the university got a look at it. There was something inside, some kind of chemical, something that could affect your mind. Our boys managed to synthesize it, and mixed it up with an ergot derivative, and- bang-o! Magic." He hands the bottle over to me. I hold it up to the light and watch the colors crawl and bloom over the liquid's surface.

"Don't look at it for too long," McGovern says. "And don't get any of it on your skin. A few drops of this, and you'll go screaming, pants-pissing mad. We had a volunteer who threw himself out a fifth-story window. Just like that." He looks suddenly uncomfortable.

"What do you want me to do with-" I pause, as implications come rolling in.

McGovern smiles.

"You want me," I say. "To poison the town."

"Got it in one."

"Why?"

"Psychological operations, Guilford. Remember those words. You'll be hearing them a lot in future. We're playing the long game with the Reds now, and it's not enough just to have the biggest guns. We need an edge. And to have that edge we need data."

I stare at him.

"Think about it, Guilford. Imagine if we dropped this stuff on Moscow? Imagine if we snuck it into Stalin's vodka supply? We could turn the tide of this conflict in a day."

"Or start a war."

McGovern waves this away. "You haven't seen our miracle drug in action. Hell, neither have we, on any large scale. That's why we need you. How many towns out there do you think we can experiment on? How many places where nobody will miss the locals? Nobody will find it odd if they all run mad and kill themselves?" He puts a hand on my shoulder. "And, Guilford, it might work in your favor. If these froggies cause enough trouble, Hoover might just step in and give you the resources you need to exterminate them. Get you a commendation. Get your picture in the papers. How does that sound?"

"You want me to poison the water supply."

McGovern raises his chin. "This assignment comes from the highest levels. This is knowledge we need to have. You know the locals. You know the town. Are you fit for this?"

I weigh the bottle in my hand. It feels very heavy. "Yes, sir. I am."

"Good man. Knew I could count on you." McGovern straightens, takes a flask from a coat pocket. "Snort? No?" He drinks, wipes his mouth with the back of his hand. The room is very stuffy. Tiny beads of perspiration have gathered at his hairline. "I'll want a full report. Everything you see. Take some pictures, too, if you can. Let's make this look good for Washington."

"Yes, sir."

I walk back to my car through the university grounds, past empty buildings whose original purpose is unclear. I pass by an abandoned warehouse, its windows dark, dusty eyes. In each window, an identical spider, sitting at the center of a geometric web.

I drive out of Arkham, and take the Briggs Hill Road through the ghost-town of Zoar. The sun sets in a fireball of red behind the hills, and the shadows merge into one encompassing darkness. Past Zoar, the light fades out of the sky, and the stars emerge one by one. The road narrows, and I drive through a forested hill country, lonely and unpeopled. From time to time I see movement, beyond the range of my headlights. Something in the woods, shying away from the light. Something walking out there, in the lonely country.

The land rises, and the trees thin out, giving way to rolling farmland and open fields. I pass the blasted heath, where nothing walks by day or night, and then turn northwards, following the mostly-forgotten road that leads past Newburyport. I pass no cars, and see no one. Overhead, the stars are very bright.

At last, I come over a rise and look down on the bay, still water lying glimmering in the light of the moon. Quiet Innsmouth, where the seas bring in strange tidings from the deeps, and the wind, sighing through the stones, tells tales of outer places where the star-wind pours from unimaginable gulfs. Innsmouth.

I park outside of town and walk down the chalk lane that leads into the commercial district. The countryside is silent. There are no other motors here, no commerce and no traffic. I hear my footfalls loud upon the overgrown earth.

I walk through the empty lane called Fish Street and into the ruined town square. The gulls cry loud from the nearby harbor. I light a cigarette and sit down on the front steps of the Starry Wisdom Church to wait.

Ten minutes and two cigarettes later, I hear movement behind me. Out of the shattered doors of the church shambles a hunched, fishbelly-white figure. This Child of Dagon regards me with great, white, luminous eyes. I do not recognize him, but he recognizes me.

I make the Sign of Dagon in the air before me, and he bows.

"I need to speak to my grandmother," I say.

***

The day of my fate. I stand naked, my body painted with ideograms from a pre-Human language. The bitter smoke from the incense on the altar fills my mouth and lungs, and my head swims. I swim. I swim into and out of the spaces in my, in our, head, and we swim with I together in me. We are I. I am they.

Terrible things are blossoming in the corners of my vision.

Before me stand my mother, and my grandmother, and her grandmother. The gold of their tiaras glints in the firelight, and their pale white eyes stand out stark on their ruddy skin. My grandmother traces symbols on the air, and they linger as afterimages before my eyes. I think there is something in the smoke. Something is in my thoughts. Swimming in my thoughts. Something is in me.

I feel haunted.

My grandmother throws the bones.

Somewhere a bell is tolling.

Drums run underneath the sea, throbbing onward like the pulse of the earth.

She throws the bones-

I can hear the bones humming.

Full of terrible purpose.

Reflected in the eyes of my ancestor.

She speaks, and I hear her from a place inside myself.

"The bones have spoken. Your fate is written on the stars. In the whorls of shells upon the sea's dead floor. You will go into their world. You will be as one of them. This has already happened. Is happening. Will happen."

Do you hear that bell? That bell, tolling for the dead?

"Past, present, future; all are one in Yog-Sothoth. It is written on the stars, in the entrails of my father. You will go into their world. This is your *dho-hna*."

127

That bell, tolling for the dead.

***

I drive back to Kingsport in the morning. In the privacy of his office, I show Boone the object of terrible purpose I carry. He is appropriately horrified.

"According to McGovern, this order comes direct from Washington," I say.

Boone scowls. "McGovern can take a long walk off a short pier. I didn't sign up for this."

"None of us did."

Boone looks away, out the window, over the town. For a long moment he says nothing, and I wonder if I should speak, or leave, or do some third thing. Then: "Guilford?"

"Yes, sir?"

"Tell me they're monsters."

"Excuse me?"

"The batrachians. You know them. They're not people. They're monsters. That right?"

"Sir, I've known that town my whole life..."

Boone turns back around to look at me.

"They're monsters," I say. "Beasts. Whatever was in them, whatever might once have been human, that's all gone. Cleaning them off the world, that's a public service. Anything we do to them before that's just part of the business. Like exterminating rats, sir."

Boone stares at me. His face relaxes, and he nods, clears his throat, and fishes in his coat for his cigarettes. "I understand. You would know, Guilford, if any of us would."

"Yes, sir."

Boone lights a cigarette, coughs, and sits back in his chair. "Very well. Take the team with you. Find a well or a cistern or something and...and do what you have to. God." He puts three fingers to his temple.

I stand up. "I'll be back tonight."

"Godspeed, Guilford." Boone is not looking at me.

I go downstairs, collect Pennington from his office, and together we drive down to King Street. We find Harkaway and Robertson in the Last Reef, and after Pennington shares a beer with them, we climb back in the car and drive out toward Innsmouth. Harkaway and Robertson talk about baseball, women, politics, people they've known, trouble they've gotten into and out of. Pennington stares out the window and chain-smokes cigarettes. I concentrate on the road.

The sun goes down in the west in an unearthly sprawl of colors.

It begins to get dark.

***

When McGovern returns to his laboratory I am waiting for him. He pauses in the doorway, blinks. "Guilford?"

"A porter let me in," I say. "I came back to tell you. It's done."

"Everything went according to plan?"

"Yes." I pause, look away. "It was horrible."

"I know. I understand." McGovern comes over to me, puts a hand on my shoulder. "The things we do for love of country, eh? You'll get a promotion for this, Guilford, mark my words. I could use an assistant down here, as a matter of fact. Free access to everything Miskatonic can provide. How does that sound?"

"Very good, sir."

"And I do mean everything. You wouldn't believe how many beautiful girls are walking around on this campus, good God."

He is very close to me. I can smell whiskey on his breath.

"What was it like, Guilford? What did you see? Don't spare the details, this is important."

I run a hand through my hair. "Like I said, it was horrible. Ah. I don't suppose we could stop off for a beer before I get started? I just...I need..."

"Need to relax, no, I completely understand." McGovern is all magnanimity. He raises his hand in an 'after-you' gesture. "We'll take my car. Tell you what: You've done a fine job. You won't pay for a single glass of beer tonight, Guilford. How do you like that?"

"I like it very well, sir. Thank you."

"Don't mention it, son. Come along! Our chariot awaits."

I climb into his car, and we drive to a bar on the dark side of town called The Mason's End. McGovern parks in a nearby alley, and we go inside.

Smells of stale beer, body odor, smoke. It is a weekday night, and apart from ourselves, I can see only a few hardened career drinkers, and a party of drunken college students.

McGovern orders a beer and a shot for himself, downs the latter, goes to work on the former. He orders a beer for me. I sip it. It tastes like polluted water.

"See, I was born in Boston," McGovern says. "And we Bostonians are hard-headed. Maybe those froggies are just the product of generations of inbreeding, but that doesn't matter. They worship heathen gods, and sacrifice to them, and that makes them monsters. None of this pinko moralistic bullshit." He sniffs, takes his hat off, runs a hand through his hair. "Way I figure, it's casualties of war. Goddamn amphibians probably weren't pulling their weight anyway."

"Pulling their weight?" I say.

"In the underworld, Guilford. Look." He leans in toward me, lowers his voice. "You're not a total country bumpkin. You know there's a whole network of evil strung through these hills. I tell you what, you read through the *Necronomicon*, or *De Vermis*, and it changes you. Changes your perspective. You start seeing things in a new way." He belches. His beer stein is empty. He orders another. "'Scuse. Mm. Gonna tap a kidney, back in a flash." He slides off the barstool and slouches toward the bathroom.

A moment is upon me. I take it.

He is back a minute later. "Hey, you hardly touched your beer. You going soft on me, Guilford?"

"No, sir." I take another sip. I try not to cringe.

McGovern doesn't seem to notice. He drinks off a third of his fresh beer in one go, frowns, smacks his lips. He takes another long drink, frowns again. "Bastards didn't clean the taps again. Anyway." He leans back, wobbling just a bit on his barstool. "Funny thing about all those bastards, cultists and sister-humping sorcerers and the lot, is that- and this is the funny thing, Guilford, this is- their gods are actually *really real*."

"Oh yes?" I raise an eyebrow.

"No, really. I mean it. This is the big secret. This is what they don't tell you. It's all real, Guilford. Sorcery, alien technology, the blackest devils and things from space. It's all really out there. That's why we have to be prepared. Listen, this is a secret, okay? You can't go blabbing this to Boone, or any of those other idiots, right?"

"Yes, sir."

"Good man."

We sit in silence for a few minutes. McGovern finishes most of his beer, but doesn't call for another. Tiny beads of sweat are standing out on his brow.

"...they could be watching us right now," he says.

"Pardon?"

"Things. Things on another wavelength than us. They're made of something that's...it's not like matter. They could pass right through us. But they could...change us. I mean..." He scrubs a hand across his forehead. "You read things and...and you see things. Suddenly, you're sleeping with the lamp on. I mean, I'm no pansy, going to run back home because the ghosts are really out there, but..."

He is quiet for a long moment. Then: "This world. It's like a haunted house. And...sometimes I'm not sure if we're the tenant, or the ghost. Do you know what I mean?"

"No," I say.

"We don't own the Earth. We're just...caretakers. The real owners, they're not even from this Universe. I shouldn't be telling you this."

"You look a little pale," I say.

"I don't feel so good." He sits up suddenly, looks around. "You hear that?"

"What?"

"Ah. Ah. Nothing. Ah. Let's get out of here." He slides off his barstool, staggers, gets his feet under him. "I need some air."

"Sure." I get an arm around his shoulders, help him to the door. Nobody marks our passage. Nobody sees us go.

Outside, the stars are clear and bright, even here in the city. McGovern turns his face up to the wind, but his eyes take in the stars, and I can see his fright deepen. "God, Guilford. It's so huge, it's so empty. We're not looking up, Guilford. We're not. We're looking *out*."

A moment of deja vu.

"They come from a place where things aren't the way they are here. I mean...physics...geometry. It's all wrong. It's all...haunted." McGovern staggers into the alleyway. He leans against the wall. He is sweating freely now, big droplets rolling down his pale face. His eyes are huge. "I...I...they came for me." He shakes his head like a dog, as if to clear it. "One night...I was alone...and they came to me. Offered me everything. Power. And I knew...I knew if I refused, something terrible would happen. Something terrible." Tears are leaking out of his eyes now, mingling with the sweat. "Oh god, something terrible. I'm so scared." He puts his fingers to his mouth, pulls at the lips, scrubs his hands over his face. "It's all wrong. It's all gone wrong. They...I...I didn't know they could do that to people." He looks up at me with mad eyes. "Say, boy, do you know *this*?" He makes a sign with two fingers in the air. A sign I've known since my boyhood.

"No."

"And I know the Voorish sign, too, and the Sign of Opening, and the Sign of He Who Must Not Be Named. They took me down the thousand steps to the pit, when I'd stopped screaming, and they showed me..." He sobs pushes his face into a grotesque mask with his hands. "I...I saw a shoggoth. It changed shape! Oh, god, nothing's ever going to be right again. Oh mother, I'm so scared." He looks up. "I don't feel good."

"No," I say. "You don't." I am not surprised. I am not surprised by any of it. I am not surprised because while he was in the bathroom, I poured about a third of the bottle of McGovern's 'miracle drug' into his beer.

"Oh mama. Mama, mama, mama, mama." McGovern suddenly throws back his head and howls, cords standing out on his neck. He reaches up with both hands and rakes them down his face, drawing blood. He catches the edge of one eyeball with a nail, and that begins to bleed as well. "Aaaah! Aaah-aah-a! *Aaayunglui bcoma hatur ngglr! Wza-yei! Wza-yei yoggog rrthna! Aaah! Aaaaaaaaah!*"

Every muscle in his body has gone taut. His face is frozen, mouth open, bleeding. He has bitten through the tip of his tongue, and it dangles on the end of a string of gristle. He pitches forward, his whole trunk leaning like a falling tree, and slams his face up against the wall. He begins vigorously scrubbing it back and forth over the bricks, as if trying to wipe away his features, still screaming in Aklo, hands beating a tattoo on his own thighs.

I step forward, reach into his pants pocket, and withdraw his keys. The movement, the touch, galvanizes him. He spins around to face me, and behind the bloody, ruined features I see two mad eyes, filled with more terror than I have ever seen on any creature. He shakes his head back and forth, blood flying, then turns and pelts away down the alley, venting terrible gobbling screams into the night air.

I slide into his car, start the engine, and drive out of Arkham.

***

I park the car well outside of town and lead my three companions in on foot. There are no lighted houses in this town, no streetlamps, no automobiles. It is utterly dark, and quiet enough to hear the breaking of waves on the unseen beach. The pale moon, rising over the horizon, casts a wan glow on cracked streets and tottering gambrel-roofed houses, their eyes empty.

"I know a house on the edge of town we can use," I say. "It looks down the hill towards the town square. I'll venture out from there and find the well. You can cover me from inside."

"How far?" Pennington hisses.

"A few blocks. Stay close."

132

We pass an old grocery store, its door hanging open over a splintery front porch. Only I glimpse the pale, luminous eyes that look out from that darkness for a moment as we pass. I do not turn my head. I continue on.

Two blocks later, I turn down a narrow, tangled lane that runs along the hill's edge before the town proper. Its far windows look down on the decaying sprawl of Innsmouth, as far as the bay and the black ocean beyond. I turn around and regard my three companions. I have worked with Pennington and Robertson for two years, Harkaway slightly less. Robertson and Harkaway are married. Robertson has a daughter. Harkaway is hoping for a son in the fall. Pennington has collectors-edition copies of Dickens, Poe, Twain. Sometimes, on his off days, he will go for long rambles in the town, or sit in the park and read Yeats.

My friends. My daylight companions.

"I'm going in," I say. "Pennington, you and Robertson follow close, cover me. Harkaway, if you could go around the back, check for movement, anything suspicious, then follow us inside. All right?"

They nod. They are frightened. The town is so silent. The night is so complete.

"All right. Go."

I open the door and step inside. Once through the door, Pennington and Robertson switch on their flashlights. The light picks out a bare, empty shell of a house, with a set of broken stairs leading up to a second-floor mezzanine. A closed door stands to our direct left, and a short hallway leads to the kitchen, and a back door.

Pennington taps my shoulder, points toward the rear door, and goes down the hall to check it.

"I'll check the bedroom," Robertson whispers, and opens the door. He steps inside, and I hear a brief flailing tattoo of motion as he tries to backpedal or catch himself. Then a fall, a strangled cry, and a thick splash somewhere far below. Then a second splash. Then silence.

I shut the door.

Pennington comes running back into the room. "What was that?"

"I don't know," I say.

"Where's Robertson?"

I nod at the bedroom door.

Pennington looks at it, looks back at me, and I see something cross his face. Something I've been expecting for years. Pennington is thinking very hard. "Where's Robertson?" he asks again.

"In there." I nod at the door.

As if on cue, there is another splash from somewhere beyond and below.

Pennington draws his pistol. He throws another sidelong glance at me, and then steps forward and opens the door.

My sister is there, in all her glory. She has changed so much since the days of my childhood, but I still know her. I would know her anywhere. We have shared dreams of sunless seas, and deep bells echoing on the north wind. She looks down at Pennington with her beautiful, pearlescent eyes. Her body gleams in the torchlight.

"Jesus Christ." Pennington takes a step back, raises the pistol.

A scream from outside. Pennington jerks his head in that direction. I take the pistol out of his hand.

He looks at me, eyes wide and staring, showing whites all around. Pennington is intelligent. He knows what is happening to him.

"Robertson is dead," I say. "Harkway is dead."

"You did this."

"No," I say. "I am only the hand. The instrument through which the will of Mother Hydra and Father Dagon flows. This is my *dho-nha*. This is what I am for."

The front door opens, and terrible shapes are on the other side. I can hear the Children padding down the hall from the back door. They have crept up out of the deeps to enact my grandmother's will. Our great Father's will. Our will.

Pennington shakes his head. "You don't have to do this, Paul. You don't have to..."

"I always did. I always have. I always will. Past, present, future; all are one in Yog-Sothoth."

The smells of fish and sea-water fill the room. The shapes of the children, my brothers and sisters, my kin, fill the doorway, the hallway, are crawling from the hole in the floor to join my sister. Pennington looks around at them; at their great, naked, ruddy bulk. He looks at me. "Not like this, Guilford. Please. Let me die a man's death. Not like this."

"I always respected you," I say.

"Please, Guilford."

I raise the pistol.

My hand does not shake. My aim is true.

I can grant him this favor.

I do.

I return to Kingsport in the early morning. I climb the steps to Boone's office.

The door opens. In I run.

I put a bullet through the upraised newspaper and into Boone's gut, then turn away before the paper drops and I have to see the look on his face. I walk out the door, down the steps, back to the car.

I drive to the coast, to a disused pier that juts out past the last of the hills, out into the wide Atlantic sea. The mist is still heavy on the shoreline. I step out of the car. I take off my coat, my shirt, my trousers, my shoes. I step out of my my underwear and, naked, I leap into the sea. The water hits my body like a blessing, like a benediction, washing away all the blood and dirt and horror. I swim. I swim south along the coast, down from Kingsport to Innsmouth. To quiet Innsmouth, where the white gulls tarry around a spire of rock that juts up from the bay. I climb up on that rock and watch the sun rise, and shake and shiver and cry and laugh. I wonder if I spilled some of the elixir on myself after all. I feel ill.

I feel haunted.

I sit on that rock and watch the sun come up, and dream of the moment when my task, my *dho-nha*, is at an end. When I can change, and go down to join my sister, my brethren. When I can cast away fear and guilt like a suit of clothes, and go down into the arms of the sunless sea. Then will I go down to join my sister in the deep places of the world. Then will I go down to where the deep bells toll, and there, amidst our undying ancestors, we will swim together through the halls of our fathers, in endless, timeless bliss.

Forever.

***

The man's suit is rumpled from his drive, but every hair on his head is Brylcreemed in place. He offers out a warm, dry, uncallused hand.

I shake it.

"Isaiah Snow," the man says. "Rad Div, New York. Pleased to meet you, Mr. Guilford."

"Thank you for coming on such short notice," I say.

"We felt the situation demanded it. And may I add that I am terribly sorry for your loss. I can't imagine how difficult it must be for you at this time."

"Thank you." I look away. "I was on assignment in Innsmouth. I came back to find..." I wave my hand vaguely. "My team gone. My supervisor dead. And you say Neiman McGovern is..."

"Confined in a private wing of the university at the moment," Snow says. His calm demeanor falters. "I visited him this morning. He is...very unwell. Very unwell."

"Do you think he could possibly have...?"

Snow sighs. "Mr. McGovern is not at all in his right mind. I'm led to understand that he was working very hard, researching matters the university is not comfortable disclosing. His car was found here in Kingsport. I'm afraid that, pending further information, we will have to assume that he is involved with the disappearance of your team, and the murder of Mr. Boone. Obviously, we would appreciate any help that you can give us in this matter."

"Of course," I say. "Consider me at your disposal."

"Thank you. You're local to this town, Mr. Guilford? Familiar with it?"

"I was born here."

Snow nods. "I've been led to understand that this area is prey to a lot of peculiar beliefs. Old mysticism, that kind of thing."

"It's true, I'm afraid." I walk to the window. I look out over the ancient town. "This is a legend-haunted part of the world, Mr. Snow. It's old, and it's full of superstitions. But by light, and rationality, and science, we'll drive them all out." I turn to face him. "One by one, we'll drive them all out."

Igawesdi

Cliff Biggers

"In your phone call, you mentioned a book, Mr..."

"Conroy—Edward Conroy. Yes, I did. It's an unusual book, and I had been told that you were an expert in this sort of thing."

"Thank you, Mr. Conroy. I suppose that's true, yes—I've spent years studying what are sometimes classified as "forbidden books." Which is why I was interested in the particular book that you mentioned..."

"I'm not sure that it's the sort of book you'd be interested in, Dr. Ahlstrom. It's not just the book's contents that struck me as odd—it's the book itself."

Dr. Ahlstrom did his best to maintain a professional aloofness, but his demeanor betrayed his interest. "Yes, you mentioned that. Did you bring the book with you?"

"Not the actual book, no—but I did bring some copies I made, and a few photos of the book's binding." Conroy opened a heavy brown leather satchel, removed a folder, and from that folder he pulled out a stack of pages. He placed them on Ahlstrom's mahogany desk and started to slide them across. Before he could do so, however, Dr. Ahlstrom had reached across with a bit more eagerness than he intended to display. He began flipping through them, stopping at random intervals to scrutinize the pages' contents.

There was a silence that might have seemed uncomfortable to most people, but Conroy sat patiently.

Two minutes. Five minutes. Ten minutes. Initially, Ahlstrom flipped through the pages casually, clearly expecting very little. But after a few such flips, his pace slowed; it was clear that he was reading some passages rather than superficially scanning them. Whatever was in these xeroxes, it had piqued his interest... and more.

Almost twenty minutes passed before Ahlstrom spoke again.

"It's not what I expected," Ahlstrom finally said.

"Sorry I've wasted your time," Conroy said as he reached for the copies.

Dr. Ahlstrom's grip tightened almost imperceptibly, "No—no, that's not what I mean. It's just—well, it's different than anything I've seen before.

"People are always bringing me books they claim to be rare grimoires, or a distant relative's spellbook, or an apocryphal necromantic reference. Most of the time, it is a waste of my time. Something cobbled together by not particularly imaginative Supernatural fans or would-be horror writers. The usual nonsense names mixed with genre fiction creatures and demons, some Biblical names, that sort of thing. But these pages... well, they're not like that at all."

"So they're the real thing?" Conroy's bit of a smile showed that he was pleased with what he had heard so far.

"Not exactly the real thing, as you put it. But they are the product of people who *know* the real thing."

"I'm not sure I follow..."

"You know what Wikipedia is? Well, this book is like an occult Wikipedia. It's an incredibly detailed reference volume. Cultes des Goules, the Pnakotic Manuscripts, The Unexpurgated Book of Lilith, the Zanthu Tablets, The Igawesdi, Unaussprechlichen Kulten, The Ninth Book of Moses... They're all in here. But what's significant is that they're all correctly referenced."

"So you're saying it's like a reading list, or a long book report?"

"No, no—that's not it. In every case, the books are *distilled...* and quite expertly. The excess verbiage has been stripped away, the style has been clarified to remove archaisms, but the *content* is all here. I'm basing that on the books that I'm familiar with, of course—some of the books represented in here are almost mythic, in fact. I've heard of The Igawesdi on multiple occasions, but I've never seen a copy. I've only heard of one scholar—an expert in Tsalagi culture— who ever had one, but that was decades ago. And yet your book contains what I am confident are very detailed recountings of its contents, complete with spells and incantations. It's as if experts on every 'forbidden book' had written down the most secret elements of each book. Thus the Wikipedia allusion—it's like what Wikipedia was supposed to be, a master reference produced by experts in their chosen fields."

"So you're telling me that my book is a comprehensive reference to 'forbidden books?'"

"Obviously I only had a few minutes to peruse its contents, but it seems to be quite thorough." Ahlstrom paused for effect before he continued. "However, I notice some significant omissions.."

"Omissions? You mean there are books that are not referenced in here?"

"Well, I'm only basing this on the photocopies you have here, but you did include the contents page. As I read through it, two books stood out in their absence. One is the Necronomicon, of course—I know of only one complete copy still in existence, and access is quite limited—and the other is Ascuns La Vedere."

"Ascuns La Vedere? What's that?"

"You've asked that question to the right person," Ahlstrom said with a slight laugh. "I've actually devoted much of my professional life to this book. It's a sort of occult taxonomy... a book that classifies by type and effect all the demons and horrors that most people can't see. The book purports that we are surrounded by monstrous creatures who are scarcely more aware of us than we are of them. In our case, we are simply incapable of fully experiencing them with our sensory limitations. In their case, we are so insignificant that our very existence is as unimportant to them as is the existence of dust mites to us. Ascuns La Vedere opens that world... it explains how to open the gateways."

"You're quite the expert, aren't you?"

Ahlstrom smiled. "I suppose I am. I was the first person to translate the book into English, in fact. I have chosen not to publish that translation, however, so I have the only English copy."

"I guess I was lucky that I showed this to you, then. No one else would have caught the omissions, I'll bet."

"Quite correct! I would guess that there's not another scholar in the field who would have caught that omission. But that doesn't mean that your book is worthless, by any means, just incomplete. Even so, I'd love to see a copy of the entire book, not just the pages you've included here.

"Oh, I could mail you a copy if you'd like," Conroy replied. "If you could give me a self-addressed envelope, I'd be glad to xerox the rest of the book and send you the entire thing."

"Excellent!" Ahlstrom said in a mock Mr. Burns voice, complete with tented fingers, after which he grinned briefly. Ahlstrom had became more casual, more comfortable as the conversation had turned to his own work. "I have an envelope," he said, rummaging into a desk drawer, "but I don't have any stamps."

"Not a problem--I have a few here. They're older stamps, so they're not self-adhesive. I found them in a folder in the back of my desk the other day, and just threw them in here just in case." He passed the stamps over to Ahlstrom—a mix of colorful images of varying values. "I think it's about $5 worth of stamps, total; that should do it."

"Oh, don't worry—if it's not enough, I'll be glad to pay the postage due!"

Ahlstrom wrote his address in both spaces on the oversized envelope to ensure that the envelope would get to him even if it was rejected for insufficient postage, licked the stamps, then placed them across the top right in three rows of varying lengths. He then passed the oversized envelope to Conroy."

"I look forward to reading the entire book, Mr..."

"Conroy."

"Yes, Mr. Conroy. I'm sorry--it's one of the hazards of having taught for so many years. I've dealt with so many students and so many names that they slip right out of my head nowadays. But you also mentioned something else—something about the book itself being unusual."

"Oh, yes," Conroy said, reaching for his iPhone. "I almost forgot. I don't think I've ever seen anything like it." As he spoke, he brought up his Photos folder, flipped between pictures for a second or two, then made his selection. He passed the phone over.

The screen showed a book bound in a patchwork of various leathers in various hues. It was not a sturdy textured leather, though; instead it appeared to be a very fine leather, as fine as kidskin. The pieces varied in tint—many almost the same hue, some a darker, richer tone—but the texture seemed to be quite uniform. The edges of each square were lined up perfectly, turned under and stitched so meticulously that no seams were visible.

"I've never seen a book like this," Ahlstrom said. "I'd love to examine the actual book. Would that be possible?"

"I don't have the book with me, as I mentioned when I called. Sorry."

"What about other photos?"

"Oh, yes—there are several. Just flip from photo to photo."

Subsequent shots showed details of some of the binding squares. There was something bout the texture of the leather that seemed familiar to Ahlstrom. He zoomed in to the point that pixellation began to detract from the image. "I think I know what this is," he finally said. "Anthropodermic bibliopegy, if my guess is right."

"Anthropomorphic?..."

"No, anthropodermic. Human skin. I suspect this book is bound in human skin—or, judging from the patchwork nature, human skins."

"No way!"

"It certainly appears that way. It's not unheard of, although it's quite unusual. There are books that have been bound in human flesh—not just books of necromancy, but erotic books bound in skin taken from the female breast. Even a book bound in a human face." As he spoke, Ahlstrom flipped ahead to the next picture, then the one after that. "I'd li... I'd like to see more, but the... the photos are... are.... blurry..." Ahlstrom's speech was slurring somewhat, and he seemed to be struggling to complete a sentence.

"Oh, no—the photos are quite sharp. It's your eyes, Dr. Ahlstrom—they're getting blurry."

"Wha?..." He looked up at Conroy, but seemed to have trouble focusing, and his head lolled slightly to one side.

"The stamps, Dr. Ahlstrom. The stamps were drugged. One of two stamps should have been enough to paralyze you, but I brought extras just to be sure. I was confident that you wouldn't be able to resist a chance to see the entire book once I gave you the bait.

"You were right, Dr. Ahlstrom—the book is a distillation, as you put it, of a great many forbidden books. And each chapter is absolutely accurate because it was produced by an expert in that particular book." As Conroy spoke, he rummaged thorugh his bag. Finally, he removed several tools—some quite modern, some visibly antique.

"It was one of the secrets of the Igawesdi, you see. I was a graduate assistant to Professor Ridge, who had dedicated much of his career to that book. His notes were quite thorough." He paused and picked up a scalpel, inspecting it closely. Then he removed another tool—a rod with a wooden turn handle on top and a saw-edged cylindrical piece at the bottom.

"That first piece you saw in close-up? That was Professor Ridge. He was the first who I added to the book. And the book was right—I followed its instructions, and within days all of Professor Ridge's knowledge of the Igawesdi appeared in my book, just as his translation indicated."

Other tools—a curved metallic spoon-like scoop, a dental pick, an awl. And a few small containers, along with zip-loc bags.

"Oh, and his computer? It was amazing—those files contained his correspondence with a number of scholars, each an expert on one forbidden book or another. It was a virtual guidebook, matching scholar and book. The second square? That was Dr. Mosig, the leading authority on De Vermis Mysteriis."

After meticulously arranging his tools on the desk, Conroy picked up the scalpel and leaned in close to Ahlstrom's face. "I only recently found out about Ascuns La Vedere—I can thank Professor Schwartz for that. He was quite talkative, and he mentioned your name and your work more than once." Conroy picked up his iPhone once again, then flipped a few photos forward. He held the screen up to Ahlstrom's unfocused eyes. "That square? Professor Schwartz!"

He brought the blade up to Ahlstrom's eyes... then went slightly higher, to his forehead. "The instructions were very specific—the flesh had to come from the forehead. It had to be the skin over the third eye." As he spoke, he began to cut. Ahlstrom was aware of the pain, almost as if it were a memory rather than a real sensation... but the blood that was running into his eyes was quite real. The cut was quick and clean. Then he picked up another tool, a scraper of some sort, to help him remove the square of flesh cleanly.

"It's not just the skin, though. There were very specific instructions. The third eye is the key—it allows some to see into realms invisible to most people. I'm sure you've read about it in your research, though. The pineal gland. Right here." He tapped in the lower center of Ahlstrom's forehead. "Well, it's a few inches inside, but this is where we access it."

He picked up the strange tool with its saw-edged cylinder and placed it against Ahlstrom's forehead. Finally, Ahlstrom recognized it: an old trepanning tool. Conroy lifted it above Ahlstrom's field of vision, then Ahlstrom felt the pressure as Conroy began to crank. Pressure and sound—a grinding sound that rumbled inside his head. Conroy remained silent as he cranked forcefully. Then the pressure and the noise stopped. Conroy smiled and pulled the tool back; in its cylindrical hollow was a bone white piece stained with blood.

"The most important step, though is the preparation of the skin. It has be tanned very carefully, using just the right method. Have you heard of brain tanning, Dr. Ahlstrom? It's been around for centuries—maybe for millennia. One brain is enough to tan one hide, they say. But I don't need your hide, Dr. Ahlstrom—just the doorway to the third eye. And I don't need the whole brain... just enough to fill this freezer bag will be fine." He used another tool to push deep into the trepanning orifice; he knew exactly where the pineal gland was located. He skillfully extracted it, placed it in the bag, then supplemented it with just enough brain matter to complete the tanning process. Conroy had become quite the expert—apparently practice did make perfect.

"And there we have it." He began to pack everything away once again. "In a few days I'll have your contribution to my anthology, containing an essential condensation of Ascuns La Vedere. You should be proud, Dr. Ahlstrom... you'll be published after all!"

After Birth

Brian M. Sammons & Jamie D. Jenkins

Jane stared out the window of the family sedan as it barreled down a desolate highway, bitter winter rain pelting the pane. She imagined the sting of those near frozen pellets would be less than the sting of the man behind the wheel. Her father was the chauffeur as the family driver was not required for this clandestine outing in the wee hours of this frigid March morning. Her father, Jamison Chatham III, sat scrunched in the driver's seat, his wool overcoat bundled tightly, a cashmere scarf framing the scowl that he had worn for as long as Jane could recall. But today, the deep set lines of his face seemed to be forged in steel. He grumbled to himself as he navigated the unlit, winding road. Jane was crying in silence, doing her best not to call attention to her presence. If only her mother were there. She served as a buffer between Jane and her father's ire, but this night she stayed home, curled up with a handful of barbiturates and a bottle of sherry in an attempt to chase away the shame that Jane had lowered onto the family.

Jane felt eyes on her and glanced up into the rear view mirror to see her father glowering at her. She cast her head down and began to finger the fringe that danced at the end of her own scarf. She hated that look in his eyes, that look of pure scorn. Her mind wandered to the day that began this regrettable chapter of her life. She had been ill for some time, unable to keep anything down. When the cook served her eggs at the breakfast table that morning she'd had to bolt from the room to empty the contents of her roiling stomach. As she looked up from the porcelain bowl in the servant's bathroom off the kitchen, she came eye to eye with her mother whose silhouette blocked the daylight that had been streaming through the open door. One glance told her that her mother knew.

"Who?'

"Wh..what?," she stammered. But the guilt was on her face. She could feel it glowing red as if her cheeks had burst into flames.

"Don't play with me, Jane. You know exactly what I'm talking about. Who did it? I know it can't be Jonathan because he shipped out months ago. I want you to tell me right now who did this to you." Jonathan was a reference to her betrothed, Jonathan Chamberlain, youngest son of the Massachusetts Chamberlains whose family was the wealthiest, most respected Catholic family in the state, probably in the region. And Jane was to be married to him when he returned from the war, a match that

Jane's father had been doing his best to arrange since the minute she had been born.

Jane sat still for a moment before she decided that honesty would be her only recourse. She steeled herself then muttered the name, "Thomas."

At first Jane wasn't sure her mother had heard her, it been little more than a squeak to her own ears. But the ghost-white wave that crossed her face, followed by the resounding thud of her mother fainting onto the tile floor, confirmed that she'd been heard.

Jane's condition, as bad as it was, was made worse by the fact that the offending party was the grounds keeper's son. That family wasn't wealthy, it wasn't well-received or respected. And they weren't white.

But she didn't love Jonathan; he was cold. His touch, his hand-holding, his hugs were always stiff, almost compensatory. He was a mere two years her senior but he treated her like a child. He acted as if he were doing her a favor by courting her. He may have been the *right* man for her to marry, but Jane imagined her future with him would be the duplicate of her mother's existence. She feared that she would be sentenced to a life that was void of affection, the pain of her loneliness kept at arm's length by alcohol, dulled by tranquilizers.

So this last New Year's Eve, when her mother had allowed her some celebratory champagne, she'd found herself wandering around her expansive home long after the rest of the family had stumbled to bed in a post-countdown stupor. She'd seen Thomas in the kitchen while looking for some of the party leftovers to quell the drunken hunger. She followed him back to his quarters. For a brief moment she felt beautiful and alive. And she wasn't sorry.

Jane's life from that moment of confession had been a series of arguments, chastisements and beatings. Her father disowned her then thought better of that idea. He *needed* her to marry Jonathan. But that marriage could never take place if she carried the bastard child of a Negro gardener. Jane spent her days and nights in her room, awaiting her fate. While attempting to avoid the burning stares of her angry father. Her mother sat crumpled in her bed, alternating between bursts of tears and near catatonia. The family doctor had made several visits, not for Jane's welfare, but to keep her mother sedated. They'd told him she'd received some bad news from back home in Virginia and left it at that.

A week went by, then two, with no further words on the subject from her father. Then, last night, she'd awakened to find him standing at the foot of her bed.

"Get up," he barked.

"Why?"

"Get up!"

Jane scrambled to her feet, fumbling with her robe and slippers, as her father shoved her out of her room and toward the stairs.

"Where are we going?" she asked.

"We're going to fix this problem you've created."

"But how?"

"We're getting rid of it."

"But Daddy..."

"Don't talk to me, I can't even stand the sound of your voice right now." He turned to look at her at last with his cold, hard eyes. "God damn it, girl, you've made a mess of everything."

Jane hesitated then continued, "But that's illegal *and* we're Catholic. I can't." She pulled from his grip and stood her ground. "I won't."

Jane had never seen rage like that which emanated from her father at those words. She wondered if he even *was* her father. His face was twisted and distorted, his eyes glowed. Jamison drew back his right arm and landed a blow to the side of Jane's face that sent her skidding across the floor in the foyer.

"You will never defy me, girl. You don't have a choice in the matter. You should have thought of that when you were trysting with a colored servant. You are not going to ruin our lives with your harlotry. I will rip that bastard from you with my bare hands if I have to."

Jane was sobbing and crying for her mother, but her mother was standing, arms at her sides, in the doorway of the sitting room. She reeked of alcohol; her eyes were vacant and unseeing. She knew none of this. Jamison dragged her outside where the car was idling and tossed her into the backseat, not waiting to see if she was inside before slamming the door. Jane had mere seconds to pull her feet into the car. Her father then got behind the wheel, turned to her one last time to tell her to stop bawling, then threw the car into gear and sped out onto the road. She was stunned.

***

Jane was snapped out of her reverie as her nostrils were assailed by a stench so overwhelming that she felt her gorge rise; it threatened to spew last night's supper all over her father's back seat. She reached for the crank to roll down the window then realized that it was coming from outside the car. The air was heavy with the smell of rotting fish. Jane pressed her face against the glass in an attempt to see where it could be coming from and her mouth dropped in horror. It looked like how she imagined those horrible P.O.W. camps she'd heard about from news reels of the war. There were tall, sprawling fences topped with barbed wire, her view was spotted with signs on posts that were long ago rusted beyond being readable. They passed one that allowed her to make out some words between the patches of rust: BY ORDER OF THE *rust* GOVERN*rust* THIS ARE*rust* OFF *rust*MITS. Startled, Jane looked at her father. He showed no signs of emotion one way or the other. She opened her mouth to ask him where they were but thought better of it. She wiped away the fog from the glass and continued to peer outside. She could have sworn she saw something dragging itself through the darkness between what appeared to be two houses that were now little more than ruins. When she'd gotten her eyes to focus, the car had already passed. All she could make out were buildings in varying states of dereliction. Her skin turned clammy as the cloying odor gained strength. She shuddered, pulled her coat closer around her and sank deeper into the seat. *Maybe I'm better off not knowing,* she thought.

Then the car skidded to a stop in what may once have been a parking lot, the best she could tell through the steamy window. There did not appear to be any lights outside but there were a few other cars of various ages and models parked in the vicinity. She could see the outline of a building with a few glowing windows. *This must be a mistake.* Before her brain could register that her father had parked and gotten out, the car door was opened and she was pulled from her seat by rough hands into the cold drizzle outside. It was her father. He marched her up to the door, told her to wait, then went inside. She gagged with every breath of the fetid air as the cold dampness attempted to worm its way into her winter coat. A few moments later he returned with a man dressed in what used to be a white orderly's uniform, but the white had long given way to the yellowed discoloration of age and multiple washings. The man grinned at her with a broad mouth and bulging eyes. She felt his clammy hand grasp her forearm and pull her toward the door but he said nothing. Her father never looked at her but dismissed her with a wave and a sharp "I'll be back later to pick you up" as he headed back to the car. Jane stood in the doorway, rain washing away the tears that streamed from her swollen eyes. *Where has Father abandoned me?*

The squat orderly tugged at her arm then ushered her into a cramped waiting room. There were two other women there, neither of whom would look at her. Jane busied herself again with the fringe on her scarf. It felt like hours before she heard her name. She looked up to see the smiling face of what may have been a nurse. The woman had those same wide, staring eyes as the orderly. Her smile, though broad, was bereft of warmth. Jane rose to her feet with timidity and allowed the woman to take her by the arm. The clamminess of her touch crawled all over Jane's skin. Jane cast her eyes down as the woman weaved her through the chairs toward the back of the room. She noticed that the woman's gait was more a drag; her feet never seemed to leave the ground. She looked at the door as they shuffled through. The worn letters spelled out PROCEDURE ROOM.

Upon entering the room, Jane could smell a hint of disinfectant beneath the pervasive fishy odor that served as ambiance for this whole area. There was a dull metal table in the center of the room with what looked like some bizarre handles at one end. The nurse guided her toward the table and instructed her to disrobe and climb onto it. Her words dripped from her mouth in a garbled stream. Jane was unable to decipher most of what she said and relied, instead, on her ability to understand the hand motions that accompanied the instructions. Shaking, Jane peeled off her coat, then her robe. She started to remove her nightgown but the nurse waved at her saying what sounded like that would be fine. Jane climbed atop the freezing table and sat, legs dangling over the side, awaiting further direction. The nurse was busying herself with a canister that she had pulled alongside the gurney as a door in the corner of the room swung open. A tall, blond man strode into the room, white coat gleaming in contrast to the dinginess of everything else in her sight. His smile seemed genuine. Jane felt instant relaxation. The man arrived gurney-side with an outstretched hand. Jane accepted the proffered hand and it closed around hers, pumping it up and down.

"Hello, Jane, I'm Doctor Mott."

Jane nodded a silent greeting.

"Your father told me all about your situation. Please don't worry about a thing. The procedure takes only a few moments and we will do our best to keep you comfortable. You will feel some pressure but our friend here," he gave the canister a hearty pat, "will make sure you feel no pain."

Jane exhaled. This man was the only normal thing she had been in contact with since her arrival. She found her voice.

"What is this place? Is this a town?"

"Yes, indeedy. Welcome to Innsmouth." He made a welcoming gesture with open arms then laughed. Leaning in closer, he said, "I don't blame you. I'm not nuts about it either." Then louder, "it used to be a much different place. It was once bustling and lively. But a few years back there was some...trouble, and then the government got involved and that was a real dilly of a pickle. Now with the war on, they seem to be preoccupied with trouncing the Germans and the Japs, so they've pretty much left this place, although it's still not the same as it was. But the natives are proud."

He jerked his head toward the nurse whose back was to them.

As if on cue, the nurse then moved to Jane's side and pushed her down onto the table with gentle hands, the garish smile never leaving her face. Jane was able to make out the word ETHER before a mask was lowered over her nose and mouth. The doctor said, "Here we go, Jane. Just relax. I'll see you again when it's over."

The last thing she saw before her eyes closed of their own volition were the froggish eyes of the attending nurse looming over her. Jane could no longer see, but she could hear movement around her. She heard what sounded like the rusty squeak and swish of a swinging door followed by an unfamiliar muddling of gurgles and what must have been words. She sensed something heavy moving itself toward her and her nausea returned as the fishy stench enveloped her once more. At the edge of her consciousness, Jane felt her legs being grasped by something slimy and positioned into something cold and unwieldy. *Those handle things aren't handles at all,* she thought as her hands were being strapped down above her head. She attempted to struggle but her efforts never made it past her will. Then, with no preamble, something icy forced its way deep into her. There was more pressure than pain but she felt violated by the alien intrusion. There was a forcible tugging. Jane felt as if something were trying to pull her inside out. She felt a sudden vague warmth. She cried out but nothing more than a quiet moan escaped her lips. A gurgling voice barked a command that she could not decipher, then the world went black.

***

Consciousness returned one sense at a time, but it began with pain. It was a dull, aching, hollowness, a void that felt recently evacuated. She was lying on her back on a lumpy mattress and under a stiff and scratchy wool blanket. Sound came next: a constant dripping close by, her own moans, and the creek of bedsprings as she moved. The odor she breathed in was the same mix of fish and rot that seemed to permeate this god forsaken town with a faint antiseptic undertone. Her mouth tasted stale and coppery and her tongue was a sluggish, dry sponge that was slow to stir. Jane opened her eyes and saw only dull, grey light awaiting her. Turning her head from side to side revealed that she was alone in a small room. Other than the single bed she was in, it was devoid of furnishings and warmth. The walls were bare, discolored, and warped from years of water damage. The dripping that seemed to thunder in her ears came from a bucket placed in one corner of the room. The dented tin pale was overflowing, so every drop that fell into it from the seeping stain in the ceiling caused more murky water to spill out onto the faded tile floor.

148

Hello? Jane tried so say, but her mouth still wasn't working. She attempted to raise herself up on her arms, but they felt too rubbery and weak to do the job. "Hello?" This time she managed a croak that was as audible as a whisper in church. She licked her dry lips, inhaled to fill her lungs with the foul air to try again, but stopped when she heard a scream.

Jane froze, listening, wondering if she had heard what she thought she had, when there was a second scream. This one was longer, filled with terror, and came from a woman somewhere outside of her room.

She felt her flesh tingle as goose bumps broke out all over her. She then heard Dr. Mott's cheery voice from the hallway past the open door to her room, "Well it seems Miss Watkins woke up during the procedure. I guess that's what we get for watering down the ether to try and make it last." Jane heard the man's footfalls coming closer, so she laid back down and shut her eyes until she was peeking out between the lashes of her eyelids, trying to feign unconsciousness. She didn't know why she did that, but it felt like the right course of action.

Miss Watkins, whomever she was, continued to scream.

"Damn it all," Dr. Mott said, closer to Jane's room, "Nurse, she's the last girl of the day, right?"

Jane heard someone with a mouth full of mud answer, but the voice was so inhuman sounding that she couldn't make sense of the reply.

"Well good, that's at least something," the doctor said, and now he was standing right outside her door looking in at her. Through her slitted eyes, Jane couldn't make out his face, but his silhouette gave her the impression that he was studying her through the gloom.

"And Miss Chatham, how are you doing in there?" he called.

Jane remained silent.

"Miss Chatham…"

The screaming continued.

Jane saw Dr. Mott's shadow nod, turn, and continue down the hall. "Well get in there, nurse, and shut her up before she wakes up the whole damn town. You know how they hate a fuss."

She heard someone croak out an affirmative and then the sound of the screaming intensified as the door to the room Miss Watkins occupied was opened by the doctor. "Young lady that is enough of that!" she heard the doctor shout over the hysterical screams, "Sure, this little fellow ain't nothing to look at, but he isn't hurting you. He's just sucking out that little problem of yours, and this is how you treat him?" The door closed and the rest became muffled words and hoarse pleas of "get it out of me, get it out of me!"

That was enough for Jane.

She sat up in bed and looked around for her clothes, although she knew they weren't in the room with her. *I'll get new clothes*, she thought, *I've just got to get out of here, this is all wrong.* Clad in a thin, cotton gown and nothing else, she tiptoed to the door on her bare feet and looked down the hall to where the shouts had given way to gasping sobs.

"That's it, young lady, that's it, go back to sleep," she heard Dr. Mott say.

Jane stepped out into the hall, turned in the opposite direction from that room, and took three shaking steps before she froze in her tracks when she heard what the doctor said next: "Nurse, tell the elders that we're going to have to dispose of this one once we're done."

Oh my god, Jane's mind screamed, and then she was off. Her feet stumbled across the cold, wet floor, her eyes sought any avenue of escape, and her hands grasped at each clammy doorknob as she came to them. The first door she tried was locked. The next led to a small closet of near empty shelves, the third to an unoccupied room identical to the one in which she had awakened. Next was a small office she thought had to be Dr. Mott's. There were shelves stacked with books, a desk cluttered with papers, an ashtray with a smoking cigar in it, and another pail catching water dripping from the ceiling, but no exit.

There was one door left in the hallway, so when she found that it was unlocked, Jane rushed inside and shut it behind her without looking. *There has to be a back door out of this place, there just has to be*, she thought as she turned around and looked at the room she had entered. Doing so caused her lips to twist into a grimace as her mind tried to make sense of what she saw before her. It was like looking at old photographs, showing a mix of people she recognized and complete strangers, in locations both familiar and exotic. Little by little she pieced together the whole from the parts, but every revelation that came to her only brought more questions.

In the center of this room a pulsating, misshapen mass of diseased flesh twitched and shuddered. It was larger than her father's car and it excreted foul fluids that ran off in filthy rivers across the floor to disappear down a crusted drain some feet away. Several bladders across its slimy surface inflated and deflated in rhythmic unison, giving it the impression of breathing. It was spotted with yellow, puss-leaking orbs that could have been eyes if the idea was not repulsive and crazy. There were six large growths sprouting from it at random and ranging in size from about six inches in diameter, to close to three feet. The organic membrane they were made out of was translucent, so Jane could see that they were filled with greenish fluid. Also, inside each pustule, a small, dark shape floated. No, not just floated, but wiggled and even swam. Each bulbous sack held something that was alive.

"No, no, no," Jane whispered. Despite her better judgment, she took a few steps toward to the unwholesome creature to get a better look at the things it contained.

The growth closest to her was the smallest, and what it held was a tiny, dark, curled shape that was unrecognizable to her. The next largest sack held something more defined, and Jane recognized what it was from illustrations in her high school biology book. The third was even more developed and bits of anatomy such as hands, feet, and facial features were identifiable. However, the full extent of the nightmare became clear to Jane when she looked at what was swimming in the fourth embryonic tumor. What was in that growth was not human, or at least, not completely human. While it still had the basic shape, the outline was marred by webbing between the fingers of its tiny, grasping hands, eyes that were too big for its face, and along its back was a raised growth that could only have been a dorsal fin. The fifth monstrosity was even more alien looking than its smaller brethren. The sixth unborn child, for Jane had to admit to herself what they were, was far more fish-like than human. Covered in scales with a lipless mouth filled with sharp teeth, it had claws at the ends of its fingers, fluttering gills along its neck, and bulging, unblinking eyes that were locked on her. Then, when Jane brought a hand up to her mouth to stifle a scream, the two-foot-long terror used its claws to puncture the external womb that held it and began to tear its way to freedom. Fetid green fluid burst forth as the newborn poked its misshapen head out of the wound to let loose a croaking cry.

Jane spun on her heel to flee the abominable sight, only to see that her escape was blocked by a grinning Dr. Mott and the frowning nurse from before. The doctor held a bundle in one hand, something wrapped in a towel that dripped.

"Nurse, if you would, please see to the little one." Dr. Mott said.

The nurse pushed past Jane, giving her a snarl and a fresh whiff of her putrid scent as she did so. She reached out to the mewling freak and picked it up like a loving mother, soothing it with throaty cooing sounds.

"What are they?" Jane asked, voicing the question that had tormented her since she laid eyes on the horrible things in the quivering fluid sacks.

Dr. Mott stepped toward the woman, smile still affixed to his face, and said, "You see, there are them from the deep that wish to breed with us, always have for some reason I don't quite understand, myself. They're willing to pay for the privilege, too. So some years back, the people of

Innsmouth took them up on their offer, and things were fine for a while. Then the government came, killed a lot of folks, both deep ones and those like my nurse here who were half and half, and that was that. But then the war started and suddenly the army had other fish to fry." Mott stopped, thought about something for a moment, and then giggled. "Ha, fish to fry."

Dr. Mott, having backed Jane farther into the room by his slow, steady advance, turned to the large, shuddering, organic mass. He opened up the bundle he was carrying, revealing a small, membranous pouch. He held the small meat sack out to the amorphous thing which responded by growing a fleshy stalk and extending it to what Mott offered. Once the stalk connected with the pouch, it retracted until the sack hung from its side, parasite like.

The doctor wiped his hands on the towel with unconcealed disgust before dropping it and turning back to Jane. "Once the government was out of Innsmouth, the deep ones wanted to go back to their old arrangement, but they're not stupid. They didn't want the government back down on them. So they reached out to those desperate, stupid, or greedy enough to listen to them," at that, Mott's grin turned sheepish, "and well, new ways were thought up to give them what they want. Sure, it's a lot slower, but it's safer, and them from below are nothing if not patient."

"It's monstrous," Jane said.

"Nonsense, all we do is take what you throw away and use it. You obviously didn't want it, anyway."

Dr. Mott pulled a syringe from his pocket and filled it with a yellow fluid from a vial in his other hand. Jane didn't like the look of the needle or what was in the doctor's eyes, so she tried to make a run for the door. Before she could do anything, the strong, sweaty arms of the nurse were around her, pinning her own arms to her sides. The nurse proved to be quite stealthy despite her looks and had crept up behind Jane who was struggling to understand everything she had seen and heard.

"The problem now is if anyone finds out about this, well they just wouldn't understand." Dr. Mott said, walking forward, the syringe poised to sting the struggling woman. "So we can't let you leave, I'm afraid. And then there's your family. They're going to have to go away too, or else they'll come looking for you."

Dr. Mott jabbed Jane in the arm and pressed the plunger home.

"Honestly, Miss Chatham, you've made a real mess of everything."

Rehab

Kevin Wetmore

"You know this is for your own good, right?" said her mother/manager/monster a little too insistently.

Stephanie rolled her eyes, mumbled something like "whatever" and went back to flipping through the tabloid.

The Lexus moved slowly down Pacific Coast Highway in the Thursday rush hour traffic. Her mother/manager/monster glanced over at the paper in Stephanie's hands and let out a disgruntled noise.

"Ugh. That photo. I think that's from before midnight. You weren't even eighteen yet. We're going to have to sue them. I'll call Darren when I get back home." Darren was the high-priced attorney who handled all of Stephanie's legal matters. He had been on the phone a lot lately.

"I don't know why," Stephanie asked innocently, "It's a good picture."

"Jesus, Steph," sighed her mother/monster/manager. "You just don't get it and you don't get how many problems this causes for you and me."

On the cover was a photo of Stephanie from last week, outside a club in Hollywood, celebrating her birthday by vomiting vodka and pills all over the sidewalk and a bouncer. Tourists with camera phones looked on in fear and amusement, but nothing like concern. Under the image blared the caption "'Good Girl' Gone Bad! Is 'Abby' Out of Control?" Abby was the character Stephanie had played on the tween show *The Good Girls* since she was twelve, which had led to roles in several tween films, always playing the adventurous nice girl who wins the affections of a good bad boy. Now just eighteen, she wanted to break out of the child star image.

Stephanie did not see what the problem was. She worked like an adult. She earned money like an adult. Now she was an adult, legally. She should be able to party and drink and do what she wanted to like an adult. And if she wanted to get drunk to celebrate her eighteenth birthday, what was the problem? Everybody did it. Her mother/manager/monster quit her job as a PR hack for some studio to become her manager when she first signed with the television show, so the family's bills were now all paid by Stephanie, too. From her point of view, that meant nobody could tell her what to do anymore.

But her mother/manager/monster and her agent, Guy, both thought this "scandal" merited action. "Nobody wants to see a little girl drunk in public," her mother told her the next day in an "emergency meeting" (Guy's words) at their Brentwood home with Guy and Darren, the latter of whom was wisely staying silent for this debate.

"I am not a 'little girl,' *Mother*," she barked coldly back from under her hangover, angry in the knowledge that even as a legal adult now she still looked fifteen on camera.

"No," said Guy, "You're a eighteen year old alcoholic. So next Thursday you are going to the Tillinghast Center in Malibu."

"You're sending me to fucking rehab?" Stephanie practically shrieked.

"Yes," said Guy. "And apparently just in time."

"What about the babysitting feature?" Stephanie had just booked the lead on a feature film in which she played a teen babysitter who developed a dangerous crush on the father of the family. She thought it was the next logical step in her career and would get audiences following her into older roles.

Guy and her mother/manager/monster exchanged glances.

"Yes, uh, the good news is that we got the studio to push back principle photography for a month, so we're OK," Guy assured her with a smile.

"So what's the bad news, then? You said that was the good news, so there must be some pretty fucking bad news too."

"If you do not complete rehab or if there are any further incidents in public before, during or after, the studio will exercise their opt out clause and you will be very publicly booted from this film," said her mother. "Which means..."

"Which means kiss any other chances at doing features goodbye. I get it."

"Not just that," said Guy, "Dave and Brannon said if that happens then your character is going to get written off of *Good Girls*."

"What? They can't do that! Those fuckers! The network won't..."

"The network is the one pushing them to either shape you up or ship you out, sweetie," yelled Guy. Regaining his composure he looked her in the eye and laid it out: "It's rehab or the end of everything. Your choice, sweetheart."

Which is how she found herself in on the road to Malibu in sunglasses and a baseball hat, her trademark blonde curls pulled back into a severe ponytail so no one would recognize her. Guy had sweetened the deal by promising to book her on a number of daytime chat shows when she got out to talk about how she took control of her life and her problems, and she is back and better than ever and all that BS. The public ate that crap up. But now she had to put up with her mother/manager/monster for the entire ride into the hills above the Pacific.

The grounds of the clinic were lush and they saw some people in the distance, reading, walking and playing horseshoes. Stephanie rolled her eyes. This was going to suck.

At the front desk a professional young woman took their name, had them sit and fill out admitting forms. Ten minutes later Stephanie's mother/manager/monster brought the forms back to the receptionist, who accepted them without looking at them and then silently slid aside a panel in the wall that moved to reveal a door.

"Stephanie Thomas and Rhonda Thomas to see you, doctor."

"Show them in, please," came the unseen response.

"Dr. Tillinghast will see you now," she said curtly to them and they gathered their possessions and entered the office.

Sunlight filled the room, the cathedral ceiling making the space seem huge and contemplative. One wall was all glass, looking out at the Pacific, beyond the complex. Another wall, opposite, of framed certificates, diplomas, photos and plaques sat behind a desk, four chairs arrayed in front of it. A man stood at the desk with a file in hand, looking up as they entered. White haired, he could have been anywhere between forty and seventy. He looked to be in great shape - healthy, smiling, friendly - in a lab coat over a professional but casual shirt. Stephanie could not see his feet but would not have been surprised if he were wearing sandals.

"Ms. Thomas," he said, extending his hand to Stephanie. "And Ms. Thomas," he repeated, shaking her mother/manager/monster's hand. "Please, make yourselves comfortable," and gestured to the chairs while taking a seat himself behind the desk.

The chairs, she had to admit, were very easy to make yourself comfortable in.

"I am sorry to learn of your recent issues," he began. "May we open with honesty? You know you are an addict, yes?"

Stephanie just stared. He smiled and went on as if she had agreed with him completely.

"You are addicted to alcohol at the very least and you have a very public record of the use and abuse of a number of substances." He consulted the file again. "Marijuana, prescription pills, recreational drugs and, if the tabloids are to be believed, cocaine at least once."

Stephanie just smiled at him.

"Yes, doctor," her mother/manager/monster finally answered for her. Stephanie ignored her.

"No worries. We are going to cure you of your addictions and even your desire to use these things."

"How might we be doing that, doctor?" Stephanie began, a mocking undercurrent just behind her voice. "Maybe my self-esteem is suffering, so we'll make me feel better? Maybe I need to eat vegan, or meditate, or firewalk, or punch a doll that stands for my inner child or her?" she said, jerking her thumb to her mother/manager/monster.

The doctor smiled indulgently. "Nothing like that. Those don't work, or at least they only address the symptoms and leave you in a state where you can fall back into a state of addiction. In short, Ms. Thomas, they are bullshit."

Stephanie smiled at that. Maybe this place wasn't what she feared.

"We use state of the art technology to help you overcome your addiction. My great uncle Dr. Crawford Tillinghast invented a device called the Tillinghast Resonator. We use it to cure you of all your addictions."

Stephanie's smile slowly became much more plastic. "A machine, huh?"

Tillinghast's smile became even sharper. "Not just any machine, Ms. Thomas. Like my great uncle, I am a researcher of the physical and metaphysical. Your addiction has numerous causes, but we will treat you in a manner that cures all. Would you like to see the device?"

Stephanie nodded and out of the corner of her eye saw her mother nodding too.

Dr. Tillinghast stood up. "Follow me." He led them out the office and down the hall to a doorway. "This is the treatment room," he told them as he opened the door and they stepped through.

At first, Stephanie was reminded of an upmarket massage parlor. The walls and floor were light beige, soft unfocused light came from recesses in the walls and ceiling. In the center of the room, the machine stood on a table next to a reclining chair. Dr. Tillighast flipped a switch and the machine began to emit a low, purple light. A sight hum, not unpleasant, filled the room.

"Scientific study and reflection have taught us that the known universe of three dimensions embraces the merest fraction of the whole cosmos of substance and energy," Tillinghast said, looking at the machine with something that resembled love. "This machine will generate waves acting on unrecognized sense organs that exist in us as atrophied or rudimentary vestiges. Someone your age should respond especially well."

"Why?" asked Stephanie, unable to take her eyes off the machine. The light, the hum felt almost hypnotic, drawing her in.

The doctor turned to her, the side of his face closest the machine bathed in a low violet glow. "The machine resonates at frequencies that our neural pathways respond to. If you've become addicted to something, the machine, over the course of treatment, erases those pathways and reshapes them so that you are not only no longer addicted but that you will not experience any cravings or become addicted to anything else. You will begin to sense the world in a different way and no longer need alcohol or drugs."

"So what's age got to do with it? I mean, could you use it on her?" Stephanie asked, gesturing again towards her mother/monster/manager, who scowled. The doctor turned his face to the older woman.

"Young people's neural pathways continue to develop until their early twenties, we've learned. That's one reason why they continually make poor decisions: their brains are not wired to make good ones yet." He turned back to Stephanie. "Nothing personal, Ms. Thomas. That's also why we won't use this technology on anyone older than twenty-three. The pathways are more set in older people and so certain side effects would kick in."

"What kind of side effects?" asked mother/manager/monster.

"Nothing serious, I assure you," Dr. Tillinghast smiled. "Mostly hallucinations and perhaps some tiredness and irritability. That's why everyone here right now for treatment is twenty and under. And we are very discrete. We cater to an elite group of individuals who value their privacy. We value your privacy as well, which is why we are the best."

"It's not plugged in," Stephanie observed.

"No," said the doctor with a surprised smile, as if he had underestimated her and was suddenly impressed with her ability to observe. "Well spotted. The Resonator is not electrical in any sense you'd understand. It has a chemical battery of sorts but it runs on a patented technology that only the Tillinghast clinic has. It generates its own power. It is, I assure you, safe and effective."

He turned off the machine and pointed to a dial. "We also take many, many precautions. The procedure is completely safe. The machine was just set to a level of one, the lowest possible setting. That, young lady," he said to Stephanie, "is where your treatment begins. At the lowest level. Then, over the next ten days to two weeks, we will increase the potency of the waves. Please note that the device goes to seven, and we never go above three for safety's sake. The device is still effective at the low levels. We have a one hundred percent cure rate with it."

"What happens at seven?" Stephanie asked.

"Your head explodes," the doctor calmly replied, then after a beat burst into laughter. "I'm kidding of course. The higher levels have produced no worse than bad headaches and some visions, not unlike a bad hangover. As we are trying to rid you of hangovers, it makes sense to stay low."

He turned and Stephanie looked back at the machine, as if reluctant to leave it. She followed the doctor and her mother/manager/monster out of the treatment room and back to the doctor's office.

"You will have a private room with private bath, take all meals with the other clients in the common dining room, although the staff will bring any food or drink you'd like to your room any time day or night. You'll undergo treatment twice a day for two weeks and we'll see how you're doing. You will have no contact with the outside world (my apologies, Ms. Thomas, but it's necessary for your daughter - we want her to focus on getting better). No cell phone, no internet, and you may not receive any mail or packages. We want to keep you away from the things that got you in trouble in the first place. Your mother will return here two weeks from today for an evaluation meeting. It's my hope that you will go home on that day, cured of your addictions. Now, will that be credit card, cash or check?"

Her bags were brought to her room, which was small compared to what she was used to, but comfortable and tastefully decorated. She unpacked her clothes and had just jumped on the bed with a magazine when there was a knock at the door and a young African-American man dressed all in white opened it after a moment.

"Time for your first treatment," he said.

"Already?" she asked.

"You want to wait to get better?" he said, unsmiling.

She put the magazine down on the nightstand. "Wow, you guys don't mess around here."

In five minutes she was in the treatment room in the recliner. The young man, who never gave his name, waited until she seemed comfortable and then flipped the switch and adjusted a knob. The low hum from earlier rose up. The purple glow grew until it infused the room.

"I'll be back in forty five minutes," he said.

"Wait," she called. "What do I do?"

"Just lie back, relax and let the treatment work."

God, she was going to be so bored.

Except she wasn't. The sound and the light worked sort of like a sensory deprivation tank. She began to see lights and sparkles in the room. She felt her breathing deepen. Wow, she thought, this could be addicting. It's like a magic mushroom with no side effects.

She drifted for a while, neither asleep nor awake but riding the twilight. The lights occasionally flickered on and off like fireflies.

Then, out of the corner of her eye, it looked like there was a snake on the table moving past the device towards her. Wait, not on the table. It was moving through the table. Snapping into alertness she turned and looked. There was nothing there.

For the rest of the session she sat there staring at the table but nothing happened and she felt no different when the man came back in the door without knocking and turned off the device.

"How do you feel?"

"Fine, I guess. Like, are you supposed to see things and stuff with this thing?"

"Some clients do; some don't. I wouldn't worry about it. Dinner is in an hour and a half." With that he deposited her back at her room and walked away without another word.

She suddenly felt tired and, although she began flipping through the magazine again, was asleep in ten minutes, waking only when a low, unobtrusive announcement let her know dinner was being served.

She walked down the corridor, out of the women's wing to the central hub and found the dining room. The food did not smell bad. Christ, for what she was paying it should be organic, gourmet, four star cuisine served to her on golden plates. Instead, she found it was healthy, simple and very tasty. She looked around the room at the dozen or so "clients" dining in small groups.

"Mind if I join you?" said a voice behind her.

Without looking, she responded, "Whatever."

A young man, looking roughly her age dropped into the chair opposite her. He immediately began to shovel the food into his mouth as if he had been lost for three days. "Say what you like about this place, the chow is some of the best I ever had."

He was a day or two unshaven, and it suited him, unlike most who tried the look. His eyes were a piercing pale blue and his features sharp. His thick black hair fell just right around his face, framing it as if calling attention to it as a work of art. Stephanie knew she knew him from somewhere.

"Hey, aren't you.." she began.

"Yeah," he laughed back. "Aren't you…"

"Yeah," she smiled.

"Booze, pills, weed, harder stuff?"

"Take your pick. You?"

"Sex."

"You're shitting me."

"Nope. I am a sex addict. I am in almost constant need of sex."

"Really?" she grinned at this tidbit.

"It's not fun or funny."

"Life's rough for Tyler Lee of 4Ever."

"Oooh, poor little rich girl from the TV. No sympathy for the hardworking man with an addiction to sex."

"I wish I had your life," she said, thinking of her mother/manager/monster.

"No you don't. You should try being in a boy band."

"As if."

"Much harder than your job."

"Bullshit."

"On tour 250 days out of the year? More or less living on a tour bus? Not seeing family. Not able to go out in public. No social life. Underage girls throwing themselves at you, trying to sneak into your room."

"'Underage?' I thought you were seventeen."

He smirked and looked around. "Can you keep a secret? My official bio says I'm seventeen because I look young. I'm actually twenty-four." He returned to shoveling food into his mouth.

"No fucking way!"

"Shhhhh. Look, it's good for business. A seventeen year old singing about love and dating to fifteen year old girls is fine. A twenty-four year old doing that is statutory and creepy."

She giggled. "OK, I'll be cool. How do you like it here?"

"It's cool. Tillinghast is arrogant, but knows what he's doing. I think the treatment is really working."

"How long you been here?"

"Day eight and no more urges," he announced proudly.

"Hey, that's cool," she said and meant it. "Maybe you can be my rehab buddy," she said standing up.

"Maybe. Welcome to the Tillinghast Team. A little purple light and everything's all right," he joked. She smiled at that and left the dining hall to return to her room and watch some television. As long as she was here, she may as well relax and see what the competition was doing.

On her third day at the clinic, they turned the resonator up to two. "You're responding well, more rapidly than the average client here," Dr. Tillinghast told her. The lights became even brighter. She felt warm while it was happening, but afterwards clammy skin and a headache brought her low. She returned to her room and crashed for hours, only emerging at dinner time, barely able to walk to the dining room.

Tyler was already at the table, again eating as if he had never had food before.

"Look what the cat dragged in," he drawled, smiling, when he saw her.

"Shut your fucking mouth," she responded, ignoring the food and getting coffee.

"Now is that how a good girl talks?" he grinned.

"Sorry. Fuck yourself hard, no lube, is what I meant."

"Play your cards right…" he began with a smile, then stopped, frowning. "Just kidding. I don't do that anymore." He looked at the mug in her hand. "Yo, you need more than that. The resonator can knock you on your ass when they crank it up. You need some sugar or some solid food, not caffeine."

"Whatever," she mumbled back, but got up to check out the buffet. Nothing looked appealing, so she had the staff make her a smoothie. When she got back to the table, Tyler was on thirds.

"Off the drugs and joining overeaters anonymous next?" she sneered.

"You know us addictive personalities." He looked up at her. "You know, I got here the week before you did and my third day was rough, too. Now I'm just feeling so alive. Like everything just looks different. More vibrant. I have this huge appetite for everything. Y'know? For, like, life!"

"Everything, huh? Even underage girls sneaking on the tour bus?"

He stopped, put down his fork and looked at her as if he might snap. Then, suddenly, he smiled and said, "You know what? Not really."

Later that night, she awoke incredibly thirsty. Something else seemed off. She had been having a nightmare, but now, awake, none of that mattered. Leaving her room, she strolled the corridor and turned down the male dormitory wing. She found Tyler's door and let herself in.

He was asleep on his bunk, the sheet pulled up halfway over his body. She closed the door and crossed to his sleeping form. She stood for a few minutes, just staring at him, then began to pull the sheet off his body. She could not explain it, but although she had no appetite for food, she found the treatment had somehow awoken a powerful physical need in her.

He was in great shape (must be all that dancing, she thought), and only wearing boxers. She climbed onto the bed and straddled him.

"Hey, Tyler," she half whispered. He stirred. "Wake up, I need to talk to you."

He opened his eyes, groggy and half awake.

"Steph, what the fu…" Before he could finish the words, she covered his mouth with hers and began grinding against him on the bed. For a second he responded, his tongue flicking against hers and she felt him begin to stiffen under her. Then his eyes opened wide as he became fully awake and he pushed her up.

"What the hell are you doing, Steph? Seriously, what is wrong with you?"

"C'mon," she purred. "I'm eighteen. It's not like I'm a virgin. We're both adults. It'll be fun." She leaned back in, prepared to kiss him again.

"Stop it. STOP IT! You have to leave now." With that he began to scramble back, trying to get out from under her.

"You know you want to," she said, leaning in to kiss him again while reaching down between them.

"NO!" he yelled and bodily threw her off him, off the bed, to the floor. She was more shocked and surprised than hurt.

He sat up in bed and just looked at her. "What the fuck is wrong with you?" he asked. "I am a recovering sex addict. I have been in treatment for a week and a half and you come in here and…do…this? What the fuck? Am I coming to your room with vodka and E?"

Suddenly, he clutched his head and let out a small shriek. His eyes were clenched tight and for a second she thought something from the inside was pushing against his forehead. (Did I really see that?" she thought). As soon as it had begun, it passed. He began to breathe again and looked at her in pain but with cold distain.

"Seriously, Steph, get out and leave me the fuck alone!" And not waiting for a response, he pulled the sheet up over himself, turned his back to her and made as if he were going back to sleep.

"Fuck you, you fucking homo!" was all she could think to say before storming out and slamming his door.

Afraid that she might have woken those in nearby rooms, she ran down the corridor back to the central hub. She found herself in front of the treatment room. No one around. She tried the door. Open.

The next thing she knew, the device was on and she was in the chair. Sitting up, she turned the knob to four.

She sat back and breathed heavily. "It's just for a few minutes," she told herself. "Just to calm myself down." She closed her eyes.

When she opened them, there was a room in the room. She could see another space, almost identical to the treatment room, overlaying it. It was trippy, but not terrifying. It was like being at a laser show at the Griffith Planetarium on X, seeing both the real world in all its intensity, but also this even more real world on top of it. It was also, she realized, like being in an aquarium. She could see little fishes darting throughout the room.

"Hello, Nemo," she giggled, "Your dad's looking for you!" She giggled some more, then realized she should go. Turning the machine off, she opened the door a crack. Seeing no one, she moved once more down the hall. She figured Tyler would apologize in the morning, and after that she'd ask him if he had seen the fish. Otherwise she'd ignore him. Serve him right for passing up this sweetness, she thought.

He was not at breakfast. Remembering his headache and the bulge in his forehead, she decided to take the high road and check on him. She knocked on his door, but there was no answer. She tried the knob and the door opened easily. Tyler was not there and the room was devoid of his possessions. It was as if he had moved out during the early morning hours. It wasn't because of her, was it?

"What happened to Tyler?" she asked the attendant who activated the resonator for her. The young Latina woman, dressed all in white with her hair pulled back in a severe bun, simply said, "I'm afraid we cannot discuss patients with other patients. I'll be back in forty-five minutes," and quickly whisked from the room.

The resonator, only set at two now, simply glowed and hummed and did nothing for her. She contemplated turning it up, but since there was no clock in the room she had no idea when the attendant would come back and she figured turning it up on your own would be frowned upon. She spent most of the next hour bored and slightly concerned for Tyler.

She ran into Dr. Tillinghast outside the room right after her session. "What happened to Tyler?" she asked.

"Now Ms. Thomas, Stephanie, you know we do not discuss our clients with other clients." He then grinned and looked around to see if anyone was in earshot, then leaned in conspiratorially and whispered, "But I can tell you he has left here, satisfied with his treatment and ready to begin a new, addiction-free life."

"He's gone?"

Tillinghast laughed. "Yes, Ms. Thomas. And you will be, too, someday soon. Once your treatment is over and you have overcome your addictions, we send you home."

"But when I saw him last night, he had a terrible headache and I swear I saw…"

Dr. Tillinghast's eyes narrowed. "What do you think you saw, Ms. Thomas?"

Stephanie shuddered in horror at the image in her head of something inside Tyler's forehead pushing against his skull, his skin, seeking to get out of his head.

"Nothing, I guess."

"All right then," Tillinghast smiled. "Besides if you saw him late last night, that would mean one of you was out of bed and perhaps in the other's room. That would be against policy and a serious temptation for Tyler."

"Oh, no," Stephanie asserted. "We both couldn't sleep and just ran into each other in the dining room for a late night snack."

"I see. No harm," he said.

"Out of curiosity, what would happen if someone in their mid-twenties used the machine?"

"What an odd question. Why do you ask?"

"No reason, just curious."

"As I said, headaches and tiredness, nothing worse. Enjoy your treatment this afternoon."

He walked away whistling a tuneless song.

Her afternoon treatment at a setting to two was even more boring and useless than the morning session. Tyler's absence at dinner left her sitting alone and annoyed at the situation.

That night, she again awoke at midnight to a quiet and sleeping center. Slipping out of her room, she moved purposefully to the treatment room.

Sitting at the edge of the reclining chair, she initially turned the knob to four and the second room burst into her perception. She could see, just out of the range of clarity, vague human-shaped entities in that room, considering her it seemed. Perhaps if she turned the level up they would come into better focus, she reasoned.

She turned the device to five. Simultaneously three things happened. First, a supernova exploded behind her eyes. She could barely see and her head felt too tight. Second, she felt a warmth spreading between her legs. She was not filled with desire, but a strange mix of desire and satisfaction. Third, she noticed the figures were still out of focus, but it was now obvious that she had their attention. The air was also filled with undulating things. She giggled because they looked like eels. Despite the pain, she knew she had to see more, and, reaching over, turned the device to seven.

Malibu police are reporting an early morning automobile accident on Pacific Coast Highway took the lives of television star Stephanie Thomas and singer Tyler Lee of the group 4Ever. The two were in Lee's Porsche Boxster allegedly exceeding the speed limit when the car struck a cliff and then rolled into oncoming traffic. One witness on the scene described the scene as "gruesome" and "grisly," although another witness said it looked as if the bodies had almost disintegrated on impact. Police had no comment as the investigation is ongoing. The two celebrities were never linked publicly, but Thomas's mother, Rhonda Thomas, who also was her manager, in a statement to the media said that they were "close friends, nothing more" and asked for privacy and understanding as the two respective families mourn their loss. In lieu of flowers, donations may be made to the Tillinghast Foundation to support their work with young people facing particular challenges.

Unsung Heroes

Don Webb

Hitler's interest in the final battle with the USA is something of an historical curiosity. Although as early as the mid-20s Hitler had referred to an ultimate conflict between Germany and America, the attack on Pearl Harbor shaped American perception of WWII as an American response to Japanese aggression. Hitler's interest in the USA is usually footnoted in three facts that seem small in the vast tapestry of the Second World War. The first was the creation of the Amerika Bomber. A project of the Reichsluftfahrtministerium, a bomber that could travel from Germany to New York had the blessing of Reichmarschall Herman Göring, who poured many marks into the project in 1942. The inability of Germany to develop an atomic bomb combined with the decrease of German aviation-production halted the process. The two attacks on American territory – the U-boat attacks on Cape Hatteras, North Carolina and Essex County, Massachusetts are almost unknown to the average American citizen. The former battle was waged by fishing trawlers retro-fitted by the US Navy and is a stirring tale of co-operation between the government and local industry. The later incident is somewhat shrouded in mystery because of the somewhat secretive nature of the good citizens of Innsmouth, Massachusetts. The Germans had dispatched two U-boats, one aimed with a special radio device perhaps to be used in a propaganda campaign. A small group of Americans disabled one of the boats, which was found ashore near the town of Rowley, Massachusetts. The German sailors were dead, seemingly slain by their own guns. The front of the submarine had been torn open. The United States government quieted any press about the incident. In fact the only surviving account of the battle have been found in German records, of the return of one U-boat from a skirmish with Americans. Oddly enough these are not standard German naval records, but an account in the files of Himmler's Ahnenerbe division, which focused on occult and pseudo-science "Ariosophy" – or beliefs of a secret Aryan tradition.

"Little Known Skirmishes of the Battle of the Atlantic"
Capt. William Henderson USN retired

The great excitement I feel at being chosen by Reichsführer Himmler to oversee the *Studiengesellschaft für Unterseegeistesurgeschichte* is unbounded. Before the coming of the NSDAP, my theories had been regulated to the ash heap of occultism. Himmler sees the truth.

Our Aryan ancestors had not only ruled the primal world of land but the seas as well. Three-quarters of the Earth is covered in water and it is only logical to assume the Will-to-Power that enabled us to claim the earth before the coming of the sub-humans had likewise lead us to conquer the seas. The legends of Atlantis, Mu, and R'lyeh all point to a bygone age of Aryan undersea folk. Of course Jewish science has done much to discredit this. Only the ever-healing movement of history has begun to reveal the watery glories that will empower the Thousand Year Reich.

I am sad my mother had not lived to see my triumph. I was a sickly and ugly, the butt of school room jokes and a crude prank at the gymnasium. Unlike my brother who has Aryan good looks, I was the asthmatic child of the shadows. The one who reads too much, who fantasy is morbid, whose interests are dark. Had it not been for the coming of Hitler, my life would be overlooked, my monographs on the secret side of history ignored, and one burning dream of finally being part of something great – something that defied the ages – would be like a vision conjured by hashish. Hitler, through the kindly face of Heinrich Himmler , had offered me salvation. What could I do but offer it back? I will be a hero of the Folk! A man whose name is known for a thousand years. Herman Mueller, discoverer of the undersea Aryan people. Heil Hitler! Heil Mueller!

I had found the story of the undersea Aryans in the Pacific. I had begun my researches with *Antediluvian Folktales, Typhonian Tablets, Migrations of Extinct Branches of the Genus Homo* and the much debated *Cthaat Aquadingen*. I was able to locate Ponape as a likely site of an underwater civilization. In 1889 Spain sold the archipelago of Ponape (together with the Marianne and Palau Islands) to Germany. Certain ruins were discovered in Nan Madol suggested the existence of a high level of civilization which did not match the brown skinned natives. According to the locals the cyclopean stone works were a mere minor construction, an embassy as it were for, for a sea dwelling race known as the Fischvolk. These immortal (!) creatures came to the land to trade gold and platinum jewelry for human workers and in exchange for mysterious (runic?) rituals being performed according to astronomical events. The Fischvolk were said to be in the service of a "Returning Savior" – clearly a folk-metaphor for the future Reich, much as the fictional (?) work of Bulwer-Lytton *The Coming Race.* Two of the Fischvolk named Olosohipa and Olosohopa told the natives that a kingdom long-ago submerged by historical accident would re-emerge on the land when the "stars were right." Until that happy time the Fischvolk would maintain the undersea world and certain land-dwellers would be tolerated. The leader of the re-emerging Reich would be named Cthulhu. This name, when analyzed by the runic principles discovered by Guido von List reads Fire and Force is Vitally Locked, Until Outer Space Vitality Returns. (Kennaz, Thuriasz, Uruz, Lagaz, Hagalaz, Uruz). Significantly the same name had been discovered by Dr. William Channing Webb's during a runic expedition to West Greenland in 1860. Unfortunately Lutheran missionaries destroyed much of the lore these primitive brown people had of the white people from sea. The locals killed off the missionaries in 1910, and a rather crazed ship's captain shelled the island in 1911 – claiming that "Fischvolk were the world's biggest threat." After the Jewish-engineered defeat of the war, Germany lost claim to the island, and it became a Japanese possession in 1919. It remains a major source of platinum for the Japanese Empire despite the geological fact that platinum does not occur on coral islands.

I was fortunate to gain some sketches of jewelry from Nan Madol made by a German missionary. The brooch and tiara he sketched show a massively detailed artistic form reminiscent of Celtic gold work. The undersea imagery bespeaks a vitality, almost a cruelty, that is the very soul of the Aryan confronted with sub-species. I had discovered this all by 1936, and had written two monographs on the possibility of an Aryan homeland in the Pacific. Indeed because of my work (and to be fair Karl Haushofer) the Japanese were granted the status of "Honorary Aryans" in 1937. It was fate, the ever-healing force of history, that enabled me to discover the Fischvolk were not a solely Pacific concern. My article in *Idunna* showing the Nan Madol tiara was read by an American scholar, Dr. Charles Evertt, who provided me with the news that similar jewelry was on display at a museum in Innsmouth, Massachusetts. He believed that the artifacts were from the South Sea trade that had enriched many coastal towns in that part of America called "New England." I set out straightaway to become an expert on Innsmouth.

The results were collected in three papers for the Ahnenerbe – the last one of which drew the attention of Himmler himself. The small town of Innsmouth had undergone an expansion due to the introduction of exactly the same sort of gold and platinum trinkets that are now flowing into Japanese hands shortly after a Captain Marsh had visited the region. At first I assumed that Captain Marsh had merely begun a trading relationship with the inhabitants of Nan Madol, but such seemed unlikely given the Spanish control of the region. But certain other facts came to play – Marsh not only had the trinkets, but his fishing trawlers began to show remarkable catches. He seemed to be possessed of a superior aquatic technology than other fishermen of New England. In addition to this he (and his family) cast off the strictures of Christianity preferring an older vitalist religion based on bloodlines. It took me many months to accept that the return of the undersea Reich believed in by superstitious South Sea islanders was begin accepted (and prepared for) by tough logical Americans – in a region dominated by chalk white Aryans. What we were struggling for in Germany by political means was occurring naturally in America in accordance with cosmic principles. The obsession of the Innsmouthers with blood-lines could only mean one thing – they had begun to interbreed with undersea Aryans. A strain of immortal, strong, wise herrenvolk was coming into being in America. Of course it was no surprise that as Hitler had come to awaken the land-dwelling part of the Aryan brotherhood, the undersea portion would be casting off its aeons long slumber as well.

The political aspect of this miracle could hardly be over-looked. If we could reunite the sundered halves of the Aryan world, we could become masters of the world decades sooner. On one hand we would have a built-in enclave on the American coast – a port friendly to our U-boats that could be used to deliver soldiers to American soil. We could avenge ourselves upon the Americans for their involvement in war. On the other hand, great secrets of Aryan science could be added to the war effort. Clearly all history was moving to this moment.

Himmler summed me to his castle at Wewelsberg. He cried with joy when I showed the evidence I had collected on Innsmouth and the undersea Aryans. This was the omen that the Reich had been waiting for!!

Now only practical matters remained. How did we contact the Fischvolk? They must have maintained secrecy for years for a reason. The rising of the undersea Reich must be fragile in some manner, or it would have long ago occurred. Was there a natural/cosmic reason that this had not been manifest? I had not considered this obvious question, and when Himmler asked it; I felt ashamed.

"I am a scholar, not a political scientist, Herr Himmler."

I thought he might have discovered my shameful interlude at the asylum. When I was seventeen a beautiful tall blonde girl named Helga Curfman had pretended an interest in me, She had told me that she had dreamed that we should be lovers. It was Destiny, she told me. I had never kissed a girl. Near our school, the Heinrich Schlemann Oberschuke, was a municipal barn, the kind that dotted Berlin in those days. She told me to strip naked and light a lantern, she would join me at night. It was cold and I was shaking with lust and coughing, longing and goose-pimples. The barn door opened. I raised my lantern and in rushed dozens of my school mates – both male and female. They pointed at my naked body. They laughed. They threw excrement on me. I had a breakdown after this. I never finished the gymnasium. I never ventured into business like my successful brother. I became a haunter of libraries, a husband to piles of books, a ghoul feeding on missing lore and grateful for the adventures of others. But Himmler smiled at me and gave me the keys to my kingdom.

"Do you know that Germany lost is greatest scientist in 1931?" He asked.

"I do not know of whom you speak."

"Just as it needed a child of Austrian culture - Hitler! - to put the Jewish politicians in their place, so it needed an Austrian to cleanse the world of Jewish science." Said Himmler.

Like many scholars I had remained in my own field. I had not heard of Dr. Hans Hörbiger, who had developed the Doctrine of Eternal Ice, which refuted the "general relativity" of Jewish science. According to Dr. Hörbiger, ice was the basic substance of all cosmic processes, and ice moons, ice planets, and the "global ether." The earth had a series of encounters with great ice moons – each almost destroying life as we knew it. The ice had almost destroyed the Aryans several times, but our evolutionary response was to grow in might and main. Clearly the undersea Aryans had been developing a great civilization in the Pacific; surely I had noticed how Aryan the heads at Easter Island were? But the Earth's previous ice moon (whose fall had produced the myths of the Flood and Atlantis) had not destroyed the Aryan Pacific Empire, but forced an evolutionary change on our brothers. This also explained why the Pacific seems to be such a large zone without land. The land here was buried under the ice. How long our brothers must have labored to rebuild what was once theirs. As we – the Aryans of the North – had struggled against sub-human hordes, so they must have struggled against giant octopi and fierce whales!

"But flesh is stronger than ice!" said Himmler, "And the Aryan spirit is stronger than time!"

I was filled with rapture. Here was a man who Understood! All of the days at being laughed at by degree carrying scholars, even mocked by my own family were over. I was to be part of the redemption of the world. God, the real God, the God of the Folk had chosen me. But my joy expanded even more. I was not the mere scholar, the mere messenger of all-healing history. No. Himmler said I was to be the ambassador to the watery realms. I would go to the sea near Innsmouth and reunite the halves of the Teutonic race! I would be having an adventure rather than reading about one.

We began researching this question at once. We must not assume that the undersea Aryans even knew of our presence. Atlantis had sunk, or as we now know been destroyed by an ice moon, millennia ago. The

Fischvolk might assume that they alone are the true bloodline, and might have their own plans for world salvation. They might distrust land dwellers, or be frightened by the large numbers of Jews that live among humans. As Herr Himmler pointed out, there were an exceptional number of Jews living on the eastern seaboard of the United States. Likewise the undersea Aryans might not speaks we do. In the cold and stormy world they inhabit they might speak only by thought – indeed which might have been how our ancestors communicated with one another. It was perhaps not until the coming of the Jew were words needed. Does not the Jewish religion says that the Word was God," instead of "God is the Blood.""?

At first we began looking for psychics, Germans with strong minds that could communicate silently. But our experiments were failures. Then an investigator in Munich contacted Himmler. Dr. Robert Schuss had been concerned about the communication problem. How could the lighting fast minds of our generals communicate with the average foot-solider? He had been working on a "telepathy-radio" and was hoping for funding. He had worked out the telepathic problem, but had not solved the distance problem. He could broadcast or receive thoughts from about thirty meters, but no further. Abs a communication device, he felt he had failed, but hoped that with Reich backing, this could be the ultimate communication device, or perhaps the ultimate propaganda device. Himmler contacted me at once, and we began trials. We choose non-German speaking inmates from the camps. There was some worry that such non-Aryan minds would be too primitive to receive our signals, and certainly too dim to broadcast to our minds. But the test seemed valid; our minds might be very different than the undersea Aryans. Perhaps (since they were most likely a telepathic race) their minds might be stronger than ours. Perhaps we (because of the excitement of being associated with Hitler) might have superior energy to theirs. So we tested. Their thoughts toward us were so vicious. They couldn't understand the greater good we were doing the world. But we could understand them even if they spoke Hungarian and read Hebrew, or spoke French and Ladino. We could understand them. And we could communicate, "Lift your right arm or the guard will strike you!"

The range was about thirty meters in air, twenty five in water, five through stone. The machine was not large. It could be fitted into the nose of VIIC U-boat. The U boat could keep its mine-laying capacity, but would lose its forward torpedo tube. This meant it would have to escorted by a second U-boat into the American waters. The Americans never had any true sense of fear. At the beginning of the war, they had only one anti-submarine boat acting as a coast guard in the Atlantic. It would be easy to mount a large submarine invasion. Himmler persuaded Hitler to allow us to try and contact the undersea Aryans of the Massachusetts' coast before any other war effort. He loved tales of the undersea Aryans. The discovery of such a proof of Aryan science coupled with the strategic edge of having an Aryan presence in America would be a war changing moment.

Our U-boat was renamed the *Cthulhureich*. Our protective boat remained the U72. The captains of both boats hated me and my mission. Fortunately Himmler had sent nine SS guard with us. Five in my submarine, four in the other sub, so that we would arrive safely. My men were tall, cruel blonde beasts – the image of what I wanted to be. I was short and dark and after Helga no woman have ever looked twice at me. My brother looked like Thor, but with my weak right eye I was Odin, ever prying into mysteries. I would be the savior of the folk.

It took five days to cross the Atlantic. We sailed on the surface the first four days, but made our approach to the Massachusetts coast underwater. If our information, bought from an Innsmouth inhabitant for much gold was true, the American government had tried to destroy the underwater settlement in 1928. The puny human attack had not destroyed the Fischvolk's city of "Y'ha-nthle" – a clear linguistic cognate to Walhalla. I had guessed that Y'ha-nthele lay about two kilometers east of Cape Ann. It would lie in a trench of course. The captain worried about the depth and warned me that he could only remain in the trench for two hours at a time. Even the guns of my guards didn't deter him. So I knew he must be speaking the truth. We found nothing during our first four days of searching. On the second dive we stayed a bit too long and a rivet in the hull imploded, shooting into the chamber like a bullet unleashing a stream of freezing sea water. We would surface at night, and twice sent small boats ashore to examine the town of Innsmouth, which seemed to be rebuilding.

One night I overheard one of guards talking to the captain. If we found nothing in a week's time, I would be killed and they would return to Germany. The mission would never have happened and there would be no official embarrassment. I was not surprised. I had heard of other "erasures." But I was deeply sad. That night I prayed to Cthulhu that I might meet with success.

And my prayers were answered.

We found another small trench, unmapped, half a kilometer east and two kilometers north. Our searchlight showed towers covered in mother-of-pearl. Strange minarets, oddly portioned frustra, delicate and cruel spikes. Dolphins, squid and enormous jelly-fish swam all around. The city suggested some alien thought. I thought it was perhaps a symbol, a bind-rune, of strange glory. I had never seen any architecture as lovely, but it suggested the magnificence of cathedrals, the moonlit beauty of the Taj Mahal, the strange film sets of Hans Poelzig. I gazed at it with rapt eyes. It frightened the sailors, even the captain. Good! It should terrify the world. In my mind I already saw the strange spires topped by swastikas.

Then we saw **them**. Two meters long with scaly backs and white bellies. They lacked the beautiful Aryan heads and blond locks I was expecting, having fish heads – an irony upon mermaid legends! They had large sharp gills on their necks, and vast cold eyes bulging on each side of their face. They did not like the searchlight, so I do not know their true color, although I suspect it be gray green. Their long paws were webbed and they carried small rods – either some wonder of Aryan science or some artifact of eldritch wizardry. Seven of them approached our craft. Our captain began shouting orders to leave. One of my guards silenced him. I sat in the radio-telegraphy device and with all my might I sent my thoughts toward them, the mantra of Aryan power that Dr. Webb had recorded almost a century before in Greenland: *"Ph'nglui mglw'nafh Cthulhu R'lyeh wgah'nagl fhtag!"*

The Fischvolk convulsed with surprise (or perhaps laughter?). One swam up to our submarine and placed her hands on the craft. I could hear her voice in my mind. She sounded like a schoolgirl I had known in Berlin decades ago. The cruel girl that made fun of my defective eye and my short stature. Her German was almost without accent.

"Dreams from the sunken City enflesh themselves in Hydra's spawn. The will of the Old Ones High Priest is undying!"

Evidently this was a counter-call or litany. I did not know what to project, so I improvised, "Sister of the Folk, I greet thee! I am come to reunite the Aryan people. The ice-moon is long gone and we are preparing to scourge the land of inferior races."

Again the Fischvolk convulsed. I felt waves of humor. This must have been much-longed for news.

The ambassador asked me, "Who are you that thinks of Great Cthulhu? "

"I am Herman Mueller of the Thousand Year Reich!"

More laughter.

"A thousand year Reich! That must be a long time to your people."

"We have heard that you are undying."

"The dreams of the Old One's High Priest are undying. They were old on Yoth of the Green Star, they were old when they seeped down to this world and you were not yet monkeys. But we are not undying. I am

173

scare three thousand years in age. What do you want Herman Mueller of the Thousand Year Reich?"

"I am come to reunite our Folk."

The Fischvolk spasmed again. I grew afraid. Could it be that this was like the false tryst where Helga had humiliated me? Did I hear **her** voice from this bacitracin abomination? I formed in my mind the emblem of the swastika, surely that would kindle their Aryan blood, even it was as cold as the sea.

She sent a Symbol back to my mind. A nine lined star that cut the surfaces of my brain to visualize it. Their language or dreams was alive! It crawled in my mind. These were not Aryans. These were not humans. These were not on the same level of being as we were. Our thoughts are not alive our words do not crawl and thrash in the same darkness of our skulls. I heard the sailors around me scream. My guards had drawn their guns.

To kill themselves!

To free themselves of the single Symbol, or Word or living Nightmare that she had placed in the machine. Into our heads. Then she smiled at me and sent a second picture. A silvery and rainbow colored wall of the Cthulhu chapel in the city below. I could see that it was covered in hieroglyphics, a long verse that she had simply thought the first word of at me. I could feel that first killer thought dissolving like sugar in tea. It was flowing down my brain and through my spine into my blood. It was water that burned. It was stone that blew with gale force. It was space that sucked time into it. It was the aethyr, the merest breeze through which great Cthulhu sent his dreams. It was changing my flesh. Taking something from it, and adding a great deal more.

"Would you like to be part of the Million Year Reich, Herman Mueller? You could not be as useful as a dolphin, but we love you Herman. Your deep hatred of others, your loathing of inferior races! These are precious things. We would be very amused by your tales of the land world. We think humans make great pets."

The Fischvolk were all laughing. I tried to throw back images of German power. The torch lit parades, the camps of starving men, the V-2 rockets, the Olympics.

And they laughed and laughed.

"I will think another Word for you little Herman. It will change your eyes so you can see us. Would you like to be my husband little Herman, we are building up the city on the land. We have to say certain things in the air at certain times. Your children would be" – she paused looking for the idea – "your children would be rich. We gave Marsh gold, the Japanese want platinum, the humans of Cornwall simply want fish. We are very giving. We would make your children very long-lived. You would say immortal."

I felt her Love. And it was great and deep and alien. It was like the ocean and it consumed everything. It was like hunger, or fire. It was like the feeling I had listening to Hitler's speeches but raised to the millionth power. And I knew my intentions, my will, my self – didn't matter in this equation. Then she drew back. The telepathy-radio was smoking. The air of the sub was filled with smoke and the smell of blood and the moans of the dying. I thought of killing myself, but I imagined my Word-changed flesh might not die. At least not die in the way I meant that word.

In the movies it is always at this point when the mad scientist throws a switch to destroy his laboratory. I knew nothing of what switch to throw. I couldn't blow up the *Cthulhureich*. The other submarine was not in sight. I swept the searchlight this way and that. The Fischvolk have begun *tapping* on the sides of the boat. It is a game. A game for the young ones of a few thousand years age. All of our dreams are nothing to the dreams of Cthulhu. The outcome of the war, the Thousand Year Reich, nothing. Of course they hadn't moved their city when the U.S. government shelled them. We don't move a tent because a few mosquitos come along.

My dream to be part of something bigger will be fulfilled. Just not the savior. A jester, a butler, a servant to a trusted dolphin perhaps.

(For Arnold Federbush)

The Litany of Yith

Brett Davidson

"There was one thing I did not tell you," the Time Traveller said to me in a sharp whisper, though the room now was empty but for us. He had dismissed the rest of the party, but he had kept me aside just as I reached for my coat. His tale was, as you have seen, remarkable enough, with its marvels piled precipitously high. A further complication, another chapter, would bring the whole edifice crashing down in the eyes of the skeptical reader. This he knew, and this he had not told to the others. For some reason of his own though, he felt that he could tell it to me – perhaps because, as a visitor to England, I might be somewhat lest prejudiced than the others. I hardly think that it was my easy credulity that made me a prospect; he was no panderer and would have been insulted by the gaping acceptance of a naïve listener. Nor would he have wasted his time with a man of great scientific expertise but so rigorous as to be ossified in thought. Instead, I think he chose me because I was a student, a man young and curious but no child and with my curiosity brought into focus by the disciplines of scholarship – or so I flatter myself.

"I only found it after I had returned, wedged in the frame of my machine," he explained. "Some opportunist perhaps jammed it there while I was… *distracted* by the hostile fauna. It appears that not all of that community were, are, will be predatory brutes."

The object looked like a bundle of seaweed and indeed as I took it, I smelt the brine and felt its rubbery texture and the grit of a sandy encrustation, grains of which scattered across the small table between us. The weed though was simply a binding and I could see that it was not merely tangled, but deliberately knotted. My host had already undone some of the knots, enough to be able remove the contents and presumably examine them, but he had thrust them back within. "Take a look at it," he said, and leant back, watching me intently to observe my reaction. "Remember that I know that you are an expert in strange documents and-"

I interrupted him: "Hardly an expert, I would say. I-"

He raised a hand impatiently. "A *specialist* in philology then. In any case your professor vouches for your talent and tells me that you promise to take up his own position in time. Now then, think of the great range of human history, the diversity of tongues and scripts that you have read and think most especially of the tale I have just told and of the still greater reaches of time that I have crossed. Imagine the years, that desolate beach under the cooling sun and the *inconceivable* gulf of time that stretches between now and that age."

I did indeed, and I shivered a little as I gingerly untied the remaining knots to reveal what they held. It was a manuscript, as he had implied, though it was not paper. Whatever it was, it reeked awfully and I peeled apart its layers while trying to have as little contact as possible. When I saw what was written on it, I jerked back as if burned. It was unbelievable.

"Aha!" my host said with a grim smile. "You see?"

I did see. The words on the slimy sheets were quite clear: they were in a recognizable Latin script and their language was English.

"This is impossible or it is a joke," I gasped.

"I assure you that it is neither."

"But how could this be?" I asked.

"It simply is. Read it," he insisted.

Carefully I spread the first sheet out. It was in fact more of a membrane than any kind of paper, almost translucent, and the smell of the sea and something else unidentifiable made it something quite repellent – and yet its text made it utterly compelling. I began to read...

"No," I said throwing it down. "I can accept your story up to a point. I saw your model machine vanish and I accept that it was no trick; I saw the flowers that you brought back and I know that they are like none that bloom today, and so I am forced to believe you – to a degree – but this, this is too much."

"Imagine *my* shock," he said calmly, "when I discovered that I was neither the first nor the last man to reach the end of time."

I took a deep breath and bent my head once more to scan the lines.

***

... at one moment I was in my accustomed theatre at Miskatonic University prepared to expound on some point on... well, I forget what now. My life in that time was like a nauseous recurring dream; the same events occurred over and over and seemed sometimes disturbingly but vaguely familiar and then disturbingly unfamiliar and yet forever cyclic. Such is the life of routine.

Then I found myself awake and my senses were sharp, far sharper than they had been. They were also far stranger and I was dizzy and overwhelmed at once with a suite of such novel and odd impressions so that I was unable to make sense of my surroundings or even myself. I thrashed about in a panic, hitting things while sharp jabs of sensation that might have been light or sound stabbed back at parts of me painfully until I began to realize that I had senses and this pain was in fact information of a sort. I forced myself to be calm and eventually an impression of looming masses of clustered points that I think had colors – though what colors! – became comprehensible as something akin to sight. Things did not *move* quite as I thought they should, but *displaced* themselves and they had no edges but rather flickering, coruscating borders as the points became brightly near or dimly far so that they had the immateriality of clouds and yet the glittering rich saturation of a jeweled tapestry, though one that hung not in a flat plane, but in three or more dimensions.

My other senses were just as problematic. Touch was uncertain, felt more as a mixture of the haptic and the vibratory. My skin seemed to have no suppleness and little sensitivity to texture directly, but nonetheless I could feel the slightest currents in the air tugging at bristles of hair and when I stroked my fingernails over even the smoothest surface it rattled as if I dragged a nail across a washboard.

This sense of "touch" seemed to overlap my hearing, which in turn seemed like an inversion of my breathing as if a church organ used to producing notes drew in air and felt them instead – but really I find both touch and hearing, like sight, purely arbitrary terms in attempting to describe my sensorium and there were other senses such what I think is an awareness of magnetic fields that are entirely beyond description in terms you would understand. There is then no way that I can fully explain to you what and how I felt and "saw"; suffice it to say that I saw, I felt and I heard. Smell at least functioned normally, though under the current ambience, I wished that it did not.

What then did I make of what I perceived about me? *That*, I must tell you, was horrible. The tapestry that I beheld about me was quite as full of chimerical grotesques as the imagination of any medieval weaver, and then some. Indeed, the person who had woven this must have eaten some ergot on their bread. Let me describe to you the beings I saw about me and challenge your credulity: To begin, think of a praying mantis, but altogether stouter, almost beetle-like and with many more legs which are as elongated as a cricket's. Imagine a plethora of ruffles under its abdomen beating ceaselessly at the air with the sound of a gentle rhythmic whisper. Imagine at the end of its thorax not the rather elegant valentine of a mantis's head as we know it, but two swollen orbs restlessly swiveling, their surfaces elaborately and densely studded with jewels like those famous Easter eggs made by Fabergé. These, I supposed, might be their eyes, compounded of myriad lenses like the eyes of insects, or they might be something else entirely. Its arms, folded in a sanctimonious posture like the insect I have recalled did not end in hands, but what seemed like the aggregation of the contents of a kitchen drawer. The frivolous thought occurred to me – as if trying to distract me from an insidiously dawning realization – that if one were to patent a practical replica of such an appendage, one would have a universal tool that one could carry in one's pocket and which would make all others redundant. I imagine a lot of money could be made from such a mimetic invention, but I am no practical businessman.

I made to scream at the sight of these weird things and to my utter shock I could merely hiss while I felt as if my whole face came apart. Sharp plates spread and scraped like the opening blades of scissors, but far more complicated in their action. Suddenly the thought that I had repressed came upon me with its full, dreadful force: I had metamorphosed into a nightmarish efflorescence of hinges and articulated blades, and I was one of them!

I trembled and thrashed violently – or rather I attempted too, because my hosts had shown some foresight in restraining me with some silky elastic cords. I could move – somewhat – but I could not raise myself and I could not reach out beyond the slab on which I lay. This was for the best, considering the harm I might have done myself, but it did not bode well. Was I to be straitjacketed permanently? That may well be the case, because how else could I explain my circumstances except with a diagnosis of insanity? I was at once vividly aware that I was a *beetle* and yet I remembered too my life as a man. There is an old parable told by Chuang Tzu of a man who awoke under a tree and remembered that he had dreamed of being a butterfly, but then wondered if that he was in fact a butterfly now dreaming that it was a man. It is an interesting conundrum, but one I would rather have saved for discussion in the common-room than had as first-hand experience.

Am I then a man or am I a beetle? Be that as it may, I see things before me and they affect me and I must deal with them and thereby control the affect that they have on me. Let me then describe what I see and what I make of it and you may judge for yourself. This is the rule I imposed upon myself in order to maintain my grip upon reason, and as I demonstrated personal restraint, I needed no external restraint and the cords were released and eventually I was even permitted to wander with guidance throughout the domain of these creatures, learning as I went.

My discoveries since my first awakening have not been particularly cheering. I surmise that the time is very late in the history of the world. The sun is nothing like the warm and dazzling orb you know. It is instead as swollen as a tumor and colored the red of embers. It squats on the horizon beyond an oily sea, lethargic and unmoving while a cold wind blows eternally. Limp black vegetation of a kind like seaweed and like tough leather in texture drapes itself in layered heaps of gray dunes that undulate down to the shore where feeble waves roll in with tubercular gurgles and mutterings. Now and again I see things like gigantic white crabs roaming the littoral zone. Perhaps they are distant, degenerate cousins of my hosts.

I would say that this earth that was ours is at the brink of its ending, but it seems to me that there will be nothing so dignified as an end. Instead, its dreary senescence will be forever, pointlessly attenuated.

My hosts have made their redoubt here by this beach. As befits their insectile appearance, they are as busy as bees. Unlike bees however, they do not store honey, but knowledge. Their civilization transcends is dubious and meager environment and is, I must say, a grand and noble thing – all the more so because of the hopeless conditions outside. They are industrious and ingenious, filling their vaulted basalt halls with extravagant machines as visually delightful as the innards of a pocket watch, all composed of glittering crystals and concentrically oscillating movements that quivered and sang like crickets on a spring evening. *Contra* the sound of the lassitudinous surf, it is quite reassuring.

These beings – we – have a name of course.[5] *We* who call *ourselves* the Great Race of *Yith* – the name is the sound of a scraped claw and an indrawn breath – have an interest in those who are themselves interested. According then to their interest they have devised a technique by which they are able to open "windows" into time. As the recent demonstrations of Hertzian waves in our own time have shown that information can be propagated across space without physical contact, the Great Race have earned their sobriquet by collecting information propagated across *time*. In particular the information that they are able to collect is *thought*. To further my analogy with this wireless telegraphy, as a transmitter-receiver of Hertzian waves may be turned in various directions and it may be tuned to send or receive at different frequencies, so too do their transmitter-receivers of thought may be directed to different

---

[5] If I ever find myself back in the age of the bright sun and in a university, I swear that I will devote myself to the study of pronouns and tenses in all the world's languages and perhaps I will be able to write a more consistent account of my experiences, but to avoid ridiculously compounded clauses, I use "us" to denote both humanity and the beings of the future and now to denote whatever time I may be writing of and leave it to the reader to deduce from context which I am describing.

eras, and by exquisitely fine tuning, establish a link with an individual mind to passively listen to it, or to actively influence it. It is by this means that my thoughts have been drawn from my brain at the end of the Nineteenth Century have been drawn out and projected into the brain of this beetle-like creature at the end of the earth's time.

I am by no means unique. The Great Race are nothing if not systematic and there are many more like me, all organized and put to task quite logically. The people and beings they have dredged up from the past to relate their own histories all by and large people whose vocations it has been to do so. It is an efficient approach, I must say, though they make appropriate boogie-men for scholars: "Do not study too well," one could warn, "or the *Yith* will snatch you out of your own head and reveal to you the logical end of all scholarship. Instead have a drink, blur your senses and forget what you have read today." Perhaps that is why so many scholars are drunkards.

The scholarship of the Great Race is very sober, and not cruel. I was eventually led from my place of awakening to my place of education or assimilation and their attitude was quite solicitous. They do not treat me as a prisoner or patient, I who am so strange here, but more as a kind of prophet, a madman touched with holy visions such as the Russians call a *yurodivy*. I soon learned, as I have mentioned, that I was far from being the only one such; rather there are many of us, all with our own particular mania and we were all indulged avidly. I prided myself on my fluency in languages when I was… human, but my grasp of the language and scripts of these beetles came to me too fast even for someone such as me to have acquired by learning. Instead, it seemed as if the knowledge had always been latent within me and its resurgence merely required the triggering effect of what passed for pen and parchment. This seemed common to us all and accordingly, we are each given a booth in what I shall call a scriptorium, furnished more or less comfortably or at least of shape and form that is convenient to my body (I do not imagine that any man of the Nineteenth Century who was not a professional contortionist would agree however!).

My acquiescence to apparent confinement and labor may seem odd, especially to the self-styled humorists among the scholarly community (of which there are too many), but industriousness is the cardinal virtue of these creatures and they find work to be its own comfort. I was not therefore unhappy, instead I experienced the constant pleasure familiar to any writer in being able to give coherent form to my otherwise chaotic thoughts. It may seem trivial to write of the minutiae of mundane human life, but to an intelligent beetle, the most ordinary to us is the most enchanting and I could indeed, as William Blake wrote, see infinity in a grain of sand – or in my case, the items on the menu at the Café Royale, the results of horse races printed in *The Times* and remembered chatter over whether mauve or yellow was this year's most fashionable color. Imagine if you will a child given a jigsaw puzzle with an infinite number of pieces; rather than being daunted with the prospect of a seemingly futile task, the child is overjoyed with the assurance that they will never run out of pieces to connect. It is not so much the pieces that matters as the sense of "eureka" in perceiving their assembly into a pattern that gives pleasure. Such it is in the scriptorium.

My mania or my task is the late Nineteenth Century, but of course I am not alone and my many companions each have their own niches. To one side of me there is an individual whose speciality is Byzantine mosaics – which is surely an appropriate metaphor for our general creation – while on the other side there is an astronomer and fifteen places down there is a being who claims to be transcribing his conversations with Machiavelli. If this is an asylum and we are all mad, then it is not without its pleasures. For instance, many supposedly established historical facts are undermined or even contradicted by these chronicles. Is it because of the wandering capriciousness of my imagination, or because the witnesses who were present at these historic events have knowledge beyond what has been officially recorded. History as we read it has been written for the convenience of the victors after all and one wit of our time – the time I imagine as such, I mean – has described the official register of the peerage as the greatest work of fiction that the English have ever produced. Then too there are many, many portraits of Renaissance popes and cardinals with their "nephews" standing in the background which anyone can guess to be their bastards. In these latter-day texts, such guesses are confirmed. Time travel, I realized with some *schadenfreude*, would be an excellent tool for blackmail.

There are also the accounts of the "past" that are to me actually the future, and reading those, the pendulum of my emotion swung far away from anything like amusement; if the past is scandalous, your future is terrible. There are revelations of such depths of human depravity I could never have imagined in my worst nightmares that have filled me with utter despair of humanity itself. I can write the word "Auschwitz", but while I could warn you of it, I am so overcome with sickness that words fail me. It is knowledge such as this that makes me wish that I am indeed mad, because sanity would be still more awful knowing what I know. Better one man be mad than an entire world! If the latter were the case, then oblivion and the wasteland outside is all we deserve!

These secrets that I have seen – trivial, enlightening, amusing and awful – imply collectively an insidious dread. There is declared in the fact that what I had once thought to be the future is written as *fait accompli.* It is but one immense mechanism, a clock made of gears grinding upon gears, regular but inflexible and lubricated with a slurry of the blood and ashes of men and none of us can ever be anything more than tiniest complicit wheels within it... and having become the past, that awful machine has seized itself to hold in complete unalterable stasis all of the atrocities committed by man and nature. As the thousands of beetles scribble ceaselessly in their booths, I imagine that for each of them there is another life fixed within that machine, a tiny figure stretched and broken upon a tiny cogwheel.

Fleeing the thought of the bloody rigid clock, now and again I wander in that wrack of a world under the red sun and I become glad of my protection. Strange as I am, strange as my companions are, we have a purpose and this damp twilit shore has none. I do not spend long outside before scurrying back under cover to write and write some more in the stone hall filled with singing machines and busy scribes. Do you see then why I found my strange embodiment ultimately reassuring and comfortable?

This then is the peculiar entwinement of horror and hope that I have found at the end of earth's time. I found a strange wonder and nobility in the task of the Great Race, which I shall now describe to you. Observing one scribe, I was shocked to discover that it was working on what I could describe as an historical kaleidoscope. As it scratched away at its plaque, I leant over to read and found to my shock that this creature was *chronicling the work of another scribe.* Tremendously intrigued by this I rushed to another and then another in the same row. All of them were writing of the experiences of scribes stationed far in the past relating events still further in the past, leading further and further back into time to the distant prehistory of earth when the Great Race occupied other bodies. According to their descriptions they were even stranger than the coleopterous things that toiled here: they were roughly conical creatures that looked like a bouquet of lilies and clawed fronds mounted in a long pleated skirt that moved it about by a kind of rippling or sweeping motion – at least that description is the best I could make sense of their words and sketches. In any case, as I peeled back one strange mask to reveal another, that mask too lifted to reveal still more weirdness. Those creatures were themselves recording the events of a time and place that could not have occurred at any time on earth and could only have happened upon a planet of another star still further back in time.

The project of the Great Race not one of idle curiosity. They would not employ their great resources to reach through time if it were of passing interest. It is, I have come to realize, their creed, the eternal mission to record. This great litany upon which they collectively toil is the very essence of their being and purpose. Unable to achieve immortality in any material form, they leap across the aeons in mind, and at each stop, they establish what we could call a civilization and which they think of merely as a base camp or reference tableau. They have, I realize, created a great encyclopedia in time and space, its chapters scattered across the eternal cosmos. At any point, on any world and at any era they can open a page on another and read it as it is being freshly written!

These *Yith* know of course the horror both explicit and implicit of which I have written because they write of it too in the manifold recursions of their encyclopedia. It is their technique for crossing time and space extra-corporeally that is their liberation from determinism – provided that they keep moving and never linger in one era or place. Now, they sense that their time here has ended and more and more often their compound eyes swivel away from the dark, vermillion-lit sands of this terminal beach and towards the stars twinkling distantly in the sky above. They are ready to flee once more across the reaches of space and time, these cosmic nomads. Already they have selected their recipients and measuring them to fit. They will take with them the sum of the earth's history as they have trawled it up from the past, and the history of all their previous abodes too. When they can carry no matter, of course memories are the most precious things to them and they are nothing if not thrifty. Perhaps they are even honorable in doing so, ensuring that mankind, a brief player in the theatre of life before collapsing into decadence and oblivion will be remembered in still more distant aeons. The fact will remain thought that we are but a medallion, a bauble in the forever-reaching hands and they have far brighter prizes.

Perhaps before they leave they will cast my consciousness back to my human vessel in old, vanished Arkham, but I think that I do not want that. I will beg, if it is worth anything, to go with them and leave this manuscript for some other traveller to retrieve should there be someone in some age who can contrive to replicate their traversal of time with a machine of his own. Who knows? Perhaps it will find its way back to an age not dissimilar to my own where my words can be read.

***

The tale of the temporal abductee came to its tentative end, but that is not all I have to relate. There is one more thing I must tell you, which is the reason why the Time Traveller held me back me and myself alone to hear his secret. The author of the manuscript who said that he was not sure if his name was real or whether it was some convenient fiction to cover an amalgam of the temporal gleanings of the Great Race was not so confused as he thought. He had a name and that name has cast a shadow across my life, bringing an awful dark enlightenment to me. It will inspire me to take up the reins of scholarship at Miskatonic University and there teach, and to delve into the libraries in search of records of similar cases of which I have already heard rumors. It will lead me to teach and its echo will wake me from my dreams at night relieved to be released from them but ridden with doubt and trembling and it will lead me to drink too, no doubt, so that my days become like a recurring dream, familiar and unfamiliar at once.

I know this because the name on that manuscript was my own.

All revelations have implications. I have learned my strange fate, and with it by my own circuitous route, like the Time Traveller I have learned the fate of humanity too: futility, decadence and extinction. I will work as a scholar to recover, preserve and transmit knowledge, but all the while I will know that will be as if I am shoveling water up a hill, because our mere human institutions will crumble into dust, our dying exhalations will be swept away by the wind and memory of everyone who has ever been will be doused with the last spark of consciousness of one of those barely sentient Eloi of which the Time Traveller told.

Can this fate be changed? Now knowing, can I perhaps to take up some other vocation or perhaps like that writer friend of the Time Traveller, pen warning polemics in the hope of diverting the progress of history towards another, better end? I would have grasped at that thought as hope if I were the man that I had been just one night before, but now the uncertainty of an unmapped future horrifies me too.

I am in a bind and I see only one way out of it. I may be mad, I may be fated to madness, I may be fated to madness because I have convinced myself of it. However, I will follow the path that I see laid out for me into the shadow of determined fate and I will stumble along under the gloom of fate and the haze of dread and drink and be tripped so that I stand upon that beach under the dying sun. There will be the solution to my dilemma. There I will see what lies beyond the end of the last sentence of that manuscript. These beings of *Yith* have recorded our history and surely they cannot but have judged us by such horrors as this "Auschwitz" – whatever that may be – and I wish to enter a countering plea in the record if I may. The Time Traveller, as we have arranged, will follow me by means of his own machine and together we will meet the Great Race on the everlasting eve of their departure and we will speak to them, we will beg, even. "Do not forget us," we will ask. "You who live forever take care to remember us and do not let mankind live in vain. Let me continue to be one of the authors of your Litany."

After that, I do not know what will happen, and I will be free at last of that awful, bloody machine of fate that my future self has, will have seen. Perhaps I shall see a new sun upon another shore. I can only live now with the conviction that this better future *must* be possible.

The Third Oath of Dagon

Robert M. Price

1. *Multi-Culturalism*

"I tried to reason with the fellow. Just because the Divinity School has adopted an interfaith curriculum doesn't mean each and every class session has to take that approach. You just cannot approach Christian theology that way if you're describing its history and development. I don't know *what* they're doing over in Systematics these days, though I'm sure we'll all be obliged to find out at the next faculty meeting." With that, Professor Oldstone took a listless bite of his sandwich. He had made it himself this morning in his campus apartment, but he had already forgotten what he had put in it and seemed almost indignant tasting it, as if someone else had failed to get his lunch order straight. In reality, it was something else, much else, that he found distasteful. And it left him feeling quite full, for he had had it "up to here." His lunch partner, a younger man, Simmons from Pastoral Counseling, tried to smooth the older man's ruffled feathers.

"Ben," he said, "I know I haven't been here nearly as long as you have, so I haven't seen such drastic changes over the long haul, but the student might have a point. Many scholars would agree with him that Christian history has a pretty dark side lying beneath its progress. Its triumphs have been made at the expense of other faiths. It didn't happen in a vacuum. Our own state..."

"You mean Commonwealth."

"Uh, yes, Commonwealth. Anyway, it's seen more than a little repression, even persecution, of rival faiths in its short history."

"Paul, I'm guessing you aren't thinking of the Indians, or the Quakers."

"You're right, Ben, I'm talking about 1928."

"Everybody's talking about 1928 these days, it seems." In fact, the campus of Miskatonic University was locked in perpetual tension, up to and including legal and governmental actions back and forth, all relating to the events of eight full decades earlier. For all that time, all parties had been content, some said forced, to maintain a discrete silence. Everyone had his own version of the events of those far-off days, some speaking of them as if they were but yesterday's news, and in general no one could quite agree on what had happened, nor who was at fault. It appeared, as far

187

as the newspapers knew, that the federal government had launched a full-scale naval attack on the coastal town of Innsmouth in Essex County. The effects of the attack had been felt more broadly, with some damage to property, in adjacent Newburyport and Ipswich, but swift assurances, not without threatenings, from the government agents had served to choke off further inquiry. Sleeping dogs lay until 2003, during the aftermath of the 2001 al-Qaida attack on the World Trade Center in New York ("that Babylonish burg" as Professor Benjamin Oldstone always called it). Old suspicions had led the local arm of the newly formed Homeland Security Department to cast a squinting eye upon Innsmouth, which had of course rebuilt itself in the interval, repopulated largely by the same stock of Polynesian islanders with whom the native Yankees had long ago intermarried, eventually sacrificing their Caucasian identity. As conspicuous foreigners, complete with an alien religion, and with an inherited tendency to keep to themselves—and especially when one recalled the destruction of 1928—they had begun to look newly suspicious to their fellow New Englanders.

The people of the shadowed town protested at what they considered unmotivated government surveillance, even profiling. And as far as terrorism was concerned, no one could prove that the Innsmouth townspeople of eighty years previously had ever been inclined to it. After all, it was the U.S. government, not the Innsmouth population, who unleashed terrible weapons of mass destruction offshore. The real historical parallel, urged the eager lawyers representing the aggrieved immigrant town, was the case of the abused American Indians of the nineteenth century. That and the internment camps for innocent Japanese citizens during World War Two.

Massachusetts public opinion was divided, and the issue dominated discussion both among pundits and pub dwellers. The notoriously liberal Commonwealth government, sovereign within its territory, had acted unilaterally to appease the complaining ethnic minority, offering what some regarded as a token gesture of opening up college admissions, with accompanying financial aid, to Innsmouth youth. It was easy to extend the policy even to private institutions by manipulation of tax laws and their application to these latter schools. Innsmouth freshmen, hitherto present only in tiny numbers even in the town's own junior college and adjacent Aylesbury State College, began to make their surprisingly voluminous presence known at Harvard, MIT, Wellesley, and Amherst, with the largest single concentration, surprisingly to some but not to others, on the maple-shaded campus of Miskatonic University in the sleepy town of Arkham.

Miskatonic's student body was very liberal, very open and accepting, especially of a new victim population. No one objected to the new Kanaka Student Union, nor to the hiring of a chaplain representing the obscure faith of most of the Innsmouth students, the Order of Dagon, though some complained this ought to be classified more as a Masonic Lodge than a religious denomination.

One of those who made this protest was, of course, Professor Oldstone, the senior professor of Historical Theology in the Divinity School of Miskatonic, a private university whose sponsorship by the Congregational Church (long since merged into the ultra-Modernist United Church of Christ) had been nearly forgotten. But not by Professor Oldstone. While he was perforce tolerant of whatever cultural mutations might manifest on the University campus as a whole, he became quickly and fiercely defensive whenever the invisible wall between the rest of the institution and the Divinity School threatened to be breached. He raised an eyebrow but no protest when the school authorities allowed a group of students to form a Wicca coven on campus and even to gather in their circles on nights of the full moon in the quadrangle. Such things, he thought, taking his long view of school history, would one day be seen as childish embarrassments dismissed with a pained laugh by succeeding generations of alumni.

Oldstone had not expected to find many of the Melanesian-derived students of Innsmouth in his classes, especially in view of their attachment to the Order of Dagon, which was apparently the sole religious allegiance available in their decaying town. What interest could they have in the Christian ministry, even as flexible as that profession had in recent years become? The professor would have welcomed Asian students. Over many years he had come to enjoy very greatly the many foreign students who came to Miskatonic's Divinity School as the fruits of overseas missions. They were invariably zealously pious and intellectually keen. Laotians, Ugandans, wherever they hailed from, they always added spice to class discussions. But this was quite different. Dr. Oldstone found his head spinning when, just before the new Innsmouth controversy, back in 1997, the Governing Board of the Divinity School had transformed the character of the school by declaring it an interfaith institution, welcoming not merely the whole smorgasbord of Protestant denominations, but the full panoply of "biblical" faiths, Judaism, Christianity, and Islam for starters, then, some years down the line, Buddhism and Hinduism, too. It was a matter of redesigning the curriculum and the library holdings and, of course, hiring new faculty trained in these other faiths when time came to replace the older generation of instructors. The septuagenarian Oldstone was the very

189

last of the old guard, though he now numbered as "veteran" colleagues a handful who had joined the faculty only a decade before. There was as yet no "Dagonite" professor, but Oldstone felt confident there would be one, probably one of the very students he now had in class, before many years had passed.

"You see, Ben, the 1928 government raid can very naturally be considered just the latest round of an age-old conflict between the Israelite and Philistine faiths, the same old conflict we read about in the Book of Judges and First and Second Samuel."

"You use too many words, my young friend. You may just call it the old conflict between good and evil, God and Satan."

The younger man's eyes darted around, alert for busybodies, and he reflexively brought his finger to his lips: "Shhhh!"

Lowering his voice, Professor Simmons continued, "Look, I know it's not exactly my field, but don't the latest Old Testament, er, I mean, Hebrew Bible, or First Testament, or whatever they're calling it now, don't they say that there never was any exodus from Egypt, that the so-called Israelites were really just one more group of Canaanites? Didn't they share the same language, the same myths, essentially the same religion? Aren't you just perpetuating the same old rivalries? Isn't it our business to make peace between rivals?"

"That is your calling, Paul, counseling, reconciliation. It's all to the good. But we can't whitewash what's really going on here."

"Which is…?"

"Well, for one thing, this noble 'experiment in ecumenism' is nothing but a last ditch effort to save the school financially. A cheap stunt to widen the student base. As such, it'll never work. But the better it *does* work, the more the Christian presence here will shrink. And in either case, the Miskatonic Divinity School the founders envisioned will be gone."

"Your facts are correct, Ben, I know. They always are. But why *not* make virtue of necessity? Maybe a genuinely new thing can emerge under the sun. Other schools have tried it. Maybe an interfaith seminary here will help bring Christianity into a new future in a new millennium. 'Behold, I am doing a new thing.' It's exciting, no?"

"But there's my other hesitation," Oldstone said, aiming his pin at the other's balloon. "This Innsmouth cult hasn't got any connection to scripture, even if I could take you seriously when you try to make it look like Philistinism was no more heathen than Presbyterianism. These Innsmouth kids, God bless 'em, and I mean the real God, the God of Israel, their religion is just some South Sea Islander paganism. They worship a big fish or something. It's an old-time totem cult. They pray to some idol to get a lot of fish in their nets and to find buried treasure. They just dress it up with a name or two plucked from the Bible by the old Innsmouth sea traders who brought them to our shores. That's what I was trying to get that student to admit in class this afternoon when he started insisting I give equal time to his own faith. But he suddenly got pretty quiet. Just quoted scripture to me. Said that soon enough I would know his faith by his works."

2. *Logocentrism*

"Jesus Christ is the Logos, the Word spoken of by the pre-Socratic Heraclitus. That Word was conceived as the principle of proportion in change, the principle by which change was kept from becoming chaos, by which stability was kept from becoming sterility. The Stoics learned it from Heraclitus, then Philo from the Stoics. From thence the secret of the Logos passed on into nascent Christianity. The hero cult of Jesus of Nazareth seized hold of the idea, and Christianity grew to be about something beyond a man. The Word became incarnate the moment Christian thinkers decided that a man, Jesus Christ, embodied this principle. Over the centuries Christianity has purified itself, and the Western world, from one degree after another of superstition. It had to, by nature, because at its heart was the very principle of rationality itself. When the Unitarians separated off from our Congregationalist forefathers, it was this that they understood: the Word came to us through Jesus Christ, but it transcends him. This is how Christianity gave birth to science, and why science eventually turned on its parent, discarding Christian faith as a butterfly supercedes its chrysalis. Some of us do not believe such a departure, such a total break, was necessary. There is more to faith than reason, and, rightly understood, the two do not collide. As theologians we want never to forget that. We hold faith in the one hand, reason in the other. We should never have to find ourselves forced to yield up one or the other."

A hand shot up. It was the talkative student from Innsmouth, a Mr. Wasserman. Oldstone felt mildly conflicted. He groaned a tiny groan, surmising rough weather ahead. But at the same time he smiled, because it always delighted him when students, of whatever opinion, wanted to join the fray. "Yes, Mr. Wasserman?"

"Sir, don't you think reason is a little, well, over-rated? I don't know what you think about Nietzsche, but…"

Oldstone replied reflexively, "He bears a mighty name! Christianity's critics are its greatest friends. It owes them the greatest debt. And much is owed to Nietzsche. Continue."

"I have to admit I'm surprised, Professor Oldstone! Nietzsche means a lot to us, too. To the Order of Dagon, I mean. The transvaluation of values, and all that. And the Superman who is to make Homo Sapiens a relic of the past. Nietzsche seems to think that the way of Dionysus is at least as worthy as that of Apollo. Ecstasy and the will to power!"

"Mr. Wasserman, do you mean to say this is the creed of Dagonism? To tell you the truth, I'm as surprised at your interest in Nietzsche as you are at mine! How on earth does he fit into your tradition? Educate me, and us, Mr. Wasserman."

The man rose to his feet. Sitting down, his face and figure had seemed almost indistinguishable amid the slouching mass of perpetually drowsy students, but now he could be seen clearly enough. Wasserman had baby-pink skin, hinting at youth, but he was nearly bald, suggesting simultaneously the newborn and the old man. His eyes bulged comically, so much so that Oldstone immediately found it difficult to take seriously what the ridiculous-looking figure was saying. But he listened as his singular student spoke.

"Actually, it's *Reverend* Wasserman. I'm Order of Dagon chaplain for Miskatonic, but I'm enrolled as a student in the Div School, too. I've had the training the Order provides, but in view of the new situation here at Miskatonic, we all agreed it would be best for me to learn more about the Christian churches, too. They haven't been open in Innsmouth for decades, you know. But we live in a wider world now. I'm sure you agree."

It made sense. He was no mere student, then.

"Then it's a special honor to have you with us, Reverend Wasserman! I hope you'll feel free throughout the semester to ask any question that occurs to you. And to enlighten us with your own point of view. Will you do that?"

"It's good to know you're so open-minded, Professor. But for the present, I'd mainly rather listen and learn. If you don't mind." His lips were flabby and wide, and it was difficult to read their subtleties, but Oldstone thought he caught a hint of a grin, even a smirk. He continued with his lecture.

"Nietzsche," the Professor said, "denied the centrality of reason. That's essentially what he meant by the so-called Death of God. There is no objective truth, never was. All so-called truth is metaphor. In our day, this insight, if you want to call it that, has been taken much further than

Nietzsche would ever have expected. In our day we have reached an epistemological stalemate in which all viewpoints are deemed equally valid--or *in*valid--since each can be judged only by criteria internal to itself. There seems to be no common ground for us to occupy to look objectively at the claims of opposing views. The result is what you see in this school: a kind of Affirmative Action of competing beliefs. Equal time for every sect and opinion. Knowledge has become politicized, which is to say knowledge has become power. Not that knowledge makes one powerful over the ignorant. Rather I mean that in our day the orthodox opinion seems to be that "knowledge" *reduces* to power. Any claim to knowledge, we are told, amounts simply to a bid for power. Nietzsche would have understood that. Maybe he was the prophet who spoke the truth before his time, after all."

Another hand went up, this time one of the younger seminarians. "Pardon me, Professor Oldstone, but did you say this Nietzsche guy said God was dead? I thought that was a joke. I read it on a T-shirt once, and on the back it said..."

"'Nietzsche is dead.' Yes, I heard the same joke. But Nietzsche meant it quite seriously."

"But what did he mean? How could he dare to say it? How could a mere human know that?"

"Good question, my young friend. Certainly no mortal mind can fathom God. It is going too far for us even to affirm that God exists as a being like ourselves. As far as we can know, there is no being out there named God who observes our theological debates and is quietly cheering for his favorite side in the argument. That's idolatry. You have to grasp that God-language is what we call a 'language game,' a system of expression appropriate to the discussion of certain questions of morals and meaning, to be employed like numbers in math. Beyond that, it just doesn't make sense to say much."

Reverend Wasserman, the Order of Dagon chaplain, just could not resist a comment. "Maybe we can speak of a God really being dead, Professor. Some of us think you can. And such a God may not stay dead forever."

3. *Phallocentrism*

As the semester proceeded, Professor Oldstone heard less and less from Reverend Wasserman and precious little from the other Innsmouth students, of whom he eventually realized he had surprisingly many. They were all quite bright and tested quite well, though of course it would be their term papers that told the tale. For non-Christians, so far, they seemed to understand the basic doctrines of the faith pretty well. They hadn't been reared with Christian catechism, and it was interesting to see them trying to make sense of difficult chestnuts like the divine trinity. Their own faith, the little he understood of it, seemed to lean more toward polytheism. No surprise there. Such was true, after all, even of many Western-educated Hindus.

But the thing that puzzled him the most was the fact that several of the Innsmouth seminarians were also on the Miskatonic football team! This was possible only because the Div School, traditionally an ivory tower exclusively set aside for graduate students, had been combined with the undergraduate Department of Religion as another in a series of Draconian cost-cutting maneuvers. It meant that his classes harbored many undergraduates, and it was a challenge to teach effectively to both levels at once. But he had learned. In any case, you did not often think of ministerial students as gridiron aficionados. Would they not have to spend most of their precious weekends on church fieldwork assignments, acting as youth directors or pulpit supply in dying country churches? How then to squeeze in the pigskin and its time-consuming demands? Well, maybe it was just his age that made him cringe to imagine the effort required.

Dr. Oldstone had never been one for spectator sports, or for sports of any kind, but he began to attend some of the home football games with other Ivy League schools, just to get a look at some of his ostensibly pious students in action, slamming against their padded and helmeted rivals. There were several Innsmouth students on the team who were majoring in other fields, too, but how odd that their religion students should be among the most natural and powerful athletes! True, circumnavigating the campus, they possessed an odd and ungainly gait. But there was no sign of it when they began to dash with lightning speed among and between their opponents on the field. And when they took their helmets off for a cool breeze in stray moments, it was interesting to see how their sparkling pates possessed not even the stubble of hair the other students, with their buzz-cuts, still possessed. By now Oldstone had come to feel a sense of reluctant pride in these students of his, heathen though they might be. None had given him any reason to dislike them. The peculiar ecumenicity of the situation ill-pleased his traditional tastes, but that was the doing of the administration, not that of the students. And it didn't appear to be going badly in any case. Maybe it was a good idea, the trend of the future after all. The only mildly discordant note in all this was that the Reverend Wasserman had stopped attending class. Perhaps his parish duties were too demanding, or maybe he judged that he had learned as much as he needed to know. He was still occasionally to be seen about campus, though, and Oldstone would wave to him.

It was, then, with a note of displeasure that he noticed one chilly Friday night in early November, on his way to the Hoag Library for some late research, that the lights in the gym were ablaze and the music blaring, and the large-lettered sign out front proclaimed MIXER WELCOME FOOTBALL TEAM. No real syntactical structure there, but the banner implied the involvement of some of his religion students in what he deemed untoward activities. He swerved aside in his course and made a detour into the brightly festooned building. No one seemed in charge, and there seemed to be no program. There was recorded music blasting from the speakers, and a suspicious odor of beer mingled with the pungent reek of drugs was everywhere. The lights were shifting colors, all focused on a central dance floor, surrounded by a perimeter of shadows. And the shadows were in constant, wriggling motion, almost as if some creature of unimaginable dimensions writhed beneath a black veil. But it was no such thing. Here, too, Professor Oldstone ventured cautiously and, as his eyes adjusted, he witnessed just what he feared he would see. Suffice it to say he realized that there was as little separating the pious from the sinners as there was separating the male from the female forms huddling on the floors of the gym, the locker room, and the showers. After a quick circuit of the place, Oldstone turned and left the place without a word. Nor did he ever say anything about it to a soul. But he remembered what the Reverend Wasserman had said, some weeks before, about the Dionysian ways which his religious denomination seemed to advocate. It was none of his business. No one had appointed him campus morality policeman. But he was beginning to think maybe retirement would not be so bad after all.

The holidays passed, and, as he listened to familiar carols and watched favorite Christmas movies on television, Professor Oldstone indeed wondered once or twice whether the Innsmouth sect celebrated any version of the Nativity and concluded he would rather not know. But once he returned to campus with the New Year, he saw that perhaps they did. For it turned out a number of the Miskatonic women students were pregnant and had in fact made a covenant to have their babies together and to raise them together as far as possible. This was odd, though not unprecedented, but Oldstone somehow knew there was another shoe waiting to drop. It fell once it became known that these mothers-to-be were all new converts to the Innsmouth Dagon sect. An odd means of evangelism, the Professor thought. And he knew good and well it all stemmed from the Football Mixer a couple of months before. And then it emerged that similar pregnancy covenants were popping up on several

New England college campuses, in every case one of the schools where the Miskatonic team, filled with agile Innsmouthers, had visited to play.

4. *Eco-feminism*

Professor Oldstone ordinarily did not care to delve into "feminine" matters, as the drug store rubric had it. But he had to admit he was eager to get a peek inside the Women's Health Center, newly and suspiciously staffed by an influx of Innsmouth women students. But he knew he could not come up with any plausible excuse for going there, much less investigating. He decided he must be satisfied with waiting to see what the stork might bring.

But as things turned out, he didn't have to. Late one night, early in the new semester, he had a visitor to his office, attracted like a moth to the lone light visible. It was one of his students, one who had never said much in his class, specifically his Radical Reformation Theology course, but who had plenty to say now. This fellow was plainly Asian in origin, a diminutive but heavily muscled figure, with an oddly tinted complexion. He sported little hair, and his black eyes were squinting beads shadowed beneath beetling brows. Not unhandsome if one bracketed conventional Anglo movie star standards. The face and body followed their own authentic symmetry, and he was accordingly a prime sample of his kind. But what kind? Without thinking twice about it, Professor Oldstone took him for one of the Innsmouth students, of which there were yet more this semester. He should have noticed the fellow did not carry any of the handful of Innsmouth names: Gilman, Sargent, Shipman, Waite, etc. This man bore the tongue-twisting appellation of Ah-Poh Vankh-arek. It turned out that he was from Myanmar, or Burma, as one preferred, from the plateau region of Sung. His name, peculiar even for Burma, marked him as a Tcho-tcho tribesman. Not surprisingly, Oldstone had never heard of them.

"I'm actually a Pre-Med student. I'm just taking your course as an elective. I wanted to get to know you. I thought you might be able to advise me, since you've dealt with these Innsmouth students. My girlfriend was an English major and an agnostic like me. I was raised in a tribal religion back home, worshipping gods you'd never have heard of. But a little scientific education from the missionary schools weaned me away from that. I came here to study Western medicine. We got along fine at first, even though our backgrounds couldn't be more different. I was seriously thinking of popping the question. And then I found out she had gone with her room mates to a football team mixer last November. She slept with some jerk there, and now she's pregnant. Obviously, it was over between us at that point. But it's gotten so much worse that I feel I need to pursue the matter."

"What on earth happened?" Professor Oldstone shifted in his chair, almost failing to notice his leg drifting off to sleep, he was so intrigued by what his student was telling him.

"Now she's a different person. She's involved with this Innsmouth guy, ugly son of a bitch named Bill Bacharach, and she's even converted to his crazy religion."

"Ah, his religion!" Oldstone said, suddenly even more eager to hear what the young man had to say. "Can you tell me more about that?"

"Not much, I'm afraid. I only know it seems kind of like the one I was raised in, which is pretty difficult for modern people to believe. I mean, I guess I can see how the native Innsmouthers believe in it. They must have been raised in it as part of their original Polynesian culture. That's where they're from, isn't it?"

"That's my understanding," the old scholar replied, in a tone which conveyed, "Your guess is as good as mine."

"Well, let me tell you, Professor, these people really believe it. That's for sure. But what I saw with my own eyes, I'm not sure *I* believe!"

"Saw? What? Where?"

"I had to get access to their pregnancy clinic. That's what it's become, you know. And only for them. Everybody else's been hustled out. There were a couple of protests, but the administration kowtows to the demands of the Innsmouthers. Thinks it owes them something. I knew I couldn't just stroll by for a visit, but I knew there must be a way to get in and have a look for myself at what was really happening. It wasn't hard to convince the late-night custodian that I was new on the staff and to let me switch shifts with him. These guys aren't exactly Dean's List. More like 'Dean's Corners List,' if you know what I mean, sir."

"Damned if I don't! Go on. This is fascinating! You're a real researcher, by God!"

"I did my best to mop the halls and tidy up, until I found a locked section. The place is bigger than it looks from outside; connects with what I thought was still part of the campus art museum adjacent to it. I thought I was stumped but then remembered that the janitor had given me his keys. I guess they just hand them off between shifts. So I went through key after key, figuring it would be the newest of the bunch, which it was. I started peeping into rooms, expecting to find the women asleep. I didn't know if I wanted to see the girl I had been dating. But I just had to know. I did see it, but I still don't know. What to make of it all, that is."

"Can you describe what you saw?"

A distinct catch, a note of discomfort crept into the young man's voice then. His beetling brow furrowed, which made him appear even more potentially menacing.

"Well, at first, I thought each woman had a bed mate. Not a room mate, mind you, but someone right there with them in the same bed. But I brought my flashlight nearer, not wanting to shine it in anyone's face and wake them up. The sheets had fallen to the floor on account of all the motion. Each girl appeared to be hooked up with some sort of bladder or translucent sack, and fluids were rapidly pulsing from it into the sleeping bodies of the pregnant women. Their abdomens had taken on a degree of the bladders' translucency, and you could see the fetus right inside! You could see them receiving whatever the stuff was that was entering the womb from outside. And their little eyes were open, bulging. Intelligent, I would swear. *Watching* me, I swear!"

Professor Oldstone really did not know how to react. The lad's story was so outrageous as to cast doubt on his sanity. But somehow the piece, precisely for its crazy shape, seemed to fit the puzzle all the better. Something occurred to him.

"Er, you do think those things you saw them connected with, do you think they might be *alive*?"

"Um, I guess I'd have to say I just *hoped* they weren't. Because… because, if they *were*, I, uh…"

"Young fellow, did you ever hear of a *shoggoth*?" The other shook his head, in a bit of a daze brought on by his reflections. "Miskatonic's Antarctic expedition of many years ago reported finding something on the order of fossilized bacteria, though on a much, much greater scale. There were also peculiar, cloudy objects frozen into solid blocks of primordial ice, easy to miss at first, as they possessed little more color than the ice itself. When thawed out, the material that constituted them, whatever it was, simply drained away, then sublimated. Our zoologists didn't know what to make of it, but then, of all people, old Jenkins, long gone now, of the Medieval Metaphysics Department, said he had read of such entities in certain old books housed under lock and key in the Hoag Library. He said they were called 'shoggoths,' which sounds like it ought to be a Hebrew word or name but isn't. Anyway, the same word came up again in certain interviews the federal authorities had with the Innsmouthers they placed in internment camps after 1928, the ancestors of the people that are making such a ruckus these days, and of the Innsmouth students we have on our campus.

"If the outlandish things my nightmares are telling me about the Innsmouth crowd are true, I think that perhaps what you saw is a type of shoggoth, and that each one is set up to augment the genetic material passed on to these women by the Innsmouth boys they had sex with."

"Professor, I'll have to say the explanation's stranger than what it's trying to explain, but I'm not ready to rule it out. When I got over the initial shock and disgust I felt, I shone my light around the sides of the bed and saw that these sacks of stuff weren't connected to anything else. They couldn't have been equipment, machinery. And they were connected to the women's bodies organically. There were just some kind of stalks or limbs entering their mouths and vaginas. I'm guessing the one was injecting nourishment, the other genetic material. The fetuses didn't all look the same—almost like different species, all more or less aquatic."

All of a sudden it looked as if an evening seminar had convened, for now the doorway was crowded with a group of the well-built Innsmouth athletes, the one in front leveling a gun, the next one holding up a rope as if on the point of binding something, or someone, with it. Ah-Poh recognized this one as Bacharach, his rival. One of their nearly indistinguishable voices piped up, in almost a croak, "That's pretty good, both of you. I don't know which of you is smarter. But neither of you is as smart as you think."

The professor spoke, sarcastically, heedless of the danger they were now obviously in: "And certainly not as smart as you, Mr. Sargent?" He spared a glance out his office window to see what he expected: a few more of the goons waiting just outside and below. Oldstone held out his wrists. "Well, where ever you are taking us, we might as well go. I have a class early in the morning."

"You're not going to make it to class, professor. But don't worry, we've got it covered."

5. *Post-Colonialism*

It was odd that Dr. Oldstone was not there patiently waiting for the classroom seats to be filled. Everyone had assembled, though that short, stocky Asian fellow seemed to be absent, too. After the usual remarks about how long one was obliged to wait for a full professor as opposed to an assistant, an associate, and so on down the line, serious voices were raised in concern. Something had to be wrong. But then a form filled the doorway, sat down on the desk, and addressed the class.

"My friends, I have not seen you for many weeks, though I have shared classes with some of you. You may know me as Reverend

Wasserman, chaplain on campus for the Order of Dagon. I have just come from speaking with our esteemed Professor Oldstone, and he bids me offer his apologies for his absence. He has suddenly taken ill, we don't know how seriously, and he hopes to be back at the lectern soon indeed. In the meantime, though, he and I would like to extend an invitation to you. The campus Order of Dagon will this very evening be hosting a heritage festival, full of good fun and fellowship. We of Innsmouth, so grateful for the chance you have afforded us to live and move among you, want to enlighten you as to our proud culture and its implications for our common future. I know I'm making it sound like some kind of a civics lesson, but it will be great fun. I think some of you men here can testify to that, can't you?"

Several of the undergraduate athletes grunted an affirmative with knowing gusto. Everyone laughed. A few women blushed. Then Reverend Wasserman dismissed the class after a brief prayer for the quick recovery of Professor Oldstone. Then: "Who knows? You may see him there tonight!"

Wasserman greeted several smiling faces with his own moon face as he hurried across campus to the Women's Health Center. No doors were locked to him, and he strode right through to the back section, paying but little heed as all visible staff suddenly rose to their feet at his hurried passage. He walked on past the rooms which the Tcho-tcho Ah-Poh had searched a night or so previously. The young man's visit had not gone unnoticed, and his eavesdropped narrative to his professor had only confirmed his guilt.

Opening the door of a store room at the very back of the building, the chaplain greeted the bound and gagged forms of Professor Oldstone and his Burmese apprentice. "I hope you are not too uncomfortable, my friends, but you will not be in this predicament for long in any case. Tonight you will leave this confinement for good. You will join the festivities planned for this evening. There will be a traditional bonfire, and the general aspect of the event will be much like one of last semester's pep rallies. But this time you two will be the stars of it. I am going to tell you what will happen to you and why. I do this for one single reason. Professor, you were fair and kind in your dealings with me, and for that I wanted to spare you your role in tonight's ceremony, but my opinion did not carry the day. I felt, then, that I at least owed you an explanation." The man he spoke to was eying him intently, his alertness inspired by genuine curiosity as much as by a desire to discover any details that might help him devise an escape.

Wasserman took a quick survey of the room, then reached for Oldstone's gag. "Nobody could hear you anyway. Er, have they taken you to the bathroom?"

Oldstone worked his aching jaw, then said, "Yes, at gunpoint, but I'm not complaining about it."

"Good. And sorry."

"You know, Reverend, in some societies they used to fete the sacrifice as a king for a day, give him a banquet for a last meal."

"So you do surmise what is to happen tonight." The Burmese's eyes widened.

"I think I do. What I don't have a clue about is why you are planning to do such a thing and how on earth you can possibly expect to get away with it."

Wasserman smiled. "It is merely the difference between today and tomorrow. Today we are playing by man's rules, rules that have become highly advantageous to us. Yours is a civilization of advanced decadence. It stands for nothing. It has lost its way. Its only zeal is to make way for those who would destroy it. Theirs are the rights it would protect. Such an invitation we can scarcely decline. It would be ungracious in the extreme. For many decades we have planned to wipe away your people and your civilization. Eighty years ago, as I imagine you know, we had come rather close to executing those plans. A freakish chain of events temporarily derailed our program. Innsmouth, really a kind of a mock-up stage setting, was destroyed. Government bombs and torpedoes did minimal damage to our true home, off the Devil Reef. The fools had no idea how deeply we had built--and lived. But they had been warned. The element of surprise was no longer ours. Not unless we waited. So we did. For a time when we could count on your help to overcome you. And that we will do tomorrow. When reason abdicates to unreason."

"Are you planning a terrorist strike of some kind? A bomb? A pathogen? And what have I and my young friend here to do with it?"

"Professor Oldstone, I am surprised you, as a theologian, would think in such mundane terms. We hope to usher in the apocalypse. Or to break one of the seals of the apocalypse. What we have done here, we have done in several other places in New England, enough to establish our beach head. We will perform the ritual of the Offering of Death and of Life. To open the way, the blood of the vanquished must be shed. But it must be coupled with the birth of new life, life of the kind that will prevail in the new era before us. This is why we have initiated your females, leading them to take the Third Oath of Dagon. By this, they open their wombs to become as many gateways for the advent of Father Dagon. The birth of their young will coincide with your deaths, and the portal will open. Then there shall be vengeance for eighty years ago. An Arkham for an Innsmouth, an eye for an eye, a tooth for a tooth. You can understand that. I know that you do understand it, for the day you have long feared has come: your white, male, European, rationalistic anthill is about to be ground under the heel of hordes of those you so long oppressed! What you called madness and savagery is about to trample underfoot the castles of your intellect! And your best and brightest will rejoice to see it happen! At least until they, too, are swept away in the same tide, without even time to wonder why. It will be quite a sight! Quite a change! Quite a conflagration, and you yourself shall be the fuse."

Oldstone didn't need the gag. He could think of nothing to say.

6. *Clash of Civilizations*

The athletic field was crowded, mostly by Miskatonic students and various Arkham townies, though there were many present from other surrounding communities, including Aylesbury and Ipswich. Most were soon too drunk to know exactly what was going on. Their jovial hosts from the Kanaka Student Union had seen to it that everyone had more than enough to drink, including a potent rum that no one had tasted before. Something from the South Seas. There was a lot of cheering, as if for a sports rally, though there did not appear to be a game of any kind in the offing. By now no one saw anything amiss in that. But there were cheerleaders, the light of the bonfire reflecting off their naked flesh as they gesticulated wildly, yet in practiced steps that would have done a circus contortionist proud. Indeed, the girls appeared practically boneless in their sensuous movements. Neither did they miss a beat in the strange cheers in which they led the crowd. The mass of half-coherent revelers managed to repeat chains of words, or at least syllables, they had never heard and could not understand. But their pronunciation got better and better with each rote repetition.

The lights of the Women's Health Center were on and remained on. Two hooded and handcuffed figures were escorted out of the rear of the building and up onto a structure built only hours before. They were taken up into what looked like a press box, only there were no lights or visible windows in it. No one really noticed, though.

Professor Oldstone and the young Ah-Poh were able to shed their loose hoods by a few violent head shakes. They had been left to wait alone and were so securely bound, no one felt they needed to guard them.

"This is such infuriating foolishness!" blurted the professor. We're going to get our throats slit as part of some fool costume party, and then these idiots will see that the only apocalypse that comes is when the police catch up with them!" He cursed a blue streak, while the other remained taciturn. Finally he, too, spoke, but it was with a subdued tone, one more of reverence than of resignation.

"I am no longer so sure there is nothing to this but fanaticism and superstition, Professor Oldstone. Ever since I saw what I saw in those hospital beds—it is not easy for me to dismiss it as you do, as some unknown science."

"Nonsense, my boy! It's just like that Manson Family business forty years ago when that crazy man thought Armageddon would ensue if he sent some idiots out to stab Sharon Tate to death. Well, you and I are Sharon Tate, don't you see? And nothing's going to happen except that we die. Unless you have some plan?" This last he said with a hint of hope that he consciously denied himself. He thought he was merely being sarcastic.

"Professor, I believe something is starting to happen out there! Listen!" Indeed, strange drummings with intervals of flutes replaced the chanting. The crowd was hushed, itself something of a wonder given the circumstances. Suddenly, hands appeared and ripped away a bedspread that had covered a window looking down on the field. Someone evidently thought the captives should see what was coming. And something was.

There was a vague image illumined by the bonfire, much like a lowering cloud bank or a wall of smoke. But it appeared more solid than that. It was unstable, seemed to shake as if with a wind, though there was no other evidence of one. All this the two captives saw through the dulling emotional veil of impending execution. But new terror galvanized them when a sudden motion revealed the detail of a scaly and webbed claw. That was enough for Ah-Poh.

"That's got to be their Father Dagon, don't you see that?"

The door burst open, and here came the roughneck Bacharach, holding a knife that he manifestly could hardly wait to use. His face was of a naturally malevolent caste, but tonight it was transformed by religious ecstasy, that ecstasy in which the foulest deeds of murder look like pious sacrifice. He dragged both men to their feet and shoved them out onto the rickety platform. All eyes below were focused on the bulbous apparition looming above them, trying, probably, to discern some stable outline.

Apparently their blood had to be shed precisely on schedule, maybe no sooner than the first woman gave birth to her loathsome spawn over in the Women's Center. So for the moment they had time to breathe. Ah-Poh stared at the thing he called Father Dagon, transfixed.

"Snap out of it! Don't be like one of them! At least die in possession of your senses, man!"

"Perhaps I may do more than that," answered the sweat-beaded Tcho-tcho. I have not told you that I was raised in the line of the high priesthood of the Sung religion. I incurred great guilt by turning my back on it and taking the path to the West. Still, they paid for my education, and my brother took the priestly office. Perhaps, though, our gods have not turned their backs upon me. Perhaps they may yet listen to the sacred summons that I know as well as my own name and genealogy. And they are no friends of the accursed Dagon. Cover your ears, Professor."

That wasn't possible, the hands of both being tied. But he decided he would oblige the man by trying not to listen. Oldstone figured he could do worse than pray to his own God, and he began with the Lord's Prayer. Then he came up with some psalms. He reflected, with a nervous inner laugh, that this way, if they did manage to get out of this alive, the credit wouldn't go to these Burmese gods alone!

Ah-Poh was reciting the praises of his lords Lloigor and Zhar, how they had in the past bested the enemies of the men of Sung, enslaving the gods of lesser nations. He bade them stir from sleep and come to the rescue. He detailed the blasphemies of the devils Dagon and Hydra, and their spawn. He begged his twin deities not to let their foes triumph this day, for their names' sake to vindicate this, their priest.

There was more, but Oldstone was trying not to listen. Still, what he heard had a strange and powerful effect upon him. He began to doze and to dream, but with none of the usual transition. He thought he beheld a clashing of two, no three, vast forms, high above the earth. Occasionally he thought he saw anthropomorphic limbs, sometimes tentacles or crustacean claws. Sometimes it looked as if there were a giant Manta Ray among the combatants. But he felt he was seeing a kind of dream symbolism rather than a real visual representation. Would he see anything at all if he were awake? And like many dreams, it was not clear how long it lasted.

7. *Orientalism*

When he awoke, the first thing he noticed was that, thankfully, he was not tied up. Instead, he found himself in a bed in the University infirmary. As soon as a nurse checked on him and found him rousing, she darted back into the hall. In mere moments, here came a hoard of men in suits. For a split second, he feared it was more of the Innsmouth welcoming committee. Instead, it was a collection of campus security, town police, FBI, and Homeland Security Department officers. Oldstone's was the ease of an innocent conscience, so he welcomed their thronging presence. No different, really, from one of his classes, though usually they were not squeezed into quite so tight a space.

They had their questions aplenty, but Dr. Oldstone was in no particular position to answer any, beyond the narrow sphere of what had happened to him and to his student. Come to think of it, the young Burmese was nowhere to be seen. "Can anyone tell me what happened to my student, er, Ah-Poh-What's his name? If anyone got us out of that mess, it was he."

The police sergeant replied: "He's on his way back to Burma. Said he had made a sudden change in career plans."

"Oh, I see. Well, he's certainly good at what he does."

"Dr. Oldstone, do you know what happened to the Innsmouth students?"

"What do you mean? They're not... dead, are they?" He thought his question might raise dangerous suspicions, but he really had no idea what they meant. What could have happened to the whole *bunch* of them?

"They're all gone. Just gone. You've been out for two days, Professor, but as near as we can surmise, the lot of Innsmouth students must have cleared out of here on signal for some reason. Funny thing is, they're gone from all the other regional schools where so many of them had enrolled, too."

"But there were plenty of other students at that rally, or party, or whatever it was. Surely they saw something...?"

"Sorry to say, not a one of them remained conscious through the thing. All hopelessly drunk. On what, I'm sure I don't know."

"I suppose you sent men to Innsmouth. Maybe the students just all went home. Some holiday we didn't know about?"

"We did try that. They weren't there. And, uh, neither was anybody else. The whole place was deserted. We even broke into all the old tenements with windows that had been boarded up for decades. I don't care to tell you what we found there. There's still a special investigation pending. But none of these students, that's for sure."

Professor Oldstone was actually asking himself whether these young men had been... vaporized or something once the Burmese deities had gotten the upper hand. But that must have been an hallucination, mustn't it? But then, here he was alive.

"Ah, officers, what about the impregnated women? They were all due at the same time, were they not? Did any of them deliver? The

Innsmouth boys were the fathers. No sign of them? No clue from the mothers?"

The head of campus security took his hat off and rubbed his forehead. "That's not a pretty detail, I'm afraid. They all aborted, spontaneously. Don't ask me how. And it gets worse. You may know that most of these young women had previous boyfriends who weren't exactly pleased when their girlfriends left them to shack up with these balding, bugged-eyed foreigners. Well, let me just say, in the wake of this, they've revived the old college sport of goldfish swallowing..."

"But the girls themselves...?"

"In shock. No clear memory. One went completely insane."

***

The next semester started on schedule with no real problems except for the sudden drop in student enrollment. The University missed the extra tuition, but the absence of the Innsmouthers made for less tension. No damage at all had come to the campus during the ill-fated Dagon rally. As Professor Oldstone had suspected, it had been a contest between Principalities and Powers on an etheric level. Something he had no theology to explain.

It was the first meeting of his course on Medieval Metaphysics, a dead course he had decided had best be revived. He was beginning to set the scene historically and culturally. Then a voice interrupted him. It was one of the new religion majors, and he was loaded for bear.

"It is only fair to serve notice, Professor, that if at least half the course is not devoted to the thinking of Muslim savants, I will be informing your superiors and perhaps even bringing suit against the school for betraying its much-vaunted 'ecumenical' policy."

Oldstone shook his head. "Here we go again."

Down By the Highway Side

Paul R. McNamee

Jeb Barksdale waited outside the terminal, stoically ignoring the sweltering Mississippi heat. The wide brim of his Stetson hat kept his neck shaded but he still needed sunglasses to deal with the early afternoon glare. His feet sweltered in their tight, polished cowboy boots. His hand moved to his throat, loosened his bolo tie, and undid the button at his throat. Too damn hot, after all.

The bus rolled in with a stink of diesel and asthmatic brakes, wheezing and squealing to a stop. A faded, mildew spotted sign on the side of the bus advertised "Thrills in Vegas!" A few travelers staggered off the bus, blinking in the sunlight. They all looked rumpled and groggy. One or two lit cigarettes and greedily smoked.

Barksdale remembered those days. They were not far behind him. Cold turkey on the plane, on the bus, in the smoke-free hotel rooms. Nearly leaping out of his skin to get outside where he could smoke. Or hide in a bathroom stall where he could do worse.

Barksdale continued to remember it as worse, not better. He shook his head and turned his attention elsewhere before any craving started. His body was clean now. They kept telling him it was all in his head, now. His behavior and his choices would be his own.

He started humming a Hank Williams tune, and then thought about how Williams had died drunk in the backseat of a car, so he hummed something by Johnny Cash instead. At least Johnny had conquered his demons well enough in the end.

The driver, a short and stocky Hispanic man, finished unloading the bags, took some tips in a callused hand. The arrivals walked off into the Jackson afternoon, muttering about cold drinks, lunches, and their plans for the afternoon and the evening.

The driver eyed Barksdale and his one small suitcase.

"You it?"

Barksdale looked around. He hadn't really noticed. No other passengers milled outside and no one emerged from the air-conditioned building. No one else had arrived to share his lonely vigil. Looking up at the windows of the bus, he saw no remaining faces in the vehicle. No holdovers would be continuing on from Jackson.

"It appears I am," Barksdale said.

"I'll take your bag, sir."

"Much obliged."

Barksdale handed over his ticket. The driver stuffed it in his oversized pocket. He looped a paper luggage tag through the handle, ripped off the claim number and gave it to Barksdale.

Barksdale took it with a small laugh.

"Expecting a crowd?"

The driver shrugged.

"Policy. Besides, Memphis is a popular destination. Never can tell."

Barksdale boarded the empty bus. He chose a window seat in the middle of the bus for no particular reason, other than to watch the countryside roll by. The seat felt cushy for his posterior but with his lanky frame no bus seat would ever be comfortable. When traveling, Barksdale only found comfort in first-class airplane seats, and those days were long gone.

Barksdale gazed out the window, saw a tall man standing outside the terminal door. The thin, tanned-skinned man stood straight as a pine tree. His bus line livery fitted him as royal attire. He regarded the bus with a baleful stare. Then the regal man turned and entered the terminal. Barksdale thought the man must be a bus line official of some sort. Manager of the terminal, perhaps.

The driver shuffled up the stairs. His brown eyes regarded Barksdale in the hanging mirror. Then the engine coughed to life, and the bus rumbled out of the Jackson terminal.

A normal drive up 55 to Canton, Mississippi would have taken a mere thirty minutes. But buses took their time, and summer road construction added to the travel time. Barksdale fidgeted in his seat. He scolded himself, told himself he just needed to get through today. When the fidgeting continued, he told himself he only needed to get to Memphis in a few hours and then he could take it from there. Finally, he reminded himself beyond Memphis there would be money, and whether he wanted sobriety or he wanted substances, either way he had no money for it now. The stint at the Copper House in Jackson had run his last savings account dry.

He tried to bring songs and lyrics to mind. That always helped for distraction, too. Outside the window, old flat rural roads still crossed each other. They had been the major roads before the interstates had arrived. One particular cross road grabbed his attention. Bare and desolate, marked only by one of the largest, fattest girthed tree Barksdale might ever had seen. The gnarled tree threw strange patterns of shade and sunlight on its rough-barked surface. Barksdale almost saw faces in the bark of the trunk. Tortured faces and evil countenances.

Barksdale had been a country singer all his life. He had made a life of it, as ragged as that life might have become. But now a song from his youth came unbidden to his mind. A blues song. He had heard plenty of blues, too, along with everything else growing up in the hill country of Mississippi.

Standin' at the cross road, believe I'm sinkin' down

Peculiar that song should jump in his head after all those years. Barksdale supposed the imagery triggered the memory of the song, but it disturbed him nonetheless. He sure had sunk down. Oh, he had sobriety but nothing else. Was sobriety a great thing when there was nothing else? No more hiding from his mistakes and failures. At least in a haze of booze and drugs he had pretended otherwise.

Bad thinking. Dangerous thinking.

Barksdale's hand reached into his pocket, and his fingers rested on the square metal shape of his cigarette lighter. Damn fool for that, he thought. A smoke wouldn't be far off and after that? He cursed himself for holding on to it after rehab. But, like his pocket knife, he'd owned the lighter since his teenage years. They'd been through so much together. If it wasn't in his pocket next to his knife he got jumpy, felt wrong. Even rehab hadn't erased the sensation.

He swore to himself he'd pawn it off in Memphis, if he had time.

His mind scrambled for other songs, he couldn't find any. His brain had stage fright.

"Hey, driver, sir!" Barksdale raised his voice over the street rumble but did his best not to be too loud. "You got a radio on this bus?"

"Yes, sir."

Barksdale requested a Jackson country music station, and cringed when some pop singer came on and pretended she knew about trucks and twangy guitars. Eventually a few more tolerable songs came into the mix, but most of the songs were still too far from country roots for Barksdale's liking. Still, the songs were perky and proud and almost enough to shake off the dark blues.

Standin' at the cross road, dark gon' catch me here

Almost enough.

The bus turned off 55 into Canton and pulled into a local motel parking lot which served for the terminal. Stops away from the bigger cities and towns lacked dedicated terminal buildings. A few people waited to board the bus.

Barksdale stared out the window, and one passenger caught his attention. A young black man, dapperly dressed in a suit coat and tie, banded fedora on his head, guitar case in his hand. The other passengers lined up their baggage, got their claim tickets and boarded the bus. The man in the fancy hat waited until everything had been loaded and then he talked with the driver. The driver paused, considered, nodded and shrugged.

The driver wrapped the baggage claim ticket around the handle of the guitar case, tore off the stub and gave it to the man separately and left the guitar case with the man. The man stuffed the stub into the lefthand pocket of his suit coat and passed some amount of cash bills into the driver's hand. He tipped the fedora to the driver in appreciation, and boarded the bus with guitar case in hand.

The man shuffled to the empty row of seats in front of Barksdale. He put the guitar case on the aisle seat, and took the window seat for himself.

"That must be one special guitar," Barksdale said.

The young man smiled. "Oh, yes. I never let it out of my sight if I don't have to."

"But I saw the driver hand you a stub," Barksdale said. Suspicion flashed in the young man's eyes. "Sorry. Just saw it out the window. People watching, not spying."

The young man's countenance brightened again. "Yes, well. I do that just in case I need to stow the guitar after all. I will if I need to, but I don't like to. Could be too crowded by the time we get to Memphis. Though, I think we'll be okay today." He glanced around the still nearly empty bus to make his point.

"Will you get your money back of the guitar goes with the rest of the luggage?"

"Reckon not. A little bit of a gamble, but would I be a bluesman if I didn't gamble?"

"Ah, the blues." Barksdale nodded. "Have you been out on the road long?"

"Playing my way up to Memphis," the man said. "Are you a musician?"

"Have you ever heard of Jeb Barksdale?"

The young man thought about the name. "Country music singer, right?"

"Right," Barksdale smiled. Country music fans barely remembered him, never mind some young blues player. He had faded years ago and stayed out of sight and out of mind thanks to his addictions. "I am Jeb Barksdale."

"Well, ain't that something. Mister Barksdale," Thompson began to say.

"You can just call me Jeb," Barksdale said.

"Fine. And you can call me Lonnie." The young man proffered a hand to shake. "Name's Lonnie Thompson."

They shook hands as the bus rolled back onto 55.

"Is there a gig waiting for you in Memphis, or are you going to try busking on the street to drum up interest?"

"Oh, both," Thompson said. "Gotta promote the gigs and if I get extra money in the hat during the day, it's all good!"

"When will you find time to sleep?"

"Ah, coffee and what-not."

"I'll give you some free advice, son. Stay away from the what-not," Barksdale said. "It didn't do me a lick of good in the long run."

Thompson nodded.

"I mean that. You're heading to Memphis to play and you've got a career ahead of you. Me? I'm heading to Memphis because I'm on my way through and maybe on my way out. Now, maybe I'd be on my way out anyway. But the bad stuff's got a strong way of hurrying the process."

"I do understand," Thompson said. "You say you're just going through Memphis, though? Headed to Nashville?"

"Nashville?" Barksdale barked a bitter laugh. "Nashville is a young man's game. Or maybe it could be an old man's game. But a burnout's game? Not really. I'm headed to Branson."

Branson. Barksdale could barely admit it. The place where performers go to die. Well, maybe not die. The place performers went to fade away even more than they already had.

Barksdale saw pity in Thompson's eyes. Anger must have flashed across Barksdale's face, because Thompson dropped the pity and looked away out the window.

Barksdale sighed.

"Yup, it's Branson for me." Barksdale spoke quietly, forcing the anger to go away. "Washed out."

"Does calling it 'the Oldies circuit' make it better?"

"No, no it doesn't."

"I didn't think it would." Thompson gave Barksdale another friendly smile, and Barksdale grinned, too.

"Lots of tribute bands, too. I guess I'll be my own tribute band, until someone comes along who is better at singing me than me."

"If it gets you on your feet and gets you paid, it can't be all bad," Thompson said.

Barksdale thought about that. He had drummed up the gig himself. No agent. No manager. It might have been the hardest work he'd done

211

since he walked away from his father's leather trade and tried his hand at singing for a living. He felt a touch of pride.

"Enough about my fading star," Barksdale said. "Tell me about your blues. What style?"

"Style?"

"Jump blues, Texas blues, Jimmy Reed shuffles, Piedmont, Delta?"

"For a country fellow, you know something about the blues. I'm impressed."

"Now, don't you confuse country boy for country singer. Country singer might or might not know about some blues. But I am a country boy from Mississippi, too. I heard plenty of blues growing up. Not just the records. I watched old men wail out blues on their porches, too."

Thompson nodded vigorously. "That's the way to learn! The records are good to listen and learn but nobody can get you inside the blues like the old ones. They can let you in on secrets."

"There are still secrets in the blues? I thought they'd all be played out by now."

"It's the old men who can tell you how to make the deal," Thompson said.

Barksdale shifted uncomfortably in his seat. As far had he had come, as much as he had seen, as long ago as it had been since he set foot in a church, Barksdale believed in his heart he was a good ol' boy, and he still held an overall belief in a higher power of God in some fashion. Any talk of the Devil made him alternately jumpy, angry or defensive of whatever good faith in God he might have left.

"Now, don't tell me you went down to the cross road and sold your soul to the Devil, Lonnie," Barksdale said. He tried to make it sound like a joke. Could a man really meet the real Devil in the middle of nowhere? Barksdale wasn't sure he wanted to know the answer.

"Not at all! Devil's too much of a trickster and all he does is tune the strings. Spanish tuning! Anybody knows that these days. No sir!" Thompson flashed a smile and a laugh. "Nyarlathotep is the one who tuned my guitar. Not just the strings. He tunes the instrument. See, the devil, you know, he just tunes up the strings, hands it back to you. Nyarlathotep changes the wood, the neck, the curve, the tuners. It all just resonates like nobody ever heard before! Make a lot of people hear your music."

"Nyarla...-?" Barksdale asked. Had he heard the name before? A demon or another name for Satan or some heathen god's name buried in the Bible somewhere he'd forgotten. Or maybe it was one of those voodoo devils. Barksdale recalled some of the odder blues lyrics he'd heard, and he recalled learning some of the imagery was voodoo related - John the conquerer root, hot foot powder, power over wind and sky.

"Nyarlathotep," Thompson said, slowly sounding out the name for Barksdale. "The guitar just vibrates when you hit the right note. Like nothin' you ever heard. Shakes with the whole fabric of the universe."

"Son, I'm just a country singer, but it sounds like you've moved out of the blues and into some hippy New Age shit."

Thompson gave a courteous smile. "I'm just searching for that note, you know?"

"What note?"

"Everybody knows the saying, right? Blues takes five minutes to learn, but a lifetime to master," Thompson said. "Well, imagine the idea on smaller scale. There's a note out there. Somewhere between the frets of a guitar, somewhere between the holes of a harmonica. One note. If you play it, you own it. One note, you make the people cry if you want to. One note, you decide to be happy and they're happy. You want the crowd jumpin' up and dancin', you got that, too. But you need to find the note. Find that note, you'll be as famous as you want to be."

Thompson glanced around, shifted in his seat to get a better view at the back of the bus. After he completed his observation, he turned to Barksdale again. He leaned in close to Barksdale, over the back of the seat.

"I think I know where to find that note," Thompson said.

"Really?"

Thompson nodded.

Barksdale glanced out the window, barely noticing the the sunny day clouding over as the bus rolled north.

"What's this Nyarlathotep look like? Not everybody can say they met the Devil - a devil, anyway. What's he like?"

"Oh, he's all kinds of shapes and things. Could be birds, or mushrooms, or shadows in the woods," Thompson said. "Like the Devil, though, he takes human form when he needs to. Tall, thin black man - African maybe but more like an African Egyptian, your know? Big head, tall forehead. Look right at home you put one of those pharaoh hats on his head!"

Barksdale laughed at himself. He felt nervous. Was he upset about the talk of deals with the Devil? Well, a devil, anyway. Whatever the hell this Nyarlathotep was. The cross road deal story was always just a way to drum up publicity. It might have also been a way to keep other bluesmen off your back. Back in the day, fierce musical competition meant men died in all kinds of seedy fights and disagreements. Sonny Boy Williamson - the "first" Sonny Boy - stabbed to death with a sharpened screwdriver.

Then again Robert Johnson's deal with Satan didn't keep him alive. Someone hadn't been frightened enough. They poisoned his drink, and it took Johnson three painful days to die.

But it was an old story and young bluesmen needed new tricks. So Thompson had created his own spin on the old story. Why not? But it was just a story. And if the young man had talent, he didn't need stories.

"I tell you what. Not a whole lot of people on this here bus. How about you play a song for me, Lonnie? Everybody else, too."

"What if they don't like the blues?"

"Don't like the blues?" Barksdale feigned incredulity. "Then I'll sing 'em some of my country songs after. We're in the South, aren't we? Fifty-fifty chance they'll go for one or the other!"

"All right then," Thompson said. "I'll play for anybody, anywhere!"

Thompson unsnapped the latches on the hardshell guitar case. When it opened a hint of stale cigarettes, spilled beer and a strangely reminiscent damp earth scent reached Barksdale's nose. It took Barksdale a few moments to identify the earthen smell. Mushrooms. Wild woods fungus, earth and rotten leaves.

Although Barksdale only ever strummed a few chords for fun and stage presence, he knew craftsmanship when he saw it. The guitar was a custom make. No brand name or logo appeared on the headstock. Barksdale did not catch a glimpse of any lettering or designs on the body - either back or front - as Thompson pulled out the instrument.

The guitar sported an unusually dark sunburst finish, with bright shiny fret markers. The frets did not appear to show any wear, but Barksdale could sense the guitar's antiquity.

One blemish marred the guitar body top, near the upper edge. Something gray and sickly white, like fungus, with a strange shining black and purple swirl in the center of the blotch. Fungus would have explained the mushroom scent sure enough. The bright, light shellacking had been applied over the blemish. Not as a repair, though. The guitar had never been re-shellacked. It had been crafted and finished over the blemish originally. The blemish appeared fungal and wet under the shiny reflective surface.

"Beautiful guitar," Barksdale said. "But that spot sure is a damn shame."

"It's the mark of Nyarlathotep," Thompson said. "Don't affect the sound any."

Thompson slid an old oversized glass aspirin bottle onto his left little finger. His right hand cupped the guitar strings without aid of a plectrum or fingerpicks. The fingers started a walking descent measure to intro the song.

As soon as the first lyrics spilled from Thompson's mouth, Barksdale understood Thompson's mastery, despite Thompson's youth. The spirit of an old bluesman hovered around the song. Barksdale could feel it, feel the utter confidence in Thompson's performance.

Early mornin', fishin' to get you off my mind
Early mornin' now, fishin' to get you off my mind

"That's it, Lonnie!" Barksdale grinned. "Sing it!"

Thompson smiled, nodded at the encouragement.

But when I got to that creek, lord
Stone sentinels in the pines

An odd direction for simple blues lyrics to take. But Barksdale couldn't deny the words power. He'd heard some haunting blues in his day, but the reference to stone sentinels chilled him to the bone. He was inside the forest, inside the song along with Thompson, and he wouldn't get out until the song finished.

Sticks in the pathway, owls hoot in day
Sticks in the pathway, owls hoot in day
Crows are cawin'
Lord, lord. Bound to lose my way.

"Play that guitar!" Barksdale shouted. "Play that note!"

Thompson's voice fell silent as he let his guitar and his hands tell the story. His thumb worked the rhythmic bass notes while his fingers plucked out a solo - alternately reflecting the melody and improvised notes. With each pause between measures, Barksdale grew more excited.

"Where's that note, Lonnie?" Barksdale teased. "C'mon, we've got to hear it!"

Thompson ran the glass slide up the neck.

And found the note.

The note rang out from somewhere between the strings, someplace askew from the sounding body of the guitar. The note came from nowhere and everywhere, a single note containing a hidden symphonic cacophony bursting out from between the atoms of the air. Barksdale smelled sulphur, saw cavorting demons, strange beasts among cold stars, and colors seared his mind.

An emotional tempest slammed through Barksdale. He seethed with anger, wailed in anguish and wanted to jump into the aisle of the bus and dance for pure joy. The conflicting feelings threatened to tear his mind into pieces. The harmonic frequency of the note carried bone-pulverizing low tones. The note held a siren's song, inviting obliteration on jagged rocks of derangement.

Someone screamed, someone cried. The bus driver convulsed but somehow retained some measure of control. The brakes slammed hard, tires screeched, the bus crookedly swerved into the breakdown lane. Some passengers tumbled out of their seats.

Then the note and its madness faded out at last. The note had only held for one or two seconds. Barksdale gasped in relief. He had been convinced the ringing lunacy would never end.

Except for the idling engine, the bus fell silent.

No one appeared hurt, but they might all have been in shock. Those who had tumbled to the floor stumbled back into their seats.

No one applauded. No one smiled. No one requested another song. No one could look each other in the eye. Everyone retreated into their own silent thoughts.

Barksdale looked out the window. The road signs indicated the 55 and route 82 intersection. They were somewhere around Winona. Droplets of water ran down the dark glass. "I don't recall rain on the radar."

Thompson's looked at the window, out the window, like he could see further into the gathering night.

"No, not at all," Thompson said, his voice betraying a shaky nervousness. "Ain't right. Ain't right!"

The rain hit the window with fury, getting heavier. Thunder and lightning crashed.

Thompson muttered. "I don't think I was supposed to play that note. Not now. Too soon. Time ain't right. Time ain't right!"

Barksdale preferred not to think about that musical note ever again. He had decided it had been the tires. Wheels whining over slight ruts in the pavement. Strange harmonics. Nothing more. His mind wouldn't let him consider the details any deeper.

Barksdale heard wind, and a low throbbing rumble. Trees flailed violently. Barksdale hadn't heard the sound in years, but he instantly recognized it. So did some of the other passengers and panic etched over their faces. The sky darkened as though night had arrived.

"Tornado!" someone hollered.

The whirlwind tore through the trees and slammed into the bus. Windows cracked, splintered into tiny fragments and safety glass still gave way under the pressure. The bus tires on the left side lifted off the shoulder of the road, and then the wind got underneath. The bus flipped and rolled.

It felt like a giant hand had picked them up in an equally large tin can and started shaking. At one point, the bus went end over end.

Barksdale felt soft heavy objects with the occasional hard angle slam against his body. The other passengers. Elbows, knees, chins painfully colliding. His back exploded with pain as he crashed down onto the top of a seat back, nearly cracking his spine in half.

All the fury and movement stopped. Barksdale didn't move for a long time. The sound of howling wind retreated. Barksdale heard sirens in the distance, groans, sobbing and hysterical screaming inside the bus. Too terrified he might shift a broken bone, Barksdale remained motionless until he realized he wasn't one of the screaming people. Surely if he'd broken something he'd be screaming. He stood up, looked up through the window hole.

Someone urged him upward, he clambered over seats and he felt his body lifted up and out through the bus window. Through his daze, he found himself standing on top of the side of the bus. The bus had rolled over multiple times across the highway and had come to rest on its side. Police, fire and other rescue personnel had arrived. Some civilians stopped to help, too. Someone with a pickup truck brought a step ladder, which Barksdale used to climb off the bus. He sat down heavily on the wet ground by the roadside.

Hands put a shiny reflective space blanket around his shoulders. Barksdale glanced up to see a paramedic - one who had helped lift him clear earlier.

"Just take deep breaths, keep the blanket on. The rain's cool. Keep the shock away, stay with us."

Barksdale could not find his tongue. He nodded his thanks and understanding.

The accident scene solidified into reality around him as his shock waned. Red fire and ambulance lights, orange tow lights and blue police lights, road flares and police spotlights lit up the night. He scanned the stunned faces as they milled around the roadside.

"Lonnie?"

Jeb didn't see Thompson. He glanced at the bus and saw no more rescue activity. On the roadside, someone pulled a sheet over the driver. Whether the man had been thrown clear or dragged there to die, Barksdale couldn't determine. He saw no other bodies. Stretchers bore some people.

A face drew Barksdale's attention. He felt a chill. The regal man from the Jackson terminal. The man mingled with the bus passengers. Probably performing the duty of condolences and promises of investigations. How had he arrived on the scene of the accident so quickly? Strange coincidence the man had been in the vicinity.

Barksdale took a long look at the man. Tall, regal. Tan-skinned with a high forehead. A forehead that would not appear out of place beneath an Egyptian pharaoh's headdress. The man's gaze fell upon Barksdale. Barksdale thought the man's eyes flashed in a strange, deep black and purple swirl of sickening color. A trick of the flashing lights, certainly.

Maybe the man would have a roster of passengers, and Barksdale could bring the disappearance of Thompson to his attention. Like the driver, a freak flip might have thrown Thompson clear of the bus and no one appeared the wiser.

Barksdale approached the man, turned his attention briefly to the woods. When he returned his gaze to the crowd of injured and their rescuers, the regal fellow was gone. Out of sight around the back of a vehicle, probably. Barksdale desperately wanted to believe he didn't feel a chill climbing over his soul.

Barksdale grabbed the large arm of a paramedic. The man's hair had grey at the temples and Barksdale could feel muscle under the dark skin.

"Can I help you, sir?"

"Can't find the man I was sitting with. Thompson. Lonnie Thompson. Had a guitar. Would've held onto it to the last if he could have. Young fella. Blues player."

The paramedic's eyebrows lifted.

"Lonnie Thompson?" The paramedic shook his head. "The only Lonnie Thompson I know playing the blues 'round these parts died fifteen years ago. He was young then, but he's long dead. Died young."

"Dead?"

"Shit, sure!" The paramedic gave a rueful smile. "Died around here. Poisoned by a jealous girlfriend, they figured. Classic stuff. Real Robert Johnson, right? Thompson's gal cooked him some cream of mushroom soup. Only it was more cream of toadstool." The paramedic shook his head. "Bus driver kicked him off the bus right around here. Thought he was just another stumblin' drunk. Someone found him by the highway side, called it in. Never forget that one."

"You were there?"

"Shit, sure. Never saw a black man look so pale. Caught his last breaths, but we were too late." The paramedic rubbed his chin with his large hand. "Must be some other whippersnapper lifted the name. Not like Thompson's using it anymore."

"Yeah, yeah I guess. But you haven't seen him?"

"No, no. I ain't."

"I'm worried he got thrown clear or something," Barksdale said.

"I haven't heard anything, but it's a little crazy right now. He'll get tended to."

The paramedic turned his attention back to splinting a woman's injured arm.

A movement at the edge of trees caught Barksdale's attention. The myriad flashing lights and oncoming darkness of night played tricks. Barksdale saw a man running down the embankment toward the woods, stumbling in a drunken, breakneck gait. Barksdale recognized the cut of the back of a suit coat, and a fedora on the head.

"Lonnie!"

Barksdale looked for help, but at the moment other needs held every rescue personnel's attention. He spotted the regal man again. The regal man's gaze held Barksdale's eyes and Barksdale could not deny the shudder convulsing along his body from head to toe. Barksdale looked to the woods, and so did the regal man. And then the regal man disappeared again. Barksdale thought he saw an another outline in the woods who looked like the regal man, too. No man could have traveled so fast.

Someone screamed in the woods.

Barksdale ran into the woods, his vision barely able to pierce the gloom. A rotted log gave way under his foot and he sprawled onto the ground, a stench of mushrooms and rot assailing his nostrils. He dug his lighter out of his pocket. Again, he swore an oath to throw it away but it would need to happen later. He needed the light now.

The log he tripped over rotted as he watched. Sickly white fungus with black and dark purple swirls expanded rapidly over the surface even as Barksdale watched. Barksdale whipped the lighter about, thought he saw movement in the shadows, but saw nothing definitive. Once or twice, the wind soughed in the trees.

And then Barksdale knew he wasn't looking at a log, at all. Somewhere under the mass of consuming fungus, he caught glimpses of white bones, patches of brown flesh both desiccated and wet with slimy moisture. Fungus enveloped the fedora brim as he watched.

Barksdale stared at the consuming fungus, watching its baleful progress, until nothing remained but the left hand suit coat pocket.

After the chaos of the crash, the police statements, reclamation of luggage, transfers, and the overdue departures, the substitute bus pulled into the Memphis bus terminal after midnight. The bus line provided for the overnight stay, and everyone received a hotel room and meal voucher for the evening.

Before heading to the hotel, Barksdale went to the lost and found desk.

The regal man waited behind the counter. He no longer appeared quite so official as a manager. The regal man was just a desk clerk now.

"Can I help you?" The voice held beauty and madness.

"I'm here for a guitar," Barksdale said. He handed over a yellowed luggage ticket.

The clerk nodded, and then spent long minutes in the back room. He returned with a guitar case in hand.

"How long ago did you lose this guitar?"

"I thought you'd know how long," Barksdale said.

The clerk, the regal man, feigned innocence. "Judging from the stub - fifteen years?"

"Got a little sidetracked in Winona."

The clerk double-checked the tags. "The dates and claim numbers match," he said. He shook his head. "Something this old should have been moved along to the auction block years ago! You're lucky."

Barksdale took possession of the guitar.

"I don't know about luck," Barksdale said. "But I'm just a strummer so I don't think I'll be playing anything too fancy. Maybe just enough to get back to where I was."

The regal man gave a sardonic grin.

Barksdale headed out to find his hotel room.

The next morning, Barksdale traded his Branson ticket for a ticket to Nashville.

In the Forest, with the Night

Aaron J. French

We stood in the field, Alex on my left, Kristine and Diane on my right; Jess was in the middle in his black cloak, complete with cowl, a rope tied about the waist. The costume had looked totally absurd when he showed it to me online; doubly absurd when it arrived in the post and he'd put it on. But for some reason, now—out here in the night, with the trees and stars behind him—seeing him dressed this way gave me chills.

Lightning flashed, triggering thunder, and the dark purple clouds mounted toward the big bright moon currently casting its glow upon the forest. The air smelled of pine needles, sap, and musk.

I looked at Alex, whose hand I held, and saw he had his eyes closed. His broad, bearded face and round chest gave him the appearance of a football player. But he was bookish at heart and had never set foot on a football field. He preferred the chair at his computer desk to anything else.

His lips rambled slightly and I knew he was chanting the mantra Jess had instructed us to chant. Jess had plucked the mantra out of that fucked-up book, the one he held in his hands. The book, too, had been acquired on the Internet.

Jess thought himself an occultist, but in reality he was just a single child and high school dropout, the guy who hated his mom and preferred alcohol to attending college classes. It didn't seem likely he'd amount to anything.

Except for tonight.

Tonight he had... changed in the most subtle way.

As soon as he'd put that black cloak on, his eyes had gone bulging and mean, and he looked serious as a heart attack. Once he began reading from that book, I saw him grinning, almost fiendishly beneath the cowl, his voice inflections different, lower in tone, articulated.

The guy was taking all this very, very seriously. I wasn't sure if that was an improvement or a type of teenage regression. Jess spent most his time in the bars around campus, getting drunk and trying to pick up chicks: succeeding in the former, failing at the latter. In a way, it was nice to see him applying himself.

I turned to Kristine, who held my other hand, and she too had closed her eyes, muttering the mantra; beyond her Diane, a bit taller, appeared in the same state of concentration. Both girls were attractive—

Kristine a little full-figured, Diane tall and thin. Blondes. This was the second time I'd ever met them outside of class. Both were in Professor Vadalini's course on Quantum Physics. A specialty seminar, being held this semester only. Jess, Alex, and myself—all fans of the outre, and science nuts too—were taking Dr. Vadalini's course, even though we didn't need the credit.

But I still couldn't figure out how the hell Jess had convinced these girls to come and do this. It really made me chuckle. I mean, this was the first time Jess had *succeeded* in picking up chicks!

I seemed to be the only one with my eyes open. Even Jess, where he stood in front of the circle, his head bowed reading in the book, had his shut. How the hell that was possible, reading with closed eyes, I had no idea—which led me to believe he was simply making shit up, and not actually reading.

I also wasn't repeating the mantra. Why the hell should I? This was all a silly fantasy for Jess and Alex. I didn't subscribe to their occult bullshit. Modern Darwinist and proud of it. But they had managed to get the girls to come. That was cool. I hoped we'd all get drunk afterward.

My attention returned to Jess, listening to the steady stream of weird syllables and unusual phrases pouring from his mouth. None of it English, nor a foreign language I could recognize. It sounded like gibberish.

***

After a while, I started getting angry. There was something about all this that just wore on my nerves, like sitting through a fucking church service. I'd done enough of that as a kid. Mom and Dad basically hogtied me every Sunday and dragged me to the car. There had never been anything more offensive to me in my youth.

Then I noticed what Jess was doing. Every couple of beats his eyelids would flutter, just enough for him to glance at the page. So *that's* how he was "reading" with his eyes closed. No magic, as usual; just sneaky illusions. I smiled, relishing my own sardonic humor. Funny to see them taking this all so seriously. It showed how much smarter I was.

A sharp movement—a shadow, but different—caught my attention in the nearby pines. I turned, peering across the grass to where, yes, a shape was slipping in and out of the trunks.

I squinted as more moonlight freed itself of the clouds. I spotted a creature, an animal, a deer perhaps, hiding, ducking, dodging. I'd have called it a deer and satisfied my apprehension but for one thing: it had octopus tentacles—like the stems of an undersea plant—trailing along behind it.

Jess's stream of alien speech oozed into the night, filling the air. I glanced at each of them—Jess, Alex, Kristine, then Diane—and saw that none had noticed the creature, their eyes still closed, lips muttering.

Maybe I had imagined it.

Nothing to be afraid of.

But when I looked again toward the screen of trunks and shrubs lining the patch of grass where we stood, sure enough the creature was there, now stationary, half concealed behind a pine trunk, its face glaring out. It wasn't a human face but something like a crazed demon: an angular jaw, nostril holes, high, bony brow. Its eyes: wide, yet slitted, bright red.

Staring at me—

But wait... *was* it?

Why not staring at the others?

Then I realized—

The creature had noticed my eyes were open.

I hadn't closed them like everyone else.

I had *looked.*

Now whatever weirdo shit Jess had summoned—from whatever crazy-ass freako source on the Internet—was here, staring at me. The Laws of Science be damned because I was fucking seeing it, *right now, in reality*, and no amount of blinking could remove it.

Suddenly it took flight, wings, more like gauzy sea fins, hoisting it up through the canopy where it thrashed among the branches. A moment later it broke free, soaring like a star into the night sky.

"Holy fuck!" I screamed.

I couldn't help it. The sight was so shocking, so terrifying, that it knocked out my normal capacity for self-control. My body thrummed like a drumhead, and my heart was tapping out the marching beat of Notre Dame. I was sweating, and for Christ's sake, I think I might have pissed myself—

Jess's eyes snapped open. He looked demonic. "Will you shut up? You are fucking up the ritual."

"But look!" I pointed to the sky.

***

Alex, Kristine, and Diane opened their eyes; because they were facing the same direction, with Jess facing toward us, they all saw it. Strangely enough, neither of the girls screamed—but Alex did, a hoarse, male cry—and for some reason that was worse. I glanced over at Kristine and Diane and saw them gazing skyward, eyes bulging, mouths agape, teeth apart.

We no longer held hands.

The link had been broken.

The creature became more visible, although its jerking movements made getting a clearly recognizable image impossible. Round, larva-like body; viscous wings; clawed hooves; and that face—horrible, with buggy eyes and sharp teeth. It compared to nothing I'd ever seen in my life.

Jess wheeled, lifting the cowl back off his head. I couldn't see his face when he screamed but the emotion in his voice was petrifying.

"Night Gaunt!"

I had no idea what those two words meant.

But as I watched, paralyzed, the creature came swooping down out of the sky, descending like a nuclear missile to the place where the five of us had gathered. I saw it close up for a second, and I marveled at its waxen, fleshy body and its fecal, primal reek, before its snapping claws closed firmly around Kristine, lifted her off the ground, and carried her off to the stars.

Diane screamed: shrilly. I screamed, Alex screamed (had Jess screamed?)—fuck it, we all screamed.

The creature—is Night Gaunt what Jess had called it?—flew clutching Kristine over the clearing.

With one sharp clench of its sharp teeth and bear claws, and with an excruciating *crunch* that made me want to vomit, the poor girl exploded in a spray of blood and bone. Chunks of gore rained down, thumping against the grass.

The Night Gaunt then circled overhead, screeching a triumphant cry of mayhem and rage, and within seconds was diving toward us again hungry for more—more death, more blood, more carnage.

We scattered, fleeing like roaches from the light. Alex and Jess went left, and Diane and I went right. By chance, the creature followed them. The consolation was mitigated when a scream traveled up over my head. The Night Gaunt had caught another; again the crunch, splash, and the scream was silenced. Distant behind me, recognizable thumpings...

I could no longer emote or feel upset; I was numb. Whatever sadness I experienced over the fact that one of my longtime friends was most likely dead was relegated to my subconscious. We escaped into the trees, running up against a small, narrow ditch. I managed to hurdle it, but Diane lost her footing and went down. The scrambling of her limbs was followed by a shriek of pain.

"Please, wait!" she cried.

I was roughly ten feet ahead of her. My nerves were shot and my adrenalin was pumping. I could no longer experience *fear*, per se, but rather a madly driving *push* to run, run, run. I could see the outskirts of the forest ahead, which led to the cars, to the street, to civilization, and safety.

***

"Please..."

She was back behind me. Should I leave her? Should I go? Or should I...

I turned and there she was lying in the rocky, weed-choked ravine. Her face was black with dirt, her legs bent unnaturally behind. She reached to me with a clenched and tortured fist.

Christ, she's hurt.

I had the flash of a memory, of accidentally hitting a cat with my car in the neighborhood I lived in with my parents as a teenager. It had been my first car, and the poor cat had come out of nowhere. As I looked back in my rearview mirror to see it twitching on the asphalt, a voice in my head said, *You did that, it's your fault. Now it's your responsibly to make it better. Go on—help!*

But I hadn't helped. I was afraid, for one thing, of its bloody fur and twisted body; and for another, I didn't want anyone knowing I'd hit it. I'd been speeding and my parents might've taken the car away. So I drove off, leaving the cat in the road. But I never forgot.

I squatted on my hunches, taking Diane's hand. Her skin felt icy cold. I pulled slightly; she groaned.

"How badly are you hurt?"

She looked at me with glazed eyes and nodded. "Shin, ankle..." she said. "I sprained it. What the hell was that thing?"

"No time to talk." I wedged my arm beneath her, attempting to move her upright. When I had her standing up, both her arms around my neck, and mine at the small of her back, I couldn't help but grin. I was her knight in shining armor.

We turned back into the forest and I heard Jess's voice raise up through the night...

"No... no... noooooooooooo!!!"

...followed by terrible screams, and the savage wails of the Night Gaunt, and then finally the end, silence.

Were they both dead now? Did it even matter? I imagined myself floating in a tiny cloud, into which nothing could penetrate, and outside of which nothing was real, like being in a dream.

Diane nudged me. She wore the pleading, frightened countenance of a child. *Save me*, her expression said.

"Get us out of here, Tom."

Her use of my first name brought me back to reality. I didn't want to die here, not like this. *Stupid Jess!* I was really going to miss him. I tightened my grip on Diane and started off into the trees.

It came up behind us almost instantly. Diane started screaming and digging her claws into my neck. The pain made me move faster, but her added weight impeded the escape. I had to struggle to battle through the dense shrubs and foliage.

The Night Gaunt kept at our backs. I sensed it more than saw it; heard it, too, screeching like an eagle, diving in the treetops and snapping branches. I wanted to rescue the poor girl. Hell, I'd wanted to rescue that cat years back. But sometimes situations are cruel. Things go badly and things get worse, and then survival is what matters.

The Night Gaunt dropped through the branches directly over our heads. It screeched, and Diane echoed its piercing cry. My heart pounded as I attempted to hurry us forward. No use; her weight was too much.

I saw the Night Gaunt lunge at us and without thinking I shoved the girl into its gnashing claws, falling back onto my butt.

It gathered her greedily to its bosom, claws enfolding around her. I smelled the thick putrid stench of its hide. Wings beat the air and the last thing I saw was her face—her horrified, pleading face, stretched like an O—as the Night Gaunt launched itself up into the canopy and disappeared.

You did that, it's your fault. Now it's your responsibly to make it better.

My stomach sank, but this wasn't the time for shame or regret. I could hear the Night Gaunt making quick work of Diane, could hear her blood pelting against the trees—which meant it would soon come back again. I had to move it—*now*.

I got to my feet and started running back through the forest. I felt blind, running along a dark tunnel with no distinguishing light at the end. The only hope was my car, my escape back to the "real" world.

I ran with everything I had.

Eventually I reached the edge of the woods and came in sight of the dirt lot where we'd parked. I'd been running so long my whole body burned and itched. My legs felt like jelly.

I gasped and panted my way through the screen of trunks (was I sobbing too?) and made a break for my Honda. The girls' car stood darkly beside it. And there it would stay, too.

At some point the Night Gaunt had backed off its pursuit, gliding instead high above the treetops, keeping watch. Tracking me. I could still hear its beating wings but couldn't tell where it was.

With rubber fingers, I reached into my pocket and retrieved my car keys; dropped them; retrieved them again; got myself in the driver's seat and closed the door, blocking out the forest and the sound of the Night Gaunt's wings. I engaged the ignition. So far, so good. I reversed and backed onto the highway.

The road seemed empty as my headlights cut through the night, paving a swath of dark asphalt. The cab smelled faintly of Jess and Alex, which I found vaguely disturbing. The hum of the engine lulled me.

"Oh Goddammit!" I screamed suddenly, slamming my palm against the wheel. This all felt so crazy—I didn't even know if I was going in the right direction. I kept moving: anything, even getting lost, was preferable to the forest, the death, and the Night Gaunt.

I depressed the button to roll down the window, felt the cool rush of air, and stuck out my head. Listened. All I heard was the engine and the wind. The sound of beating wings was gone.

I turned on the radio, a classical station—Strauss, I believed—and drove. Kept driving till the lights of town appeared. I recognized where I was finally and took the corresponding road to my downtown apartment.

I parked, went in, and locked the door. The interior was silent. The Night Gaunt flashed before my mind's eye, and I switched on the light to make it vanish. Earlier, before leaving to perform Jess's hare-brained ritual, we'd had a few beers here in the kitchen; the empty bottles stood where we had left them.

The horrible incident had left me feeling queasy, so I threw on my pajamas and got into bed. I had to leave the light on, though. I tried to sleep but kept tossing, turning, seeing Diane in the gulch reaching for me, and Kristine carried into the sky to be obliterated, Jess and Alex's awful screams, but most of all… the terrible, beating wings of the Night Gaunt.

My thoughts ran erratic; my body tingled with nervousness and fear, and I sweated even though there was a chill. Should I call someone? The police? Would they believe one word I said?

My stomach formed knots at the thought of police officers standing at my front door, and I groaned as I rolled onto my side, then onto my stomach, but nothing could put me at ease. I was tortured.

I got up to peer out the window, searching the stars and clouds and moon, looking for the beast.

Where had it gone?

Suddenly a mental lightbulb went on.

I returned to the kitchen, grabbed a beer, and plopped down at my desk, switching on my laptop. I signed onto my email account and scrolled through my messages. A month ago Jess had sent me a link to the place where he purchased the goddam book that caused all this. That seller, I decided, was the person to contact.

I found Jess's email and followed the link. It sent me to eBay, a seller named *mythosdealer93*. I clicked the name and saw a picture of a gaunt, austere man with black hair and pale skin, wearing a tuxedo. In his profile picture he stood before a ruinous building beneath a sunset sky. It said location Bali, Indonesia.

Who the hell was this joker?

I searched through his available items: books, mostly; several creepy little bronze statues; ornate mirrors, hooded cloaks, a dagger; even a miniature stone altar.

"What a bunch of freako shit..." I murmured.

Mythosdealer93 had a seller rating of ninety-nine percent. I considered, with a chuckle, a negative review I could write: "Terrible seller! Beware! Items summon otherworldly beasts that will eat you!"

I clicked on the Contact Member link and wrote a brief paragraph explaining who I was and what had happened. I hinted at the Night Gaunt but kept it ambiguous in case there could be a court case in the future. But I described how my four friends had been gruesomely murdered and ended the message with, "I blame you for all of this," then hit SEND.

"That ought to get his attention."

Not a minute later I heard the notification ding that I had received an email. My heart leaped into my throat.

"Nah-huh, no way." Probably just a spam advertisement.

But when I switched tabs to my inbox, I saw in the bar-line of the new message the name Mythosdealer93. There was no subject.

"Son of a bitch..."

Swallowing my terror, I clicked the message.

***

Tom:

Thank you for getting in touch with me. I must admit that butchering your friends earlier this evening made for a fine time. However

I was rather disappointed that I didn't get my claws into you. You looked so supple and moved so limber. I appreciate your sending me this email that I might locate you again. Let us now finish what we have started...

I hadn't stopped reading even a second when I heard the tap on the window to my right. Slowly, I turned my head in that direction. Through the narrow part in the curtains, I could see...

"*Oh fuck...*" I whispered.

Then I jumped out of my chair as glass shattered and the room filled with noise, screams, wings, and whooshing air...

CONTRIBUTORS

Rebecca Allred lives in Salt Lake City, working by day as a doctor of pathology, but after hours, she transforms into a practitioner of macabre fiction, infecting readers with her malign prose. Her work has appeared at Hellnotes, Freeze Frame Fiction, Sirens Call eZine, in *Vignettes from the End of the World*, and *Gothic Fantasy: Chilling Horror Short Stories*. She hosts a weekly flash fiction writing challenge at The Angry Hourglass and is a proud pack member of the Flash Dogs, contributing to their annual charity anthology. When she isn't busy rendering diagnoses or writing, Rebecca enjoys reading, drawing, laughing at RiffTrax, and spending time with her husband, Zach, and their kitty, Bug. You can keep up with Rebecca at diagnosisdiabolique.wordpress.com or follow her on Twitter @LadyHazmat.

Cliff Biggers first discovered the wonders of H. P. Lovecraft thanks to a 1965 Belmont paperback; two years later, he bought his first Arkham House hardcover, and thus began a lifelong addiction to horror fiction. Cliff has written for a variety of comics publishers, including "Earth Boys" for Dark Horse and Isaac Asimov's I•Bots for Tekno, and is the author of the upcoming novel 1967 Wayside. in addition, Cliff has written for DC Comics, Dynamite Entertainment, and IDW Publishing; he is also the editor and co-publisher of Comic Shop News, a comics industry promotional newsmagazine that recently released its 1470th weekly issue.

Matthew Carpenter is a practicing radiation oncologist. He has been a devoted fan and collector of all things Lovecraftian for more than 40 years. After writing numerous reviews of Cthulhu Mythos books on Amazon, for a few years he wrote a column about the state of US Lovecraft fandom for the Japanese magazine Night Land. He has had one story published in a chapbook by Rainfall Books but it was a terrible pun that no one understood but him (And he still thinks it's funny.), and no one else would accept (Maybe they didn't get it?). Lately he has appeared as a regular panelist on the Sunday webchat for the Lovecraft eZine. This is his first effort at editing an anthology (Thanks Ulthar Press!). He lives in Peoria, IL with his wife, Isabelle, and two teen age sons, Ethan and Sam.

Brett Davidson describes himself as an eclectic dilettante, perennial opsimath and practitioner of cat fu while his friends describe him as Hannibal Lecter's nicer sibling. He is a New Zealander who grew up in Edinburgh's southernmost clone, Dunedin, and now lives in his country's capital, Wellington. In fact, 'New Zealand' is only the name given to the exposed highlands of a sunken continent called Zealandia (it's true, look it up). Moreover, giant squid are frequently caught in its waters. All of this delights him.

    As for the bare facts of this temporary concatenation of transient cells, an entity had the name 'Brett' bestowed upon in some time in 1967 and has continued to accrue mass since. Since some of those cells are neurons, they have been put to use in education and academia so that he now has qualifications in fields as diverse as industrial design, architecture and English literature and he has taught in all of these areas to make a meager excuse for a living.

Long fascinated by weird fiction and science fiction, Brett has turned his hand to writing and has a number of creative and critical works to his name, a number inspired by that other writer of weird fiction, William Hope Hodgson. His first novel, *Anima*, has recently been published by Utter Tower. Naturally you are advised to buy it.

Seán Farrell is a 25 year old human from Killeshin, Ireland, who currently works in advertising in Dublin. He graduated from Trinity College Dublin (the same college that features in The Horror at Red Hook) with First Class Honours in English Studies. In Trinity he discovered the works of H.P Lovecraft, and has never looked back since. He also managed the famed Sellotape for a period, while simultaneously acting as trequartista/box to box dynamo in a fabled partnership with John Colthurst. He counts this as his crowning achievement in third level education.

His favourite writers are Samuel Beckett, James Joyce and Karl Peters. His favourite person is his girlfriend Laura. He lives in Ranelagh with his housemate (also his favourite pig farmer) owenfrog. In his spare time he likes to read, play football with 50 year old men, cycle with delusional Newcastle fans and settle.

He's finding it hard to fill this 500 word bio, so he's going to quit while he's ahead, and ask that anyone wishing to contact him can do so at farrelsj@tcd.ie

Aaron J. French is a book editor for JournalStone Publishing and the Editor-in-Chief for *Dark Discoveries* magazine. He has edited several anthologies, including *Songs of the Satyrs, Monk Punk & Shadow of the Unknown Omnibus*, and *The Gods of H.P. Lovecraft* (Winter 2015) from JournalStone Publishing, which includes new Mythos work from the biggest names in horror fiction, including Adam Nevill, Laird Barron, Bentley Little, Christopher Golden, Jonathan Maberry, Joe Lansdale, and Seanan McGuire.

2014 saw the publication of *The Chapman Books*, a supernatural thriller collection from Uncanny Books featuring Aaron's novella "The Stain." His single-author collection, *Aberrations of Reality*, was published by Crowded Quarantine Publications and it is the first book to collect Aaron's fiction focusing on the occult, metaphysics, and the weird. His zombie collection *Up From Soil Fresh* was published by Hazardous Press in 2013; also in 2013 "The Order," an occult thriller novella about a Lovecraftian secret society, was published in the *Dreaming in Darkness* collection. Look for Aaron's brand new hard-boiled Lovecraftian novella "The Dream Beings" forthcoming from Samhain Publishing in January of 2016.

Jamie D. Jenkins is a fan of all horror mediums and has devoted over a decade to celebrating the genre in one form or another. She began writing film reviews, soon transitioned to conducting interviews, then to having her own editorial column where she enjoyed stretching her legs in research and non-fiction writing. From there, she became the editor of The Chainsaw Mafia, then the Director of Marketing for Viscera Film Festival, a festival dedicated to highlighting women horror filmmakers, which led to her writing and directing her own critically acclaimed short film "Secret Shopper." For the past several years, she has been behind the mic as host or co-host of a half dozen genre-related podcasts including her labor of love, Lycan It!, a podcast which strictly discusses werewolves. Most recently, Jamie has begun to tap her inner storyteller via fiction prose with this tale and one that will be appearing in the upcoming anthology Summer of Lovecraft.

Paul R. McNamee was born and raised in Massachusetts, where he still lives with his wife, kids and cats. He discovered H. P. Lovecraft during college, drifted, found other literature, then stumbled into Robert E. Howard. All things pulp and weird (with the help of friends) brought him back to horror and the Cthulhu Mythos. A few of his stories appeared in online venues, and he had a sword-&-planet tale in the illustrated print anthology *Strange Worlds*. He is very happy to be appearing in a Lovecraftian anthology. His blog can be found at; http://paulmcnamee.blogspot.com

Christine Morgan works the overnight shift in a psychiatric facility, which plays havoc with her sleep schedule but allows her a lot of writing time. A lifelong reader, she also reviews, beta-reads, occasionally edits and dabbles in self-publishing. Her other interests include gaming, history, superheroes, crafts, cheesy disaster movies and training to be a crazy cat lady. She can be found online at https://www.facebook.com/christinemorganauthor   and   https://christinemari emorgan.wordpress.com/

Robert M. Price, a fan of H.P. Lovecraft since the Lancer paperback collections of 1967 appeared, began writing scholarly articles and humorous pieces on H. P.L and the Cthulhu Mythos in 1980. His celebrated semi-pro zine *Crypt of Cthulhu* began as a quarterly fanzine for the Esoteric Order of Dagon Amateur Press Association in 1981 and made it to 109 issues. Contributors included most of the rising stars of Lovecraft scholarship as well as renowned Cthulhu Mythos writers. In 1990 Price began editing Mythos fiction anthologies for Fedogan & Bremer, Chaosium, Inc., and others. His own fiction has been collected in *Blasphemies and Revelations* from Mythos Books. He has continued the adventures of Lin Carter's Sword-&-Sorcery hero Thongor of Lemuria, as well as those of Carter's occult detective Anton Zarnack.

Steven Prizeman is a freelance writer and graphic designer based in the small town of Amersham, Buckinghamshire, southern England – the last home and final resting place of Arthur Machen, who, like H. P. Lovecraft, is a strong influence on his short stories.

His fiction springs from a variety of sources – love of history, the landscape (and what it might conceal), the writers he admires, and a constant stream of odd ideas for which he has no one to blame but himself.

He has published three novels, all available from Amazon:

- *Arise, Black Vengeance*: a blood-soaked, Renaissance-set, Young Adult epic.
- *Huck*: a reworking of the adventures of Tom Sawyer and Huckleberry Finn, based on the premise that the ghosts and superstitions in which the protagonists believed were real.
- *Nietzsche Against Dracula*: a confrontation between the world's most egomaniacal philosopher and the definitive literary vampire.

His short story 'Books (Misc)' was published in the December 2014 edition of *The Lovecraft eZine*.

Sample chapters from Steven Prizeman's novels, and several of his short stories, may be downloaded free of charge from his website: stevenprizeman.com.

Pete Rawlik, a long time collector of Lovecraftian fiction, and is the author of more than twenty-five short stories, a smattering of poetry, the Cthulhu Mythos novel *Reanimators*, *The Weird Company,* and the forthcoming *Reanimatrix*. He is a frequent contributor to the *Lovecraft ezine* and the *New York Review of Science Fiction*. In 2014 his short story *Revenge of the Reanimator* was nominated for a New Pulp Award. He lives in southern Florida where he works on Everglades issues.

Damir Salkovic is an aficionado of weird and macabre tales, presently residing in Arlington, Virginia. His short stories have been published on the Tales to Terrify podcast, the Lovecraft ezine, in the Schlock! Bimonthly magazine and in anthologies by Schlock! Webzine, Source Point Press, Parasomnia Press, Apokrupha, Villipede Publications, Miskatonic Press, Mad Scientist Journal, Thirteen O'Clock press, the Black Library Bolthole and Emby Press. He earns his living as an accountant, a profession that lends itself well to nightmares and harrowing visions.

Brian M. Sammons has been writing reviews on all things horror for more years than he'd care to admit. Wanting to give other critics the chance to ravage his work for a change, he has penned stories that have appeared in such anthologies as Arkham Tales, Horrors Beyond, Monstrous, Dead but Dreaming 2, Horror for the Holidays, Twisted Legends, Mountains of Madness, Deepest, Darkest Eden and others. He has edited the books; Cthulhu Unbound 3, Undead & Unbound, Eldritch Chrome, Edge of Sundown, Steampunk Cthulhu, Dark Rites of Cthulhu, Atomic Age Cthulhu, World War Cthulhu and Flesh Like Smoke. He is also the managing editor of Dark Regions Press' new Weird Fiction line. He is currently far too busy for any sane man. For more about this guy that neighbors describe as "such a nice, quiet man" you can check out his very infrequently updated webpage here: http://brian_sammons.webs.com/ and you can follow him on Twitter @BrianMSammons.

Jonathan Titchenal has been reading and writing weird fiction for many years, both in the Lovecraftian genre and others. In recent years he has been published in the Das Krakenhaus collection *The End of the World as We Know It*, and is currently at work on an epic fantasy novel. His favorite horror movie is *John Carpenter's The Thing*. He lives in Milwaukee.

Don Webb is from the place in Texas with the most Helium and Plutonium -- Amarillo. He is the Head of the Humanities Department at Goodwill Charter School in Austin, TX. He lives with his lovely wife and two tuxedo cats. He has been writing fiction influenced by Lovecraft since 1986. His latest collection is *Through Dark Angles* from Hippocampus Press

Kevin Wetmore is the author of *Post-9/11 Horror in American Cinema* and *Back from the Dead*. He has also published essays in *Rue Morgue*, *Gothic Studies*, *Horror Studies* and many other magazines and journals. He has also published over a dozen short stories in such anthologies as *Enter at Your Own Risk: The End is the Beginning*, *Moonshadows*, *History and Horror, Oh My!*, *Book of the Dead*, *Dark Tales of Elder Regions*, and *Midian Unmade*. An actor, director and stage combat choreographer, this native New Englander now calls Los Angeles home.

While the other children were playing outside in the fresh air, *Susan Hicks Wong* was scrunched down in a tattered armchair inhaling the miasma of H.P. Lovecraft, Edgar Allen Poe and Shirley Jackson. After stints as an art director and textile designer, she now travels wild and free across North America as a long haul truck driver with her husband. She attended the 2013 Odyssey Writer's Workshop, an experience she would recommend for aspiring speculative writers. Susan reads and writes as the prairie rolls past and she still loves the funk of decaying old books.